HORROR HOUSE

"Young lady, I wouldn't spend a night in that house for all the wealth in the York coffers."

Cathy closed her eyes and shook her head. "I don't want to go into this again. I have to go back there. I have no choice. What you've just told me makes me sure that my brother's mind is still alive, and that means he is still alive, even if he's in another form."

"But that entire hill could be a cemetery! The authorities will be moving in at any time, so you won't have to expose yourself to any of this danger."

"And when the authorities move in, how can we be sure that those crazy people won't try to eliminate all of the evidence against them?" Cathy demanded. "I have to get Mikey out of there before this all blows up. Really, I appreciate your concern, but I'm not going to change my mind, even if I have to die for it. . . ."

Other Leisure books by Steve Vance:

THE HYDE EFFECT

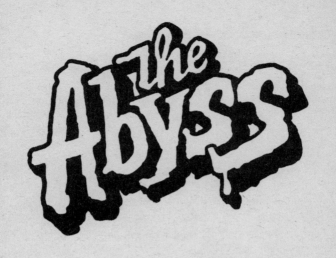

STEVE · VANCE

Book Margins, Inc.

A BMI Edition

Published by special arrangement with Dorchester Publishing Co., Inc.

Printed in the United States of America.

Prologue

Wednesday night, September 7.

The rain came down incessantly, angrily.

The windshield wipers beat with all the energy that the little car could generate, but at best they were merely shifting one sheet of water aside so that another could take its place. The heavy storm clouds blocked out whatever light that the sky might have had to offer. All in all, the young couple could just as well have been driving along at the bottom of the sea.

"Mikey, maybe we should stop somewhere until this blows over," Nona Lockwood suggested nervously, using a tissue to wipe the misty windshield in front of her husband.

Michael "Mickey" Lockwood (who had been married to Nona for all of three days and was still finding grains of rice in his hair) forced a smile and a short laugh. "Hon, if we stop now we're liable to float away completely," he said, but the tension in his voice was thick. Mikey was a good driver, though not always a confident one.

"But I can hardly see the road at all! Shouldn't we pull onto the shoulder for a few minutes?"

Mikey continued to smile, though his tone was firm and calm when he replied, "I can still see the center line out of the corner of my eye, babe. If we stop on one of these soft shoulders, a couple of things are sure to happen. First, we'll sink so deep in the mud that we'll have to call a tow truck to get out, or second, we could drift directly into the ditch. Try to relax. I'm holding the speed down, and as soon as we get to that little town, we'll find a place to stay for the night. What time is it, anyway?"

"Um, almost midnight," she answered, squinting at her wristwatch.

"Why don't you check the map again? I promise that we won't get into a fender-bender on our honeymoon."

"There aren't any other cars out tonight to endanger *that* promise," Nona said in mock seriousness. "All of the sane people are inside in bed."

Actually, his reassurance had eased her fears. Mikey Lockwood had that effect, usually radiating competence and reliability. Nona squeezed his arm lovingly.

Five minutes later, the headlights managed to pierce the wetness enough to illuminate an orange sign. "WELCOME TO EUPHRATA, INDIANA," it read. "POPULATION 10,000. WE BELIEVE IN THE GOLDEN RULE."

"Sounds like a real friendly place, Mrs. Lockwood," Mikey said.

Nona laughed, relieved. "It sounds biblical to

me. I wonder if there's room in Euphrata for a 'Mikey' and a 'Nonnie.' "

Euphrata proved to be as tightly closed as the main vault in the bank where Mikey worked over weekends. The only cars visible sat securely locked in overnight parking spaces, and just a few dim security lights shone in the stores. Though the streetlamps were on, the continuing, powerful rain made driving a rather dangerous exercise.

"Well, thanks for your open-arms greeting, Euphrata, Indiana," Nona observed as they crept past the city limits sign on the west side of town. "It looks like you've already begun breaking your promises to me, Mr. Lockwood."

Mikey slowed to a complete stop, not in the least worried about traffic, and took the unfolded map from Nona. After examining it for a few moments, he sighed and rubbed his neck. "Nothing until we hit Tiverton, and that's fifty miles southwest," he said.

Disappointment welled in Nona's voice. "Oh, Mikey, that's too far away. I'm exhausted, and I know you must be, driving all day long. At this rate, it'll take us two more hours to get there."

"I didn't see any hint of a hotel in Euphrata, did you?"

"No," she admitted reluctantly.

"Hmm, fifty miles, fifty miles," he muttered. He *was* tired—very. "Let's give this metropolis one more chance, shall we?"

Carefully avoiding the shoulders, he steered the blue Volkswagen in a slow U-turn and slipped back inside the city limits.

The second survey proved to be no more successful than the first. If Euphrata contained anything remotely resembling a hotel or a boarding house, it was securely camouflaged. The skies seemed to possess an unending supply of rain, however, and it continued to pour down upon the little car.

"Strike two," Mikey said in a resigned tone. "Want to go on one more tour and try for strike three?"

Nona shook her head. "No. We've covered every inch of this place. I guess we'll have to head for Tiverton. If you want me to drive for a while . . ."

Mikey patted her hand. "Don't worry about me. If I start to feel sleepy, I'll just poke my head out the window."

Another slow, tight turn aligned them to the west again, but just as Mikey began to accelerate as much as the circumstances allowed, a dazzling blue light flashed through the rain from behind them. The first moving vehicle that they had encountered in over an hour proved to be a police cruiser.

"Damn," Mikey whispered as the brilliant light glared into his eyes from the rearview mirror. He hardly ever swore, but then he'd been driving for a decade without a traffic ticket, too. "I guess two U-turns was pressing my luck."

Even though the patrol car didn't utilize its siren or loudspeaker, Mikey knew that the light was flashing for them and pulled over in front of a hardware store.

"I hope that the jail's dry, at least," Nona commented in a valiant attempt at humor.

The patrol car slid into the space next to them. Mikey took his driver's license from his wallet in preparation for the ordeal, but he kept his window tightly closed until the lone officer appeared from the other vehicle. The policeman looked like a huge, orange-colored bear as he lumbered around his car, glanced at the rear of the Volks for the plates, and lumbered toward the driver's window in his bright rain gear. He tapped on the window, and Mikey was rather surprised when he rolled it down to find a smiling and obviously mature face a few inches from his.

"Trouble, officer?" Mikey asked, hopelessly.

The round, grizzled face continued to smile. "That's about what I was going to ask you folks. Saw you pass the station twice in the past few minutes. Not lost, are you?"

Mikey had to force himself to suppress his relief; maybe his driving record was still intact. "Oh, no, sir. I mean, we know that we're in Euphrata, but we'd like to find a place to spend the night. There don't seem to be any hotels or motels in town, at least none that we can find."

"We'd really like to get out of this weather," Nona piped in.

The policeman smiled even broader upon seeing the young woman and chuckled a deep laugh, again reminding Mikey of a bear.

"Honeymoon, eh?"

Mikey nodded.

"Best wishes to the both of you." The policeman straightened up and glanced about the empty street, as if he were searching for a stray hotel or two. He seemed oblivious to the rain. "Well, there's a nice motel about six miles west of town—Ed Stern's place, clean cabins," he told them after he'd stooped back to the window.

"Where do you young folks come from?"

"McKeesport, Pennsylvania," Nona responded.

"Real nice city, real pretty. You going to spend your honeymoon here in Euphrata?"

"Actually, we're just passing through," she continued. "We're headed for Kansas City."

"That's a long drive. I'd guess money's a problem?"

"Who doesn't have that kind of problem?" Mikey asked. He was a little uneasy over Nona's dismissal of the small town as a honeymoon site and the way that the cop might take it.

"That's the gospel." The policeman drew in a slow breath. "Let me give you two a break. Ed Stern's motel is a really fine place, but to be honest, his prices are a little steep, especially with out-of-staters. Right up there on the hill to the north of town," he pointed off into the darkness, "is the old York house. If the moon was out, you could see it as clear as could be."

"Is it a hotel?" Nona asked.

The policeman grunted a deep, bass laugh. "Not exactly, ma'am; at least, it's not licensed as one. But the York place has been a sort of informal boarding house since it was built, oh, nearly seventy years ago. The Yorks are a fine lot of people, and they'll only charge seven or eight dollars a night for the two of you."

Mikey didn't care for the idea of staying at a private residence, but there didn't seem to be any sign of the storm abating. "We wouldn't want to disturb anyone this late."

"No need to worry about that, son. Somebody is always awake at the York home. And they must have at least a dozen bedrooms. I'd say that that's the biggest lodging in the southern half of the state.''

Nona gripped her husband's arm with excitement. "Let's try it, Mikey. Even if it's ten dollars a night, we'll be better off than any other hotel or motel.'' She was acutely aware of their financial situation.

When Mikey didn't respond for a few seconds, the policeman straightened again and wiped away a trickle of rain that had found its way beneath his hat and onto his forehead. "Well, friends, I can't stand out here in the rain all night. Those are the only two places hereabouts that rent rooms, so the choice is up to you.''

"Sure, and thanks a lot, officer," Mikey replied.

"Don't mention it. Happy honeymoon." The policeman trudged carefully through the rain toward his car, but he stopped before opening the driver's door and called, "One more thing, son!"

Mikey had rolled his window up, but he cracked it enough to answer, "Yes, sir?"

There was a trace of amusement in the policeman's voice when he said, "The limit for U-turns in Euphrata is two in a twenty-four hour period. You're there.''

"Uh, yes, sir. Thanks again.''

The patrol car started up and pulled smoothly out of sight, leaving the couple alone once more.

"If this is a marriage of equality, my vote goes to the York house," Nona stated. "We could get a good night's sleep, a home-cooked breakfast, and then we could use the money we save to detour south and visit Wyandotte Cave.''

"Hey, I thought it was a law that a bride-to-be had to tell her groom before the ceremony if she had an interest in speleology, but I suppose we'll have to learn to put up with each other's eccentricities if we hope to make this thing work. How do you feel about hunting mastodons with bows and arrows?''

"Hunting?''

"Never mind. Okay, let's give the York place a try.''

The little Volkswagen responded once again to the demands made upon it and began to creep through the flooding streets. Mikey was so intent on his driving and in locating the York home that he didn't notice that one of the parked cars he passed on his way out of town was the same marked police car that had stopped him only minutes before. But the man in the police car definitely noticed him.

The man's right hand was still damp with rain as he lifted the microphone from the police band radio and keyed in the dispatcher. "Louise, honey, this is Baxter,'' the big man said cordially. "Do me a favor, if you don't mind. Fix me up a phone patch to Cecil York. Yes, ma'am, we've got a little business to talk.''

Chapter One

Friday afternoon, September 9.

The new guy was watching her. She could feel his eyes running up and down her back as she talked to Monica. In fact, Monica's overly plucked eyebrows were using semaphore to keep her advised of the boy's inspection.

Well, let him look, Cathy Lockwood told herself. He hadn't become an embarrassment yet, and he *was* kind of cute, even if his studied New York accent was a little too much to be believed. He might be worth a look or two himself.

"All I can say is I hope that the boys do better tonight than they did last Friday night," Monica Pettis said between bouts of eyebrow-signaling. It was clear that she was quite interested in the new guy, but she went on with her account of the Eastpoint High Cougars' wretched performance in their first game of the football season one week before. "I mean, how can we be expected to inspire school spirit when the team is on its way to the wrong end of a thirty-six to zero massacre?''

"Tell me about it," Cathy sighed. But part of her was still wondering when the new boy would summon up the courage to introduce himself.

"But that highkick routine should do the trick tonight," Monica assured her. In demonstration, she hitched her right leg up to chin level, a move which drew a round of applause from the male students who were lounging about in the classroom.

"You're a hit," Cathy said laughing, her blue eyes sparkling.

Monica bowed melodramatically. "Thank you, thank you all. Autographs will be available for a small fee immediately following the performance." She leaned close to Cathy and whispered, "God, girl, how do you get your kicks so high? I think I just destroyed any chances I had for a future family."

"The secret is in clean living and a steady diet of anabolic steroids," Cathy whispered back.

Monica rolled her eyes. "Oh, I'm sure! When you put something unnatural in the Holy Temple . . . well, that'll be the day."

Suddenly the atmosphere of the large, breezy room shifted into reverse as Mrs. Reilly, teacher of History and Political Interpretation, entered the room. Mrs. Reilly was all right, but she *was* a teacher, and there are some gulfs that can never be bridged.

"Playtime is over, ladies and gentlemen," the short, gray-haired teacher declared. "Everyone to your places, if you can find them."

Cathy and Monica moved to their desks along

with the rest of their junior classmates. Monica, though, was still excited over the coming evening's cheerleading acrobatics.

"I predict that we'll have the place rocking tonight," she said, leaning across the aisle and keeping her voice low. "Unless the stands are filled with the living dead."

"Or Myrridge outscores us thirty-six to zero," Cathy added.

"It seems that Ms. Pettis and Ms. Lockwood would like to direct the class today, my friends," Mrs. Reilly said coolly. "Now, which of you would like to lecture us about the role of the Catholic church during the Renaissance. Ms. Pettis?"

Monica lowered her head and said, sort of into her left shoulder, "No, ma'am."

"Ms. Lockwood, perhaps?"

Cathy sighed, though not loudly enough to be heard. "I'm sorry, Mrs. Reilly," she responded.

"I see. If there are no other volunteers, then, shall we get on with the rise of modern European civilization?"

And so class proceeded. Because it was a Friday afternoon, with the final hours of the school week slipping away, no one—least of all Mrs. Reilly—expected any serious studying to be undertaken, even though the usual plastic facades were employed by all involved. The Friday night ritual awaited, and after that the weekend. With her brother and new sister-in-law honeymooning in Kansas City, Cathy had the apartment completely to herself, and the variations on that theme seemed boundless and enticing.

Perhaps the reason that the arrival of the

school's psychologist/career counselor, Janet
Shelby, into this typical lazy afternoon setting
seemed so jarring was the fact that Eastpoint
High School possessed a modern, thoroughly
efficient intercom system. Under normal circumstances, any summons from the office would have
come via this system, and Mrs. Reilly would have
responded by way of the controls on her desk.
Therefore Janet's arrival in person created an
expectant hush over the class.

"Please excuse the interruption, Mrs. Reilly,"
Janet said from the doorway, her usual cheerful
tone subdued and a bit halting. "I need to speak
to you in the hall for a moment."

Mrs. Reilly was just as confused as the
students, and for an instant her face reflected
this. She covered the uncertainty quickly and pro-
fessionally. "Don't think of this as a reprieve,
ladies and gentlemen," she advised the class as
she walked toward the rear of the room. "Just
think of it as an opportunity to quickly memorize
the major Renaissance artists and sculptors while
I'm away." Then she stepped into the corridor
and closed the door.

"Maybe the Big One is on the way and the
faculty is being evacuated first," Monica
theorized in a whisper.

Cathy smiled. "Into the mine shafts, Dr.
Strangelove. Women, children, and home ec.
teachers first."

"My motto is: 'When the Big One comes, the
hell with sexual equality; just keep out of my
way.' " Monica stared past Cathy's shoulder
briefly and then said, in an even fainter voice,
"The new guy's still gaping at you like a starving
man at a meal."

"Good," Cathy replied. "If he's not a total, machoed-out nitwit, maybe I'll—" At that moment, Mrs. Reilly entered the room and Cathy shut up just as abruptly.

Mrs. Reilly returned very slowly to the head of the class. There was none of her commanding presence about her, and when Cathy saw her face she was stunned by the stark whiteness of the woman's usually ruddy complexion. Yet, there still were no danger signals in Cathy's sub-conscious.

"Cathy Lockwood," Mrs. Reilly said, "you are to accompany Mrs. Shelby to Mr. Curran's office." She took a breath and quickly added, "The other members of the class will open your textbooks to page thirty-four."

What on earth have I done? Cathy thought. A call to the principal's office generally meant a disciplinary mission, even though she was a 16-year-old junior with decent grades and no catastrophic bad habits. Almost numb due to the complete unexpectedness of the summons, she slipped the strap of her purse over her shoulder and stood up.

Monica flashed her a weak grin and a thumbs-up.

Once in the hallway, Cathy's thoughts remained on the possible reasons for the call and why the school psychologist had delivered it personally.

Janet Shelby was short, petite, 31, and so youthful that the students felt comfortable in calling her by her first name, a liberty which she encouraged. At the moment, however, she wasn't very cooperative.

"Mr. Curran will explain," she answered

simply to all of Cathy's questions. Then she would strain to produce a smile that was weaker than Monica's and pat Cathy's arm. "It'll be all right," she would add.

The first hints of the seriousness of the situation began to appear. When they passed the large window facing the eastern parking lot, Cathy saw the police car sitting there, among all of the new and battered student vehicles.

"Oh, God," she whispered. "Something's wrong. I mean really . . ."

"Mr. Curran will—" began Janet.

The explanation came to her in a burst of inspiration. "My car's been stolen, hasn't it? I must have left the keys in it again, and after I promised Mikey that I'd guard it like a trooper."

But the keys were in her purse.

"He's really a terrific guy, you know, um, Mikey," she continued hastily, recklessly. "He's worked at that bank for almost eight years, driving that same old Beetle, and what does he get me for my sixteenth birthday? A new Camaro."

They arrived at the principal's office.

"Mr. Curran will explain," Janet repeated helplessly.

"He's my whole family . . . I mean, he's raised me since our parents . . . were killed. I was only six and Mikey was sixteen, a decade between us, and we had to stay in a foster home until he turned eighteen and got a job with—"

"Cathy, please, let's go inside," Janet said, taking her hand.

Cathy pulled away and backed across the hall. "I don't think I should go in there. I have . . . I need to get back to class before Mrs. Reilly . . .''

"No, dear, you have to come with me.''

"Leave me alone!" Cathy screamed.

The door to Mr. Curran's office opened, and the principal stepped toward her. It was written clearly in his eyes. "Cathy," he said in almost a croak, "come inside."

She moved like a zombie. With Curran at her right side and Janet at her left, she allowed herself to be led inside and seated on a cold plastic sofa. There was a solemn policeman waiting for her.

"Miss Catherine Ann Lockwood?" the policeman asked.

"Yes," she replied.

It obviously was a very difficult moment for the officer as well. "Your brother's name is, uh, Michael Nathaniel Lockwood, is that correct?"

"Of course it is." She wasn't even trying to think now; everything was happening on its own. "Did you know he's on his honeymoon? He married Nona Byers last Sunday. She's lovely, a lovely person . . ."

"Miss Lockwood, the police in Tiverton, Indiana, discovered a blue Volkswagen in the Ohio River this morning."

"That's not ours. Mikey's a wonderful driver; he's never even had a parking ticket."

The officer coughed nervously. "A, uh, body was found inside, and credentials in the wallet identified it as Michael Lockwood. I'm sorry, Miss Lockwood, but your brother is dead."

"No . . . I'm sure there's been a mistake." Curran put one hand on her shoulder, and suddenly she understood that denial couldn't change anything. "Oh, my God!" she cried.

They tried to comfort her, and Janet brought Monica, her very best friend, into the office, but there are times when comfort can't be given or accepted. She didn't collapse into hysterics, but she couldn't keep from crying, either, not even when the policeman's duty compelled him to relate all of the information that had been gathered in the case.

A terrible rainstorm had covered the southern half of Indiana on Wednesday night, and the Indiana police had theorized that Mikey, tired from a long drive and almost blinded by the rain, had simply misjudged the approach to a bridge and driven into the river. The searchers had been alerted by an anonymous phone tip late Thursday morning that a small car was being swept downriver, but they hadn't located the Volkswagen until the next day, that Friday morning. Even after recovering the car, they had been unable to find any trace of Nona's body since the door on the passenger side was missing, and her family was being notified at the same time that Cathy was hearing the awful news.

Mikey had certainly died in the car during the initial crash. The windshield had been shattered, and he had been decapitated.

After several calls were made, Monica's mother arrived at the school with her personal physician, and the doctor administered a sedative after they had returned to the Pettis household. Cathy hadn't resisted the drug, because she knew now that sleep was her only escape.

With her parents dead in an airplane crash and now her only brother taken by another horrible accident, Cathy Lockwood was all alone. She had no other living relative.

Cathy was spared any thoughts for the rest of
that horrible day and night. While the Pettis
family took it upon themselves to cope with the
details of the tragedy, she remained asleep—a
dreamless, medically induced sleep.

Mikey's body arrived in McKeesport by police
transport at six that Friday evening, but there was
still no trace of Nona. Due to the nature of the
death, an autopsy was legally required, and, even
though a positive identification would rest on
Cathy, the rules were bent in this case. The
autopsy was performed on Friday night.

The body was in very poor condition. Using the
Thursday anonymous tip as a guide, it was
reasoned that the car had been in the river for at
least 30 hours, carrying Mikey's body as it was
swept downstream by the rapid currents.
Relatively little was determined from the autopsy
other than the fact that Mikey most probably had
not drowned, reinforcing the theory that he had
been decapitated upon impact.

There did appear to be a trace of alcohol and at
least one other unidentifiable chemical depressant
in Mikey's system however. The medical
examiners had expected as much.

In other words, all indications were that
drunken driving had led to the fatal accident.

On Saturday, reality intruded into Cathy's life
again.

Though Monica's parents objected strenu-
ously, the McKeesport police arranged for
the required positive identification, which, under

other circumstances, would have been made prior to the autopsy. It took place in a quiet, comfortably furnished room at the city morgue. Due to the installation of a sophisticated closed circuit television system, the person making the identification of a corpse was spared the ordeal of actually having to enter the refrigeration compartment where the bodies were kept.

"We understand how difficult this will be for you, Miss Lockwood," a compassionate employee of the morgue assured her as she assisted Cathy to a seat before a television screen.

"Your brother had a small, half-moon birthmark on the rear of his left calf, is that right?"

Cathy sat down slowly. It was all so much like a dream. "Um, yes, his left leg." There were stretches of the morning about which she could recall absolutely nothing probably due to the aftereffects of the sedative, but she knew that really wasn't the cause. "It's strawberry-colored. Mikey calls it his werewolf stigmata . . . I mean, he used to."

Monica began to sniff softly, and Mrs. Pettis put her arms about both girls. "It'll be all right," the woman promised. Everyone seemed to be promising her that now.

"Please watch the screen, Miss Lockwood," the kind attendant said.

Cathy slowly looked up. On the blue-tinted screen, a pair of hands belonging to a man pulled open a heavy metal drawer, and a white sheet came into view. The hands carefully drew back the sheet to reveal the swollen lower legs of another man. They were lying downward, and a reddish splotch was visible on the left one, in spite of the awful discoloration. It could have been the birthmark.

It took several seconds and two attempts, but finally Cathy was able to whisper, "Yes, that's Mikey." She wondered why she wasn't crying.

The attendant touched a button next to a condenser microphone below the TV screen and said, "Thank you, Frederick." The hands closed the drawer and the picture winked off. Then the woman turned to the policeman who had accompanied them and asked, "Is that satisfactory?"

He nodded.

"Let's go, Cathy," Mrs. Pettis said.

As they started to leave, Cathy thanked the attendant for her kindness and unable to prevent herself, asked, "Was his face too bad . . . too injured to be recognizable?"

Without pausing to think, the attendant replied, "Well, it wasn't available, since the head wasn't found . . ." She broke off, her eyes revealing sudden comprehension. "You didn't know?"

"No," Cathy said. Now the tears came. "I thought that it was in the car."

There was nothing more to be said or done in that place of the dead.

Had she been in any condition to oversee everything, Cathy probably would have set the funeral for Monday, or possibly Tuesday, so that some of Mikey's out-of-town friends could attend. But the Pettises were still handling these details, and she was glad to leave them in control.

Due to the condition of Mikey's body, the

funeral was on the next day, Sunday, one week after his marriage.

The afternoon was bright, warm, and only a little windy. There were over a hundred people in attendance at the chapel and almost as many at the short graveside ceremony. Mikey had been loved and respected by practically everyone he knew. There were even a few former classmates of his at the service from several states away, despite the short notice they had received. He had been class president during his senior year.

Cathy made it through the service as bravely as she knew he would have wished. More than a dozen of her and Mikey's friends invited her to stay with them until she was able to straighten out her life, but she managed to convince them all, including a very reluctant Mr. and Mrs. Pettis, that she needed to spend another night alone in the apartment that she and her brother had shared for over seven years.

Cathy was still legally a minor and had no source of income of her own, so keeping the apartment was out of the question. She had discovered on Saturday that she was the sole beneficiary of two rather large life insurance policies that Mikey had taken out, the total of which would run to over $100,000, but she wouldn't be able to claim the money until she turned 18. Uncharacteristically, the normally prudent Mikey had not been able to set up a workable financial package that would have protected Cathy *until* her 18th birthday, but then again he hadn't counted on dying at the age of 26 either. Knowing that she would be moving out soon and into the Pettis household, she needed to sort through their possessions.

Mikey's things were almost all ready to go, anyway. He and Nona had already leased another apartment in the same building, giving Cathy her longed-for independence and themselves some privacy. They had planned to move into the new place upon returning from their honeymoon on Monday.

Cathy finally fell asleep sometime after midnight while looking through a family album that contained dozens of photos of her parents, even more of her, and only a few of Mikey, with his chocolate-brown hair—the same color as her own—his slightly lopsided grin, and those shoulders that had been forced to accept an adult's responsibility long before he reached an adult's age.

School on Monday was out of the question, of course. She even was considering quitting altogether and looking for a job, but whenever that thought lingered with her for more than a second or two, she would hear his voice saying, "Kitty Cat, even if you don't learn to tie your shoes in college, tough it out because just the possession of that piece of paper can cover a multitude of incompetence." Never having had the chance to attend college himself, he'd learned that the hard way.

It was nearly noon before she got up in response to a worried call from Mrs. Pettis. Cathy hadn't found herself hungry since Friday, and today proved to be no different. Fixing herself up just a little, she slipped on a pair of jeans, an old blouse, and a scarf about her long hair in preparation for another day of getting the apartment ready for moving out. Even though she was surrounded by reminders of him at every turn, working seemed to ease the continual aching within her.

She didn't think to check on the mail—three days of it—until mid-afternoon and then almost by-passed the opportunity. She certainly wasn't ready to begin reading even sincere condolences or the con games initiated by the obituary page freaks, but it would give her some excuse to get out of the apartment, if only long enough to reach the first floor mail boxes.

She met just a few people in the hallway and the elevator, but they all knew her and what she was going through. Their words were spoken in low, almost apologetic tones, and Cathy accepted the sentiments in the prescribed civilized manner. Sometime soon she would be able to appreciate the very real sympathy that they were expressing, but right now she could only pretend.

At first she only noticed the usual mail: a store's salespaper, a bill, an overdue notice from the public library. Then a post card stopped her cold. It was addressed to her in Mikey's unmistakable handwriting from somewhere called Euphrata, Indiana. She flipped it over, both eager and reluctant to read what were undoubtably his last words to her.

September 8 (a.m.)

Hi, Kitty Cat!

Having a wonderful time; hope you are, too (I know how you *love* school). Stayed overnight at a real Stardust City type of place, whacko deluxe. These people would make the Addams Family feel commonplace. Tell you more when we get back. Nonnie wants to tour Wyandotte Cave today, so we're going underground, I suppose (henpecked already!).

Don't forget your keys again. And always remember, I love you, kid.

                                        Mikey

"I love you, too, Mikey," Cathy whispered. She prayed that somehow he heard her.

Another neighbor stopped by to speak to her, and Cathy tucked the mail beneath one arm. She was on her way up again, alone in the elevator, when the thought came to her. She reached for the post card so hurriedly that she dropped everything on the floor, but the card landed with the message side up.

"Hi, Kitty Cat!" it said. "September 8 (a.m.)."

According to the Tiverton police department, who had located the car on Friday, they had acted on a tip from an anonymous caller who had seen the little blue car floating half-submerged in the rain-swollen Ohio River outside of that town early on Thursday morning. The man had claimed his sighting had taken place at about 6:00 a.m. September 8th had been last Thursday.

Cathy's heart began to pound. The elevator doors opened on her floor, but she ignored them. If this witness had seen Mikey's car at eight in the morning near Tiverton, how could her brother have written and mailed that post card to her from this other town before 6:00 o'clock and then driven off a bridge at Tiverton the same morning?

She had to find out how far Tiverton was from this . . . Euphrata place, the place which had stamped the card with a September 8th postmark. It was so faint a mark that she couldn't tell if that were an a.m. or p.m. above the date, but since Mikey had written "a.m.," she accepted that.

Even as Cathy ran from the elevator for the road atlas packed away in her apartment, she knew instinctively that there was something very wrong with all of this.

Chapter Two

Monday morning, July 10.

Generally speaking, waking to music from a clock radio is considerably better than being aroused by a jangling alarm, Euphrata had only one radio station which played country and western music religiously. Greg Hoode hated country and western music—religiously.

This might have come as a surprise to those who knew that Greg originally came from the traditional home of country music, the deep South—Atlanta, Georgia, to be specific. He simply had resisted the attractions of what he referred to as "nose-twang tunes" for all of his 17 years, despite the fact that he was a great admirer of most other forms of music, even a little classical. Of course, Greg Hoode was about as atypical a 17-year-old as could be found in the eastern half of the nation.

For one thing, he was rich—rather, his family

was rich—and on his next birthday in eleven months he would receive enough stock in the Hoode Pharmaceutical and Electronics Industries to make him worth roughly $13,000,000. Among his other singular attributes were an I.Q. of 143 which he seldom bothered to display to its fullest extent, his 52 and 2 record as a light middleweight (156 pounds) amateur boxer, and the manner in which he conducted himself as if none of these things meant very much in the overall picture of his life.

One trait that he did have in common with a number of other 17-year-olds was the fact that he had hardly any idea of what he wanted to do with the rest of his life.

On that Monday morning in July, more than ten months after Cathy Lockwood learned of her brother's death, Greg Hoode was pleasantly surprised when his clock radio went off at 9:30 to the strains of "Pauncho and Lefty," by Willie Nelson and Merle Haggard. That was one of the few country/western songs that he liked.

The Euphrata sunshine streamed cleanly into the bedroom and across Greg's bare chest as he lay and listened to the song. He had to admit that, in spite of all of its other faults, this small town had beautiful weather.

Another great day in Heartland, U.S.A., Greg told himself.

The song ended and the local announcer chirped, "Would you just look out your windows, Mr. and Mrs. Euphrata? Another glorious day in Heartland, U.S.A."

Greg nodded and rolled easily out of bed. He could tell at once that a brisk shower would be needed to shock his system into complete attention, so he paused only long enough to dig some fresh underwear from a dresser drawer before proceeding into the bathroom that connected with the guest bedroom.

Greg had no brothers or sisters—though he did have a first cousin who had to meet life day after day with the name Robin Hoode—so naturally, his parents had lavished just about every excess available to them on their single offspring. They wanted their son's life to be absolutely perfect, and it was this desire that had resulted in Greg's summertime stay in "Heartland, U.S.A."

Mark and Elaine Hoode, Greg's father and mother, were young, wealthy, neither too liberal nor too conservative politically, and in one way very old-fashioned—they thought that they could decide his matrimonial future better than Greg himself. Their very eligible son had begun seeing a good deal of pretty but socially unprominent Julie Ardeth Newman around Christmastime, and alarm bells went off all over the Hoode household. Sensing that the summer would be a most fertile time for the budding romance, his parents had carefully pressed Mark's older brother Daniel to invite Greg to spend that time in quaint, picturesque, and isolated Euphrata, Indiana.

Greg could have resisted. Though he got along well enough with his family, he did have a strong streak of independence. Still, he and Julie weren't really *that* close, and his parents *did* endure his potentially dangerous boxing addiction in spite of their misgivings, so . . . what the hell! He had decided that he could live with all of that unhealthy country air for three months.

Of course, he hadn't realized at the time that friendly little Euphrata would be as deathly dull as it turned out to be.

"Can I fix you brunch, Gregory?" Diana Meredith, the cook/housekeeper in the Hoode home, asked as Greg entered the kitchen.

Though he was as financially secure from the profits of Granddad Hoode's Industries as Greg's branch of the family, Uncle Daniel lived in a relatively modest house and employed only three servants. Perhaps this was his concession to small town life.

"Thanks anyway, Diana, but I'll just grab a sandwich until lunch," he answered. "I don't want to put you to any extra trouble."

"Oh, it wouldn't be trouble at all," she said. Diana was in her mid-forties and was one of the nicest people Greg had ever met. He just couldn't convince her that he didn't eat breakfast. "Eggs and bacon?" she continued. "Ham?"

Greg stepped to a cabinet and began searching for various sandwich makings, including peanut butter and bananas. "Really, Diana, I'm not too compatible with cooked food in the morning."

Muttering to herself about the importance of the day's first meal, the housekeeper left Greg to his own devices.

Greg's uncle, Daniel Hoode, was 42, four years older than Mark, Greg's father. He had two daughters and a son of his own, but they had lived with their mother for five years following their parents' divorce. Daniel had always been a sort of playboy, intent on discovering just how much pleasure his inheritance could bring him, so it had been quite a shock to the other family members when he had retired a few years following the divorce to quiet little Euphrata.

Daniel was sitting in the den scanning through several out-of-town newspapers when Greg entered. "Ah, the Golden Boy arises," he said, referring both to Greg's light blond hair and his boxing career. "Another big day planned?"

Greg was fond of his uncle, so he didn't answer with the first thing that came to mind. "Sure, I thought I'd try out Euphrata's version of hang-gliding, riding a shopping cart through the parking lot of the Food King." Instead, he said, "You bet, Uncle Dan. I thought I'd go over to the gym and work out this morning, maybe get in a little sparring if I can scout out a partner. How about you?"

Daniel, a tall, tan-complexioned man with dark hair and a quick smile, laughed and shook his head. "Not even Diana at her most intimidating could drag me into the ring with the next Olympic champ."

Greg had come rather late to amateur boxing, but he had shown enough natural ability to be considered a serious contender for an Olympic berth in three years, if he could keep his nervous parents from reading too many AMA reports until that time.

"Besides," Daniel continued, "I've got to be in the office right after lunch. There are some business matters I want to attend to before tonight's lodge meeting."

Greg smiled to himself. It was still hard for him to imagine his worldly uncle as a member of a

bucolic lodge, wearing a furry little hat and
reciting secret pledges. Maybe I'm just a stuck-up
snot, he thought.

"You are planning to keep tomorrow night
free, aren't you?" Daniel asked.

"No plans so far," Greg replied, though he had
given a short, inaudible sigh of dread before
answering the question.

"Good. The induction of new members is set
for then, and I think you're going to be pleasantly
surprised by how much you'll enjoy the
meeting."

"I'm sure I will," he managed to respond in a
moderately cheerful tone. "Catch you around
suppertime, then." He headed for the door.

"Don't decimate the county's population of
young men in the ring or young women out of
it!" Daniel called after him. "And be here at six-
thirty or face the wrath of Diana!"

For all of his inherited wealth and social status,
Greg Hoode cared little for trendy clothing or the
fancy toys of the rich, aside from his home video
and stereo equipment naturally, but he absolutely
had insisted that he be allowed to bring along his
brand-spanking-new, midnight blue Porsche.

Needless to say, there was not another car even
approaching it in Euphrata or the surrounding
vicinity.

Since the day was admittedly gorgeous and he
had next to nothing to do to pass it, Greg drove
lazily through what passed for downtown
Euphrata with his windows down and a Bob Seger
tape at high volume. He drew a few looks from
the women shoppers and a traffic cop, but most

of the town had become inured to him during the previous month.

"Hey, Jan-Michael!" a girl's voice called to him. "How's it shaking?"

Greg hit the brake and whipped his head around to find the girl standing across the street and a half block behind him. Though he already had encountered most of Euphrata's small teenage population, this girl was still an enigma. Not even Frankie Holloway at the bus station could put a name to her for him.

Red-haired, tall, slender, and definitely worth a few thousand second looks, she was maybe 18. She had first spotted him cruising around in the Porsche only days after he'd arrived in town and hailed him with a shout of "Jan-Michael!", clearly a reference to his strong resemblance to actor Jan-Michael Vincent and one that had been made many times before. But each time that she made verbal contact, it was from a considerable distance, with a street or parking lot acting as a buffer zone. It was obvious that, for some reason, she didn't want the two of them to meet, and so far she had been too quick for him. Maybe she knew he'd only be in town through the end of August.

Even before Greg could swerve into a parking space, she had disappeared into a department store. Probably suffers from a Mata Hari complex, he thought, turning down the avenue.

"God, he's cute," Lynette Madison sighed slowly as she watched Greg Hoode cruise away from her in that devastating car. It was obvious that he was looking for her, too, but he hadn't seen her slip into the aging, green van that was parked next to the entrance to Alpert's Oldtime Department Store. "I wish that we could pick *him* up for one of the monthly meetings, and I'm sure that there are plenty of other girls who agree with me on that."

The second occupant of the van, her father, snorted a short laugh. "The gentle sex," he observed wryly. "Cannibal maidens from Mars would be more appropriate."

Lynette shook her head. "You know what I mean, Dad. Just for fun, not for . . . *that*."

"Whatever, you can just forget it. He's local and therefore out of the question."

"He's been here a month. Does that make him a local?"

"And he has to leave in another month and his folks have more money than even the Yorks, so we certainly don't need any trouble from them. Got me?"

Lynette nodded reluctantly even as the Porsche disappeared around a corner.

James "Jimbo" Madison started up the van. "Good. Save those winsome pouts for the game we're tracking. The old man is pretty upset that we haven't provided him with more entertainment this month, and if we don't meet our quota for tonight and tomorrow night . . . well, there will be hell to pay, that's all." He swung the vehicle into a southbound lane.

Lynette realized at once where they were headed, and her greed for a night with Greg Hoode vanished before a wave of adolescent revulsion. "Oh, Daddy, the freight yard? But they're all so dirty, and they paw at me like I was some kind of toy or something.''

Jimbo sighed this time, and his regret was deep and sincere. "I'm sorry, baby, but if we come up empty again today . . . and I don't have a better place to get them, do you?''

Lynette decided to play the martyr a bit longer, reasoning that she could use the leverage at some point in the near future when something else she really wanted came along. "The old man is turning into an addict," she muttered. "Before you know it, he'll be using fifty a month.''

The van drifted slowly toward the one place in the little town where the outside world made regular contact, where the poor and homeless occasionally paused in their cross-country wanderings. A sign on either side of the vehicle read, "EUPHRATA WELCOME WAGON.''

The gymnasium contained a pool, some Ping-Pong tables, a basketball court, a small weight room, and a pair of punching bags, one a speed bag, the other a heavy bag. Greg was interested in these, of course, but when he carried his kit through the front door on his way to the men's dressing room, he realized he was a little late. The Kamikazes were already utilizing both of the bags.

"A touch late this morning, aren't you, Hillbilly?" Paul Lattwig called across the gym. Lattwig was around 19, a big, husky local who had driven down to Tiverton a few years ago to begin taking karate lessons. Now he was a black belt with a cluster of pie-eyed teenaged boys around him who were dedicated to learning the intricacies of Asian mayhem.

A couple of his ardent students were awkwardly kicking the heavy bag at the moment, while a third tried to set the speed bag into the sweet-sounding rhythm for which it was designed. He was missing every third punch.

Greg paused at the door, considering whether or not to fade away before the matter escalated. For no discernible reason, the aggressively confident Lattwig had taken a quick and intense dislike to Greg upon his arrival in town a month earlier. Greg could see no reason for the animosity; certainly, he had not initiated it. Maybe it was just the old boxing vs. karate conflict.

"Good day to you, too, Lattwig," he responded, continuing toward the dressing room.

Paul grinned in a rather nasty way. "Sorry that the bags are occupied, but you know how it is. First come, first served."

"Wouldn't have it any other way," Greg said. "I guess I'm stuck with the pool today."

Since Euphrata had no other public swimming pool, the gym was very popular during the hot summer months. It was crowded that morning, especially with squealing, enthusiastic youngsters, but Greg managed to engage in lively conversation with several attractive, relatively more mature swimming partners as he exercised what he felt to be his rapidly atrophying body. It was nearly lunchtime before he figured that his fingers and toes had wrinkled enough and headed back to the dressing room.

Lattwig and his fellow Kamikazes were arranged about his locker in what they intended to be casually intimidating postures.

"You know, you've got a lot of outstanding qualities, Redneck," Paul said coolly, his eyes half-lidded and bored but his tone decidedly serious. He stood around six foot one and weighed perhaps 190, which made him some two inches taller and thirty pounds heavier than Greg.

"That's damned nice of you to say, Lattwig," Greg replied as he stepped among the circle of white-robed figures. He was able to maintain a calm exterior, but he also was carefully examining the possibilities. There was no one else in the dressing room, and four of the six guys facing him were significantly larger than he. "I'll try to think of something nice to say about you if you can wait five or ten years." Taking a towel from his kit bag, he began to walk toward the showers.

One of the boys stopped him with a heavy hand on his left shoulder. "Paul was talking to you, Hillbilly," the Kamikaze said.

Greg felt it beginning in his stomach, a cold yet tingling electricity that mixed fear, rage and joyous anticipation into a single alloy, the same sensation that had preceded each of his 54 amateur bouts. He stared evenly at the boy.

"Lattwig," he said, "you'd better order your trained ape here to take his hand off of me or he'll be on a liquid diet for the next few months."

Several of the other boys hooted derisively, and Paul smiled. "A number of outstanding qualities," he repeated, "including a wide streak of bluff. Let's not cause any ill-feelings, Willie. This is just a get-acquainted meeting, after all."

The big guy dropped his hand. Greg stood still, though he had shifted most of his weight onto the balls of his feet. With only a pair of wet trunks

and a dry towel for protection and outnumbered
six to one, he knew that he would not be the
betting favorite if this confrontation developed
further. "Gregory Hoode, Atlanta," he said, "in
case you forgot."

"How could we forget one of the famous
Hillbilly Hoodes from good ol' Georgia? The
Hoodes with their Electric Soda Pop millions and
their midnight blue Porsches and their adorable
accents, who think that they can take over a town
for the summer and leaves all of the local po' boys
strangling in the dust."

"Oh yeah, territorial imperative," Greg said,
understanding now. "Afraid of losing the home
court advantages, is that the problem, Lattwig?"

The bushy-haired martial arts expert seemed to
be frozen for several seconds as his eyes bored
into Greg. Finally, with a nod of his head, he
moved several feet from the others and swiftly
went through a series of intricate and impressive
punches, kicks, and leaps aimed at no visible
opponent. Paul called it his *kata*; Greg considered
it to be shadowboxing.

"No threats, Hillbilly," Paul stated, grinning.
"Euphrata is a friendly town. Just don't think
that you can move in and dazzle us with your car
and your money."

Greg knew that he had to answer the challenge
somehow, just as he knew that it would be idiotic
to charge the six of them. So, still dripping from
his swim, he casually walked out of the dressing
room to where the punching bags hung, now
unmolested. His bag gloves were still in his kit in
the locker, but to go back for them would be an
admission   of   weakness.   After   mentally

apologizing to his bare knuckles, he started the show.

The speed bag is the small, inflated leather sack that is hung from an overhead frame and designed to aid a fighter in sharpening his hand speed and punching rhythm. It's generally the first training technique a young boxer is introduced to, and Greg was particularly adept with it. The brown bag became a dull blur as it danced before his fists, and the sounds that filled the gymnasium as it rebounded from the frame were like machine gun fire.

Greg turned it all on. He had very fast hands, and he geared them up, threw in a few headbutts to break the monotony, and even punctuated the action with shots from both elbows. The bag seemed to be ready to snap from its metal ring and soar into the far reaches of the swimming pool when he ended the display with a powerful overhand right. It swung freely for almost half a minute longer.

Laughter and cheers erupted from those in the crowded pool.

"Atlanta is a friendly town, too," he told the obviously impressed Kamikazes. "But we don't care for threats, even when they supposedly aren't threats."

Fifteen minutes later, showered and dressed, Greg returned to the parking lot to find the word "Hillbilly" scratched into the beautiful, blue paint job on the driver's door of his car.

Chapter Three

Early afternoon, Monday, July 10.

He was an outsider, he would be one all summer long, and he was damned sick of it.

Greg wasn't a Paul Lattwig, who needed a horde of admirers, but he did like to have a few friends around from time to time, if only to let him know that he was still a member of the human race. Friends had proven to be rather scarce in Euphrata, Indiana.

The townspeople were cordial enough, aside from Lattwig and his pals, but behind the smiling exterior mask there was a protective shell that said, "You have to be a member of the inner circle to be of any worth in Euphrata, and, fellow, you definitely are eccentric." Even the few dates he had had since arriving in town had left him with that feeling.

Though Greg was used to insincere friendship from people who envied his advantages, he had been totally unprepared for this particular reaction.

He knew where the scrawl on his door had come from, of course, but he had no proof, and the hospitable town authorities never would have helped an outsider prosecute a local for so minor an offense. He contemplated tackling the whole gang and gaining some measure of revenge before he was overwhelmed by their sheer numbers. Instead, he drove to a nearby hamburger joint and ate lunch while feeling exquisitely sorry for himself. Then he cruised over to the bus station.

"*Hola, compañero*!" Frankie Holloway shouted across the otherwise empty station as Greg entered. "What's on the agenda for the rich people today?"

"Travel, ace. How much would a bus ticket to Little America, Antarctica, cost me?" He walked to the counter behind which Frankie sat and dropped into a contoured plastic chair.

Frankie pretended to consult a chart on the counter. "It says here that a trip of that length would run approximately seventy-three million dollars, plus your firstborn male child and one dark blue Porsche." Frankie was 16 years old, black, thin, and had lost the use of his legs a dozen years earlier in an automobile accident.

Greg sighed loudly and massaged his eyes. "The money's in my wallet, you'll have to take an I.O.U. for the kid, and there's a Porsche parked outside that's about ninety-eight per cent the right color."

Since he had met no one in the mood to buy a bus ticket all day, Frankie left his post and motored his electric wheelchair around the counter to a point where he could see the car in the adjoining parking lot. "Oh, Jeeze!" he cried, as if struck by physical pain. "That's a desecration! To do that to a defenseless automobile! Man, I dream about that car at night—and sometimes on the job, too."

Greg worked up a tired laugh. "Sorry to shatter your fantasy, Francis. Maybe you'll find a nice four-door to fall in love and settle down with."

Frankie continued to stare at the rudely etched word on the door. "Damn, man, who did it? I've got contacts. I'll have them hit."

"Who else? Paranoid Paul and the Brain Damaged Five."

"And still they live?"

"Well, I am negotiating with a mysterious Algerian for several mid-range nuclear weapons, but other than that no retaliation has taken place."

Frankie shook his head, and Greg suddenly realized how authentic the other boy's sorrow was. He turned the wheelchair about to face Greg again. "I hate that, man, really. Those stupid jerks, especially that Lattwig. Somebody should put the skids to him and damned soon."

"Don't worry, *compadre*, what goes around comes around." Greg sat straighter in the chair. "But I didn't come here to dwell on my losses. Let's talk music, and when the next bus gets here, we can drop all pretenses of modern liberalism and chauvinistically rate the female newcomers."

If Greg had made one friend in Euphrata, it was sharp-witted Francis Albert (after Frank Sinatra) Holloway. Frankie couldn't carry a tune in a bucket, but he knew practically everything there was to know about American music since the turn of the century. Though he had been in Euphrata for much of his life, Frankie was a member of a very small local minority, and, like Greg, he saw through the friendly faces to the ultimate rejection that lay behind them.

A half hour later, they were discussing the relative historical importance of Chuck Berry and Buddy Holly when the 1:45 bus arrived, only seven minutes late.

"Shall we rate by the numbers or letters?" Frankie asked as he zipped back around the counter to his position.

"Let's be sophisticated and erudite about this, shall we, Francis?" Greg responded loftily. "Complete silence equals no interest, a soft moan means mild interest, and a winner rates the full-blown, on-the-floor convulsion."

Frankie laughed. "Ah, sexism is my life, but you may not have that many choices. Euphrata is not a hotbed of comings and goings, in case you haven't noticed."

"Tell me about it," Greg muttered.

It turned out that Frankie was right, to an extent. No one boarded the bus when it stopped and only two people disembarked. The first was a small, bright-eyed, sprightly woman who fairly bounced down the steps with a suitcase in her left hand and a birdcage in her right.

The lady—who looked so stereotypically the senior citizen but moved with so much bubbling energy—stopped before the counter and placed the birdcage directly before Frankie. She seemed to be inviting his response.

"How are you, Miss Amelia?" Frankie asked with what seemed to be genuine delight. "I didn't think you'd be leaving your sister's until Friday."

"Now that I'm back home, I'm just perfect, Franklin!" she answered. "How nice to see you, too. Say hello to Franklin, Benjamin." She held up the birdcage.

"How you doing, Benjy?" Frankie said, still smiling.

"Prettybird," the parakeet chirped.

Miss Amelia continued. "I was going to stay at Bertha's until Friday, but her health . . . my, my, she's in such poor shape."

"Sorry to hear that."

"Well, at ninety-one you have to expect as much." Suddenly, the sparkle returned to her eyes. "But good news! I've convinced her to spend the rest of the summer with me here. Two months in Euphrata will cure her arthritis and give her the lungs of a twenty-year-old."

"I sure hope so, Miss Amelia. Should I call a taxi for you?"

The woman looked startled. "Heavens, no! It's only six blocks, and the walk will do me good."

After Miss Amelia had left, Greg cocked an eye at Frankie and asked, "Franklin?"

He shrugged. "It beats what she used to call me —Fletcher."

Greg chuckled. "She does get around well, though."

"You don't know the half of it, bruddah. Remember Miss Bertha, her ninety-one year-old sister?"

Greg nodded.

"Her *younger* sister."

Greg coughed with surprise. "Just how stupid do I look to you, man?" he asked.

"Right hand in the air, man; that little woman is ninety-four."

"Jehosephat! Ninety-four? She looks at least forty years younger than that!"

"There are a lot of real old folks in Euphrata." Frankie paused and gave Greg a peculiar look. "Who knows? Maybe there *is* something in the air around here."

Greg started to respond, but at that moment the second passenger finally made her way from the rear of the bus and stepped down from it.

"Frankie, you're just about to witness an epileptic seizure," he whispered. "All of my hormones are hormoning, and I think I'm in love."

The second passenger was a young woman about 17 or 18, tall, about five-feet-seven, and the most gorgeous vision he had beheld since leaving Atlanta. She had brilliant blue eyes and deep, rich brown hair that fell in glistening waves about her shoulders. The blue blouse and skirt that she wore set off her eyes perfectly and complimented her trim, athletic figure.

The girl carried a single, small suitcase and moved with confident purposefulness as she entered the station and walked to Frankie's counter. "Excuse me, I wonder if you could call a cab for me?" she asked crisply.

"Sure could, Miss," Frankie said, lifting the receiver of his telephone. He was impressed with the new arrival, too, but he was even more fascinated by Greg's open-mouthed awe and the young woman's apparent ignorance of it.

Before Frankie could begin dialing, Greg had virtually levitated himself out of the molded chair and stepped to the girl's side. He caught the other boy's hand and guided the receiver back to its cradle. "Just a moment, Franklin," he said smoothly. "Before our attractive guest is subjected to the exorbitant rates charged by the local cabbies, let's not forget to tell her about the special service being offered this month by the Euphrata Tourist Council."

The girl turned to face him.

"Tourist Council?" Frankie repeated in amused tones.

Go for it, Hoode, he told himself. "Sure, the motion that was passed at the last city commission meeting." Even as he spoke, he saw in the girl's perceptive expression the realization that what he was spouting was nothing more than hogwash, but she didn't seem too upset by this, and he was enjoying himself for the first time in days, so what the hell? He plunged ahead. "Let me introduce myself. I'm Gregory Hoode, head of the Euphrata Tourism Council's official welcoming committee. It's my duty and pleasure to provide you with transportation for a general tour of all of the interesting sites in our fair city."

Frankie laughed aloud at that.

"All of this is, of course, free of charge as a goodwill demonstration of our intention to increase tourism in this area tenfold. Franklin, tell this young woman how well-trained and highly qualified I am for this particular position."

Barely able to compose himself, Frankie said, "Miss, I wouldn't trust this guy with my prize collection of antique bubblegum wrappers, even if I had one."

"See?" Greg continued, undaunted. "May I take your suitcase?"

The girl smiled, in contrast to her former serious demeanor, and replied, "Thanks, anyway, Mr. Hoode, but I believe I'll stick with that taxi."

"I understand. I can see that you realized that everything I just told you was a cloud of hot air—except for my name—but the offer itself was legitimate, and it still stands. I'd be glad to take you wherever you'd like to go this afternoon. I'm free for the day, and my car's right outside."

"What a car," Frankie moaned softly.

The girl hesitated. Up close like this, Greg could see that his instincts hadn't failed him; she was truly naturally beautiful, with skin like pale, clear velvet and soft but distinctive features.

"I really appreciate the offer, but I think it would be wise if I took the cab," she finally said.

Greg couldn't fault her for her caution. He grinned and nodded. "Of course, I can appreciate that, but the car remains at your disposal if you change your mind." After all, where was he going in Euphrata on a Monday afternoon?

Frankie rang up the only local cab company and discovered that two drivers were off-duty, two others were carrying fares, and the remaining fifth car was being repaired. It would be at least 40 minutes before a cab could arrive.

"Is there anyone else you could get in touch with, a relative or a friend?" Frankie asked.

She shook her head. "No. No one."

Greg had already gone down swinging, so he raised his eyebrows with interest but said nothing.

The girl consulted her watch, apparently eager to get underway. After a moment, she said, "I suppose you'll think I'm awfully opportunistic, Mr. Hoode, but if your offer is still open, I'd like to take you up on it."

That's good enough for me, he thought instantly. "Believe me, I'd much rather be a taxi driver than a bus station groupie with Mr. Holloway," Greg stated.

"I didn't think that the authorities would give your license back to you so soon after that conviction for driving while legally insane," Frankie muttered good-naturedly.

Greg took the young woman's suitcase. "I'm his idol and role model," he told her, inclining his head toward Frankie. "He tries to emulate me in every way." They left the station together.

Dropping the suitcase in the back seat of his car, Greg opened the passenger door for the girl and then slipped behind the wheel. He hoped that he had successfully screened her from the embarrassment scratched into the driver's door.

"Well, all I need to know now is our destination," he said to her.

"Oh, I'm sorry. Um, can you recommend a nice place to stay?" she asked.

"As far as I know there's only one motel in the whole area."

"Don't you live in Euphrata?"

"I'm here for the summer."

She smiled slightly. "I thught that you sounded a little out of place. The south?"

"Atlanta, Miss. . . ?"

"Pettis. Catherine Pettis. Call me Cathy."

"And I'm Greg."

The small smile flickered again. "Not Robin Hoode?"

"That's my cousin," he answered, "and she's not used to the wisecracks yet. As I was saying, I'm staying here with my uncle for the summer, and so far it seems like this summer started years ago." He started the car and pulled out of the lot.

"You sound as if Euphrata isn't exactly your idea of a resort location."

"Watching a paid political broadcast is exciting in comparison."

"That bad, humm? Well then . . . Greg, if there's only one motel, I guess that's the one I want."

"It's Ed Stern's place, and it's four or five miles to the west of town." Greg hoped that he recalled the correct location; he'd passed the motel only once himself.

It was too beautiful a day to think about secrets.

Pamela Durben had never visited Indiana before, and as she passed through its summer glory in full bloom, she had to wonder why that was. A professional photographer of both landscapes and urban skylines, she had taken award-winning shots in 42 other states during her career, but somehow or other, the nation's 19th state had never seemed to offer any of the compelling yet not overexposed images that she liked to focus upon in her work. In fact, had she not been commissioned to compile this extensive national photographic record, she might well have overlooked Indiana, one of the most beautiful of all the states, for years to come.

With her trained eyes searching the vast expanses for just the right scene, Pamela was almost able to sublimate the persistent question that slowly was becoming a nagging pain in her relationship with her husband.

Then the van topped a deceptively small hill, and the vision that greeted her from the other side eradicated all of these troubling thoughts from her mind, however temporarily.

"Kevin, Kevin! Stop here! This is great!" Pamela said excitedly, already scrambling into the rear of the van for her camera equipment. She certainly didn't need the miniature lens that dangled about her neck to tell her that this one was right.

Behind the wheel, Kevin Durben chuckled indulgently and swung the vehicle to the right-hand shoulder of the road. He was a hefty, tall man at 29, with curly brown hair and matching beard and mustache that gave him the air of a genuine outdoorsman who filmed macho beer commercials for money, not fame. Actually, Kevin had a decided preference for fine wine and nights spent at the symphony over beer and camping.

"Better hurry while the light is exactly right," he told his wife in a teasing tone as she struggled to open the sliding side door with both arms filled with equipment.

"Oh, if only you would help instead of hinder!" Pamela said in exasperation.

Still laughing, Kevin strolled to the other side of the van to lend his assistance.

Indeed, he had to admit it was a magnificent vista. The two-lane highway that they had been traveling while visiting some of the less well-known communities in Indiana rose straight and smooth over the peak of this seemingly insignificant hillside and then dropped like a shot into a vast, shallow, idyllic valley on its other side. Green pastures were separated from either side of the road by weathered brown fences, and a few spotted cattle grazed amid the lushness with such deliberation and at such distance that they appeared to be mere details in this Cinemascopic, Rockwell painting. Far away—two miles or more—a single farmhouse stood halfway up the side of the next hill.

"God, isn't this perfect?" Pamela asked. "The colors, the composition, the spatial contrasts . . . it looks like some huge cosmic being came down with a magic brush and painted it just for us."

"A rainbow brush," Kevin observed. "That's where the colors come from."

Pamela leaned over to spot the camera atop the tripod. She was 28, just a year younger than her husband of 18 months, and her figure was very nice and well-rounded, though she was convinced that someday she would have to lose those ten pounds that she had been promising to eliminate for the past dozen years. Kevin—and most every other man who saw her in blouse and jeans, as she was now—knew that Pamela didn't need to drop an ounce. Her short hair was a color that lay intriguingly between deep red and rich brown.

"Kev," she stated thoughtfully, "I believe we have our cover shot . . . right here." She snapped the first of what promised to be a number of pictures of this scene.

"Let me see now," he responded in mock confusion, "will *this* cover shot replace the cover shot we took of the old country church in Vermont, the shot from New York Harbor, or the Amish couple in the wagon in Pennsylvania?"

"So maybe it'll be part of a montage. I wish that it was cold enough to have some smoke puffing from the chimney in that farmhouse."

Kevin leaned against the fender of the van. "Ah, but then how green would our valley be?"

"Good point, Watson."

Pamela continued to snap shots of the valley with enthusiasm, and though they all seemed to be of the same angle to Kevin, he waited patiently, fully aware that his talented young wife was capturing a different nuance with each exposure. She really was terrific with a camera. The traffic was so light here that only one picture was ruined by the appearance of an auto from over the far hill.

Though Kevin was patient, his mind could wander after some minutes of staring at the same scene, and it did. Pamela was bent forward behind the camera with what seemed to be inexhaustible stamina, and her rear was thrust provocatively toward him in the tight jeans. He knew that this was an entirely unconscious pose on her part, but such knowledge didn't make the sight any less appealing. He felt the urge coming on, sort of like the onset of a welcome fever, even as he realized that there would be no release for it here and now. In a year and a half of "legal" lovemaking, he had never convinced her to do it outside.

Instead, he reached out and slapped that round fanny, a slap with some real zest in it.

"Damn it, Kevin!" Pamela cried, standing sharply and covering the offended area with her hands. "That really hurt! Ow . . . I wish you'd stop doing that all the time!"

"You mean you don't love it?" he asked with feigned innocence.

Pamela rubbed herself and tried to control the flare of temper that threatened to spoil what had been, until then, a very special moment. With some forced willpower, she finally answered, "Honey, you know I don't mind open displays of affection—I love them—but that felt like more than just play. That was painful."

He stood and took her in his arms. "Don't you know that I'd never intentially hurt you? Sometimes I just feel like I'm going to explode if I don't touch you."

"Touch me?" she repeated uncertainly.

"Like this." He kissed her slowly and passionately. A couple of cars passed rather close together, and their passengers were treated to something of a public display, but neither of the two even noticed them.

"You know," Pamela whispered happily, "that helps, but it's not what hurts."

Kevin's eyebrows did a Groucho dance. "Want me to kiss that, too?"

A while later, on the road again, they passed a sign that said, "EUPHRATA—FIVE MILES."

"Euphrata?" Kevin mumbled with a quizzical look. "Isn't that a river in Mesopotamia or something?"

Pamela fought briefly with an obstinate map that was threatening to devour her. "Well, according to this, it's a little blue patch on the highway. Maybe they have a sandwich shop; I'm starving."

"A BLT on stone-ground whole wheat, and hold the cow patties."

"You are so urbane," she replied, sighing. "It won't hurt to look, since we have to drive right through it, anyway. You know, some of the best atmospheric shots can be found in these out-of-the-way places."

Kevin continued to grin. "Yeah, like this week's high society wedding."

As the miles passed, the occasional rustic dwelling began to appear by the roadside, but it still seemed as if they were a considerable distance from anything that deserved to be called a town. Pamela tried to focus her mind on the photogenic surroundings, where they would enter Illinois after completing the Indiana shootings, how hungry she felt—anything to keep her thoughts from returning to last night and the things she had heard in the hot darkness of a little Piqua, Ohio, hotel room. But like a probing finger at an open sore, she found herself drawn back to it by a magnetic intensity.

And, almost against her will, she began to speak of it, "Kev, maybe you should let me do a little more of the driving on this grand tour."

"Why?" he asked, still light-spirited and unsuspecting. "Do I frighten you?" He gunned the engine playfully with the clutch in.

"You know you don't. It's just that I feel . . . like you're trying to overdo it just to make sure that I meet my deadline on the book. Two and three states a day is quite a load."

"Not for me. You're art and I'm transportation, remember? Your eyes have to be free to roam the scenic splendors of our great nation without being locked into observing the basics of the highway, which, I might add, you're not all that familiar with under the best of circumstances.''

Pamela gave him a frisky punch to the ribs.

In a somewhat more serious tone, Kevin added, ''Don't worry about me, babe. I've got the stamina of a mule, and there are still six weeks left before I have to report back to Durben, Durben, and Schallert. It don't hurt to be the son of the founder, what?''

''True enough,'' she admitted. ''I just want to be sure that you're not overtaxed. Last night . . .''

''You were disappointed in last night?'' he shrieked comically. ''Oh, my lord, it must be premature celibacy attacking in the prime of my physical youth! I suppose I'll have to resign from this marriage and open a chain of cut-rate monasteries. Or maybe I should just stop making it with the coffee shop waitresses while you're in the powder room.''

Her mind told her to laugh with him and allow this potentially ugly moment to evaporate before it really began, but her heart wouldn't listen. ''You had that dream again last night,'' she said quietly.

That immediately lowered the temperature inside the van by a few dozen degrees. Kevin turned his face from her to fasten his eyes on the empty road ahead, and his wide grin disappeared behind the veil of his thick beard. Pamela regretted the words even as she said them.

Support him in this, she told herself. Show him that you're always going to be here for him, that he can tell you about whatever it is that comes to him in the depths of the night and forces him to cry out and whisper apologies to . . . someone.

''You know, I don't mean to jump the gun, but I'm pretty sure that this marriage is going to work,'' she said weakly in the following silence. ''We can talk about it, Kev. You can tell me what it is that causes these awful nightmares, and maybe that would—''

''There's nothing to say,'' he interrupted sharply. ''They're just stupid dreams, that's all. Sorry I woke you.''

''Dreams—or the same dream?'' she asked. ''You always say the same things, the same regrets . . .''

''What the hell difference does it make?'' he demanded a little more loudly than he had intended. ''Dream or dreams, it's still ridiculous. What do you want me to do, start psychiatric counseling? Or just get separate bedrooms?''

''Talk to me, hon. A problem shared is—''

He laughed suddenly, bitterly. ''Not this one, believe me. Nothing's going to help this, Pam.'' His voice fell to an almost inaudible whisper. ''Not unless you can come up with that old time machine and send me back there again.''

Pamela looked at her husband, who now seemed to be consciously avoiding her, and she felt her heart breaking a little more. God, she loved this man, and she knew that he loved her, too. But it appeared that he didn't love her quite enough to trust her with his secrets, even though they were threatening to destroy him during the night, while she lay helpless at his side. What could it be? He came from an apparently loving family, and he'd never lost a close family member; as he told her, even his grandparents were still living. As the middle son of one of the East Coast's top lawyers, his youth had been privileged, to say the least, though that hadn't affected his character in any visible or adverse way; never in the military, it couldn't be some terrible war story that was haunting him.

As much as anything, Pamela was afraid that he never would trust her enough to tell her.

''It's nothing to be ashamed of,'' she said.

He briefly looked at her, then, and she saw something deep and shining—but with an awful, fearsome light—in his eyes, as if a curtain had been lifted for just an instant. It descended just as quickly.

"Let's forget it, Pammie, okay?" he asked. There was a trace of real pleading in his voice.

"Baby, I want to," she answered, "but I hate the thought that there's something you feel you can't share with me."

He again faced her, his eyes unreadable now and his expression unlike any she had ever seen in her husband, when it happened. Perhaps he had been ready to open himself to her, or perhaps he had been determined to end the discussion for good; but the words never came, because a large, ancient pickup truck loaded to bursting with farm produce approached the stop sign at the end of a road which intersected with the highway and passed it without slowing. The truck swung directly into their path.

"Kevin!" Pamela screamed.

Kevin snapped his eyes around no more than a heartbeat before the inevitable collision, but in that brief moment, he was able to whip the van to the right in a desperate effort to ride the shoulder behind the antique truck. He almost made it work.

The head-on crash was avoided by Kevin's maneuver, but the left rear side of the van pounded into the corresponding fender of the truck. Pamela may have screamed—she never knew—but in the following second all conscious reaction left her. She wasn't wearing her seatbelt, so she was tossed about the interior like a pebble in a whirlpool, while the van spun from the highway into the comparatively soft earth of the shoulder. Rather than helping Kevin to regain control, however, the dirt grabbed the smoking tires much more severely than the paving had, and the vehicle tumbled madly down the incline next to the road.

It was a preview of hell for Pamela. The world seemed to be exploding all about her, and everything from her bags of clothing to her expensive camera equipment was transformed into dangerous implements. She was thrown against a window and snatched away just as quickly to be pounded by the headrest of her seat as she flew across it. Cannons erupted viciously all about her as something cold and metallic smashed into her ribs.

Though she wouldn't know this until much later, the rickety truck which had been the cause of it all was knocked to the other side of the road, the driver hardly injured.

The deadly roll of the large van came to an end only when it reached the bottom of the slope and plunged into the trunks of the trees that grew there. With a final, awesome peal of thunder, the wreck finally ground to a halt. It was almost like death.

Pamela didn't lose consciousness until after it all was over, for some strange reason, and when she did it was only for seconds. Her eyes flickered open, the lashes coated in something thick and heavy that she was too dazed to recognize as blood, and she opened her mouth to draw in another breath, which was her first since the collision. Her lungs and chest hurt, but dully, practically like memories of old injuries. It was quiet and she didn't know where she was.

The insulation of shock kept her removed from the sharp agony of the moment, until she heard someone call her name from very far off. Kevin! With realization came the pain, and she began to scream and cry at the immensity of it.

He managed to drag himself into the overturned van sometime later, and though the fact that he was still alive should have assured Pamela, when she looked at her husband the anguish of her own body receded behind the sorrow she felt for him. His face was all bloody, from his scalp, his nose, his mouth, and his ears, and he couldn't walk when he struggled to reach her due to the awful damage that had been done to both legs and one side of his hips. He was bleeding somewhere in his throat, too, and every time he exhaled a gasping breath a pink cloud of mist sprinkled upon her. If Pamela could have moved, she would have taken him in her arms to soothe away the hurt.

"Shhh, okay, baby, it's okay," he whispered, and only then did Pamela realize that she was crying. "We're both alive, there's no fire, and the ambulances will come very soon. We'll be all right, I promise you we will."

"Your face is cut," she sighed weakly.

"Hey, don't worry about me." He tried to grin. "I'm too mean to be hurt; you know that. Can you move? Can you crawl?"

"I think I—oh God, Kevin! It hurts! Jesus, it hurts all over!"

"Okay, okay, I'm here right beside you, baby! I swear I won't leave you!" A panic that he hadn't felt for his own safety glowed in his face now. "We're going to be fine, baby. Try to ease your breathing—don't cry! Don't move! Help is coming. God, Pamela, hold on! Hold on for me, baby!"

She passed out again.

Consciousness was fleeting during those next minutes. Pamela's heart would continue to pump energy throughout her broken body, and some of this would reach her mind and awaken her to the fact that she was lying in the overturned van, bleeding to death. Then a new wave of agony would flood through her and drown all awareness momentarily.

When she finally came around for a relatively substantial amount of time, she was drawn out again by Kevin's voice.

"Down here, mister!" he was shouting. "We're here, in the van! You gotta help my wife! She's hurt!"

Pamela couldn't speak or move now, but she did hear a couple of men slowly descending the long slope down which the van had tumbled. Their grunts of exertion and curses when they fell or snagged themselves on the shattered trees and bushes came to her as clearly as if her spirit were hovering invisibly out of her body next to them. When they reached the side of the van, all that she could see of them were the high-topped, brightly polished boots so favored by small-town police-men.

"You okay in there?" one of the pair asked.

"Okay?" Kevin repeated incredulously. "We're hurt, man! Get us out of here, to a hospital!"

The men stooped to peer into the van, and, yes, they were even wearing dark glasses.

"How many of you in there?"

"Two! My wife and I! I'm all right, but I think she's dying!"

Really? thought Pamela with startling calmness and clarity. I didn't know . . .

The policemen stood again to take themselves out of her line of vision. "Damn," one of them said with little attempt at hiding his anger. "I knew old Cleotis was going to cause something like this one day. The old bastard should have been grounded twenty years ago."

"Well, bitching about him doesn't do us any good now, does it?" the other responded. "What are we going to do about them?"

"Let me think a minute, will you? Hell, what do the plates say?"

"Uh . . . New York, Erie County. Isn't Buffalo in Erie County?"

"Why are you asking me? You're the geography nut."

Kevin's voice was raw with both pain and fear when he interrupted them. "You've got to help us, officer! Please!"

The first cop employed a plastic tone of reassurance in replying. "Don't you worry, sir. We'll take good care of you and your little lady." To his partner, he continued, "Man, Buffalo is a big place, and if they're from there, somebody's liable to come looking for them. You know what I mean? Maybe we'd better call Tiverton for an ambulance."

"I don't think they'd last until an ambulance got here, Wally. Why don't we take 'em in the cars?"

"The way they're bleeding? Shit, Matty, we'd never get that off of the upholstery!"

They think we can't hear them, Pamela told herself, because she couldn't speak to Kevin. They think we're almost dead already.

"Well, we can't just walk away."

"Why not? We could say we didn't find the wreck until *after* we—"

"Come on, Wally. Being careful is one thing, but that's sick. Let's get them into the car. We'll put them both in mine, so don't worry about your precious upholstery."

"Are you going to take them all the way to Tiverton?"

"Nah. Just to the Yorks'. Maybe the old man will even be able to use them, and we'll get bonuses next month."

The first man laughed grimly. "Yeah, bonuses or butt kickings."

"Just give me a hand with them, all right?"

When strong arms lifted her from her place amid the wreckage and began the trek up the hillside, the pain became too much, and Pamela slipped without resistance into a quiet place that was beyond its reach.

Chapter Four

Midafternoon, Monday, July 10.

The drive from the bus station was quite enjoyable, as far as Greg Hoode was concerned. Cathy Pettis proved to be as intelligent and convivial as she was attractive, and she displayed a ready sense of humor, always a plus in Greg's estimation. There were always more than enough serious people in the world to fill the needs of any masochistic moods he might pass through from time to time.

But Cathy was hiding something. Greg didn't consider himself a Sam Spade type or anything, but it would have been hard to ignore the fact that a slight tenseness entered her voice when the conversation centered about her reason for visiting Euphrata. She had neither relatives nor acquaintances in town and claimed to have come simply to spend a quiet week's vacation. Greg didn't bring it up, but he had some trouble with the thought that anyone would voluntarily vacation in Euphrata.

The pair had just cruised past the city limits when they encountered two police cars, lights flashing and sirens wailing, making tracks in the other direction. Greg pulled to the side of the road until they passed and then drove carefully until he reached the site of the wreck, only a quarter-mile away. This certainly was proving to be an uncommonly exciting day in old Euphrata.

It was a two vehicle accident. To their left, far down a steep slope and surrounded by eight or ten excited locals, lay a fairly large blue van that Greg didn't recognize from anywhere about town. It was really busted up, making Greg glad that he hadn't been in its path when it left the road.

"I hope no one was killed in that," Cathy said with apparently sincere concern.

I don't see how they could have avoided it, Greg thought. He pulled across the road and came to a stop on the shoulder just before where the van had crashed. "Need any help down there?" he called through his open window.

Only one of the curious men looked up at his question. "No thanks, young fellow. The deputies have carted the folks off to the Yorks'. Move along and keep the street clear."

"Right, can't keep traffic backed up," Greg answered with a grin, since aside from those already parked, there wasn't a sign of a car in either direction. He eased back onto the highway.

"They must have hit a vegetable supply truck," Cathy commented while she regarded the littered road before them. Smashed crates of tomatoes, cabbages, potatoes, and practically every other locally grown food had been scattered with mad abandon. It made for a colorful and fragrant obstacle course that Greg maneuvered through.

A short distance away on the right side of the road sat a fragile but seemingly indestructable old red truck, still on its wheels and a third full of produce. A white-bearded little man was standing next to it arguing vociferously with a couple of onlookers and occasionally kicking the severely crumpled rear fender.

"There's your culprit," Greg said, indicating the enraged man with a motion of his head. "Traffic Ticket Louie, the worst driver it's ever been my misfortune to encounter on a public street, and that's saying a lot when you remember that I live in Atlanta."

"He certainly looks upset over the whole matter," she agreed. "Doesn't seem to be injured, though."

"The ones who cause it seldom are."

"He must be eighty years old. It's a wonder that he's still able to drive."

"There are plenty of spry senior citizens around here," Greg pointed out from a fresh memory of Miss Amelia. "I only hope that the cops get those other people to the hospital in time."

"How far away is it?"

Greg considered for a moment before realizing, with a start, that he had no answer for that. "You know, I have no idea. I can't recall ever seeing it."

Cathy gave him a bemused smile. "Nice little place you have here, Mr. Hoode."

They left the accident scene behind. Luckily for

Greg, only one primary highway ran through
Euphrata, and Ed Stern had been smart enough
to select a location on it to set up his motel. The
Porsche stopped before the main office only 15
minutes after having left the bus station.

"This is it, the Euphrata version of the
Waldorf-Astoria," Greg said. "If you don't
object, I'll take your suitcase inside." He opened
the door.

"Greg," Cathy said, placing a hand on his
shoulder, "I really don't mean to impose on you,
but I'd like for you to wait inside with me while I
speak to the manager, if you will. I may not be
staying here."

Ah, another puzzling facet of this mysterious
woman, he thought. Some things just get better
and better. Why not stay aboard for the ride?
"You're in charge, Miss Pettis," he said,
laughing.

Stern's Motel was actually a pleasant arrangement of 26 individual cabins around a kidney-
shaped swimming pool that was open to guests
only. The office looked like any of the other
cabins and was identifiable only by the sign in
front of it. The interior was air-conditioned and
lighted with muted fluorescent fixtures. A middle-
aged man with only a ring of dark hair and a
rather substantial midsection looked up from a
crossword puzzle magazine when they entered.
He switched off a small radio and stood behind a
mahogany desk.

"Afternoon," he said in a friendly manner. He
looked pointedly at their bare ring fingers. "What
can I do for you young folks? A couple of
cabins?"

"I'm just the driver," Greg answered. "This is Miss Pettis."

The man obviously was relieved that he wouldn't hve to inquire about their marital status. "Ed Stern, Miss Pettis, the name on the sign. If you're interested in a place to stay, I'm sure we can help you."

Cathy seemed very interested in the decor of the office. Greg could almost feel her readying herself for the coming moment. Her voice betrayed none of her nervousness, if indeed she had any, when she said, "Before I make up my mind, Mr. Stern, there are several questions that I need to have answered."

"I'd be pleased to help you, Miss Pettis," Stern said.

"Thank you. First, are there any other hotels or motels in the Euphrata area?"

Stern simply grinned. "Nope, we've sort of cornered the market. We don't get a lot of tourists here in the best of times, so the industry has never really gotten started. But I make a decent living, and I can't complain. A lot of people prefer to have Euphrata remain their little secret."

"Such as the National Insomnia Control Society," Greg commented almost inaudibly.

"Okay," Cathy continued. She seemed to have a mental list of questions all ready. "Do you keep a log of everyone who registers here, and, if so, do you mind if I see it?"

"The law requires that we maintain a register," Stern replied. "I don't have any objections to letting you look at it. Do you have a particular date in mind?"

A new excitement glistened in Cathy's eyes. "Last year," she said quickly, "September seventh and eighth."

"Just one second," Stern said. Rather than leaving the desk, the man turned to what Greg had taken to be a television set and switched it on to reveal the screen of a computer terminal. "September seventh . . . and eighth. There we go." He swiveled the screen about so that Cathy and Greg could read the information that was displayed upon it.

There wasn't much. "September 7—Peter Jackson Samples, checked out September 10; Mr. and Mrs. Matthew Scoonover, checked out September 13. September 8—Mr. and Mrs. L.B. Maretta, checked out September 9."

Greg could see the excitement draining from Cathy like a current of light that has been shut off. Who was she looking for?

"Would it be much trouble to backdate the records to, say, September fifth?" she asked.

"Not a bit," Stern answered in a jovial tone. His heavy fingers danced with incongruous speed over the keyboard.

The first listing was replaced by: "September 5—Jason Plummer, checked out September 6. September 6—none."

Stern read the disappointment in the young woman's expression. "How about the fourth?" he asked. "Or the nineth or tenth? I love playing with this thing."

"No," Cathy responded slowly. "They wouldn't have gotten here by the fourth."

"Well, we do have the actual register in storage, if you'd like to check out the signatures.''

Some of the enthusiasm returned to Cathy's voice. "Yes, I'd like that."

As if in keeping with some sort of cosmic balance, a good deal of Stern's enthusiasm for the task vanished. Sorting through back registers wasn't as much fun as playing with the computer, it seemed, but he maintained a professional smile and left them to find the appropriate book.

It took just over ten minutes, about what Greg had expected. The only names listed on the dates in question were the same ones that had been displayed by the computer. Getting into the spirit of the activity, Greg carefully and surreptitiously checked the pages for any signs of tampering, but he was unable to detect any.

"Anything else, Miss?" Stern questioned after a proper length of time.

There was little energy remaining in her tone when Cathy said, "Just one more thing. Would you consider your motel to be a family operation?"

"Sure would," he replied proudly. "The Stern Motel stands for decency and security, no cohabitation without benefit of matrimony, no alcoholic beverages, and even all of those who use the pool are required to—"

"That's not really what I meant," Cathy interrupted. "Is the business *run* by your family, your wife and children?"

Stern didn't try to hide his confusion. "Well, since you're being specific, I'd have to say no. I put in most of the time here in the office, and I've got a night manager, but he's no relation. The wife never has shown much interest, and my kids

are all married and live upstate now. I hope you
don't mind me asking, but are you always this
careful about where you check in?''

"Yes, Mr. Stern, I am. These days everyone
always should be just as careful as possible.
Thank you for your time and help." She turned
to leave.

The man looked even more startled. "You
don't want a cabin?"

"No. I'm sorry, but this just isn't the place that
I am looking for."

Picking up the suitcase, Greg caught the
befuddled and somewhat angry expression that
Stern was aiming at the two of them, and he really
couldn't blame the man. So he shrugged and, on
impulse, pulled a ten dollar bill from his wallet
and handed it to the manager.

"For your trouble," he said.

Stern didn't refuse the money. In fact, his
harsh stare softened a little, and he said, "Miss?"

Cathy stopped at the door and turned back to
face him.

"If you wouldn't be comfortable here, there is
another place in town that occasionally takes in
boarders. They're a private residence, not
actually a hotel, but—"

"Where?" she asked avidly.

"The York place would be your best chance.
It's that large, dark house on the hill overlooking
town."

"I know it," Greg said. "Never been there, but
you can't miss seeing it."

"It's a family business?" Cathy inquired.

"A private residence, like I said. And it's got a
real solid reputation around town. The Yorks are

probably the richest people in this part of Indiana, except maybe for that Hoode fellow who moved here a while back.''

"Thanks again," Greg said.

"Yes, thank you very much," Cathy added.

The two young people left the office and returned to the Porsche. Even before she spoke, Cathy's eyes were asking a question that Greg could read.

He decided to save her a little embarrassment. "I'm pretty sure that I know the way to the York house. How about if I drive you up and check this joint out?"

She tried to remain calm. "I shouldn't put you to any more trouble, Greg, but I really need to get to that place. If you wouldn't mind . . .''

"You couldn't keep me away from there with a ten foot pole."

They headed back toward Euphrata.

The passage by the wreck site was even a little slower, because enough time had passed to allow more people to stop and gawk at the damaged vehicles and more stray dogs and cats to investigate the strewn produce. Traffic Ticket Louie was still resisting the pleas of concerned friends to allow himself to be taken somewhere for examination, and he was still giving the helpless truck hell with lusty kicks and punches. Greg couldn't smother a laugh at the sight.

Just before they passed the city limits sign, Cathy said, "I'd like to repay you for what you gave Mr. Stern, Greg. If you'll tell me how much it was . . .'' She began opening her purse.

"Oh, no, forget about that," Greg stated. "If money stays in my pockets too long, it has a nasty habit of reproducing. That bill started out as a quarter this morning.''

"Must be a terrible burden to you," she said, chuckling. "But really, I can't continue to impose on you this way."

"I said forget it, didn't I? Remember that rich Hoode guy that Stern mentioned? He's my uncle Dan, the one I'm spending the summer with, and my branch of the family has more money than he does." Normally Greg didn't reveal things like this to new acquaintances, having found that friends won by his wealth were about as permanent as the rare and light Georgia snows. But he really didn't want to take Cathy's money, and she was proving to be the most intriguing individual he had met in quite some time.

A kind of melancholy entered Cathy's attitude in response to Greg's last statement. "It must be wonderful not to worry about money," she said as she watched the passing scenery. Euphrata was beautiful in its own way. "Mikey and I always had to be careful with every penny."

"Mikey?" he asked quietly.

"My brother."

He decided to press his luck. "Is he the one you're looking for?"

She turned to stare directly at him. "My brother is dead."

"I'm sorry."

An uneasy silence filled the car.

The York Mansion was only a little more difficult to reach than the motel had been. Because of its size and position atop the towering hillside, it was almost always in sight as they wound along the narrow street leading up to it. Greg made one wrong turn that dead-ended at a deserted animal hospital, but it was easy enough for him to backtrack and continue the climb. Finally, the road they were following changed to a long, wide driveway that delivered them to the front porch of the mansion.

And it was a mansion in the richest sense of that word. Three stories high, it consisted of a huge central section, large enough to be a boarding house by itself, and two opposing wings to the east and west. It was painted predominantly in a dark, hushed green, and an oversized garage abutted the end of the eastern wing. A lush, healthy and well-kept lawn seemed to buoy it like a green sea, and an imposing sundeck thrust out from near the top of the central tower.

"It's magnificent," an awed Cathy said. An entrancing smile lit her face and chased away the shadows that had darkened her upon the mention of her brother. "It looks like a presidential retirement home."

"It's even bigger than I had thought," Greg agreed. He'd been in many beautiful and ostentatious homes in his time, but the York mansion would have held its own with any of them. "I'll bet that it has at least sixty rooms."

"No wonder they can take in guests." She fell silent again as Greg slowly maneuvered the car up to the front veranda. As he cut the engine, she asked, "Do you think that they keep a register?"

"I doubt it," he answered. "It's really not a hotel."

"But wouldn't they have to be licensed in some way?"

Greg considered this before replying. "Take my word for it, any family that can own and maintain a residence this size in a community like Euphrata can decide for themselves which laws they'll recognize and which they'll ignore." He took her suitcase and stepped from the car.

There was no one in sight as they crossed the spacious hardwood porch, and when Greg pushed the doorbell, no one responded to the rolling chimes. The front door was open, however, and by placing his face close to the heavy screen, he was able to see the darkened foyer beyond.

"Looks as big as the lobby in the Omni," he reported. "Nobody in sight, though."

"Surely someone's here," Cathy said. "They wouldn't go away and leave everything open this way."

Greg tried the doorbell again, and the sound pealed within the depths of the huge structure. On a staircase at the far side of the foyer, a small, white figure appeared, descending quickly.

"Bingo," Greg muttered. "That woke up somebody." He drew back from the screen door with a number of tiny red checkerboard squares impressed on the tip of his nose; under other circumstances, Cathy would have laughed at the sight.

The white figure came silently and ghostlike to the front door. She was a girl, about 15 or so. Barefoot, she was no more than five-foot-two and possibly 100 pounds. The wide eyes that peered out at them with an evident touch of fear were pale green, and the hair that fell lifelessly over her brow was a white-blonde that was lighter in color even than Greg's. She would have been very attractive had she made the effort and done away with the frightened doe expression. She was holding a large stack of freshly pressed white sheets and was standing so close to the door that Greg could feel the clean heat radiating from the bedding.

"Y-yes, please?" she asked with a severe stutter.

Greg was convinced that she was as terrified by the two of them as she looked. He decided to handle this very carefully. "May we come in?" he asked.

The girl didn't answer for a moment, as if she were trying to form an understandable answer within her mind. Then she gulped a breath of air and replied with a question. "Delivery?"

"What?" Greg responded.

"Delivery? You bring one?"

Cathy caught the meaning of the hesitant, whispered words. "She thinks we're delivering something from town, Greg."

The girl nodded. "In the back, please," she said laboriously.

Greg smiled and shook his head. "We're looking for a room. At least, Miss Pettis is, and we've come to ask if you have one to let."

"Room?" the girl repeated.

Brain dead, Greg thought.

Cathy stepped close to the door. "That's right. I'm willing to pay, of course."

The girl seemed to notice Cathy for the first time, and several long, embarrassing moments passed as she stared at her, lips parted and mouth slightly open.

I wonder if I looked so vacuous back at the bus

stop? Greg asked himself in amusement.

Eventually, the girl literally shook herself and whispered, "No room. Go away, please." Then she turned away from the door.

"Hey, wait a minute!" Greg said. "There's not one empty room in a building this size?"

"Ohhh," the girl sighed. The emptiness of the sound sent a chill up Greg's spine.

"I think we'd better go, Cathy," he said, taking her arm.

"I don't know . . ." the girl whispered. "The boy should be at the door . . . I don't give the rooms . . ."

"Is there someone else we coud speak to?" Cathy asked.

"Delivery?" the girl responded pleadingly.

"Jeeze," Greg sighed.

Another voice from within the house came as a sudden shock. "Gretchen! Why are you standing there in the doorway, you silly thing! Get those sheets upstairs, right now!" It was a woman's voice.

If the girl had seemed perplexed by the situation before, the introduction of this new element completely unraveled her. She gave out a short cry, dropped the clean sheets, and then began scrambling about to pick them up. "I'm sorry! I'm sorry! The people!"

"This place is like a zoo," Greg observed in an aside to Cathy, "and we haven't even been inside yet."

"I know," Cathy agreed. There was something in her tone that was almost as disconcerting to Greg as the maid's rising hysteria. "Gretchen!" she said sharply. "Is that your name?"

The girl looked up from the floor. "My name," she managed to answer, if it were an answer.

"Good. Gretchen, my friend and I would like to come inside and speak to someone else, someone in charge. May we?"

Again there followed that long, uncomfortable pause until Gretchen, reacting as if it were her own idea, rose on her bare feet and pushed open the screen door. "Please!" she said earnestly. "Come in and . . . uh, come inside, please, and sit down." Then she practically pulled the two of them into the high-ceilinged, cavernlike front room.

Urged on by fervent tugs and pushes, Cathy and Greg crossed carpeting that was royal purple and so thick that it sprayed across the tops of their shoes like foam from the ocean. They settled side by side on a luxurious sofa the size of a bed. Lifesized portraits decorated the polished oaken walls, and an ornate chandelier, looking like some sort of stupendous crystal wheel, hung above their heads.

The air seemed heavy with the scent of honey.

"You sit here, right here," Gretchen directed. She patted their knees carefully, as if she were afraid that they would run away unless they were properly handled. "I . . . um, Herm—Madame come, okay? Okay?"

"That's fine, Gretchen," Cathy said slowly. "We'll stay here while you run and get Madame."

"Okay!" The girl gathered up the fallen sheets and sprinted swiftly up the spiral staircase.

As Greg's eyes swept the room, he muttered, "I

have to admit that this is without a doubt the best decorated asylum I've ever visited.''

Cathy placed her purse on her lap and sat very straight. She looked both excited and slightly uneasy. ''That's cruel, Greg. I don't like to laugh at problems that people haven't brought on themselves.''

''Let's not jump to conclusions. I know a fellow back in Atlanta who makes Cinderella here look like a member of the Manhattan Project because he puts any and everything into his veins or up his nose.''

''I doubt if derision is going to help to improve his condition.''

Greg sighed good-naturedly. ''Cathy, my dear, I believe that a touch of derision can help *any* situation.'' He glanced again at the elaborate and sometimes startling—such as a stuffed brown bear—furnishings in the large room. ''And this situation definitely needs something.''

''I think I've found the place I've been looking for,'' Cathy stated quietly.

Greg responded with a quizzical stare.

After a time, he remarked, ''The air freshener in this place sure smells unusual.''

''That's honey,'' Cathy told him.

''A little strong for my tastes.''

''I think it's lovely. It's always been one of my favorite scents.''

For a number of reasons—the oppressive grandeur of the house, widely varying personal conflicts, and old-fashioned caution among them —the two dropped the conversation, so that the only sound within the room was the steady clicking of the pendulum of a huge grandfather clock actually built into one wall. The silence lengthened slowly into several minutes.

Greg was just becoming convinced that Gretchen had not run upstairs to fetch "Madame" but to hide beneath a bed, when a newcomer walked into the room. It was another girl, though she appeared to be somewhat older than Gretchen and considerably more ostentatious. She even wore shoes.

"How do you do?" she said in a calm, self-possessed voice. "I am Noleta Evangelista, though I prefer to be called Noleta Thrush." She was taller than Cathy, perhaps five-feet-nine, and as slender as a reed. She was also very attractive, with dark brown eyes and black hair that reflected her apparent Spanish heritage and a snow-white complexion. She was dressed in a long, mauve gown that appeared to be ideal for a fashionable evening party but seemed a little much for that early in the day.

Greg's Old South upbringing had caused him to come to his feet when the young woman entered the room, but when she extended her right hand toward him, limp and with palm down, his social training did not include a ready response. He had never seen a man kiss a woman's hand other than in films and on television, and he sincerely doubted that it was a common Indiana custom. Somewhat embarrassed, he took her hand in both of his and shook it gently. It was soft and surprisingly cold.

"It's certainly a pleasure to meet you, Miss Thrush," he added lamely.

She flashed a dazzling smile. "How charming you are!"

Greg coughed slightly, as he always did when embarrassed. "And I am . . ." he began.

Noleta pressed her fingers to his mouth and said, "No, please let me!" She paused for a moment and closed her eyes while her lips moved silently. In a moment, she opened her eyes again and said, "I feel that you are called . . . Greg or Gregory, though I cannot fasten on the last name. Is this correct?"

"Hey, that's right!" he answered, genuinely surprised. "Have we met?"

"I think not." Noleta turned to face Cathy, who still sat on the sofa. "And you, dear, the echoes in my mind tell me that you are . . . Catherine or Cathleen, known generally as Cathy. At least, that is what I hear through the vibrations in the psychic continuum."

"Cathy Pettis," she said, though her tone was hardly as amazed as Greg's. "That's really astounding. How did you know?"

Noleta waved her hand in casual dismissal. "A minor talent. Mental telepathy. I've been proficient at it for all of my life, and it really makes things rather a bore, knowing all of the intimate little secrets about a person as soon as I've met them."

"I can imagine."

Greg was fairly open-minded, but he wasn't at all sure that he believed what this girl was telling him, no matter how good-looking she was. Still— he glanced about at the sheer depth and width of the room—he and Cathy had not been speaking very loudly, so it would have been extremely difficult for anyone to have overheard them. Who else in Euphrata knew Cathy's name? Only

Frankie, and he wouldn't have set them up for some sort of practical joke like this, not even with his warped and wild sense of humor.

"Won't you have a seat?" he asked, not certain if proper manners dictated that he make this offer to someone who lived in this house.

"How gracious of you," Noleta said, smiling as she eased herself onto the sofa next to Cathy. Greg took an armchair facing the two of them. "Now, may I ask what brings you two attractive young people to our home?"

"Why don't *you* tell *us*?" Cathy suggested.

"Quite wise of you," Noleta replied without any evidence of offense. "It's said that one should never take too much of life at face value."

Especially in this place, Greg thought.

Noleta closed her eyes once more. "Hmm, it's rather transparent, actually, and not a true test at all. You wish to rent a room, do you not?"

She hadn't directed the question at either Cathy or Greg specifically, but Cathy responded quickly. "I must stop doubting your abilities. I would like to stay here for a few days. Mr. Stern at the motel couldn't offer me a cabin, but I've heard wonderful things about the York mansion."

Noleta opened her eyes. "These are much nicer surroundings, in any case. I have dwelt here on the York estate for almost six years and have enjoyed every moment."

"Oh? You're not a member of the family?"

"Oh, no. My actual surname is Evangelista, as I told you, which is Spanish for Gospel singer, though I prefer to be known as Thrush. Less religious, more melodic. I was born in Spain, in

Cadiz actually, and I lived there until the age of thirteen. I have worked diligently at ridding myself of an unattractive accent. Would you say that I've succeeded to any real extent?''

"Definitely," Greg replied with honesty. The girl sounded like a native American, though slightly affected.

"Thank you. The rest of the story is that I came to this wonderful nation along with my parents, my father being an official ambassador to the U.N. Only months later, a girlfriend and I were touring some of the lovely countryside by car, along with our chaperons and security agents, when we were attacked by representatives of a fanatical Basque separatist group. All of the other members of my party were killed, and I was severely wounded and captured.''

"I remember a little about that," Cathy said. "Six or seven years ago. There was a very big diplomatic dispute.''

"Yeah, but that took place in New York, and the girl was never found," Greg added. "The Spanish government had a fit.''

"Why not?" Noleta asked blithely. "My parents certainly had a right to be distraught. I was their only child, after all.''

Noleta was looking away from him, so Greg rotated his forefinger in a circle before the right side of his head to indicate his impression of the girl and her story. Cathy saw him and could barely repress an agreeing nod.

"I'm glad to see that you survived and have fully recovered," she said tactfully. "Why haven't you returned to your parents?''

"Oh, I do love and miss them," Noleta

admitted, "but I could never leave here."

"Not without getting dumped into a psychiatric ward," Greg whispered to himself.

"Pardon?" Noleta asked brightly.

"Uh, I just said that I wonder where the maid's gone," he improvised, hoping that he didn't look as red as he felt.

"I suppose you're referring to Gretchen. That creature is totally unreliable. She probably forgot her name again before she reached the second floor."

"I hope that I'm not being rude, but what exactly is wrong with that poor girl?" Cathy asked.

"Rude?" Noleta repeated. "My dear, it's exceedingly difficult to insult someone who has the mind of a ripe tomato. And that undoubtedly is underestimating the tomato."

Greg saw Cathy wince slightly. She really *was* sensitive about the problems of others.

"Is it a problem that she was born with or the result of an accident of some kind?"

"Congenital, probably," Noleta stated. "She's been an idiot for the entire span of my stay in the mansion. She has periods of lucidness when she becomes almost human, but they invariably are followed by complete regressions. And the most intriguing part of it is that when she's intelligent, she knows that a return to cretanism is just around the corner. On the average, she's a goose, awakening in a new world every day."

"Is she a York family member?"

Noleta covered her mouth with her hands and giggled. "Now, if I were a York, that would be a most rude remark! I doubt that she even has a last name.''

Let's move on to other matters, shall we? Greg requested silently.

As if in response to this, another figure suddenly appeared, descending the stairs. It was a rather heavyset, middle-aged woman in a yellow jogging suit and running shoes. She had short brown hair and a hearty smile on her lips.

''Good afternoon, you two,'' she said in a friendly voice. ''Am I right in assuming that you're here to look for rooms?''

Greg stood again. ''Well, one of us is. I'm Greg Hoode, Daniel Hoode's nephew.''

The woman reached the ground floor and strolled over to where the small group had gathered. ''Hermione York. Very glad to meet you, Greg. Oh yes, I've heard all of the local girls whispering and giggling about the new dreamboat in town for the summer.''

Noleta sniffed and imperiously turned away from the conversation.

Greg simply coughed again. ''This is Cathy Pettis. She just arrived this afternoon and is looking for a place to stay.''

''It's very nice to meet you, Ms. York,'' Cathy said.

''Hermie, please. Everyone calls me Hermie,'' the woman stated.

Without speaking, Noleta stood and quickly walked from the room.

''Well, everyone but Noleta calls me Hermie,'' she said in amusement. ''Noleta is very ladylike, and jogging and nicknames don't fall under her definition of ladylike behavior.''

Cathy smiled sympathetically. ''Well, uh,

Hermie, from what little I've seen, you certainly have a beautiful home.''

"Isn't it, though? Grandfather Cecil built it some sixty-eight years ago. You'll have to meet Grandfather; he's a real character.''

"I wouldn't want to bother him . . .''

"Don't worry about that. Grandfather's ninety-eight years old, and he still can jog me into the ground.''

"My, ninety-eight,'' Cathy commented with real interest.

"Euphrata has a lot of healthy elderly people,'' Greg pointed out, repeating Frankie's words.

"Euphrata has a lot of healthy people, period,'' Hermie corrected him. "It's a marvelously robust area.'' She directed her gaze to Cathy. "Where do you hail from, Miss Pettis?''

"West,'' Cathy answered. "Kansas City.''

"I imagine that it's a fascinating place.''

Greg said nothing, but he knew that the bus that Cathy had arrived on had been westbound rather than coming from that direction. A mysterious beauty on a strange mission, a luxurious mansion full of definitely out-of-kilter people . . . A cynical portion of Greg's mind began to consider the possibility that his Uncle Dan, realizing how boring this vacation was proving to be for him, had hired a scriptwriter and a troop of actors to set up this whole performance for his benefit.

"And an attractive young lady like you is traveling alone?'' Hermie asked.

"That's right,'' Cathy said, volunteering no further information.

"All righty, I believe we can find you a nice, cozy room for a few nights." She muttered several unintelligible observations to herself as she catalogued the available rooms. "There's a really comfortable little nook on the third floor with an excellent view of the meadow to the east. You'll catch the morning sun, and—"

"That will be fine," Cathy interrupted. "How much will it run per night?"

"Oh, let's say something nominal. With meals tossed in, would five dollars be within your budget?"

"Perfect. I don't know how long I'll be staying."

"Don't worry about that, honey. We're hardly structured here. I'll call for Gretchen." She stepped across the room and pressed a call button set in the wall. "Gretchen, report to the lobby, please." Releasing the button, she added, "We'll have you moved in in a jiffy. Is this all of your luggage?"

The jittery little blonde appeared in the room in less than a minute. Though he found her rather cute, Greg was still a bit uneasy at her return. He knew that he was being ridiculous, but when he considered that behind those clear, shining eyes was a mind that gained and lost intelligence with the ease of a switch being flipped, there was the barest trace of queasiness in the pit of his stomach. He just couldn't seem to bury the feeling.

Hermie produced a large key from the top drawer of a desk and handed it to the young maid. "This lady is Miss Pettis, and she's in the McKinley room, third floor, east wing. Got all of that?"

Gretchen's lips trembled slightly as she struggled to find the words. Finally she said, "East wing, 'Kinley room, Miss Pettis, y-yes, ma'am."

Hermie ruffled the girl's hair affectionately "We name all of our bedrooms after presidents," she explained. "You've drawn the William McKinley room."

"McKinley was assassinated, wasn't he?" Greg observed.

Hermie winked conspiratorially. "That's right. Gretchen, take the lady's bag and make certain that the room is well-aired and the bed has fresh linen. I have to get out and into the athletic struggle before I gain five pounds just by standing here and breathing."

Gretchen reached for the small suitcase, but Greg stopped her by raising his hand. "Let me get that," he said.

Hermie had been walking toward the front door, but she stopped and said, "Don't bother with it, Greg. Gretchen is a little bundle of energy."

"I'm sure she is, but well, I'm from Georgia, and we're still kind of socially backward down there." Greg rebelled against the smug and largely groundless prejudices that much of the nation held against the Southeast, but that didn't keep him from using those same prejudices when it suited his purposes. "Besides, I've carried this thing so much today that I'm starting to walk at an angle without it," he added, slipping Cathy an "I'm-just-kidding" look.

"Far be it from me to discourage a chivalrous man," Hermie said. "Lord knows, we see fewer and fewer of them as the years go by."

"Thank you," Gretchen whispered faintly.

"But you both must attend the customary 3:30 tea so that you can get acquainted with the other guests and some of the townspeople," Hermie ordered with a firm, but smiling expression.

Then she trotted out of the front door in search of slimness.

The York mansion had no elevators.

Cathy was just a little out of breath when they finally reached the top floor and began the long walk to the east wing. It was evident when she said, "I'm surprised that Hermie needs to jog at all if she climbs these stairs more than once a day."

"I'm surprised she *can* jog," Greg said. As an athlete, he had highly developed stamina, but he had been out of training for several months and understood what Cathy meant. "What about Mr. York, Gretchen? He's almost a hundred, isn't he? Surely he has a private elevator."

The girl continued to pad down the hallway ahead of them. "No elevators, only stairs," she replied. Then she sighed, "Lots of stairs."

The McKinley Room seemed to be at least three blocks from the lobby, but it was just as cozy and comfortable as Hermie had promised. While Gretchen opened the one window and turned down the bed in preparation for the change to fresh linen, Cathy explored its closet and fine furnishings. In spite of the seriousness of her motives and the pain that she was still experiencing, she realized that she very easily could have fallen in love with that particular eighteenth-century room.

"I wonder what this second door is for?" she asked, referring to a slim panel almost completely camouflaged by the wall covering.

"Servants' passageway," Greg answered authoritatively, and indeed, he had seen many like it before. "It opens to a second corridor system that runs as a companion to the main passages throughout the house so that the servants can carry food and other deliveries to the guests without assaulting the sensibilities of the other residents."

"How thoughtful," Cathy observed, "and tyrannical."

The only incongruous note in the decor was a large, metal animal's head that was mounted on the wall above the bed like a trophy.

"I suppose you know what that is, too," she mentioned idly.

Greg looked up at the equine head, with its wide, flaring nostrils and vicious teeth bared threateningly. "It looks like a dragon to me. Gretchen, does old man York like dragons?"

At the sound of her name, Gretchen looked at the head, rolled her eyes, and said in a furtive voice, "Master York, he . . . ooohhh!" It was perhaps the most eloquent assessment of her feelings that she was capable of giving them.

Greg laughed. Suddenly he realized that the queasiness was gone; he was beginning to like this kid.

The honey scent that had filled the air downstairs was still noticeable here on the third floor, though it was not so powerful as it had been below.

Cathy put aside her favorable impressions of

the room and its antique vanity table and
elaborate, fourposter bed to reestablish her
purpose for being there in the first place. Walking
to the heavy door, she pushed it shut and slid the
bolt into place. Gretchen was too busy with her
scrutiny of the room's corners and closet to
notice this; Greg noticed but said nothing.

Continuing with her mission, Cathy returned to
the bed and opened her suitcase. Sorting among
the clothes, she quickly pulled out a framed
picture and then tapped Gretchen on the
shoulder. The girl had been so occupied with her
hunt for dust that she was taken totally by
surprise, emitting a short, piercing cry and
scrambling into a corner of the room with her
arms frantically covering her face and upper
body.

Greg had been in the ring with enough hurt
opponents to recognize an instinctive reaction to
expected pain when he saw it. Gretchen was used
to being physically assaulted. He felt the heat
rising from his neck upward. Despite his love of
boxing, wherein two trained and voluntary
opponents pitted their agility and power against
one another, he found no pleasure in violence
outside of the arena, especially (chauvinistic or
not) violence against women and children.

Cathy was horrified by the reaction she had
accidentally caused. Pursuing Gretchen, she said
urgently and comfortingly, "I'm sorry. I'm sorry,
honey. I didn't mean to frighten you. It's all
right. No one wants to hurt you!"

Gretchen remained huddled in the corner,
trembling like a terrified little animal. "Sorry,
sorry, sorry, sorry . . ." she whispered

desperately.

"Damn!" Greg hissed. He was both embarrassed and angry at the display and the obvious reason behind it.

Very slowly, the girl became calmer as Cathy stayed by her, repeating reassurances and stroking her hair.

"That's better, much better," Cathy chanted quietly. "I'm so very sorry. I didn't mean to scare you."

Gretchen wiped her eyes with the back of a hand and sat up. "Sorry," she said for the twentieth time. "I . . . stupid, stupid and . . . stupid . . ."

"No, you aren't; I just startled you. Here, stand up." She helped the girl to stand and then led her to the bed, practically having to force her to sit on it. "Listen to me just a moment, Gretchen, I need to ask you something, and it's very, very important. Do you understand? Good. Do you feel like you're ready to help me?"

Gretchen nodded.

"Wonderful!" The look returned to Cathy's eyes, that eager, powerful look that Greg had seen before in the motel manager's office. "You're going to have to think really hard about this, okay? How long have you worked here at the York home?"

Gretchen's reply was nothing more than a vacant stare.

"Gretchen, listen to me!" Cathy ordered sharply. For an instant, Greg thought that she might actually slap the girl. "How long have you worked—and lived—here in the York house? Has it been since last year?"

Gretchen sighed, obviously deep in thought, and worked her bare toes in the deep pile of the carpeting. "Long, long time," she eventually said in a hollow voice. "Always."

Cathy sighed, too, but with frustration. "Since last September? That long?"

"Years and years," was the reply.

Biting her lower lip, Cathy took the picture from the floor, where she had dropped it at Gretchen's unexpected panic, and held it before the girl's eyes. "Have you ever seen these people before? Did they check in here last year in September?"

Gretchen took the picture from Cathy's hand and stared intently at it, saying nothing. The internal struggle to please Cathy could be read in her eyes. Greg stepped to her side to get a better look. It was a wedding picture, crisply photographed and in clear focus. The white-gowned, smiling bride was an attractive woman with auburn hair and green eyes. The groom seemed rather tall next to her and had dark brown hair and blue eyes . . . just like Cathy's. It obviously was her brother.

"Gretchen, do you understand?" Cathy asked after the silence had lasted for most of a minute. "Have you ever seen these people? The man?"

Gretchen touched the bride's face with a finger. "Pretty," she said quietly. "Pretty girl." Then she touched her own cheek. "Ugly," she added.

"No, no," Cathy said, her expression beginning to show her exasperation. She took the picture from Gretchen. "She's a pretty girl, and *you're* a pretty girl. Have you seen the pretty girl or the handsome man?"

Gretchen's response was almost inaudible. "Long time ago."

"Where?" Cathy demanded. "Here?"

"Go now," the girl stated as she stood. "Got to go to work."

Cathy caught her wrist and held her. "Did you see them here?" she repeated urgently.

"Go now," Gretchen said. "Please." But Cathy wouldn't let go of her. She touched Cathy's face with her free hand and said, "Pretty girl, too. Go away. I don't want . . ." Then she slipped free and ran to the door, where she fumbled for a moment with the deadbolt lock before escaping into the hall.

"Phew," Greg whistled. "Why do I get the idea that I'm wrapped up in a mystery that's fit material for an Alfred Hitchcock film? Maybe this *is* the Bates Motel—or the Twilight Zone."

Cathy slowly replaced the photo in her suitcase and closed it. "I apologize, Greg. I realize that I owe you one tremendous explanation, now that I'm sure I can trust you."

He grinned. "If you can trust ignorance, I'm the most trustworthy dumb sucker alive, but don't do anything because you feel obligated to me. All I've provided has been a little gasoline." Actually, he was about to self-destruct from curiosity. This was, by far, the most interesting afternoon he'd passed in Euphrata.

"No, I want to tell someone—but not here. What time is it?"

He glanced at his watch. "Five after three."

"We have twenty-five minutes until the tea, then."

"You're going to stay here?" he asked,

startled. "This place is like something out of Stephen King!"

"I'm staying here just as long as it takes. Would you like to walk around the grounds? We could talk."

He looked out over the garage at the wide, immaculate lawn that stretched beyond the window. "Sure. It looks like I'm not going to wake up from this one, so I might as well have it explained to me."

Chapter Five

Late afternoon, Monday, July 10.

Extreme pain and the cloaking nothingness of shock alternated like sides of the same coin to maintain an unbreakable grip on Pamela Durben's mind. When she was still, possessed of no movement other than the weakening pounding of her heart, she could slip from the unbearable present into another state that may have been closer to death each time, but was also soothing in its insulation from the torture that was consciousness. When the two policemen had taken her from the wrecked van, the agony was so focused and sharp that, for a moment, she had actually wished that she *would* die, if only to be rid of it. The trip up the roadside slope was hell.

When they reached the top, there had been no waiting ambulance filled with trained medical people and the drugs that would course through her system to root out the pain and give her relief.

Instead, she had been thrust with little concern of her suffering into the rear seat of a police car with flashing blue and red lights; even those lights had hurt her.

She could feel parts of herself grating together inside her body, and the blood swiftly flowed out to envelope her in a warm and sticky film that was as much a part of her departing life as each breath that fled raggedly through her throat. She called weakly for Kevin.

But he couldn't come to her. While she lay, suffering in the back of the car, the two policemen returned to the van and carried her husband up the same incline to join her. The pain of his injuries was so great that it drove groans and sharp gasps from him, and she knew that Kevin never complained or moaned that way, except when he was trapped in the night by the dream.

When they reached the car, rather than putting him in the back with her, where there was no room, the men actually sat him upright on his shattered pelvis in the front seat. A steel mesh curtain separated the two of them; though she understood that there was no room for him back here amid all of her agony, Pamela still cried out with the gulf that was placed between them.

"You've just got to hold on, baby," he told her pleadingly, twisting himself about in the seat to see her, in spite of what this action demanded of him. The fingers of his right hand gripped the metal screen as tightly as if he were clinging to the side of a mountain. "We're going to make it, but you've got to believe that with all your heart!"

"I do," she sighed, lying.

"That's my girl. We've got to fight! Don't let the bastard win! I'm sorry, my God, I'm so sorry that I did this!"

"The accident was your fault?" asked the cop who was driving in an interested, but casual tone.

Kevin stared at the man in disbelief. "No! That damned idiot pulled right into us! But please, just shut up and get us to the hospital! Pammie? Pammie, can you hear me?" His voice rose a notch toward hysteria.

"Yes," she finally answered. "I can . . ."

The trip to the hospital seemed to take forever. Pamela often drifted away from the shore of this terrible world, but always the desperate voice of her anguished husband would reach through the veil and draw her back—back to life, agony, and that shrieking siren.

She could hardly see anything by the time they stopped again, and what vision she did retain was like something seen through gauze late on a rainy afternoon, but her hearing was still sharp in comparison, and again she listened to others discuss her fate as if she were no more capable of understanding than an injured family pet.

"Got a delivery for you," said the policeman who had driven them to . . . wherever. "Fresh out of a squashed van over close to Luke Barber's farm. Old Cleotis was performing his specialty again."

"Was he hurt?" a second voice asked. This belonged to a man as well, though he sounded somewhat more mature than the wisecracking cop.

"Not to speak of. Popped his skull a little, but the old buzzard wouldn't come along because he had to stay and 'discipline' that ancient rattletrap of his.''

"Something's going to have to be done with him some day soon. Who are these two?''

"Out-of-towners. The man's license says Kevin Jeffery Durben, of Buffalo, New York. We couldn't get any I.D. on the woman, but we figure she's his wife; she's wearing a ring.''

The second speaker seemed interested but cautious. "Passing through, or does someone expect them to be in town?''

"Don't know. The woman's too incoherent to answer, and the man can't do nothing but beg us to save her life.''

"Then why in the world did you bring them here, Matty?''

"Well, we couldn't just leave them on the side of the road, could we? What would that look like?''

"Then you should have phoned Tiverton and—''

"Look at them, Carl. Do you think they'd survive a trip to Tiverton? And if they died on the way and turned out to be somebody important— that was a pretty fancy van before it got creamed —don't you know that their relatives or somebody in Tiverton would kick up a fuss about Euphrata not having a hospital or even a doctors' clinic? And there's no doubt at all that that could lead to major trouble. Wally and me figured that it would be a good idea to bring them up here, maybe have the Doc juice 'em up a little, and then decide what to do with them. Hey, they might even fit in with the celebration. Who knows?''

The second man sighed wearily. "They're here

now," he said. "Let me get Dr. Welsh and see what he thinks about it."

"That's all I'm asking, Carl."

Time seemed to have become all askew since the accident. After Carl left, an entire year crawled through Pamela's brain on plodding feet, so intensely did every fraction of every second imprint itself upon her soul, but the moment that still another man arrived and opened her shredded clothing to assess the damage, the pain took her again into the tumbling and bounding van. She moaned with all of the strength left in her, but it came out as a mere sigh.

"Cleotis certainly did a job on these two, didn't he?" the man with the exploring fingers asked dispassionately. To Pamela's restricted vision, he looked just a bit like Kevin, though those certainly weren't Kevin's loving eyes. "You were right, Matty. They never would have made it to the hospital."

"So what do we do with them now, Doc?" the policeman asked. "Is there anything that you can do for them without, you know . . . without giving them some of *it*?"

"Not a thing. Any idea where they were headed?"

"No, sir. There was a lot of busted up camera equipment in the van, though. Maybe they were on their way to the Wyandotte Caves to take pictures."

"Perhaps," the doctor allowed. "Or perhaps they were headed for the Angel Mounds near Evansville. Whatever, we can't simply let them bleed to death, can we? Carl, have your people take them inside."

"Are you sure, Dr. Welsh?" he asked. "If they were supposed to be in Euphrata, and we expose them to it . . ."

"Then I'll be in quite a fix for ordering it, correct?"

That seemed to satisfy Carl. "Okay. Do you want them in the clinic?"

"I think not. Take them to the holding room. Rubber sheet a couple of beds and secure them. I'll step in with a preliminary treatment in five minutes or so, after I've spoken to the old man."

"Yes, sir."

"Matty, you make certain that the wrecked vehicle is removed from the roadside before it can be seen by any outsiders. Keep it safely concealed until a final decision can be made regarding its disposition."

"Right on it, Doc! Just as soon as I hose out the car."

"Now, Matty," the doctor said with quiet authority.

'Oh, uh, sure, Doc, first thing."

Kevin apparently was unconscious now—at least, Pamela could no longer hear him calling to her—and without his calming influence not even the pain could keep the young woman imprisoned on this side of reality when Carl and his helpers pulled her from the car to take her somewhere inside. She welcomed the slide into unconsciousness.

When Pamela awoke, she was lying on her back in a dark place. She couldn't tell if it was dark because of poor lighting or because she was becoming progressively blind.

Her clothing was gone, stripped away while she was unconscious, and someone had sponged away the old blood before applying bandages to the worst of her open wounds. There was a pillow beneath her head, and she couldn't move her arms or legs.

"Kevin?"

At the sound of her voice someone—it was a woman, thank God—stepped to the side of her bed. "Hush, now," she said. "Doctor will be here with your treatment in a minute."

"Kevin?" Pamela repeated, more urgently. "Where's my husband?" She tried to raise herself to look about but was defeated by both her condition and some sort of retraints around her wrists and ankles.

"He's right here next to you," the woman told her. "He can't talk to you because he's asleep, but he's going to be fine. You both are."

Pamela settled back into the bed, wondering what kind of hospital this was. She wasn't really able to relax at all until she herself heard Kevin. He seemed to be unconscious and moaning only slightly with the pain, but what really had him in its grip was that damned dream again, the same dream that had tortured him at least once every week for the duration of their marriage. Pamela heard him whisper, "Angie."

Then Carl, who had removed her from the patrol car, suddenly was standing next to the attending woman, asking, "Do you need anything else from me and Jeroboam before tea?"

"Wait and ask Dr. Welsh," the woman answered.

"Hey, Carl! Carl, come here!" a man's voice

called from some other part of the big, dark
room.

Pamela slowly turned her head to the right and
was startled to discover that there were many
other people in the room, ten or twelve men and
women, old and young. What she could see of
their huge, dark-ringed eyes made them look like
a collection of ghosts. They were all sitting in
large, cumbersome armchairs.

"What do you want, Neil?" Carl asked of the
man who had shouted to him so eagerly.

Neil, an extremely slender black-haired man
with a ragged growth of beard and unkempt hair,
grinned like a cowed animal submitting to a
stronger rival and replied, "I remember one,
Carl, just this morning, and it's a beauty, I swear.
The old man will love it. I swear! If it's good, all
I'm asking is three breaths. That's all!"

"Aw, for goshsakes, Neil, we'll be down here
for questioning at six. Wait until then."

"But this is great," he repeated. "I just
remembered it!"

"Why now?" Carl demanded. "You've been
here for twenty-seven days already."

Neil seemed momentarily perplexed by that,
but only momentarily. "Why, I guess I did what
the psychiatrists talk about all the time. I guess I
sublimated because I was ashamed of it."

Carl sighed wearily, obviously not convinced.
Still, he motioned to someone whom Pamela
couldn't see and started across the room. "Okay,
Neil, but it had better be good. I don't want to
waste any time with him, Jeroboam."

Jeroboam came into Pamela's line of sight, and
she was stunned by what she saw. Though four or

five inches short of six feet in height, he must have weighed 400 pounds. His legs were like bridge supports tightly encased in blue denim, and his arms looked every bit as large. His head was a lump atop the massive shoulders with no room for or need of a neck, and beneath a thatch of straw-colored hair, his face was swollen, bulbous, and somehow remotely childlike. He was the largest person Pamela had ever seen, and though he had done nothing threatening to her, an irrational fear ran through her.

"Who's that?" she asked in an already panicky voice. "What is he going to do? Who is he?"

"Shh, never you mind," the nurse answered without answering.

Carl and Jeroboam stopped before Neil. "Let's hear it," Carl ordered.

"Yeah, I swear to God this is true, Jeroboam," Neil said as he nervously licked his lips. "See, I was bumming in Great Falls . . . that's in Montana, you know the place?"

Jeroboam was absently licking an ice cream cone that he held in his left hand, and he responded to the question with a flat, empty stare.

"Okay, well, I had just dropped off a freight there and I come across this house out in the sticks, all by itself, and I figure that there's nobody home because there's no car in the driveway and everybody has two cars now, right? So I break in only to find this broad, this really good-looking broad, but she's unconscious—you know, in this coma, and—"

Jeroboam paused long enough in his licking to say, "Lying," in an emotionless voice.

Neil's watery eyes swelled with terror. "No, man, I swear it! It happened this way!"

Carl waited no longer. Pulling out a long, leather device that resembled a policeman's night-stick, he expertly whipped the flexible rod across Neil's face. This drove the man's head back hard against the back of the armchair, both of his hands jerking upward, as if in an attempt to block any other blows, but they never rose more than an inch above the sides of the chair; that was when Pamela saw that the man was strapped to the big chair by the wrists and ankles. They all were.

Pamela screamed, and she was surprised by the volume and power of her voice. "Where am I? Oh my God, what is this place? Kevin! Kevin, help me!"

The nurse made various futile attempts to calm her, but the terrified woman had actually come into a half-sitting position before the bearded doctor materialized from nowhere to mash a clear plastic cup over her nose and mouth with angry strength. She struggled for a moment longer, before all consciousness deserted her once more. Then the dreams began.

"That man in the picture was your brother, wasn't he?"

The temperature was hovering around 90 that midsummer afternoon, but there was a lively and playful breeze to offset the heat as they walked across the rolling lawn on the eastern side of the mansion. Cathy's beautiful hair was blown about her face and shoulders, and Greg thought that this made her even more gorgeous. He was beginning to get a little worried since it had been a long time since he'd been so smitten so quickly by anyone. Certainly Julie Newman hadn't had a comparable impact.

"That was Mikey," Cathy admitted, holding the brown strands out of her eyes. "And Nona. It was taken on their wedding day, last September fourth. They died four days later."

Greg realized that Mikey was the key to this whole enigma, but it was obvious that she was going to be slow in unlocking the rest of it. "It must be rough to lose someone so close to you. Makes me realize how lucky I've been." When she didn't respond for several seconds, he continued, "I guess that Noleta is way ahead of me on this one."

Cathy laughed, a little grimly. "She's as much a psychic as she is a diplomat's dead daughter."

"Think so?"

"I don't know how she found out our first names, but she didn't blink when I called myself Cathy Pettis, though any self-respecting mind-reader would have known in a second that I was lying."

Greg was surprised at the revelation, but he handled it carefully. "That's not your name? Darn, I've always liked 'Cathy.' "

She smiled. And then she told him.

Greg held the card in his hand for a long time after he had read it.

Until that moment, all of it—the dazzling young woman on the cryptic mission, the veiled detective tactics at Stern's Motel, the literally lunatic House of York, and even poor, abused, apparently retarded Gretchen—had been a diversion, a nice way to pass another dull day in Euphrata. But now it was real.

"Hi, Kitty Cat!" the card greeted him again. Words from the dead. "And always remember, I love you, kid. Mikey."

He had no brothers or sisters, but he imagined that it must have been like losing a father or mother to Cathy. And she'd already lost them once.

"I can see what he meant about the Addams Family," he said rather lamely. Nothing else came to mind. "I wonder if he met Noleta and Gretchen?"

They had paused beneath a gloriously verdant elm, the only tree in the east lawn, while the story unfolded and Greg read the card she carried in her purse.

"It depends on what time they checked in on Wednesday night, I suppose," Cathy answered. "They probably met Gretchen in the morning."

"And the Tiverton police say that the anonymous caller claimed to have seen the car in the river on Thursday morning?"

"*Early* Thursday morning, about six, I think. And Mikey dated the card Thursday, September 8th, *a.m.* How far away is Tiverton, fifty miles?"

"About that."

"Kind of far to have driven by six a.m. *after* having had breakfast and written this postcard in Euphrata."

"Maybe they left before dawn." Greg wasn't trying to demolish Cathy's hopes, but he felt it necessary to examine all of the angles.

"That's what the police said when I showed them the card. But you'll notice that it says they were going to visit Wyandotte Cave on Thursday. According to the map, that's seventy-five miles southeast of Euphrata. How early would they have to leave in order to reach Tiverton by way of Wyandotte Cave and drive into the Ohio all by six?" There was a note of triumph and toughness in her voice; Cathy knew that something was untold in the matter of the death of her brother.

"Yeah," Greg muttered, also getting caught up in the mystery. "But the police weren't interested in this?"

"They had a closed case, and they didn't want to reopen it," she said bitterly. "They contacted the authorities here, but no one could recall ever having seen Mikey and Nona, so it was dropped again."

Greg leaned against the smooth trunk of the elm. "All right, you've hooked me, Cathy Pettis/Lockwood. Something is wrong with all of this, but maybe I'm just thick. I don't see how this masquerade is going to find out what really happened to Mikey. Why would anyone want to make you think that he didn't stop here in Euphrata? God, you don't think that he was murdered, do you?"

When she replied, Cathy's eyes were flashing like chips of blue ice. "That's *exactly* what I think. He was here; the card proves that! He was here in Euphrata on Thursday! He didn't even drink at all, not so much as a glass of champagne at his own wedding. Even I had one then!"

How far do I give in to her? Greg asked himself. She's hit me with a lot in these last few hours, maybe too much. What if I'm being taken in by the way she looks and she's really as punchy as Gretchen or Noleta?

"Greg?" Cathy whispered. "You believe, don't you? It's got to be a conspiracy of some sort. Mikey couldn't have destroyed his and Nona's lives by driving off of a bridge on his honeymoon. Can't you see that?"

But why would there be a conspiracy to kill a bank clerk from another state?

"Greg?"

But he believed her and told her so.

"Oh, Lord," she sighed in relief. "I haven't told anybody else this, not even Monica or her parents. And you came out of nowhere . . ." Suddenly, she began to cry.

Greg gently placed his right arm about her shoulders, but he didn't try to stop her tears. He realized that she needed this emotional release. As she had told him, she had kept all of this inside herself for the time that it had taken to finish her junior year of high school, work a month to raise money for the trip, and then come to Euphrata alone to find out the truth behind her brother's death. Greg had stumbled into it all merely by chance.

Cathy's tears didn't last long. She soon was wiping her eyes with a tissue and trying to smile.

"Great start, huh?" she asked. "When I find out what really happened, I'll probably stand and cry all over whoever's responsible."

"Don't give it a thought," Greg said. "When the time for resolve comes, I'll bet on you."

She laughed weakly. "Don't bet the entire inheritance."

Greg looked at his watch. "About five minutes 'til tea. You feel like attending?"

Cathy straightened and began to check her clothing. "You're damned right I do. Mikey was here and something happened during that time. I want to know who else I have to face in this asylum, as you called it, to find out what went on." She began to walk in the direction of the house, which was more than a hundred yards away.

"Just a minute," Greg said. "I guess we're both new at this detective game—Lockwood and Hoode, Investigators Extraordinaire—so I want to clear up something right off the bat. The body of Mikey's wife was never found, right?"

"Right. Apparently, it was washed downriver."

"And Mikey's . . ." He was trying to find a way to phrase this while taking her feelings into consideration. "I mean, he was decapitated . . ."

"The head was never found, either," she stated with no break in her voice.

"Okay." He took a deep breath. "Do you believe that there's any chance that Mikey's alive? That the body wasn't his?"

Cathy took his hand and squeezed it hard. "Greg, I'm praying every second that my identification was wrong. It *was* our car, that's definite, and it was Mikey's wallet, but the condition of the body after being in the rough currents for so long could have fooled me. That might have been a bruise on his leg instead of his birthmark."

"Wouldn't the bank have his fingerprints on file?"

"Inconclusive—even the police admit that. Everything was really terribly mutilated by the time that had been spent in the river.''

"Well, then, we have to keep something else in mind.''

"I've accepted his death, Greg, but as long as there's even a remote chance . . . Realistically, we'll be very lucky if we can even find out what actually happened here on that day.''

He took her arm. "Let's get back to the house and check out the lineup, shall we?''

They were halfway to the house when the horse appeared around the rear corner of it moving at full gallop.

"The Yorks must have a stable around back,'' Greg observed. "I wonder who the rider is?''

Cathy squinted. "I don't know. It looks like a little boy.''

"Whoever he is, he's in one hell of a hurry.''

The horse was a huge, black mare with a mane that streamed in the air as its hooves gouged large clods of sod from the lawn. The rider was a small, bunched figure dressed in brown clothing. His teeth were bared in a ferocious grin. Occasionally, he would emit a high-pitched cry of wordless ecstasy.

Cathy was the first to become uneasy. "Greg, he's coming awfully fast, and he's heading right for us.''

Without considering the move, he stepped in front of her. "Wild Bill seems to be trying out for the Derby, all right. I wonder what the hurry is?''

They didn't have time to ponder over reasons, however, because the horse and rider were closing on them by the second. Greg raised his hand and shouted to wave the little man off, but he was paid no heed. Clutching Cathy's shoulder, he pulled her sharply to one side, but the rider reined the horse in that direction instantly.

"Jesus!" he shouted. "Run, run for the house!" Giving her a shove, he dashed again to the side in an effort to draw the horse and rider away.

The rider jerked the mount to a stop between the two fleeing figures, as if completely stunned by this tactic. Cathy and Greg were able to see that he was the size of a child, one no older than seven or eight, but his slightly oversized head possessed the face of a much older individual. It was the face of a man consumed by the need to trample them.

"Are you crazy?" Greg demanded. "What are you trying to do, you jerk? Kill us?"

The small man snapped his wild eyes in Greg's direction. "Hyah!" he screamed, jabbing his heels hard into the animal's sides.

The horse whinnied and leaped toward Greg.

"Look out!" Cathy cried.

Greg reacted without thought. His reflexes, sharpened by years of training and competition, allowed him to dart out of the way with only inches to spare, and his resulting burst of anger drove him to leap at the rider. His right hand closed on the man's leg, and they tumbled to the ground together.

As the horse bounded back toward the house, Greg scrambled to his feet, white with rage. He jerked the befuddled midget erect and held him clear of the earth by his shirt front.

"You jackass!" he shouted. His fury was burning its way past all inhibitions, and his body was rapidly gearing up for war. "Do you realize what you could have done to us? I ought to kick your butt all the way to the house and back! You crazy—"

"Greg!" Cathy said frantically as she ran up to them. "Take it easy! No one's hurt!"

He looked at her in surprise. "Don't you realize that this idiot could have killed us?"

The midget slowly seemed to regain his senses, though his eyes still seemed unable to focus. He produced a lazy grin. "Wow, man, I feel like I've been kicked in the head by a mule. What happened?" An alcoholic breath accompanied his words.

Some of Greg's rage drained away, replaced by disbelief. "You're ripped," he said, shocked.

"Well, it wouldn't be the first time," the little man said. Then he hiccupped.

Abruptly, Greg laughed. "I'll be damned," he said. "Why else would he have been riding like that?" He hoped that there was no other reason. "Listen, fella, what you consume is your business, but the next time you're drunk and go horseback riding, don't head my way, or we may not be having this conversation again." He carefully placed the dazed man on his feet.

"Sure, man, whatever," the midget responded. "I think I'm going to ring the bell . . . if I can find it."

Cathy shook her head. "Why don't we get the Sundance Kid back to the compound? Someone at the house may be in trouble for leaving his cage open."

Greg directed the man toward the mansion only to find yet another apparition charging down upon them.

"I don't know if I can take much more of this," he said wearily.

"Mikey sure was right about this place. It's a real circus," Cathy added.

The man advancing on them like an out-of-control truck was physically the opposite of the drunken midget. He appeared to be nearly eight feet tall, and his weight must have been in the area of 500 pounds. In spite of his size, however, he was moving with considerable speed, straight for Cathy, Greg and the midget.

"Joseph!" the giant bellowed. "Are you all right?"

The midget looked up blearily at Greg and asked, "Did you say something?"

Greg pointed toward the approaching behemoth.

"Oh," he said calmly. "That's Gerhard. He's very tall."

"No joke," Greg muttered.

"Did I tell you that I've grown six inches taller in the last three months," the little man asked Cathy.

"No, but I don't doubt reports of anything that goes on around here," she answered.

"I'm going to be able to play basketball next season."

The huge man moved with startling speed and nimbleness, especially in light of the fact that most people of his size are generally cumbersome, and he was upon the trio in seconds. Greg wasn't expecting any trouble due to the midget's placid attitude, but he didn't relax his guard.

"Joseph!" the giant gasped. "*Himmels willen,*

I have been looking for you! The horse came back alone!'' His accent was heavily Germanic, and he hardly seemed to notice Cathy and Greg as he stooped easily before the midget. His voice was as deep and voluminous as empty 55 gallon drums dropping on concrete.

The little man grinned dreamily. "I was riding a horse? Man, I'll bet I had a good time . . .''

"He almost ran us down," Cathy snapped. "If he wants to get stoned and kill himself, that's one thing, but when he intentionally tries to injure other people . . .''

The giant, who, even on one knee, was as tall as she, looked sharply at Cathy, and his sheer bulk and wild appearance was such that she gasped and stepped back from him.

"Watch yourself," Greg said in what he meant to be a cautionary tone.

The big man looked at him in turn. He had shaggy black hair and wide-set, almost black eyes. "I am sorry," he said in a surprisingly subdued voice. In fact, he sounded as if he were about to cry. "I have this effect on everyone because of this monstrous, gross form. Please forgive me, I beg. I did not intend to startle you, and I would never, never hurt anyone. I am not an ogre, no matter what my size.''

The drunken midget laughed loudly. "Old Gerhard is a stuffed toy, a teddy bear," he stated. As if to illustrate this, he kicked the massive man solidly in the behind.

The giant ignored the assault and stood, dusting his right knee. "Allow me to introduce Joseph and myself. He is Joseph Trout, and I am Gerhard Klopstock. We are guests at the York home under the care of Dr. Welsh. Might I ask who you are?''

"I'm Cathy Pettis, and this is my friend Greg Hoode,'' she responded. "I registered at the house about an hour ago.''

Klopstock inclined his head politely. "It is a pleasure to meet you, Miss Pettis. Again, I must apologize for the fright I caused you and for the incident that Joseph created. He has a vast spirit in a small form, and sometimes there is a weakness for the release offered by the alcoholic beverages.''

"Better living through chemistry,'' Greg muttered. "I suggest that you keep him away from large animals and automobiles when he's so liberated.''

"Yes, yes, I am at fault. You see, in spite of our diverse sizes—or perhaps because of them—I have become his guardian, after a fashion.''

"Keeper,'' Joseph corrected, laughing and breaking into a drunken run toward the house. "Keeper, warden, custodian, watchdog, and towering redwood, but I'm getting bigger and bigger, day by day, in every way! Tea time! Everybody gets polluted, and next come tonight!''

Gerhard reddened slightly in embarrassment. "I must admit I can do little with him. But it is tea time. Would you please consent to join us?''

"We'd be glad to, Mr. Klopstock,'' Cathy said, "but one more question. This Dr. Welsh—is he a psychiatrist?''

Gerhard smiled gently. "No, Miss. Many of the residents of the York household are a bit eccentric, but none so much as to require psychiatric aid. Dr. Welsh is perhaps the most talented and brilliant physician in the world today, with expertise in practicing all forms of medicine, but his actual specialty and driving interest is the organic, not the psychologic, functioning of the human brain. Shall we?'' He gallantly held out a tremendous, crooked arm to Cathy.

She took it, though she had to reach upward to do so.

Following the mismatched couple across the lawn toward the rear of the house, Greg thought, Off to tea, which I hate. But if I'm up-to-date on my Lewis Carroll, I just may know what to expect from this particular little party.

Cathy had a preconceived idea of what the afternoon tea would be, as well, and it involved a sedate gathering of a few people, perhaps outside on a sunny day such as this, a little soft background music from the stereo speakers, small cakes or biscuits, and quiet conversation. She was right about one item; it *did* take place outside.

"Whoa," Greg whispered to her as they followed Joseph and Gerhard into the backyard, where the York family and their houseguests had already assembled for the daily ritual. "I thought Ed Stern said that they took in an *occasional* boarder."

There were more than sixty people sitting around a pair of long wooden tables beneath a group of trees. They were already well into the tea, with food and several types of beverages on the tables and more being brought by a number of servants. The conversation was loud and enthusiastic, and Gerhard and Joseph smoothly joined in.

"Well, at least there are other household employees," Cathy said. The size of the gathering was almost devastating; if there had been only a few family members and one or two guests, the suspects in her brother's murder would have been much easier to evaluate. "I was afraid that poor Gretchen had to take care of the entire house by herself."

"She's in there pitching," Greg said, pointing to the small girl, who was offering a jug of some iced drink to one member of the group.

Hermie York also was there, still in her lemon yellow jogging suit. She saw the two of them. "Cathy! Greg! Come over here and join us. Here, beside me."

They circled the nearest table and its boisterous crew to slide into a pair of empty chairs next to her. Immediately, Gretchen rushed to the spot.

"Help you?" she asked eagerly. "Iced t-tea, lemonade, coffee, w-wine, uhh . . ." Both Cathy and Greg could see the thought slipping from Gretchen's mind like sand through a colander and the panic that this was causing in her expression.

Hermie patted the girl's behind comfortingly. "Take your time, dear. It starts with an 'S.' "

"Ssss . . . sss . . . sssoft drinks!" She smiled victoriously. "Soft drinks or soda water. And to eat—"

"Cookies or cake," Hermie interrupted to save time. "And if you're really hungry, we can whip up sandwiches, can't we, Gretchen?"

"Nothing to eat for me," Cathy said. "Just a soft drink with ice, please."

Greg decided not to test his luck with Gretchen's culinary skills. "Same for me, Gretchen. A classic Coke, if you have it." He suddenly noticed that the honey smell of the interior of the house was detectable even out here among the trees and flowers, though he saw no hives. This alone would have killed any hunger pangs that he might have been suffering.

After Gretchen had hurried off with the orders, Cathy glanced about the huge, festive gathering and said, "This tea is quite an affair, Hermie. More like a party."

"Isn't it, though?" Hermie replied with characteristic good humor. "I hope you realize that not everyone here is a member of the family or a houseguest."

"No, actually, I didn't."

Hermie laughed loudly. "My darling girl, you're out of Kansas City now. Euphrata is a small town, and what you see before you is a fair sampling of our community's power structure. You have the mayor, five members of the city council, religious leaders . . . this is a daily caucus. Also featuring members of the family and our guests, naturally."

"Seems like a popular tradition," Greg said with a chuckle.

"That's a safe assumption," Hermie responded.

The noise level was so high that Cathy, who was sitting next to the older woman, had to lean toward her to be heard without shouting. "Is that your grandfather?" she asked, pointing to a small, wiry-looking man with crew cut black hair and a distinctly sour expression on his remarkably unlined face. He was sitting at the north end of the larger of the two tables and waving furiously to a young man carrying a bottle of wine.

"That's Grandfather Cecil, all right," she answered. "He'll be a hundred year after next."

"Amazing," Cathy stated. "He looks so active and vital."

"And so dangerous," Greg added. He had just witnessed Cecil as he swung a wide, hard right-handed punch at the waiter's shoulder, apparently in response to what he took to be the boy's laggardly attitude toward his work. Even more surprising was the fact that the boy was a member of Lattwig's Kamikazes, yet he took the physical rebuke meekly. Old Granddaddy must really pull some weight in Euphrata.

"Hermie, if you'll pardon my asking, do you have a doctor in residence?" Cathy asked, almost too low to be understood.

"A doctor? Dear, are you feeling ill?"

"Oh, no, I'm fine, really. It's just that Gerhard mentioned that both he and Joseph were under the care of Dr. Welsh . . ."

"And you want to know if everyone in the York household is in need of treatment, psychiatric or otherwise," Hermie said jovially.

Bingo! Greg thought.

"I realize that to you out-of-towners, many of our ways here may seem . . . unusual," Hermie began.

"I wouldn't say that," Greg commented sardonically.

"Well, I assure you that we're all just ordinary people, with our idiosyncrasies and our unique outlooks on life. We're actually a big family, and

I hope that you come to feel a part of that family, as well.''

''I may not be in Euphrata that long,'' Cathy said.

''What about this Dr. Welsh?'' Greg asked, primarily to keep Hermie talking while he continued to survey the assemblage. What did a psychotic murderer look like, anyway?

''A genius, decades ahead of his time,'' she answered. ''As well as my brother-in-law, married to my little sister, Alfreda. There they are, over there.'' She pointed to a couple at the second table. The woman resembled Hermie rather closely, except for the facts that she looked a bit taller, slimmer and considerably younger. The man appeared to be in his early forties, with light coffee-colored hair and a lush beard and mustache. Between them sat a large, sturdy baby carriage.

''They have a child, I see,'' Cathy said.

Hermie was sipping a glass of iced tea at the moment, and she almost choked as laughter overtook her. ''I shouldn't hope to have Earl as my nephew!''

''Pardon me?''

''Earl is in the buggy, but he's not their child. You see, Tony—Dr. Welsh—is a brain specialist . . .''

At that instant, Gretchen rushed up to the trio, crying and obviously frightened over something that had occurred inside the house. ''I breaked it, I breaked it!'' she whispered urgently as she tugged at Hermie's arm.

''Another disaster, today's brush with doom,'' Hermie said in mock exasperation. ''Please excuse me while I restore the natural order of things inside. Have Alfie and Tony introduce you to their pride and joy." Then she trotted off behind the upset girl.

"This is getting stranger and stranger," Gregg observed. "Tony Welsh is some kind of hotshot brain doctor who's treating an eight foot giant and a four foot dwarf, and the rest of the cast belongs in an early Fellini film. You know, this morning, before I met you, I was just another spoiled rich kid."

"It's just as weird to me, Greg. Let's go."

"Where? I haven't had my Coke, yet."

"To meet Alfie and Tony and Earl. They sound like an interesting group."

"Sure," Greg replied, standing. "It's not like I have any idea at all what we're looking for or anything . . ."

They made their way to the next table, discovering as they went that the various conversations were as colorful as the guests. One man was convinced that he could create a source of eternal energy if he could trap a beam of light inside a hollow, mirrored sphere; he had the sphere, and all he needed now was a shutter device that could admit the light to the interior and then close swiftly enough to keep the beam from escaping through its point of introduction.

Another was discoursing on the theory that on each January 1st he planned the events of the entire year to come through some supernatural agency and then commanded himself to forget everything until the next January 1st, so that life didn't lose it spontaneity.

And Noleta Thrush was deliberating whether or

not she would become an official ambassador to the U.S.S.R. so that she could use her telepathic abilities to eavesdrop on the Kremlin and relay all of the information she collected to the CIA.

"I was joking the first time, but I'm beginning to believe that this really is an asylum," Greg whispered to Cathy.

"I'm inclined to agree with you," she whispered back. "Maybe Dr. Welsh can help us find out what the York mansion really is and who might be dangerous enough to commit a double homicide."

Welsh was talking to his wife and gently rocking the covered, oversized baby carriage when they approached. He rose slightly to his feet and offered Cathy his chair. The Yorks, even those by marriage, were very polite.

"No, please, keep your chair," she told him. "Greg and I would just like to ask you a few questions, if it's not too much of an imposition."

"Normally, there would be no problem at all," he said cordially. "As you can hear, talking is what these gatherings are all about, but I'm going to have to ask that we set discussion back a bit, perhaps following dinner day after tomorrow. As soon as Grandfather York recites the canticle to close the gathering, I'm going to take care of one or two important matters in the house and then race out of here to catch a 4:30 flight to Milwaukee. I have to speak at a medical convention there tonight."

"Cutting it close, aren't you?" Greg asked.

"I don't like to disappoint the old fellow by missing a tea."

Especially since the old fellow controls the

purse strings, Greg thought cynically.

"He should conclude the gathering any minute now." Before Welsh could go on, a strange mewling sound came from the carriage. "Excuse me. There, there, little one." He rocked the carriage a bit harder, but the eerie noise—a little less than a moan and a little more than a sigh—continued.

"He probably has an air bubble, Tony," Alfreda Welsh said.

"We'll get out of the way while you burp him," Cathy told her.

"We don't burp Earl without help," she replied, "preferably from Gerhard."

Dr. Welsh laughed softly as he stood up from the table and rolled back the sun hood to take a look at the child lying in the carriage. Earl lay on his right side with the nipple of an empty formula bottle in his mouth and his long, brownish-blond hair falling lightly over his forehead. In cotton pajamas, he was the picture of a cute, sleepy baby boy except for one detail.

The baby was at least 25 years old.

It was the most catastrophic moment that Cathy had experienced since the long days following Mikey's death.

There was the creepy sensation of seeing an adult man dressed in baby clothing and being treated like a helpless infant, but the impact was multiplied by something greater than this alone. Ever since she had met Gretchen at the front door, she had realized that anything was possible in this madhouse, and somehow, amid all of the confusion and shock, something like hope had begun to grow, too. Maybe that hadn't been her brother in that wrecked car . . .

While Welsh fussed over the cranky infant/man, he had begun to talk about the most interesting medical project thus far in his career. At first, Cathy had been fine— a little repelled but fine. Then the doctor mentioned one topic that brutally ripped Cathy's self-control from her and left her standing, unseeing and unhearing, like a zombie.

He said, "And I have performed what will surely go down in medical history as the first successful human to human brain transplant."

After that, her body began operating in an automatic fashion that allowed her to appear to be normal, even though she was literally stunned. Occasionally, a word or an entire phrase would penetrate the cloud that enveloped her mind— words like "heart-lung machine," "controlled oxygen deprivation," "biological antifreeze"— but these only served to feed the budding idea that was at once impossible, unthinkable and ultimately wonderful.

She stood and was inundated by it all.

No one called Welsh crazy. There was no derisive laughter or any accusations. And skeptical Gregory Hoode, though he asked several questions, didn't express any opinions that overtly labeled Welsh as a charlatan or a crackpot.

It couldn't be, it couldn't be . . . but, oh God, what if it were?

So she remained a static scarecrow too rational to believe what she was hearing and too desperate to let it go.

Then the little monkey man that Hermione had identified as Cecil York climbed upon his chair, shouted for attention and began leading some ridiculous chant that signaled the end of the tea. Greg leaned close to her ear and asked, "Are you okay, Miss Marple? You look like you're about to pass out."

"I don't know . . . I think maybe I need to sit down," she answered slowly. "Greg, I have to talk to you—now!"

Thankfully, he understood. "Sure. We'll go for a drive and get some air to clear our heads. Dr. Welsh, I appreciate your time; you've certainly given us plenty to think about."

Welsh stopped his half-hearted recitation of the chant and replied, "Just a preview, my young friends. In a year, this will be the hottest story in the world, once I work out all of the bugs. Trade in your old body for a new, young, healthy model!"

"Greg, *please*!" she whispered.

"Yeah, uh, we have to make a short trip. See you later, doctor," he said quickly. Then, taking Cathy's hand, he led her toward the front of the York mansion.

Even as they left the miasma of insanity and otherworldliness behind, Cathy felt compelled to look over her shoulder at the large carriage and the sandy-haired man sleeping peacefully in it, sucking softly at his right thumb.

Chapter Six

Early evening, Monday, July 10.

Greg talked around the subject for as long as he could while the pair cruised about Euphrata with no destination in mind. They knew that it was there in the car with them, like an invisible, smothering vapor, so the only real question was who would broach the topic first and when.

"I'm serious now, Cathy. I really think that that place is an institution of some sort," he said, turning around in Ed Stern's parking lot for the fourth time. "There's not one sane person in the bunch."

"What about Hermione?" Cathy asked.

"Okay, she seems fairly level-headed and unthreatening," he admitted, "but maybe she's a keeper or something. That place is dangerous, and I don't think you should go back there."

"I have to. I left my clothes."

"So buy more."

"Another rich boy's answer?"

"Some people wear their poverty like a badge." There was a trace of real irritation in his tone. He wanted to talk her out of staying overnight at the mansion, and he knew that he was going to fail.

"I didn't come to Euphrata for a vacation," she remarked.

"Then tell the police of your suspicions, Cathy. This isn't some Nancy Drew comic book. If any of those people *are* killers, you can be damned sure that they'll be ready to tie up loose ends. If they have even a hint of what we're—"

"I don't recall anyone asking you to take a chance, Mr. Hoode," she said coldly.

"Hell!" He stopped for a traffic light and took the time to compose himself. "Let's look at this rationally, all right? You have a number of certifiable characters in that house, including a drunken midget who tried to trample us, a nut who claims she's going to read the minds of Moscow's top brass, a hundred-year-old servant beater, a giant who could break this car over his knee—"

"And who has never hurt anyone in his life."

"—plus one legitimate mad scientist straight out of Monogram Pictures, circa 1934! What are the odds that not even one of them is a psychotic who will cut your throat in the middle of the night? You can stay at my uncle's house."

"I have to go back. I have to find out."

"The authorities—"

"Haven't done a thing in almost a year. If it's up to me, I'll take the opportunities that I can get." She was silent for a moment, and the fire of possibility glowed even hotter in her heart and mind. "Besides, I left someone back there."

"Who?" he asked, knowing what she would answer.

"Mikey."

"Cathy, Mikey is dead."

"His body is dead, but his brain . . . his soul is still alive."

Greg pulled over to the curb. "Don't do this, Cathy."

"You heard what Welsh said about brain transplants."

"That's science fiction!"

"And what were artificial hearts and space stations and trips to the moon just a few years ago? For Godsake, they cut off his head, Greg! Why would they do that if not to get his brain?" Her tone was pleading—she wanted to believe.

"But it's still impossible, even if Welsh *is* a genius, even if he does have all of that equipment!"

"Earl—"

"Earl's a drooling cretin! If he had Mikey's brain, why would he have been reduced to that level?"

"Some kind of injury during the operation, maybe, or a reaction to being introduced to a new body."

He sighed heavily. "Nerve tissue doesn't heal. When a brain goes without oxygen it starts to die."

She gripped his shoulder with both hands. "But what if it *is* Mikey? What if he's alive? I can't walk out on him!"

Greg started the car and pulled out of the parking space.

"Where are we going?" Cathy asked.

"The library," he replied shortly.

"The library? Now?"

"You're convinced that this Tony Welsh is for real, a respected, maybe even world famous brain specialist, right? Well, if he's so all-fired accomplished, he should be listed in *Who's Who* or some other reference book. If there's no mention of him in any off the books or medical magazines, I want you to seriously consider the possibility that it's all a hoax or a sick fantasy before you have to face burying Mikey again. Is that fair?"

"It's nearly six," she stated, ignoring the question. "Most libraries close at six."

"We'll make it," he promised.

It was four minutes before the hour when they pulled into the nearly empty parking lot. The library was an old two-story building that sat alone just inside the city limits on the western side of town. It hardly resembled any of the sleek glass and steel caverns that most community libraries had evolved into; in fact, on appearance alone, it might well have been a private residence, like the York house.

"I don't think that anyone's still here," Cathy said.

"Two cars in the lot," Greg countered. "Let's go."

When they entered, they startled a pair of youngish women behind a long counter directly across from the doorway. It was clear that these two had been preparing to leave.

"Oh, hello. I'm sorry, but we're just closing. We'll be open at nine in the morning."

But Greg wouldn't be deterred. "This won't take long and it's important. I'd appreciate it if you could stay open for fifteen minutes more."

The young women glanced at one another with slightly bothered expressions.

"We'd like to help you, but that would be entirely against the rules," the first responded.

Greg withdrew his wallet. He didn't care what remarks would be made about a rich boy's solution. "I'm willing to pay you each fifty dollars for fifteen minutes."

Startled looks replaced the bothered ones. "Phyllis, fifty dollars!" the second whispered.

The first woman was tempted—her eyes expressed that plainly enough—but not even money could outweigh some sort of commitment that she had made. "You know that we have to serve dinner tonight," she whispered back, though both Cathy and Greg easily overheard. "If we're not there promptly at six-thirty, we'll be in all kinds of trouble with the old man."

The second woman sighed. "You're right." To Greg, she added, "I'm sorry, but we have to close now."

At that moment, a third woman walked into the front room carrying an armload of books. She was distinctly older than the two women behind the counter, perhaps in her early fifties, and was shorter than Gretchen. She had bobbed black hair and gray eyes behind large, round spectacles. Idly, Greg thought that these were the first eyeglasses that he had seen on a resident of

Euphrata.

"See you in the morning, ladies," the woman said as she struggled to place the heavy stack of books on the counter.

"Can I help with those?" Greg asked automatically.

The little woman jumped, apparently not having seen Cathy or Greg from behind the books when she entered the room. "Oh, yes . . . thank you, thank you," she said, allowing Greg to place the volumes on the counter. "I feel that as a librarian I have a certain example to set for the rest of the community."

"Mrs. Simpson, these people would like to use the library for another fifteen minutes or so," the first young woman said. "We told them that the hours were nine to six, but it's awfully important and Phyllis and I have to go. Could you help them?"

Mrs. Simpson adjusted her glasses and inspected the newcomers. "We don't get many last minute emergencies here," she pointed out.

"Well, this is one," Greg told her. He had slipped his wallet back into his jeans before he helped the woman with the books, but he made a motion toward it now.

Cathy casually grasped his hand. "We wouldn't take up much of your time, I promise," she said.

"Mrs. Simpson?" Phyllis prodded.

"Of course, of course. Run along, you two," the woman said. "I'll take care of this crisis and close up."

Clutching their purses and tossing quick good-byes over their shoulders, the women rushed out the door which Mrs. Simpson locked behind them.

"That's to keep us from being interrupted," she stated, "though heaven knows, we don't get very many visitors during regular business hours. Now, what exactly do you need to offset this literary alarm?"

"You have a current edition of *Who's Who*, don't you?" Greg asked.

"The most recent one." Mrs. Simpson strode quickly and purposefully into the room to the immediate left of the counter and stopped at a wall of shelves containing several sets of encyclopedias and a number of other reference works. Selecting a thick, red volume, she carried it to a table and opened it. "What's the name?"

"Welsh," Cathy said, apparently eager now to investigate the man who offered her some flicker of hope. "His first name is Tony or Anthony or something like that. He's a doctor."

"The Yorks' in-law?" Mrs. Simpson said.

"Yes. Do you know him?"

"I've never met the man, but he's sort of a folk hero around Euphrata. At least, that's what I've heard since moving to town."

"You're not a native?" Greg inquired.

"No. I was sent here eighteen months ago by the state library board to find out why practically no one in Euphrata uses this facility, and the local workers haven't quite forgiven me for being a foreigner yet. If you're interested in a doctor, a better bet would be *The Encyclopedia of American Science and Medicine*, right there at your left elbow, young man."

Greg looked at the books near his elbow and

found the appropriate one. It was gigantic, around 20 pounds and several thousand pages. "I didn't know that there were this many scientists and doctors in the whole country," he muttered as he placed it on the table. "Welsh, Welsh, I guess that's spelled W-e-l-s-h."

"Sounds right to me," Mrs. Simpson agreed. "Though I have heard it pronounced 'Welch', with a 'c-h', from time to time."

"No, it's Welsh," Cathy said with certainty. "His sister-in-law told us that."

"Hmm," Greg whispered absently as he flipped through the mountains of pages. "Here we go. 'Wakefield', 'Walls', 'Wample', 'Waterman', 'Webb', 'Webster', 'Wells' . . . 'Welsh'. 'Welsh, Andrew James', 'Welsh, Beatrice', 'Colin', 'Eugenia', 'Matthew', 'Morton', 'Peter', um, 'Thomas', 'Tyler', 'Victor', and 'Walter'. No Tony or Anthony or any variation thereof." He looked at Cathy with a slight smile.

"Maybe it *is* a different spelling," she said faintly. "Maybe he's not listed as Anthony."

"Yeah, or maybe he's just a legend in his own little community."

She stepped beside him and scanned the shelf. "Wait, here's another volume, the revised edition! It's updated." She struggled to wrestle the even heavier book onto the table.

Greg gave her a hand. "You don't give up easily, do you?" he asked, though not without some admiration. The second volume was newer than the first, by a full decade, and he quickly found the "Welsh" listing.

Again there was no Anthony.

"This is pretty recent, Cathy," he said. "If Welsh is as world renowned and respected as everyone swears, I think he'd be listed, don't you?"

She began turning the pages swiftly. "What about Tony? Is there one?"

"Cathy, the man's a fraud! Anyone who claims that he can not only transplant a human brain but already *has* is either running some kind of bunco game or is driving with one wheel in the sand."

"Brain transplants?" Mrs. Simpson repeated with interest.

"He's a nut," Greg reaffirmed.

"Just a minute!" Cathy said excitedly. "Here, right here! Read this!"

Greg looked at the listing beneath her stabbing finger. "Welsh, Stephen Anthony. New York, New York, St. Martin's Memorial Hospital (*q.v.*); innovative, revolutionary, and sometimes controversial medical doctor specializing in research and experimentation into the organic mysteries of the brain. Proposed theory of isolated cryogenic preservation of brain function following host death, partially successful demonstration with rhesus monkeys . . ." Greg's voice faded.

"Do you see it?" Cathy demanded. " 'Innovative' and 'revolutionary'! He's done it! That's why they never found Mikey's head!"

"Jeeze," Greg said, having to admit at least the possibility to himself for the first time.

"He's still alive!"

"Pardon me, but what in the hell are you two talking about?" Mrs. Simpson asked bluntly.

Greg still wasn't able to give in entirely. "Mrs.

Simpson, is there any possibility that the York mansion ever was a . . . a hospital of some kind, a treatment center for the mentally ill? I saw a movie once about an an asylum where the patients revolted, took over the staff's positions, and went on to establish their own community.''

"That might explain some of the weirdness up there," the woman agreed, "but the records say that it's simply a private residence, built early in the century for A.H. Hotchkiss by the York Building Company and taken over during construction by the Yorks due to lack of payment. The Hotchkiss family disappeared, apparently because they couldn't afford to honor the contract. Actually, Euphrata doesn't have a hospital as such."

"Not at all?" Cathy asked.

"Only an animal hospital that was started by an out-of-town concern some years ago and promptly failed. There aren't even any practicing physicians, aside from Welsh, as far as I can discern."

"Euphrata is a healthy place," Greg said grimly. "Okay, you're obviously an intelligent woman and well-educated. What do you think are the chances that Dr. Welsh, acting pretty much alone, was able to transplant a man's brain from his own body into another one?" It sounded ludicrous even as he spoke.

Surprisingly, she didn't laugh. "That's quite a question. It's like a scenario from a science fiction movie. But according to some sources, the mainland Chinese have already successfully completed a similar transplant, using the entire head, as early as '83 or '84, and reports from East

Germany in '85 claimed that surgeons there were performing such procedures utilizing only the brain itself in an almost routine manner on humans."

"Oh, my God," Cathy gasped. Her knees weakened, and Greg helped her to sit in a chair.

"Her brother," Greg explained. "His decapitated body was found in a wrecked car after he and his wife spent the night up there. She thinks maybe he was . . ."

"Earl," Cathy whispered, covering her face with her hands.

Though they were alone in the locked building, Mrs. Simpson seemed to glance furtively around the room before she took a seat next to Cathy and asked quietly, "Neither of you is from Euphrata, are you?"

"I just arrived, this morning," Cathy answered.

"I've been here since the first of June, staying with my uncle," Greg added. "Why?"

"For reasons of my own," she said. "You're the Hoode boy, yes? I've seen you in here once or twice in the periodical section, reading *Sports Illustrated*."

"Greg Hoode," he said. "And this is Cathy Lock—uh, Pettis."

"Lockwood," Cathy corrected him.

Mrs. Simpson raised an eyebrow. "Well, Greg and Cathy, I'm Louise Simpson, and if it's not too uncomfortable for you, I'd like for you to call me Louise. As to your question, I believe that it would be very unlikely that Welsh, working outside of the medical establishment, would be able to accomplish a radical procedure such as that, but since I've been here so much has happened in that place that I wouldn't rule out anything. I don't know if that's a relief or a curse to you. My only advice is not to pursue the matter on your own. Soon, perhaps before the end of the month, an official investigation will be taking place, and all of this can be cleared up then.''

''That's what I've been trying to convince her,'' Greg said. ''You can't go back there tonight.''

''You're *staying* at the York house?'' Louise asked in a shocked tone.

''I checked in this afternoon.''

''Oh, that's not such a good idea at all!'' Louise stood and walked to the counter; when she returned to the silent, waiting pair, she was carrying a small black briefcase. ''I'm trusting you to keep what I'm about to show you a secret. You may think that all of this is only the invention of a lonely widow, but I swear to you that I've been as completely impartial as possible as I've gathered it.''

Her story was strange, but nothing less believable than what they had already experienced.

As far as the official record went, there was nothing outstanding about Euphrata, Indiana. It was a town of medium size with no statewide significance of either a political or commercial nature; its steady population figures and isolationist policies had helped to keep it little more than a spot on the map. Euphrata, it seemed, needed nothing that the outside world could provide.

When Louise Simpson had arrived in an effort to drum up wider community support for the

regional   library,   she   had   immediately
encountered the cordial resistance that Euphrata
residents habitually employed when dealing with
outsiders. They were all friendly, helpful and
polite, but they made it plain that, as natives, they
were a part of some invisible society that non-
locals could never hope to approach.

Of course, a number of small settlements share
this exclusive attitude, but the longer Louise
remained, the more she picked up on a number of
slightly out-of-kilter details—such as the fact that
Euphrata had no hospitals.

No one ever seemed to be seriously ill. There
were overweight people, smokers, drinkers, and
the occasional carouser, but all seemed to be
brimming with good health. Whenever any of her
acquaintances displayed any signs of a cold or any
other sickness or minor injury, they disappeared
for a day or so and returned hale and hearty. The
phrase used for these short disappearances,
supposedly uttered out of Louise's hearing, was
"going to the Yorks.' "

On one occasion, six months before, Louise
had actually witnessed a terrible auto accident
involving four local teenagers and an elderly
produce delivery man in a pickup truck. The man
was not hurt, but the kids were in critical
condition when they were pulled from the
wreckage by the police rescue team and carried to
some unknown destination in patrol cars. Louise
saw the gaping wounds and broken, protruding
bones, and she knew that those types of injuries
were often fatal. Despite the evidence that her
own eyes had provided, three of those kids had
returned to school, apparently totally recovered,

a couple of days later, and the fourth had resumed his normal schedule without any evidence of lingering disability within the week.

When she had tried to discuss this with the others, she had been met with subtle implications that she was mistaken or had overreacted to what had been, in fact, minor injuries. Her only explanation had been provided by the muttered words, "They went to the Yorks.'"

A more sinister discovery was that, excluding the disappearances, Euphrata had no crime to speak of. Even the subculture of hustlers, sellers, abusers, and soliciters that usually existed in practically every neighborhood couldn't be found within the city limits. Transients appeared from time to time, but they were never present for two days in a row.

Louise didn't actually see any of these street people swept up or rushed out of town, but she knew instinctively that it was happening.

In addition, many people seemed to vanish in the Euphrata area. They were men and women traveling by car predominantly, seldom in groups larger than two, and almost invariably they came from out of state. Officially, none of these people were in Euphrata at the time of their disappearance, of course, but they all were within a surprisingly limited radius of the town. Most of Louise's casebook was made up of newspaper clippings concerning this aspect.

Louise really couldn't bring herself to trust anyone she had met in Euphrata, so when her suspicions became too strong to carry alone, she discreetly made a few inquiries among her state board acquaintances. Over a period of months,

she had interested a state police investigatory
panel in her theories. So far, they didn't have
enough substantial material to move upon, but
she remained in contact with a special agent in
Tiverton by telephone.

Something was going on in Euphrata, and, as
Cathy and Greg had suspected, its focal point
appeared to be the York mansion.

They were quiet for a while following Louise's
story, digesting what they had heard. They were
startled by the scope of the situation and
somewhat relieved to find that their suppositions
were not entirely imaginary, after all. And they
were more than a little scared.

"Do you think that Welsh has been treating the
townspeople—like those boys injured in the
wreck—at the house with some type of new
medicine or something?" Cathy asked.

"I'm sure he's in on it, but he's in town only
about half of each year, and I have the feeling
that this thing has been going on for a long time,
long before Tony married into the family,"
Louise answered. "I think it has something to do
with the house itself."

"Okay," Greg began uncertainly, "if the
Yorks have discovered some miraculous new
healing system, that's good, isn't it? Why would
they be involved in kidnapping and maybe
murdering travelers?"

"I didn't say that I had any answers, only clues
and theories," Louise pointed out. "Maybe
they're involved with human sacrifices. All I'm
certain about is that young mothers-to-be in
Euphrata go to the York mansion to give birth,

that you'll have to search high and low in this town to find anyone other than myself who wears glasses or is hard of hearing or has false teeth, that there are literally dozens of citizens in this area who are as lively as adolescents even though they're in their nineties, and that the state officials are so interested in this that I have a special code to relay to the task force in Tiverton for immediate assistance if I come across some solid evidence.

"I took you two into my confidence against my better judgment because of one very important element. You are not a part of this invisible clique and therefore are in very serious danger. Young lady, I wouldn't spend a night in that house for all of the wealth in the York coffers."

"Yeah, just try to convince her," Greg advised wearily.

Cathy closed her eyes and shook her head. "I don't want to go into this again. I have to go back there; I have no choice. What you've just told me makes me sure that my brother's mind is still alive, and that means *he* is still alive, even if he's in another form."

"But that entire hill could be a cemetery! The authorities will be moving in at any time, so you won't have to expose yourself to any of this danger."

"And when the authorities move in, how can we be sure that those crazy people won't try to eliminate all of the evidence against them?" Cathy demanded. "I have to get Mikey out of there before this all blows up. Really, I appreciate your concern, but I'm not going to change my mind, even if I have to die for it. He would die for me.''

What could they say to that? Was logic any defense against love?

When Pamela Durben finally awoke after her first experience with the gas, there was no way for her to be certain that this wasn't just another of those countless, incredibly real dreams that she had been trapped within while unconscious. At first she had thought that they too had been reality.

When she stared up into the face of the man that, in her earlier delirium, she had felt resembled her husband Kevin, she knew with enough certainty that she was awake.

''I dare say you feel better now, don't you?'' the man asked with a smile. Though both he and Kevin had full beards, Pamela found it impossible to accept that she had confused the two of them—not with those cold, reptilian eyes.

''Where is my husband?'' she asked faintly.

''Right here, babe, beside you!'' Kevin said from no more than five feet away, and his voice even sounded excited.

By raising her head slightly, Pamela could see him, strapped to the bed next to her. They were still in that strange room, along with a dozen other haunted-looking individuals lashed to huge chairs.

''Are you all right?'' she asked. The memory of the terrible accident was growing sharper in her mind as she receded from her dreams.

''All right?'' he repeated eagerly. ''I still ache some, but, Pammie, I'm almost healed! Goddamn, can you believe it? It's only four o'clock. We've been here just two or three hours, and my bones have knitted! The gashes and open wounds healed over!''

The bearded man above her continued to stare down with a proud expression. "And how do you feel?" he asked again.

"I . . ." she began. Then wonderingly, she finished, "I feel . . . better, much better. I still hurt, but it's like everything happened six months ago.''

That was the reaction that the doctor had wanted, and he chuckled with self-satisfaction. "You were a very severely injured young woman earlier this afternoon. I believe that you were within half an hour of death, in fact, but, with a few more applications of the vapor, you should be completely recovered by, oh, Wednesday morning at the latest.''

Pamela's incredulous belief in the man's words and her own relief from the suffering she had endured couldn't completely push away the fear of her surroundings. "Where am I? Why are we strapped down this way?''

"Where? In the only place that could possibly have saved your life. You are secured so that you don't further injure yourself before your bones have knitted completely.''

"Then what about us?" shouted one of the men from the armchairs savagely. It wasn't Neil, who was sitting quietly and wide-eyed. "Why are *we* prisoners here, you bastard?"

Pamela was aware that Carl, the keeper apparently, was in the room only when he stepped before the angry man and silenced him with several blows to the face and body.

"Enough, Carl," the doctor said casually after a few moments.

"Kevin, help me!" Pamela said in rising hysteria. "Get me out of here!" She knew her pleadings were futile and irrational, but she was so frightened that she didn't care.

"Take it easy, baby, and try to keep calm," Kevin said earnestly. "I'm sure that we're being kept here only because we're not physically ready to leave, and soon, after we've had more of that wonderful gas, we'll be released. We can pay for these treatments—"

The doctor interrupted him. "And I know that the two of you have no reservations in Euphrata and are acquainted with none of our citizens, which leads me to believe that no one knows of your whereabouts other than our little group."

"That's not true!" The desperate lie came easily to Pamela's lips. "My editor sent us here to take pictures . . ."

"She's lyin'!" Jeroboam's rather high-pitched voice came from behind her.

Pamela craned her neck back to find the massive man standing at the head of her bed. This time he was eating a candied apple.

"Fine. Thank you, Jeroboam," the doctor responded. "No one knows and no one will look —most convenient. I think that it's time for another application of the vapor, Nurse McCardle."

The memory of the earlier visions slammed into Pamela with stunning impact; most of those dreams had not been pleasant, though all had been far more realistic than any she had ever experienced before. "No, I don't want that," she snapped. "Not yet!"

The man winked at her. "You must learn to listen to your doctor, my dear. Nurse."

"Kevin!"

"There's nothing that we can do right now, Pam," he answered, and she could hear the anguished helplessness in his voice. "It is for our good, so try to relax and go with it. I swear to God I won't let anyone hurt you."

She fought anyway, not with her hands or feet since they were still tightly strapped, but when the nurse came with that plastic mask again, she whipped her head from side to side in spite of the pain. Carl caught her head in his hands and held her until the mask could be fitted against her. Even then, she held her breath for just as long as was possible.

Whether it was due to the weakness of her body or the potency of the reddish gas that hissed over her beneath the mask, she was unconscious within seconds—unconscious, but not at rest.

The second round of dreams was no better than the first, and this was one of the first things that she asked about when she regained consciousness and found that no one other than the captives was in the large room. The lighting seemed to have been turned up—or perhaps her sight had been more fully restored—and she could see everyone quite easily, merely by lifting her head from the pillow. This didn't hurt nearly so much as before, either.

"It's the gas, naturally," Albert Tarkenton said. He was the man who had been beaten into silence by Carl two hours earlier; there were ugly welts and dried blood on his face. "It heals. In that way, it's a miracle, but I think that it drives you crazy, too, if you're exposed to it long enough. God, I hope that someone finds us before that happens to me."

He and the eleven other captives, three of whom were women, were just like the Durbens in that they had been passing through Euphrata when they were abducted by these weird, conscienceless people and brought to this room. Neil and three other men were hoboes who had been picked up at the Euphrata freight yards by the so-called welcome wagon with promises of food and lodging. Two couples had been spending the night in what was called the York House (of which this room seemed to be a part) when they began experiencing the awfully realistic dreams and awoke in the chair that they now occupied. One woman had had the unfortunate luck to undergo car trouble while driving through late at night, and the other three men wouldn't talk about themselves or anything else, as if terrified that they would be caught imparting information which would have been useless anyway.

Each of the twelve had been captured during the preceding month. There had been no one in the room when the first was strapped to his chair, and no one had left since. Their bodies rebelled at the long confinement, of course, but one whiff of that gas was enough to undo any sort of damage that captivity had inflicted on them. The hallucinations also broke up the monotony, so each of them slowly had become addicted to their too-infrequent treatments.

Another reason that they craved the gas was perhaps the most basic of all—they were never fed.

The gas clearly possessed the capacity to sustain human life even when no nutrition other than water was being administered. The hunger pains were horrendous for the first few days, of course, but within a remarkably short amount of time they all became used to existing on the regular twice a day "meals" from the gas mask, three daily trips to a small bathroom for whatever function proved necessary and long droughts of metallic-tasting well water. They weren't permitted baths, though one woman who had gone through her period had been allowed to clean herself with the supervision of the armed nurse. The room would have smelled considerably worse had it not been for the pervasive, honeylike odor of the gas.

"I believe that it's a natural phenomenon," Albert continued. "It originates in the soil on which this place is built, and it seeps up through floors, walls, everything, and eats away at the brain. These people have tapped it somehow and can put it in pressurized bottles."

"But why are they keeping us here?" Pamela asked, while looking at the skeletal limbs of Neil Frazier, who had been there the longest of any of them. Though the body was maintained by the gas, it continued to feed upon itself, it seemed.

"Entertainment," Albert replied.

"What?"

"You'll see at six this evening. I told you that the gas drives them batty. Apparently, it increases their tolerance and craving for violence—man on

man, man on woman, man on child or animal,
depravity, torture, just about anything that a
normal person would be repelled by.''

"They're not going to do that to us!" Kevin
almost screamed. "I don't care what their
damned gas does for—"

"Okay, calm down," Albert said quickly. "As
far as we know, they don't intend to use us for
that kind of stuff, except to shut us up or to
punish us for lying to them. They like to listen."

Pamela and Kevin exchanged confused looks as
much as their confinement allowed. "What do
you mean?" she asked. Listening sounded almost
as frightening and sick as participation.

"Everyday at six p.m., Carl and Jeroboam
come down here and order us to tell them
something terrible that we've done in the past; it
can be either emotional or physical abuse, though
they prefer physical. And it always has to be the
truth."

"What difference does that make?" Kevin
asked.

Albert shrugged, after a fashion. "They love
authenticity."

"I mean, they can't know if it's true or a
fabrication."

Neil abruptly laughed in a high, almost lunatic
tone.

"Jeroboam knows,"Albert said with a quiet
sincerity made ever more profound by its contrast
to the panicky laughter.

"How?"

"The gas again, I suppose. It seems to bring
out the psychic potential in certain people—or at
least in Jeroboam. I've never seen anybody else

who could tell exactly what someone else was thinking that way. It's like he can tune into thought waves."

"I don't even believe in psychic abilities," Kevin stated flatly.

"Right. Just don't try to lie to him. He's never been wrong with me, and if he had more brains than a turnip, I imagine that I would be long dead and buried by now."

"Don't rush it," one of the captive women sighed with resignation.

"I still don't believe it."

Albert contorted his bruised face with something like a smile. "Good enough. You'll be getting your chance to test him soon. It should be close to six by now."

Within a few minutes the two men appeared, as Albert had predicted. Carl was wearing his usual dour expression of weary revulsion, just as Jeroboam looked as placidly thoughtless as before. For once, the titanic man was not eating.

Carl began by asking the older captives if any of them had thought up a new story with which to amuse their hosts; as Albert had previously explained, a story with the proper degree of grotesqueness won the teller a trip upstairs to present it to the Yorks in person. The old man was particularly fond of murder and torture tales.

The first twelve captives had exhausted their meager supplies of depravity days before, and of the group only Neil responded to the invitation. He began another frantic recitation involving a fellow hobo whom he had shoved beneath the wheels of the train they were both riding, but he got only a few words into it before Jeroboam mumbled, "Lyin'." Carl was free now from the restraint of the doctor's presence, and he delightedly chopped the emaciated man's face to ribbons with the leather strap.

Then the men turned to the newest arrivals.

"What about you?" Carl demanded of Kevin. "What was the worst thing you ever did to anybody?"

"Go to hell," Kevin replied.

Carl hit him on one of the knees which had been so severely injured earlier that day. Kevin cried out and cursed with words that he hadn't used since his days as a college student.

"Ready to try again?" Carl inquired.

Kevin spat at him, and the sequence was repeated. Pamela was crying now and feeling every electric bolt of pain that coursed through her husband.

"Tell him, Kevin, for Godsake, tell him something! Anything!" she screamed.

Carl grinned coolly. "But don't lie about it. Now, I know a guy like you, from the big city, has done something he's ashamed of in his life."

It took Kevin the better part of a minute to regain his breath. "Okay," he hissed. His voice was harsh with pain and fury. "I'll tell you something."

"I thought so. Go ahead, and I'll decide if you've won the trip up top or not. If it's real good, you can even make an appearance at the convocation tonight."

"I . . . I'm a lawyer, and I once defended a man who was accused of murdering his brother-in-law. Certain evidence that I located convinced me that he had done it." Kevin paused to drop his head back, close his eyes and pant for breath.

"So?" Carl prompted.

"When I told him what I knew, he promised to give me an extra, undeclared hundred grand if I got him off. I collected."

"That's it?" Carl asked. When Kevin said nothing more, he looked to Jeroboam.

"Yeah," Jeroboam responded. "He done it."

"Oh God!" Pamela gasped. Tears burned in her eyes and spilled down the sides of her head. How, how, how? They had been together on a trip, a wonderful dream assignment—how had it come to this?

"That ain't much, man," Carl stated. "The old guy won't sit up and take notice of it. Is that the worst thing you ever did?"

"Yes, damn it, yes!" he shouted.

"Neil had better stuff than that after he'd been here ten days. Jeroboam?"

The tremendously fat man rubbed his forehead with a sweaty hand. "Don't know, Carl. His thinkin's all screwy. Don't know."

Albert and the other captives looked startled. They had never known the ponderous psychic to be uncertain in his decisions.

Carl didn't seem unduly upset, however. "Let's give him time to think about it. How about you, Missy? Got any juicy morsels for us?"

Pamela saw the men turn toward her, but she felt their filthy eyes falling upon her naked flesh beneath the thin sheet. Suddenly, she wanted to throw up.

Carl barked, "Speak up, woman."

"I don't know what you want," she said. "I never killed anyone. I don't understand . . . why should you want to hear this?''

"Nothing?" Carl said. "Lady, I know that women aren't any more moral than men, just a little more devious. You'd better come up with something, p.d.q.''

"I can't think!" Her mind was chaotically swarming with snatches of her past, all of the mean-spirited, ugly, and thoughtless items that collect in the best of lives like iron filings on a magnet, but none of them would be anything but ridiculous posings to these ruthless men. "I try not to hurt people—''

Without warning, Carl reached beneath the sheet to grab the ring finger of Pamela's left hand and twist it up and back so that it snapped with a startlingly loud crack.

Pamela completely lost her breath for an instant, and then she found it with a shriek of agony that threatened to rip her throat open. Without the layer of shock that had enveloped her during the wreck, this became the single worst pain that she could ever recall. She screamed until there was no longer a molecule of oxygen left in her chest.

"You bastards! I'll kill you, you animals!" Kevin cried just as loudly. "Stop it!''

Instead, Carl took the middle finger of her pinioned hand and repeated the action. Still screaming, Pamela felt her bowels and bladder void themselves onto the bed.

"I'll kill you if I ever get loose!" Kevin repeated, eyes wide with fury.

"Shut up," Carl said. "Hey, Jeroboam, how many fingers we got left now?"

The big man frowned in concentration.

"Which hand?" he asked.

Carl found Pamela's forefinger and began to apply pressure to it. "Better come up with something, lady."

"Wait!" Kevin's roar rang out above even Pamela's screams to fill the room. Carl and Jeroboam actually looked at him. "I'll tell you something—something horrible, something I've never told anyone else! It's good . . . I mean, it's something . . . the worst thing I could ever conceive of anyone doing, and I did, I swear to you, I did!"

Jeroboam grunted in abrupt shock at the powerful waves he was intercepting, and Carl released Pamela's fingers, impressed by the display. "A good one?" he asked.

"Whooo," Jeroboam moaned. "I don't get no fix, but he ain't lyin'. Strong, strong."

"Okay, Kev, you've got me interested. Go on."

"You've got to promise to stop hurting her and give her some more of the gas," he stated. "Okay?"

"No, no . . ." Pamela cried. She hated the visions more than the pain.

"We'll see," Carl answered. "Talk."

"I want to sit up. I want to be in a chair."

Carl responded by touching a button on the side of the bed which raised its upper portion and brought Kevin into a sitting position. His arms and hands were still strapped uselessly beside him as if he were offering himself for sacrifice—which, in a way, he was.

"Pammie," he said with tenderness and calm, "I love you. I wouldn't even be telling this but for you. Try to understand.''

She could only stare at his ashen face. It couldn't be that bad. Loving, liberal Kevin Durben wasn't capable of anything that bad.

''You'd better get busy talking,'' Carl warned.

''Don't prod me!'' Kevin snapped with authority again. ''You can bet your stinking heart that this will be worth the hearing, so don't say anything while I tell it. Do you understand?''

Stunned, Carl merely nodded.

''Okay.''

And this is what Kevin told them.

It was fifteen years ago, the beginning of summer, and I was fourteen.

My family and I were at the lakeside cabin on Erie, just north of Dunkirk, and six other families were there, too, all in lodges and cabins. Each group had money, so we owned all of the land around there. It was something like a private resort.

There were seven of us kids all about the same age, and though we didn't see that much of one another throughout most of the year, we were all really close—four boys and three girls. The oldest of us, fifteen, was Derek. He was a good friend, but really tough. He looked a little older than he was, smoked out of his parents' sight, picked fights with older guys, and won most of them.

Somehow we all realized that this would be our last summer as kids, and we wanted to do something to mark it, so that we'd be able to say, ''That's how it was when I grew up.'' But we didn't know what. It didn't matter so much during the day, because there was always so much to do, but at night we could feel it slipping away from us—youth—and we knew that we had to do something that was really dumb, stupid and childish, something that only adults could get away with, using adults' brains and bodies.

We thought of sex, but that wasn't really the answer. For one thing, Derek and Mona were already doing it, sometimes with each other, but for the rest of us that seemed a little like incest. We were really brother and sister bonded, the way only kids can be. My real older brother was away at college, and Derek was much more a protector and confidant than he had ever been.

So, as ridiculous as it may sound now, we began to read a little porn at first, but, in spite of how we tried to act, that bored us. At the end of each day, the seven of us would meet in a cabin that was going unused that summer—the O'Donahues were in Europe—and we would read our scandalous magazines and pathetic little paperbacks out loud, so everyone could join in the fun. Sometimes we would act them out. If we'd had VCRs then, we would have watched R and X movies, and maybe that would have been enough. Maybe it never would have happened.

After a few nights, we noticed that it was the violence more than the sex that intrigued us. We'd all seen *If* by then—God, how I wished I looked like Malcolm McDowell—and that became sort of our ideal—the kids, us, rebelling and using adult weapons and tactics against the world that had made them. We were all convinced that the Russians would bomb us in '76 anyway, while everyone was blithely celebrating the Bi-Centennial, and when you're chicly fatalistic, the ultimate implications of what you do don't seem to matter much.

We drifted away from porn toward real books, respectable novels that dealt with interesting themes, like *First Blood*. We read that a long time before Stallone made the movie. And *Open Season* was another big favorite. It told of these good ol' boy hunters who every year vacationed at an isolated lake to hunt and fish. On the way there, though, they would always pick up a couple of drifters, usually a guy and a girl who would be the quarry for that year. Yeah, that book may have incited the first inklings of the plan in us.

By accident, then, we had stumbled upon the last kids' lark that we would do with our lives. Of course, the guys in *First Blood* and *Open Season* got killed at the end, but we wouldn't. It was all just a fun fantasy then, nothing serious.

There was a novel about a man who made war films in the Philippines, and used real ammunition on the actors, one by Ed McBain about a woman who kidnaps a man and holds him for ten years or something, and another that was my favorite that dealt with a secret club in which the initiation was to murder three people, one of whom you knew personally. That may have been inspired, pardon the term, by the Zebra killings out on the West Coast.

The turning point came when Wesley brought *The Collector* by John Fowles to the meeting. It was a little cerebral for us—hell, the second portion, where the kidnapped girl sets her feelings to paper, was just plain boring to us. Nuclear disarmament marches? Artistic and unfulfilled love affairs? We skipped most of that, but the book did have the girl dying and the kidnapper getting away scot-free, hinting that he would do it all again. It sort of set our target as an attractive woman. The girls mock-bitched a little about equal rights and all, but we understood that a girl would offer less of a threat and . . . more fun.

Besides, it was all in fun . . . then.

I don't know who brought the next book—yes, I do, but I won't say, just like I won't say the title of the novel. I've been trying to forget all of that for fifteen years, even though I've read it word for word at least a thousand times.

It was a newly published book, and I don't think that it enjoyed any real success, though it was reviewed in the *New York Times Book Review*. They didn't like it. To us, however, it was a heavenly revelation.

It combined the best elements of *The Collector* and *Lord of the Flies,* the only good novel we'd ever been forced to read in school. It had an attractive young woman as the captive and the kids in charge. God, this is so . . . I'm sorry . . . yes, yes, I'll go on.

The book was about a bunch of spoiled rich kids like us who overpower and tie up their live-in babysitter while their parents are away for a week or two. At first, they do it only as a game, so that they and their friends can enjoy freedom from adult rule for the week, even though the girl was only twenty or so. But things progress, as they always do, and they begin to torture the babysitter and then to rape her. Finally, they realize that they can do what they honestly have always wanted to do and kill her. They wanted this from the start, but they didn't recognize it early on in themselves. So they strangle her, shoot a tramp, and blame it all on him. And, of course, they get away with it. That was the most important part—what Leopold and Loeb couldn't manage.

That book was almost three hundred pages long, and we read it aloud in one night.

I remember Derek said it first: That's who we'll kill.

We all laughed, naturally. It was only a joke that we had been playing with, mulling over, planning for about a week. That's who we'll kill!

And we all laughed.

For one thing, we didn't have a babysitter. We were the oldest kids at the lake, and since the smaller ones were never allowed to bother us during those summers, we were pretty much on our own. Even our parents didn't pay much attention to us. Oh, don't worry, I'm not going to try to blame everything on parental neglect or any of those handy excuses. I know who was responsible—and who is now. The point is, our parents were having their vacations and we were having ours, all in the same general area, but not really together.

So who would we have kidnapped? There was no one.

Derek woke me the next morning early, about six-thirty, and I'd only been in bed since four. We were going to drive down to Cleveland to a big summer festival they were holding there, almost a hundred miles away. I told him to get lost, that I was too tired to go anywhere. Then he said that we all had to go, because that was where we were going to do the thing. I didn't completely understand then, but I went, and you can bet that I was excited.

Derek didn't have his license, of course, but he drove all the time, anyway; he looked about seventeen. His folks were gone for the day, leaving behind their huge, beautiful RV, and that's what we went in.

How can I explain? We still thought it was a big joke then. No one knew where we were going, the adults not even aware that we'd left the lake. So we started to plan as we traveled. This is how we would do it *if* we did it for real, though we never would hurt or kill anyone, especially not a girl.

We got to the festival early, just after it opened. It was almost like Disneyland with rides and shows. Man, we forgot all about that kidnapping garbage for three or four hours and just had a time of it. It wasn't until we broke for lunch that it came up again.

Now we're going to do it, Derek said, and go out with a blast.

Damn, man, you're crazy, somebody else said. It was Peter, I suppose, the only one of us who really resisted the idea. I'm not going to spend the rest of my life in prison for rape and murder, no matter what that stupid book said.

It won't be like that, Mona told him. We'll take her, to show that we can, drive her around in the camper, scare her a little, and then let her go out in the sticks somewhere and be back at the lake, a hundred miles from here, before she reaches a telephone. No one will even suspect us.

She was convincing. She could charm a mouse into a snake's mouth. Maybe that's what she did.

So we did it.

We came up with a half-assed plan that was so haphazard and ragged that it worked. Mona and Donna went to the first aid station—we'd seen earlier that it was staffed by a couple of young student nurses—and they told one of the girls there that their little brother had fallen in the park and maybe sprained his ankle. Because they were girls and such good actors, the nurse didn't think twice about it. They led her to a wooded spot, away from all of the park visitors, and we all jumped her—everyone except Peter.

It was supposed to be easy. After all, she was only one girl against us boys, and even though she was older than we were—nineteen, we found out later—she fought like a tiger. I got my forearm into her mouth the first thing, so that she couldn't scream, and there are scars from her teeth there to this day; she bit all the way through the towel I had wrapped around it. For a while, I thought that she was going to get away, but we couldn't just let her go then, could we?

Finally, Derek really got mad and started using his fists. It almost made me sick to see what he was doing to her, but I didn't do anything to stop it. Peter was so scared and upset that he was crying, and later we all called him a fag for the way he acted.

Anyway, while she was out, we carried her through the woods and to the RV, which was parked at one end of the lot all by itself. Inside, Derek had two sets of handcuffs and a leather mask, a hood really, with zippers over the eyes and mouth so that she could be rendered blind and gagged by closing them. Now I understand Derek better, and I know why he would have those things, but then I just thought that it was cool.

We cuffed her ankles together and her wrists behind her back and put that Godawful mask on her. Then we left.

Even then, that far into it, I think that we all looked at it as more a joke than anything, Derek and Mona included. Even me, with my bleeding arm. Derek started driving north, and before we realized it, we were back at the lake, and it was late.

What's the matter with you, man, are you crazy? We can't let her go here!

It's late; we'll take her somewhere tomorrow.

What about tonight?

We've got the cabin, stupid, and nobody but us ever goes there.

That's where we put her, still cuffed and masked, crying inside the leather. Suddenly it wasn't fun anymore.

I didn't sleep at all, because every time I closed my eyes, I saw prison bars before them. I was so scared that I vomited. I could only pray that the sun would hurry and rise so that we could carry her away into Pennsylvania or maybe Virginia, and let her go and be done. I kept hearing those terrible sounds that she made and the way she trembled all of the time.

We didn't let her go the next day. I think it was because Derek was mad at the way the girl had scratched him during the capture that made him want to punish her a little more. And Mona—who knew what she was thinking? She was wild, really.

We didn't touch the girl. We went about our usual routines the next day, or tried to, but just knowing that she was in the cabin was like a powerful scrambling signal that interrupted our thoughts every few seconds. I couldn't concentrate on anything. I kept creeping into the cabin to look at her, sometimes struggling, sometimes just lying still and defeated. I wouldn't say anything, in case she could identify me by my voice later, after we turned her loose. We all had the same idea, and at one point late in the day, all seven of us crouched around her and watched like silent statues for a solid hour. She knew that we were there somehow, and that only made it worse.

We've got to do something with her, Michele said the second day. She's going to die in that mask, and she's messed and wet herself. We have to let her go.

No, not yet, answered Mona, and because Derek backed her up, we all agreed.

We opened the flap over her mouth and gave her some water. She was pathetically grateful. When she asked what we were going to do with her, Derek told her that she was a political captive of The People's Revolutionary Campaign, or some garbage like that, and she wouldn't be harmed if she cooperated. I could tell she didn't believe any of it. After all, who was *she* to be captured by a political party? But she promised not to resist if we took the cuffs off her wrists and ankles. We didn't, and that night she escaped.

Somehow she managed to get the cabin door open—we were so cocky that we didn't leave anybody on guard—and she hopped into the woods, though because of the mask she couldn't call out to anyone or see where she was going. It must have been a night of hell for her, but, if anything, it was worse for us when we found her gone the next morning. Peter actually said that he was going to kill himself, but Derek slapped him around and knocked the idea out of him. We hunted her all the next day, but we didn't find her until dusk, half-dead from fear, hunger, thirst, and the injuries that she had inflicted on herself while trying to escape blindly that way.

It sounds crazy now, but we felt betrayed by the girl, and we all went a little . . . insane. The seven of us stayed at the cabin for the rest of the night. We tore off her clothes and . . . we did everything that had been in the novels and more, everything short of killing her.

The next two or three weeks we really . . . they were enjoyable for us. We became worse savages than Golding had ever imagined in *Flies*. We acted as if she deserved it for trying to escape. I can't . . . no, don't interrupt . . . I won't tell you that now, damn you!

Yes, I remember every second of it, and it cuts into my heart like a razor when I think that even Peter, even Michele . . .

Well . . . give me a minute . . .

Okay . . . a really strange thing happened then, in July. We had looked at her as a thing rather than a person, a thing that we were doing; even the girls felt that way. But in July, it all became kind of boring, and we were practically able to ignore her. Sometimes no one would go to the cabin to feed her or clean her for two or three days at a time, but finally we began listening to her when she was ungagged to eat.

Her name was Angie, Angela Broughton; she was nineteen, a student nurse who was engaged to be married . . . and she was a person, not some kind of masturbation tool. There's a psychological phenomenon—I think it's called the Stockholm Syndrome—and it develops between captor and captive. I began to like her. Throughout the month, we left her ungagged much of the time while there was someone there to talk to her, though we kept her hands chained almost all of the time. After a while, even that seemed to stop hurting. She was afraid that she would go blind in the mask, but even though we liked her, we couldn't chance letting her see our faces.

She was actually a sweet girl, intelligent and thoughtful . . . oh my God, Angie! I could have let her go a hundred times, a thousand! But I didn't.

There were times when it was almost like she was in charge of us, and only those small links of steel chain kept her from reversing the roles entirely. But Derek and Mona kept . . . using her . . . and some of the rest of us did, too.

We told her that we would let her go at the end of vacation, when we would be going back to Canada, which is where we said we lived. She seemed to be able to accept that. It wasn't easy, but she stopped crying and screaming. Then came August, and it was the worst.

We were all really done with it now. Angie now was a burden rather than an amusement. We wished we were rid of her, but we could never sit down and decide where and when we would let her go. We remembered what had happened in the novels, of course, and we knew that somehow we would get away with it, but we didn't really want to kill her. I swear to God, we never degenerated into that. In *The Collector*, the guy had wanted to keep her forever, but she had died accidentally from disease; in the other novel, the kids really had wanted to kill Barbara from the first, so they did. We weren't like that, not even Mona.

That was fiction; this was for real.

But there was no way out of it. Angie swore that she wouldn't try to have us found and arrested, and maybe she meant it. I believe now that she wouldn't have. Could we take that chance, however? No. God, no.

We were trapped by a stupid, childish joke that had grown of its own volition, an idiotic thumb of the nose toward adulthood that had in turn devoured us. Now we had to live with it or Angie had to die with it. And we all had such bright futures.

We didn't tell her; even in our savagery, we had this small measure of kindness. We continued to treat her well, comparatively speaking, and she truly believed that within a few days she would be back home again. She talked of the things she would do, the children she hoped to have. She actually said that she had learned from the experience, and then, on one of the last nights, she told us that she thought that she would be having the baby of one of us, all of us. She promised to keep it and love it.

The final night we did it together, as we had started it together. Peter was a real case by then, but even he came. We said good-bye in the cabin and then put her in the RV. As we drove, Wesley, the sickest one of us all, began to wrap her in

heavy duct tape that he had bought weeks before
on a trip to Akron. She panicked, of course,
because she realized that we'd never do that to her
if we were going to let her go, but she was so weak
by then—and we were so strong with fear—that it
was no real struggle. He started at her feet and
then removed the ankle chains. It was harder to
get her arms strapped to her body after we had
uncuffed her wrists, but we did it. Most of us
were crying as we did.

Then we had to take off the mask, which she
had worn for almost three months. It smelled
awful naturally, and some of her hair fell out with
it, but the worst part were her eyes. After all that
time, her pupils were like black marbles, but she
could still see, even in the dark inside the RV. She
stared straight at us . . . at me . . . and she said.
Don't let them do this. You can stop them. I
didn't say anything.

Christ!

Only then did she start to scream, and I can still
hear her screams and Wesley's laughter. I-I . . .
yes, all right, don't hurt her. That's why I'm
telling you this.

Finally, her face and head were covered, but we
could still hear her a little. Derek drove all the
way to just outside Columbus, Ohio. We got out
on a deserted road, surrounded by nothing but
the night and emptiness, and we carried her deep
into the forest. Then Derek tried to strangle her.

It only looks easy on television and in the
movies. She shouldn't have been able to fight
him, wrapped the way she was, but, by God, she
did. After a while, he had to give up.

Now I tell myself that I was being merciful. I

could see how much this was torturing her, and I couldn't stand it, so I picked up a large stone and struck her in the head. She stopped moving.

Derek said, All right, now we all do it.

Each of them took the stone and hit her once, though we had to force Peter and Michele to do it. Then we left her there and drove back to the lake. She wasn't found until October or identified until a month after that.

We're all responsible, Derek said, back at the lake. We all hit her, so we don't know whose blow killed her. That means no one ever tells about this, or we'll all fry for it.

But that's not true. *I* know who killed her. It was me, that first time. I destroyed an innocent young woman and my own child with one swing of that Goddamned rock.

The room was quiet, yet filled with tension. Kevin was crying, but silently.

Carl spoke first. "Wow," he said, in admiration. "That's terrific, the best we've had since that woman who poisoned her family!"

"What in the name of God are you people?" Kevin screamed hysterically.

"Was he telling the truth?" Carl asked of Jeroboam.

The big man seemed practically awe-struck. "Ever' word."

"No, it was a lie!" Pamela cried. The physical pain wasn't as bad as hearing those words. "He was lying. He couldn't do that!"

Jeroboam grinned crookedly.

"What are you worried about, lady?" Carl asked. "They got away with it, didn't they? Just like in the books.''

"Got away with it?" Kevin repeated in whistling disbelief. "I didn't 'get away' with anything, you incredible idiot! We weren't caught by the police, but we didn't get away with anything. It's not like in the books. I haven't had one complete night's sleep in fifteen years without resorting to drugs or booze. She haunts me all of the time, and I don't even believe in the afterlife! Jesus, before I met Pamela my greatest wish in life was that I could be dead instead of Angie!''

"Hell, just because you're some weak-kneed pansy—''

"Not me alone, buddy! That murderer I defended even though I knew he was guilty? That was Wesley, crazy Wesley, and I didn't do it for the money, but because he threatened to reveal me otherwise. I almost let him do it. And do you know where Wesley is now? Dead! He migrated west and began picking up hitchhikers of both sexes and any age and doing what he did to Angie all over again. He must have killed a dozen people before a motorcycle club caught him with a victim and did it to him!''

Kevin didn't notice, but both Carl and Jeroboam were grinning ever more broadly.

"In fact, almost half of us are dead already. Peter, poor, weak Peter, who never wanted to get involved in any of it but couldn't stand up to the rest of us . . . Peter shot himself when he was twenty. The note said, 'You know why, Kevin,' and I did. And Michele, who was probably the least interested member of our group, who did practically nothing to Angie, while never trying to stop us, Michele was found cut open like a fish being prepared for dinner two years ago. She was a writer, did you know that? And a number of her most recent stories were remarkably factual, even though they were published as fiction, something that was well-known to both Derek and Mona. We're falling apart, man! It's not like the books. You don't just go on living after doing something like that to another human being!''

Carl's reply was like shattering glass in the still air. "I can."

Kevin's eyes rolled back, and he stared at the ceiling. "Is this enough, Angie?" He jerked fiercely at his strapped arms and legs. "Do you see what you've done to me after what I did first?"

"Leave him alone!" Pamela cried. "Oh God, go away and leave us alone!"

"Gas," Neil Frazier croaked hungrily. "That was a good one, a real one, so we all get some gas!"

"Later, old man," Carl told him. "You'll get all you can handle tonight." He looked to Kevin again. "You definitely are excellent. Unstrap him, Jeroboam."

An eager pleading came to Kevin's expression as Jeroboam began to worry over the leather straps which held him. "You're letting us go?" he asked.

"Just you, hotshot, and you're coming with us," Carl answered.

"But you can't leave Pam. I only told you because of her. You have to let us go!"

Carl drew a pistol from his pocket. "We'll see what I have to do, won't we?"

When they forced him from the bed, Kevin very

gingerly eased his feet to the floor and tried a little weight on legs that had been smashed almost to powder only hours before. Pain shot through his face, but it was nothing near the intensity that he had expected; he could even walk haltingly, as he proved by limping across the narrow space that separated him from Pamela.

"Let's go, Main Attraction," Carl ordered. "We're going to make you a star tonight."

"Just give me five seconds, will you?" Kevin snapped. He leaned over to kiss Pamela, who could do nothing other than stare up at him as if viewing a stranger. "I promise I won't leave you here, baby. I'll get you out of this."

She said nothing, almost as if she had been paralyzed by what she had just heard.

"Let's go, Kev."

"Okay," he sighed, touching her face lightly. He turned to follow the pair.

She spoke then, if only faintly. "Kevin."

He quickly turned back. "Yes? What is it, honey?"

"It was a lie, wasn't it? I mean . . . you won't even watch those horrible maniac movies because they make women victims. You couldn't really have done that to some poor girl, could you?"

There was a very long pause. Then he smiled warmly at her. "Of course it was a lie, babe. I wouldn't hurt anyone."

Pamela couldn't breathe again until the three had left the room and locked the door behind them.

Chapter Seven

After promising to contact Louise Simpson the next morning, Cathy and Greg left the library a few minutes following their conversation with the woman.

They drove away, still stunned by what they had learned from Louise, but the physical realities of life slowly began to reassert themselves. Emotion had carried them for a number of hours, but Greg suddenly remembered that he hadn't eaten since lunch and was ravenous. Cathy, on the other hand, had had nothing to eat since breakfast in McKeesport, and she was past ravenous and almost weak from hunger. It took very little convincing from Greg for her to agree to have dinner with him.

Though he didn't say it, he felt that it was much safer for her to have her meals outside of the York mansion.

Throughout the dinner, he tried to sway her in a subtle manner. God, what if Earl really *was* Mikey? Did he have any right to keep her away from her brother when he needed her the most? From the conversation they had had with Dr. Welsh, it was easy to see that the brain specialist viewed people only as marginally intelligent subjects for his work and wouldn't hesitate to destroy a subject whose existence threatened his own freedom.

But how could he and Cathy get a 170 pound man with the mentality of an infant out of the mansion without creating a major disturbance? And that was exactly what Cathy had committed herself to accomplishing.

Greg had no doubt whatsoever that Welsh was responsible for the impaired minds of Gretchen, Noleta, Joseph and many others and would eagerly welcome two more experimental guinea pigs. With a touch of embarrassment, Greg abruptly realized that he was more afraid for Cathy's safety than his own.

She resisted all of his attempts to persuade her not to return to the mansion anyway. They ate slowly and mostly silently in Euphrata's finest restaurant, but when the meal finally ended, her resolve was as strong as ever.

So he drove around some more, killing the rest of the daylight hours. It was 9:00 o'clock and dark before he pulled up to the front door of the huge mansion. It looked even more nightmarish silhouetted against the deep purple sky where clouds were gathering.

"How's this for an idea?" he asked before she could open the car door. "I'll check in here, too.

That way, if anything happens, there will be two of us to face it.''

"That's not so good, Greg," she replied. "The Yorks know that you're staying at your uncle's home, so if you suddenly take a room up here, that will cast suspicion on both of us. Thanks, anyway." She opened the door.

He touched her hand. "One more thing. I'll be over in the morning, so you take damned good care of yourself tonight, Kitty Cat."

Her voice remained soft and her face relaxed, but there was no mistaking her feelings when she said, "Please, Greg, don't ever call me that again." Without awaiting a reply, she walked to the door, rang the bell and entered the house.

Greg sat in his idling car and stared at the vanishing stars. It was going to rain tonight. This was the first time in eight hours that he and Cathy had been separated, and it all seemed like an elaborate dream, maybe a dream that Edgar Allan Poe once had.

He drove off slowly, listening to Peter, Paul and Mary singing "In the Early Morning Rain."

"My, out late tonight, aren't we?" Hermie asked brightly as Cathy crossed the lobby.

Cathy smiled. "Greg Hoode seemed dedicated to showing me every corner of Euphrata today."

"Ah, a trip that would take a good ten minutes, at least. If you haven't had dinner . . ."

"No, don't bother, please. Greg included the charms of The Lamplighter Restaurant in his tour. It was a delicious meal."

"It's a fine place," Hermie agreed. "Well, I suppose you're tired from your long day, so I'll make sure that your room is ready." She used the call button again. "Gretchen, come to the lobby, please." To Cathy, she added, "If you should like to watch television, I'm afraid that your room doesn't have one, but the third floor recreation hall is only five doors down to your right, and it has a nice, big, color model."

"I'm not going to be watching television tonight," Cathy assured her. "Maybe a little reading, but I'm really very tired."

"Good. You probably need a night's rest after all of the riding you've done." She heard someone swiftly descending the stairs behind her and turned to see the little barefoot maid. "Gretchen, dear, show Miss Pettis to her room and make sure that everything's ready for her retirement. The McKinley Room."

"Yes, ma'am," the girl said.

Gretchen took Cathy's hand to lead her toward the staircase, but Cathy resisted for an instant. "Hermie, is Dr. Welsh in tonight? He promised to continue our conversation this evening."

"Heavens, no. You can't keep that man around here for two days in a row," she declared. "Right now, he's in Milwaukee or Oshkosh or someplace like that."

"And Mrs. Welsh? Did she go with him?"

"Of course. That's one thing about Alfie. She loves to travel."

Cathy's spirits sank.

"Left us with that pants-dirtying ward of theirs to look after," Hermie went on. "If it's not one thing it's another with that man. But he's a genius, and they're not the same as you and I."

Hope brimmed within Cathy's chest again. Her

plans were still intact. "Good night, Hermie," she said, almost flying up the stairs ahead of Gretchen.

"Sweet dreams," the older woman called back.

Following the long walk to the McKinley Room, Cathy found the key in her purse and unlocked the door. The single window was still up, as she had left it that afternoon, and the fresh linen on the bed was turned down, awaiting her. Any mustiness that might have resulted from long disuse was masked by the pervasive honey scent.

"Window?" Gretchen asked cryptically.

"Pardon?" Cathy responded.

Gretchen's lips began to tremble as she struggled to make herself understood. Cathy's memory replayed the scene that afternoon of the girl cowering in terror in the room's corner. How many awful beatings had taken place to result in her present condition?

Gretchen darted to the open window. "Window up tonight . . . for air, or . . ." She pointed to an air-conditioning vent high on the wall. "This-this fan . . . air condition for tonight?"

"Oh, the air-conditioning, I think. It might rain," Cathy told her. "And I don't really trust night breezes that much." She slipped a dollar bill out of her purse. It was all that she could spare under the circumstances. "Gretchen, honey, look at me." She was very careful not to alarm the girl a second time.

Gretchen turned from the window she had just closed with no small amount of effort. "Yes, um, yes, ma'am?" she asked.

Cathy pressed the bill into her hands. "I want

you to have this for being so helpful. I'm sorry it can't be more, but I'm on a strict budget." If all went well, she would be gone from this place before sunrise and would never see the girl again.

Gretchen's hands failed to close about the dollar, and it fluttered to the carpet. She quickly stooped and picked it up. "Money," she said wonderingly. "Not my money. Yours." She tried to hand it back to Cathy.

"No, no, take it, please," Cathy said. "I want you to have it."

Gretchen smiled wanly, one of the few times that Cathy had seen that expression from her. "Don't need money," she said. "Don't buy anything, don't go anywhere. Townpeople laugh at me, call me 'Retard' and 'Dodo,' 'cause I'm stupid. Ahhh, nowhere to go." She handed the dollar back.

"Well, if you're sure you can't use it," Cathy said uncertainly. Her throat was tight. "Good night then, Gretchen."

The girl walked to the door and patted its heavy solidness. "Lock it, please. Take good care . . ." She broke off abruptly when she realized that she was singing rather than speaking. Speech was such a treacherous tool. "Uh . . . good night, pretty girl, and, um . . . g-good night and sleep tight." She closed the door behind her.

"You, too, you poor thing," Cathy whispered.

She did lock the door, but she didn't do anything else to prepare for bed. Instead, she opened the suitcase she had brought along, looked lovingly at the picture of Mikey and Nona for over a minute, and then drew another object from beneath her clothing. It was a small, but deadly handgun.

Cathy had never fired a gun in her life, but she had studied a library manual on how to do so before secretly taking this one from Mrs. Pettis' closet. She loaded the weapon easily enough and then took a chair before the door.

Midnight should be late enough for the rest of the household to be soundly asleep, she decided, and midnight would be when she would attempt to save her brother's life.

Greg felt like so much dog excrement as he drove back to Uncle Dan's.

It wasn't often that a guy got involved in something as wild and woolly as this deal, and how had he reacted? Heroically?

He had left Cathy back there in that place, where you didn't fit in unless you were as loony as a fly trapped inside a bass drum. So what if she had insisted? He should have insisted right back, picked her up and carried her away from that place if it came to it. And now, when it might already be too late, he couldn't even tell Uncle Dan what was going on because of some stupid promise he'd made to her over dinner.

"Damn!" he spat.

He pulled up to a spotlight. The streets were pretty much deserted, but there was one figure walking slowly before the darkened storefronts across the street. He recognized this figure as Paul Lattwig only when Paul called out, "How's it feel to be a mobile billboard, Hillbilly?"

"How's it feel to be a jerk, Lattwig?" he shouted back, too preoccupied to even work up much anger at the other boy. When the light changed, he laid down a little rubber.

When he reached the house, Diana Meredith was just getting ready to leave for her home, and it was clear the moment that he greeted her that there was something wrong. The normally cheerful and easygoing woman froze him with a look as she marched past him and through the door.

"If I ever find out what I've done, I'm sure I'll be properly chagrined," he said wearily as he entered the den.

Uncle Daniel was there, standing before a small wall mirror and enthusiastically combing his dark hair that had once seemed to be thinning but now appeared to be making a triumphant comeback. "Think about it, Greg. Diana puts a lot of effort int her meals and takes a lot of pride in the results, so how do you think it makes her feel when one-half of her audience fails to show for the presentation and doesn't even bother to phone?"

Greg slapped his forehead with the heel of his hand. "I'll be . . . I forgot completely, Uncle Dan! Jeez, I'm sorry, but Cathy and I were at The Lamplighter—"

"A new girl, eh?"

"Just met her this afternoon."

"So you'll apologize to Diana in the morning and explain about Cathy, and I'm sure she'll forgive you in time for breakfast. Now, tell me how great I look."

Greg dropped into an armchair. "You look great," he said, realizing that Daniel did look more excited than he had seen him all summer. These once-a-month lodge meetings really did a lot for Daniel Hoode, former playboy and current small-town squire. "It'll be ten soon. Isn't your lodge meeting getting a late start?"

"Well, these fellows run the old sunup to sundown routine just about every day of their lives, so they deserve an occasional all night howl. Which reminds me, you needn't wait up."

"Now, now, Daniel, is that the way I've raised you to behave?" Greg asked with a laugh.

"Just be sure that you get enough rest for tomorrow night," Daniel ordered. "That's your turn, a once in a year opportunity."

"I don't know, Uncle Dan. Since I'm only going to be here through August, I don't know if it would be fair for me to take a place away from a local in the lodge."

"Enough of that, my friend. You're in." He checked his pockets to make certain that he had his keys. "I suppose I'm as presentable as I'll ever be, so see you later."

"Have fun," Greg muttered.

He couldn't think of anything to do with himself for the rest of the evening. He could have gone driving and maybe come up with a way to kill time, but he had spent most of the day behind the wheel and doubted that he could endure five more minutes of it. There was the rec room downstairs where he could shoot pool, kill a few million cartoon aliens, or pit his chess skills against a simulated grand master, but there are few things more depressing than trying to have that kind of fun by yourself. Of course, Uncle Dan had a high resolution, big screen TV and VCR combination, but his tastes in films had never exactly paralleled Greg's, and his library had remained pretty skimpy since he moved to Euphrata.

Almost before he realized what he was doing, he had flipped open the phone book and punched in most of the number needed to reach the York house. Then his stubbornness reasserted itself. If she wanted to handle all of this by herself, why should he try to stop her? Who was she, anyway? Just a girl with a wild tale who he'd met less than ten hours ago.

He punched in Frankie Holloway's number instead.

"How's it going, Franklin?" he asked after Frankie's aunt had put him on the line. Frankie's parents worked out of town during the summer months.

"Who is this? This couldn't be the Great White Hope wasting his time on the telephone while there are girls to be dated, could it?" Frankie replied. He couldn't understand how anyone with Greg's advantages—primarily his ability to walk and his money, in that order—could ever be bored or at loose ends.

"That's me, Mr. High Life. You busy tonight?"

"Not much. Just watching the second half of a John Belushi film festival on the tube."

That was a possibility worth considering. He could always do with another viewing of *Animal House*. "Which films?"

"*Neighbors* and *Continental Divide*."

Greg whistled in disappointment. "Major league offal."

"Tell me about it, man; I've been watching the stuff. Strange how a man so talented could have appeared in dogs like these.''

"Life's weird. Well, I know that you've got to get up and go to work in the morning, so I won't keep you any longer."

"Hey, just a minute, Gregorio," Frankie interrupted. "You're not getting off that easy. How did she work out?"

Greg grinned. "Who?"

"Who?" Frankie repeated tauntingly. "You know who. Miss Vision in Blue from Kalamazoo, the incoming siren who vanished with you early this afternoon."

"Oh, her. She found me irresistable, naturally." For a moment Greg considered telling Frankie the whole story—he felt like he had to tell *somebody*—but his sense of honor managed to win out. "We made a day of it. She even introduced me to an alcoholic dwarf and a giant with the soul of a poet."

"You must have checked her into the York house," Frankie stated casually.

"That's right."

"Man, that is one weird place."

Greg silently agreed.

Frankie went on. "You know, I get to feeling pretty sorry for myself because my legs are dead and all, but when that pathetic guy hit town last summer, asking to be directed to the Yorks', I counted my blessings."

"The midget?" Greg asked in confusion.

"No, he's a wild little dude. The eight-footer is the one who can't stand up on those long, skinny legs. I'll bet he doesn't weigh two hundred pounds. And those other problems he's got— diabetes, bad feet, no teeth . . .''

Shit, Greg thought, these people can even cause
teeth to grow back. "He looked pretty healthy
this afternoon. In fact, he was even running."

"No kidding? People have a way of getting
better around Euphrata—some people, anyway."

"I guess I'll let you go, Francis Albert. I'll
probably hit the sack myself."

"I'm sure. You're probably just catching your
second wind. See you, Dempsey."

"Adios."

He stuck it out for half an hour longer by
wondering just how much of the big picture
Frankie had sniffed out. But at half past ten, he
couldn't resist any longer. He had to call Cathy
and let her know that he was still with her, that
he'd park outside the mansion in case of trouble if
she wanted him to.

He had to call her, but he couldn't. The
operator connected him with the mansion, but
whoever answered there informed him that guests
were not disturbed by telephone messages after
9:00 p.m. except in case of emergency. He was
tempted to tell the woman just what sort of
emergency *she* was sitting on, if she knew it or
not, but instead he thanked her and hung up.

At 11:00, he located a satellite station that was
broadcasting one of the top ten best adventure
films of all time, and so he spent the next two and
three-quarter hours immersed in *The Towering
Inferno*.

When Madame Hermie called Gretchen over
the intercom to come down and take Miss Cathy
to her room, the girl was curled up in an open
closet on the third floor watching the television in

her mind, the pictures that usually came to her from her pillow.

Gretchen didn't normally sleep in a closet. She had a nice, cozy room of her own on the second floor curtained off from the library, and she didn't usually go to sleep so early.

But she had kind of tricked herself tonight. Most of the house had soft and pretty carpeting on the floors, but there was one hall on the third floor that only had smooth, shiny wood without any carpet on the floor. And it was Gretchen's job to wax this hall every day after Sunday to keep it smooth and shiny, even though nobody ever came up there. That's what she was doing on the third floor when she got so tired that she crawled into the closet and fell asleep.

Though she got tired from waxing the floor, what really made her sleepy was what she did after that. The floor was so smooth and slippery when she was using the big fuzzy towel on it that she got the idea.

If she ran real fast into the hall and jumped on her knees on top of the fuzzy towel, she could slide—wow, all the way down to the other end—like she was riding fast in a car or maybe the way she saw the other people do it on the pond in town in the cold time when the water became ice. Boy, it was fun, and she had slid and slid a hundred times until she got so sleepy that she was dizzy. So when she put away her waxing stuff in the hall closet she sat down to rest for just a minute with her head against the big pipe that brought hot air from down there, and somebody made her go to sleep.

In her dreams Gretchen was smart again, not so

smart as Hermie or Dr. Welsh but smart so that
writing talked to her instead of looking like little
worms that crawled. She used to be smart like
that, and sometimes she was again. But then she
always got stupid again. She cried a little bit in the
dream, because she remembered that she would
get stupid soon.

When Hermie called her, she woke up, most of
the way. But she could still hear voices, like
dream voices, from one side of her ears, from
inside the big hot air pipe that stood against the
wall inside the closet and came up from down
there, where Hermie said "Don't go down
there!", except sometimes once in a while to clean
while somebody watched.

"Help me, please!" a girl's voice whispered
inside the pipe. "For the love of God, won't
somebody help me?"

Gretchen sat up fast and breathed in hard. That
scared her.

"Oh, please God, please let someone come!"
the girl's voice said again.

And Gretchen knew why she was never
supposed to go down there, under the bottom
floor, alone. There were ghosties down there.

Real scared now, Gretchen ran to the lobby
where Hermie was calling and took Miss Cathy to
her room.

Miss Cathy was nice and pretty and she never
tried to hurt you. Gretchen liked her a lot and
wished that she would stay in the 'Kinley Room
for a long, long time . . . but not really. If she
stayed here, she might get stupid, too, and have to
work . . . or the ghosties might come up at night
and get her. In her room, Miss Cathy even tried to

give Gretchen some money. Nobody ever did that before.

But she forgot a lot of these things when her tummy started hurting, and she ran to the kitchen to see if she could have some sandwich before she went to sleep in the right place. Cook was still there too late, and Gretchen was glad. She liked Cook almost as much as Miss Cathy.

"Well, hello there, Pretty Little Green Eyes," Cook said, and he was talking to Gretchen because nobody else was in the kitchen. "What are you doing here at this time of the evening?"

Cook was nice, because he was big and fat and laughed a lot, but not to make fun of her, and he never ever hurt her. Gretchen stayed away from most people, who probably wanted to hit her for being stupid and ugly, and she always stayed away from most men, who usually would hit even harder and try to touch her all over, in places like Miss Janie touched her in the special baths. But Cook would never do this.

"Hungry," Gretchen answered shyly.

Cook laughed. "Now, I wonder what we could do about that?" He had little bits of black hair under his nose and on his chin, like some men did.

"Ummm," Gretchen pretended to be thinking. Then she smiled. "Cookie?"

"Cookie?" he asked. "Is that what you want to eat this late at night?"

Gretchen nodded hopefully.

"Do you know what will happen if you eat cookies all the time? That little tummy will swell up as big as mine." He poked Gretchen's stomach lightly, making her giggle and then slapped his own. It shook and wobbled like Santa's on the television show last . . . whenever it was on. Sometimes, Gretchen thought Cook *was* Santa. "Still, I guess we can spare you one or two cookies if you'll promise not to get too big and fat so that we'll have to roll you around the house in a wheelbarrow to do your cleaning."

"Jeroboam," Gretchen whispered while her hands hid an evil little grin.

"Okay, you know where the cookie jar is. Go to it."

Sometimes, Gretchen forgot to look all around her when she came into a room and she could be surprised by what—and who—was in there with her. This time was like that. She turned to run to the counter where the big glass cookie jar full of pecan and lemon sandies waited for her, and her eyes were suddenly filled with the sight of food all over the big long table that was there. She saw hams and roasts and turkeys and potatoes and pots of beans and fresh bread with butter running over it like yellow rain and cakes and pies and puddings and soups and gravy and all of it was steaming hot like the Sunday meal that she carried into the dining room every time. For a moment, her mind was confused—was this Sunday?

"Oh boy," she said, low and happy. "That smells good!" Her eyes woke up her nose, and her tummy jumped inside her.

"Don't tell me you intend to eat all of that, little one," Cook said. "Then you *would* pop like a balloon."

"Can I have just some?"

Cook tried to scowl, but she could tell that he was only playing. "Oh, I guess so. What do you want?"

She had a turkey sandwich on some of that hot bread, some creamed corn, and a tall glass of cold milk. Then, with a little bit more asking, she got some chocolate pudding, too. She was eating this when *they* came in—four boys from town.

"Howdy, Mr. Davis. You ready for us?" one of the boys asked.

Cook was wiping his hands on a dishrag. "Good evening, gentlemen. Actually, you're a bit late."

"We're here, aren't we? Don't bitch about it," said another one of the boys whose name Gretchen knew was Paul. He was really a man. He was like strong and mean; he liked to pretend like he was going to kick her, and that made her scared. Sometimes he would miss.

"Never mind that now. Jerry, you and Lester go downstairs and begin setting up the folding chairs. Paul, why don't you and Marco start carrying down the food? The bread and soups first." Three of the boys said, "Yes, sir," because they didn't want to get in trouble for being lazy, but Paul just stood and looked at Gretchen. She turned to look at her pudding.

"Well, if it isn't the little retard," Paul said. "So how are you tonight, Cheesebrain?"

"Paul," Cook started to say, "if you don't mind—"

"In a minute, Borden," Paul said fast. "The big shots haven't even started assembling yet. I want to say hello to my girlfriend. I said, how are you tonight, Gretchen?"

"Hello, Mr. Paul," she answered, like in a whisper. The pudding in her bowl started to shake a little bit. "I'm f-fine."

"Glad to hear it." He walked to beside where she was sitting and put his finger into the chocolate pudding. "Don't you know that stuff's bad for your complexion? Jeeze, what a messy eater. You got it all over your mouth and chin."

"S-sorry . . ."

"Leave the child alone, Paul," Cook said like he was getting mad, too.

"You watch yourself, Borden," Paul told him. Then he flipped the pudding off of his finger into Gretchen's eyes. She tried not to cry, but it burned so much.

"That's enough!" Cook yelled real loud. "You four have been recruited tonight to serve not to cause trouble, so get about your business before I report you to the old man!"

Paul talked low and whispery, like maybe a snake or something. "Don't ever threaten me, man. I'll trash you so bad that it'll take a damned month in the clinic to get you back on your feet."

But Cook didn't back down. "Get out of my kitchen! Get to work, right now!"

The other three boys ran downstairs, but Paul walked kind of slow and picked up a big platter of bread that Gretchen couldn't even have lifted. "I'll be seeing you later, Retard."

Cook wiped Gretchen's face and eyes with the rag while he said mad things quietly to himself. Gretchen thought he was mad at her.

"S-sorry," she whispered. "I . . . no trouble, sorry."

"Shhh, you just relax now, baby. I won't let them hurt you," he said. Just then, Gretchen was sure she loved Cook. "Those young animals . . . no respect for women or their elders or anything any more. Sometimes I think that we should put them down there, instead of . . . stop crying now and eat your pudding.''

Gretchen thought of Paul's finger in the chocolate and knew that the rest of it would taste like dirt. She sat the bowl on the counter. ''Too fat,'' she said. ''Pop like a balloon.''

''Not the way you have to work,'' Cook said. ''Well, you should run along, I suppose. I have to go down to supervise—''

Gretchen got real scared and grabbed his arm. ''P-please, don't go . . . down there! Nobody go down there tonight! Please!''

Cook looked real surprised. ''Gretchen, child, what's wrong? Those profane brats don't frighten me. I could handle a dozen Paul Lattwigs.''

It was all racing around inside her head and she had to grab it to find the words. ''No, no, not the boys! Don't go down there because . . . because . . .'' Her eyes grew very big and her voice fell low, almost too low. ''There's ghosties down there!''

Cook looked at her like confused, and then he laughed. ''Oh, my dear, there are no ghosts in the cellar. Ghosts don't even exist.''

''Yes. I heard them. On my pillow.''

''On your—you mean dreaming? Did you hear them while you were sleeping, Gretchen?''

She nodded. ''Not in bed, but I was in the . . . I heard them.'' She took a deep breath. ''And they will eat you.''

He patted her shoulder, and it was a soft and nice pat, not the other kind. ''Don't worry, little one, there are no ghosts, not down there or anywhere else. Do you understand me?''

"But I heard them . . . 'Help me! Please, somebody! And when you go down to help, *chomp!* They eat you."

Cook's eyes went kind of hard, maybe a little scary. "You heard these voices?"

Gretchen nodded. "And Hermie says, 'Silly Gretchen, don't go down there ever, 'cept I go with you.' So it must be—"

"Did Hermie tell you they were ghosts?"

"No." She smiled a little bit. "I did. I thought it."

He smiled again. "Then it must be true, because you are about the wisest little girl I have ever met. I promise I won't go looking for ghosts."

She thought some more. "And Paul and Jerry and Marco and Lester?"

"Let them get eaten."

"Noooo! Nobody, please!"

It was real funny to him. "All right, I'll warn them to watch for ghosties." He wiped a little bit more chocolate pudding from her chin and kissed the top of her head real fast. "Run along. I'll see you at breakfast tomorrow morning, and we'll have hotcakes!"

"Oh boy!" Gretchen stood up and clapped her hands. "Good night, Cook, and sweet dreams don't bite."

"You, too, Little Green Eyes."

Thinking about the hotcakes made Gretchen happy for some minutes while she went to her room, but then, in the big, quiet library with all of the books that nobody ever came to read, she started to hear the voices again, like remembering though. She tried looking at a big book full of colored pictures that was maybe the best pictures she had ever seen, but they still talked in her head. She didn't want the ghosties to get anybody, but 'specially not Cook or Hermie or . . . Miss Cathy. Cook and Hermie were big grownups, but Miss Cathy was almost like her—but smarter.

Putting the book in its place, Gretchen turned out the light in her little room and left the library. She didn't like the servants' passageways that were kind of cold and maybe dark a little and scary.

But she couldn't let the ghosties come without trying to stop them.

Louise wasn't asleep at 11:00 o'clock that evening, and she wasn't watching television, either. She was too nervous to concentrate on anything other than the problem that was threatening to consume her.

What on earth had possessed her to open up that way to two complete strangers? All right, they were exactly that—strangers—and most probably not at all connected with the secret activities of this town, but the Hoode boy had been around for over a month and had an uncle living here. He could have been introduced to the seductive mystery controlling Euphrata by this time.

And what was the girl's name? Cathy? Cathy Lockwood?

Louise was alone in her house, but she still moved in a stealthy manner as she rechecked her doors and windows and took her briefcase into the kitchen. Lockwood, Lockwood. She couldn't recall the first name of the girl's brother, but

Lockwood was not all that common a name. If a Lockwood really had disappeared in the surrounding area in the past year or so, the coverage of it should be in her file of newspaper clippings.

It took only a few minutes for her to locate an article from the previous September 10th edition of the *Tiverton Tribunel* carrying the title, "PENNSYLVANIA MAN DIES IN BRIDGE ACCIDENT," and an accompanying grainy photo of a small car being winched out of the Ohio River near the city limits. The article detailed the discovery of the headless body of a Michael Nathaniel Lockwood, 26, within the car, plus the fact that Lockwood's new wife was still missing. There didn't seem to be any evidence of foul play.

Louise began to relax. This Michael Lockwood certainly was Cathy's brother, so at least she was who she claimed to be.

Actually, it had been sheer luck that she had kept the article at all. Most of the cases that interested Louise were complete vanishing acts that did not involve recovered automobiles or bodies. Only the fact that the woman, Nona Lockwood, had never been found included this incident in her sphere of concern.

Now, if only that poor girl didn't become another member of the missing before Louise herself could give the state police task force some evidence solid enough to move on . . .

Sighing, she began scooping the fading scraps of paper into the open briefcase. She should be able to sleep tonight anyway.

When the knock came at the kitchen door

behind her, Louise almost jumped out of the chair. Who could be visiting her at this time of night? And, better yet, why? The most terrifying answer also seemed to be the most likely.

"Miz Simpson?" came a deep, powerful voice from behind the door. "It's Baxter, ma'am, and I'd like to speak with you for a minute, if you don't mind."

"Oh, it . . . it's awfully late," she answered as she dumped the rest of the articles into the case, closed it, and shoved it into a chair beneath the table.

"This is real important, ma'am," Baxter said. "Open the door."

Louise got up and began walking hurriedly to the hallway. "You will just have to come back tomorrow. I'm getting ready for bed."

The preliminaries were over, it seemed, because the bolt lock exploded from the doorjamb as the door itself flew inward. A man, big and wide, stood there, and several others waited behind him.

At the sound of the breaking lock, Louise had uttered a short cry and sprinted through the dark hall toward the front door. She had known for many months that something like this could happen, but she was still unprepared for it. When she pulled open the front door, four more men stood waiting, patiently and silently. There was nowhere else to run.

Baxter ambled into the living room with the slow, muscular stride of a grizzly. He carried the brief-case in his right hand as if it were no more than a deck of cards.

"Loomis, it's mighty damned cool for a July

night," he said. "How about starting a fire in that fireplace there?" He tossed the case across the room and into the stone fireplace with a flick of his wrist.

"Yes, sir," a younger man responded, quickly rushing to follow instructions.

One of the men who had been waiting at the front door now had Louise's right arm twisted painfully behind her back, and he steered her over to where Baxter stood. She moaned slightly, both in pain and fear.

"Here you go, Bax—" the man began.

Baxter moved with the quickness of a striking snake to backhand the man in the face. "Where are your manners, Roy?" he demanded. Roy released Louise and clutched his jaw with both hands. "I know we're here to do a distasteful thing, but that don't mean we forget our respect for the lady's gender. I apologize for him, ma'am."

Louise massaged her arm carefully. She was determined not to break down in front of them. "There's no way that you'll be able to get away with this," she said. "My murder will raise an alarm with some very powerful people."

"Murder, ma'am? Why, I never killed anybody in my life, 'specially not a lady. How's that fire coming, Loomis?"

The other man had used her collection of articles to start a small blaze that was rapidly growing larger, after first having removed them from the briefcase. "It's doing just fine, Bax," he replied. "This sure is a nice case, though, real leather, and no initials or anything identifying on it. It'd be a shame to burn it, too."

Baxter chuckled deeply. "Okay, if nobody objects, you can have it."

"I object," Louise said defiantly.

"I'm sure you do, Miz Simpson, but we have more important things to talk about, me and you, like them papers burning over there and all the long distance calls you've been making for the past few months."

"It's part of my job. I have to keep in touch with the state literacy board."

"That's not who the operator says you've been phoning. We don't have the time to dance, ma'am, being that it's nearly eleven-thirty. So we're going to have to take this up in another place. Boys!" At his command, three of the men surrounded Louise, two taking her arms, while the third stood behind her. "I regret this sincerely, but we can't take the chance of you disturbing the rest of the community, you see."

Louise gasped when the gag was placed in her mouth, but she realized the futility of struggling against seven large men. She remained still even when her wrists and ankles were bound.

"Put her in my car out back," he directed. "Roy, you stay inside and prop the backdoor shut with a chair to keep the dogs and cats out. I'll have somebody over here tomorrow to fix that jamb. Be sure to lock the front door when you leave."

"Yes, sir," Roy said through his bleeding lips.

Within minutes, the house was dark, silent and empty. Only the last remaining newspaper article crackled faintly in the fireplace and then died.

Chapter Eight

Early morning, Tuesday, July 11.

Midnight came very slowly for Cathy. She sat in the chair, not sleeping, not reading, not really even thinking. She had a mission that was more important than anything she had ever known. The minutes crept by leadenly, and her resolve grew.

There was no longer any doubt that Earl was Mikey, the essential part of Mikey that is—his essence, his mind. He was her brother even though his flesh had been exchanged for that of another. He had given so much to her that she was ready now that the time to repay him had arrived. Soon she would begin her search, and when she found Mikey she would take him out of this terrible place to his real home.

If anyone tried to stop her, man or woman, she would use the gun.

She wasn't certain how she would get the large and unstable man out of the house or to the bus

stop—she might have to hire a cab for the entire
trip back to McKeesport—but there would be a
way. Once there, another long and arduous
journey awaited, of course, because she would
have to reeducate him back to being Mikey.

The tiny alarm on her wristwatch announced
that midnight had arrived at last.

Wearing soft-soled shoes and with her purse
slung over her right shoulder—the wedding
picture was in the purse, and the rest of her things
could stay behind—Cathy took the gun in one
hand and marched to the door.

The door wouldn't open.

She couldn't believe it at first. The bolt had
been pulled back, and she hadn't used the key, so
the knob should have turned freely in her hand.
But it wouldn't.

"Damn!" she whispered, opening her purse.
The room key was on top, so she quickly slipped
it into the slot and turned it. The tumblers seemed
to have frozen solid. Even though she wriggled
the key with furious energy, the lock remained
dead and the door remained closed.

"Open, damn you!" she shouted, not concerned about stealth any longer. "Don't do this to
me, not now!" She put the gun in the chair and
used both hands, but she achieved nothing. In
frustration, she kicked the thick oaken panel.

I'll shoot the lock off, she told herself.

But did you shoot the lock mechanism or the
plunger or the frame or what? And if the lock had
been turned from the outside by a member of the
York household, that meant that they were
suspicious of her. Maybe it would be better if they
didn't know that she was armed. How else could

she escape from the room?

There was the window, but one look told her that she would have to be a bird or a monkey to make it out that way without splashing all over the garage roof.

The bathroom had no windows.

And next to the closet was the featureless, narrow door that Greg earlier had identified as the opening to the servants' adjacent corridor, and he certainly should have known what it was with his background. Hope swelled within her, but lasted only until she tried to turn the miniscule knob—locked from the other side.

All right, so she was trapped in here. That had to mean that someone in the house had plans for her. Let them come, she thought.

Returning to the bed, she slipped beneath the sheets without removing her clothing and placed the gun at her right side, hidden and just an inch or so from her head. Let them come, she repeated. She would do what she had to do.

But she didn't see the faint wisp of red gas that oozed languorously out of the nostrils and mouth of the metal dragon's head above the bed, invisibly dissipating. And she didn't notice the room's normal honey smell growing even stronger than usual.

Suddenly, Mikey stood before her alive and whole.

"Hi, Kitty Cat," he said, smiling happily.

Cathy's heart stopped and then started again. Joy like a roaring fire streamed through her, and she threw off the sheets. "Oh, my God, my God, Mikey!" she shouted joyously. "I thought that you were dead!"

He caught her in strong arms as she leaped from the bed and whirled her about the little room as if she were weightless. The love that she felt for him threatened to burst her into a million glowing shards.

"Oh, Jesus, where have you been?" she cried. The joyous tears rolled down her cheeks.

"I've been looking for Nona," he answered. "I didn't mean to frighten you, but I love her, too, and I had to do everything I could to find her. But I can't find her anywhere."

"It's Dr. Welsh!" she said frantically. "He's a madman, and he uses people to experiment on in his laboratory!"

"Mad doctors!" Mikey asked . . . but he didn't sound like Mikey anymore; he sounded like Greg! "Laboratories? That's science fiction, Cathy!" It *was* Greg!

"What happened? What have you done with Mikey?" She tried to slap Greg's face, but when her hand struck, it was Mikey who winced in pain.

"Oh, wow, hon," he said, "you've really been taking your vitamins, haven't you?"

"I'm sorry! I thought—I don't know what's happening."

"It's all right now, Cathy. I swear I'll never leave you again," he said comfortingly, encircling her once more with his warm arms.

Then Cathy began to feel safe again, and just as she did, her world was torn apart once more. Welsh appeared in the room behind Mikey with a long, razor-sharp knife that actually made a high, whistling noise as it cut through the air.

Before she could react to this sudden menace, Welsh had grabbed a fistful of Mikey's hair in his left hand and had swung the long knife with the other. It sliced through Mikey's neck with one stroke.

Cathy's heart and lungs turned to stone as Mikey's body dropped from beneath his head with blood spouting in an obscene red fountain. It jerked spasmodically on the floor. The head screamed a long, thin wail that continued even as Welsh waved it about the room like a trophy. Cathy found her voice then, and her screams mixed with his in an insane chorus.

Cathy ran to the bed to find the gun, but it had vanished. She scrambled beneath the sheets, searching frantically for it, but found only that the bedclothes had taken on a life of their own and were trying to wrap themselves tightly about her in a strangling embrace like the bandages of a mummy.

It took all of her strength, but she managed to hurl herself bodily from the bed and free of the grasping sheets. Welsh was still there, towering triumphantly over Mikey's still trembling body and swinging his head like a train man with a lantern. She sprang to her feet in a catlike motion before charging at the murderer with nothing but her rage as a weapon.

Welsh remained in front of her as the embodiment of Satan until the last possible instant, when he seemed to slide to her left and swept down with that terrible knife a second time. Sheer agony erupted throughout her being. She screamed again, so loudly that she felt as if her lungs were turning inside-out. Her hands dropped off her arms onto the floor as swiftly as lead weights. Blood geysered from the stumps of her wrists.

Then she was lying on the floor between Mikey's body and her own severed hands. There were glowing streams of blood blazing through the air overhead as she hysterically flailed her arms. Welsh bent over her with the gleaming knife, his face cold and blank behind the beard. She thrust her useless stumps at him, but he dispassionately brushed them aside and drew the keen blade across her throat.

She tried to cry, "Dear God, somebody help me!" but she no longer had a voice. A cruel hand caught her hair and lifted upward, so awfully hard . . . and her head left her neck. The essence of Cathy Lockwood was concentrated in the bodiless head that hung from Welsh's left fist.

Noleta Thrush lay on the floor below Cathy, her eyes staring sightlessly and the top of her head surgically removed . . .

She was strangling!

Pain filled Cathy's mind. Water was crashing down upon her upturned face, pounding into her eyes and rushing up her nose, and someone was slapping her cheeks sharply.

"Wake up! Please wake up!" a woman or girl's voice cried.

Cathy tried to scream, but water filled her mouth and she gagged on the attempt.

Then the hands stopped hitting her and dragged her out of the torrent of water. She heard fast footsteps running away from her, even though the room was carpeted, and she was finally able to open her eyes in time to see the door to the servants' corridor slamming shut.

A wave of nausea gripped her and manifested itself as a wild coughing fit that allowed her to do nothing else for more than a minute.

"Oh God," she managed to gasp weakly. She touched her throat gingerly—her throat and her hands! It had been a dream, the absolute worst nightmare she had ever had.

She was still in the bedroom, though on the floor now. She was lying in front of the open window that came almost all the way down to meet her, and the rain was pouring outside the sill. That was the water that had almost drowned her. It had revived her instead. Someone had dragged her from the bed to the window, opened it, and thrust her face into rain to pull her from the depths of that damned, awful vision.

Mikey hadn't been here at all; he was still somewhere in this house inside the body of some other man. Cathy dropped her face into her hands as grief welled up within her.

At that instant, the thick bedroom door flew open. It slammed powerfully against the wall, creating a sound like a cannon shot, and Cathy screamed in alarm. Hermie York stood in the doorway wearing a brilliant green robe that fell all the way to the floor and hid her dark hair with a heavy cowl. The hood threw deep shadows over her face, but Cathy still was able to see blood running freely down her forehead and cheeks from fresh, deep gashes. She was grinning with a madness that rivaled anything that her relatives had ever displayed.

"Hermie!" Cathy gasped.

The insanity of Hermie's eyes changed at once

to confusion. "Miss Pettis, uh, is there something wrong? We heard . . . sounds from in here."

"What's happened to your face?" Cathy asked in a stunned voice.

Hermie's right hand fluttered up to her cheek involuntarily and came away dripping. "Nothing, dear, I'm fine. You've had a nightmare, and you're still mixed-up. You're so wet, simply drenched! Close the window and come to the bath!" She stepped into the room, and Cathy was able to see an entire hall full of eager men and women dressed in bright green robes pressing in behind her.

"No! Get out!" she screamed.

Hermie stopped, though she maintained her placid smile which looked grotesque amid her bloody features. "Why, Cathy, dear you're still dreaming. This is all an awful nightmare. Just come back to bed."

"You stay away from me!" she commanded. Her hands reached blindly for the gun, but it was still on the bed, out of reach.

"Yes, of course, dear, everything is just fine," Hermie said in a placating tone. She waved the others into the hall and slowly backed from the room herself. "You're just tired and overwrought. You need rest, that's all."

"Leave me alone," Cathy said. "Close the door."

"Good night, Cathy."

"Get out!"

The door shut firmly and left Cathy alone in the small room. She was shivering from exposure, fear, and a sense of loss at discovering that Mikey was still dead—at least in one way. The rain blew in the open window and sprayed across the back of her neck.

Scrambling to her feet, she rushed to the door and tried it. Locked, as she had known it would be. The same was true of the servants' entrance again. She was still trapped in here, unable to reach Mikey or escape. In a fury, she slammed the bolt back into place.

There, now the door would slow them down, too.

Another step that she took was to wedge the chair beneath the knob of the servant's door.

If she were to be in here until morning, then, she had to stay awake. She never wanted to undergo a dream like that again, even if it meant staying awake forever. Also, she needed the gun.

It was a terribly difficult thing to force herself to do, but she made her body climb onto the bed with those so recently monstrous sheets and retrieve the weapon. She didn't stay on the bed or return to the wedged chair. The rain—and some faceless entity—had saved her from madness and the green-robed creatures once, so she would have to rely on it now as well.

In this way, Cathy Lockwood passed the long night on the floor of the room before the open window. Each time that she felt the tentative beginnings of exhaustion or drowsiness, she used another handful of that wonderful rain to startle her spirit into life again.

Chapter Nine

Midmorning, Tuesday, July 11.

The phone rang once in Daniel Hoode's guest room, but Greg, who had occupied that room for almost a month and a half, was not shaken out of his deep sleep by the sound of it. Greg had always been the type of sleeper who could blissfully slumber through a major earthquake.

Diana Meredith lifted the receiver in the kitchen before a second ring could disturb the young guest. The call turned out to be for him anyway.

"Telephone, Gregory," the housekeeper said, knocking on his door.

Greg swam up toward consciousness through a viscous fluid that worked to drag him back toward the bottom. He heard her voice trying to convey some kind of message to him, but it had to be far too early for any type of intelligent life to exist in the world. He seemed unable to throw off a nightmare about some kind of female mummy.

"Mr. Gregory?" Diana repeated. "Did you hear me?"

With a great effort of will, he pried open one eye and tried to focus on the bedside clock which registered 7:12 a.m. Forget it!

"Should I tell the young lady to try later when you're more prepared to take her call?" Diana asked sweetly.

Greg made a distorted noise that was meant to represent the word, "Who?"

Diana correctly interpreted. "She gave her name as Cathy, I believe."

That sent a jolt through him. Cathy Lockwood and the York house all flashed into the front of his mind with the power to knock him into a sitting position.

"Gregory?"

"Right, uh, I mean I'll take it!" he shouted back. Then he began trying to work the sleep from his tongue and lips while picking up the receiver.

"Hello, Cathy?"

"Greg, I'm sorry to call so early," she responded in a calm, clear voice. "Did I wake you?"

"Well, no, not really," he answered, lying facilely. "Really, I wasn't able to get much sleep last night at all, because of . . . ah, you know, I was worried . . ."

"Let's not talk about it over the phone."

"How about over breakfast then? Have you eaten yet?"

"No, I haven't."

He swung his feet over the side of the bed.

"Great! I'll be over in ten minutes. We'll go out somewhere."

He had expected her to ask for a little more time to get ready, but she quietly said, "All right. Hurry, okay?" She didn't have to ask twice.

Greg quickly scouted out a clean pair of jeans and a red pullover and ran a brush through his hair. He had shaved yesterday, and two or three shaves a week were enough to hold him. He didn't bother with checking for stubble as he brushed his teeth.

There was no sign of Uncle Dan, which wasn't at all surprising, considering that last night had been his lodge meeting. Greg almost made it out the front door before he was trapped by the arrival of Diana.

"I was sorry to disturb you so early," she said, though her tone said that she certainly hadn't been.

"No problem," he assured her. "I was waiting for that call. And, uh, Diana, I'm really sorry about not phoning before dinner last night. I had a date, sort of, and I completely forgot."

That was all that she wanted to hear. She smiled and said, "Tell you what. I'll whip up a breakfast to set your taste buds hopping."

"Hmm, you needn't bother," he replied. "Got another date of the same sort with the same girl. I won't be back for lunch and probably not for dinner, either."

She deflated as swiftly as she had recovered. "Is there a number to which I can forward the rest of your phone calls?" she asked coolly.

"That's great," he told her while darting out the door. "Great sense of humor! I'll see you later.''

It had rained during the night, but now the bright morning sun had already burned off most of the excess dampness.

Traffic was light enough to be practically non-existent, and he parked near the front door of the York house just about five minutes later. The door opened quickly following his first ring, but instead of Gretchen, as he had expected, another young kid stood in the doorway. He wondered fleetingly if every adolescent in Euphrata took a turn as palace serf.

'' 'Morning, Miss Pettis is expecting me,'' he said too swiftly for the boy to react. Then he hustled by the startled doorkeeper and into the front room.

''Greg Hoode,'' Hermie York said almost immediately. She was sitting on the large sofa that he and Cathy had shared the day before and was sipping tea. ''How nice to see you again. Breakfast should be ready in just a few minutes, and I'd love to have you join us.''

The cloying smell of honey had already begun to kill his appetite. ''Actually, I've just come to pick up Cathy. She wants to get an early start at sightseeing today.''

Hermie laughed. ''Obviously, I haven't seen Miss Pettis this morning, except for a moment when she used the lobby phone. I must say, she didn't look as if she slept well last night.''

''Excitement.''

Cathy appeared on the staircase.

''Well, here she is now,'' he said, relieved. ''Ready to go?''

Cathy hurried down to meet him. ''I'm ready if

you are," she replied in a tone that stated that she was more than ready. She did look a little drawn, and there were faint rings beneath her blue eyes, but she still was beautiful enough to pull some of the breath from Greg's lungs as he looked at her.

"No breakfast for you, either, Miss Pettis?" Hermie called.

"Not this morning, Hermie," she answered, without looking at the other woman. She took Greg's arm and pulled him toward the front door.

"Have fun, you two," Hermie added. "Don't forget, lunch is from twelve 'til two, tea is at three-thirty, and dinner starts at six-thirty."

"Everybody in Euphrata wants to turn me into a heavyweight," Greg muttered.

Cathy wasn't very hungry in spite of all that she had experienced since she last ate, and since Greg never craved any breakfast, they settled on a little shop that handled doughnuts and coffee. She slowly and deliberately related the events of the night before, trying to maintain a calm demeanor that would give weight to the sensational content of her account.

But Greg didn't laugh at her; in fact, he seemed ready to believe almost anything after what had transpired the day before. "Man, that must have wrung you out. I had nightmares, but nothing like that," he said gently.

Cathy rubbed her eyes. "I thought you didn't get any sleep last night."

Jerk, he told himself. "A little while, after three, but that's not important. Are you sure that when you saw Hermie and the others you weren't still dreaming?''

"I'm positive. I know that I was awake. Some-body had already dragged me from the bed and pushed my face out into the rain. Hermie was there, she had come to get me.''

"I wouldn't have thought it of her." He paused. "I'm sorry to put it this way, but why didn't she take you?"

"I haven't actually figured that out yet, though I think that somehow they found out that I had the gun and was expecting trouble. They pre-sumably thought that I would be unconscious. I'm sure I didn't just fall asleep; I was too keyed up to sleep.''

Greg swirled the last of his coffee in the bottom of his cup and then swallowed it. "Don't take this the wrong way either, Cathy, but have you ever had any experience with hallucinogens?''

"What? You mean drugs?''

"Yep. Specifically acid.''

"What's that?''

You just answered my question, he thought. "LSD.''

She stared at him, as if trying to read his mind. "This may sound uncool or small-townish to someone of your background, Greg, but I haven't tried everything in the pharmacy yet.''

"Okay, okay," he said quickly. "It's just that the dream that you described, its vividness and the way things moved into the bizarre, well, it sounds like an acid trip. And when you saw Hermie for real, the aftereffects could have made you imagine the blood on her face.''

"She was bleeding, damnit!" she snapped. Almost immediately, she apologized. "I'm sorry,

Greg. You haven't done anything but help me since yesterday morning, and I know that I've been a real pain most of the time.''

"Forget it," he said. "I could do without the rich boy cracks, though."

"You've got it," she assured him, smiling. "But she *was* bleeding. I'm sure of it."

"Cath, I saw her this morning. Unless the cuts were shallow enough to be covered by makeup, she must have healed very quickly."

"According to Louise, people heal very quickly at the mansion."

"You're right." He slid his chair back from the table. "The next question on the agenda is—what do we do now? You're not considering staying there another night, are you?"

"I still believe that Mikey's alive in Earl, and I'll do whatever I have to in order to save him."

"Louise is going to call in the state police team."

"But when? After Welsh has decided that Earl is a failed experiment and stored him away with the other vanished travelers? Or maybe after the lunatic tries another experiment and puts Mikey's mind into somebody else? I can't let him do that to my brother again. You have to understand that.''

"I understand that you've got more intestinal fortitude than I could ever muster up," he said with sincerity.

"You don't have a brother or a sister."

"Yeah, right." He stood. "One thing I do understand is that there has to be a better way to go about this than having you set yourself up as a target again. What do you say to checking this out with Louise?''

"I'd say that that was the most intelligent thing I've heard today.''

Louise wasn't there.

The two young librarians were in place and quite cordial as they answered Cathy and Greg's questions. But they were not at all upset that their immediate superior seemed to have stepped into another dimension.

"We did call her house, naturally," one said, "but the operator said that the number was out of service now. She said that Mrs. Simpson had been reassigned by the state board to a branch up north. South Bend, I think.''

"I thought that she resigned," the second said. "To get married or something?''

The first young woman elbowed the second sharply. "I'm sure that she was reassigned. Why don't you call South Bend? Or maybe it was Fort Wayne.''

"We'll do that. Thanks," Greg told them as he nudged Cathy toward the door.

"They were lying," she declared once they were outside.

"Yeah. They can act about as well as I can recite Shakespeare," he said. "They've caught on to her. That's the only explanation.''

"Oh, God, do you think they've killed her?''

"I don't know . . . though it has to be a possibility. This thing is really snowballing, Cath. We can't handle it alone anymore. I'm going to call Uncle Dan and tell him everything.''

She clutched his hand. "Is that safe? The more people we drag into this, the more danger we expose them to. If we hadn't talked to Louise . . ."

"Who then? The police? I've got more faith in Dan. Pardon my lack of modesty, but he's wealthy, so nothing these people could offer him could draw him into any type of conspiracy, and he knows influential people all over the country. And he's tough as a pine knot."

Cathy sighed. "Well . . . okay. You're right; we do need some kind of help."

He trotted toward a pay phone at the corner. "I'll have him meet us, uh, at the bus station. We can trust Frankie, and there's never anybody else there." He fished a quarter out of his pocket.

It was a futile exercise.

"Not home," Greg said as he returned to the Porsche, where Cathy was waiting. "In fact, he hasn't been in all day, according to Diana. That must have been one hell of a lodge party."

"I've been thinking anyway, Greg," she said. "Why don't we get Mikey . . . Earl out of there and then go to the state police ourselves? We could drive to Tiverton."

He slid into the driver's seat. "That's not a bad idea at all. We sure can't wait for Louise to call in the troops now, can we? But it's not going to be easy to walk in there and take Earl away from that nutty doctor and his wife."

"They're out of town. Hermie told me last night that Welsh left for Milwaukee to make a speech and Alfreda went with him. They didn't take Earl with them, though."

"That's right," Greg muttered. "He told us about that yesterday right before old man York started his 'I know the words' routine."

"His what?"

"The dismissal prayer, or chant, or whatever it was, at the tea. You remember. 'I know the words to open the gates to health and joy, the words that brought the gifts of heaven,' et cetera. Don't tell me you didn't hear it."

"I was somewhat preoccupied."

Greg suddenly recalled what had been discussed just before the chant began. "Oh yeah, sorry. Come to think of it though, tea time might be a good opportunity to make a move. If everybody's outside again today—and with this weather, why wouldn't they be?—we'll practically have free run of the house. If we're really lucky . . ."

"Why should we presume good luck now?" Cathy asked dryly.

Greg nodded. "Right, but *if* we're lucky, no one will want to take care of Earl during the festivities and he'll be inside in bed."

"It's something," she admitted. "We should leave word with someone on the outside, just in case we run into some unexpected trouble."

Greg looked straight ahead, over the steering wheel and past the parking lot to the brooding splotch against the blue sky that was the York house. "I think I've got that covered, too. I thought I'd make the quick search while you waited somewhere outside, say at the doughnut shop. If I don't show up after a reasonable length of time, you can contact Uncle Dan and get the hell out of town." He took a deep breath.

Cathy paused a long while before replying. "You're expecting me to be a real bitch, aren't you? I'm supposed to rip into you for being so old-fashioned and chauvinistic and demand that you allow me to prove myself every bit as good as you are, isn't that right?''

Greg said nothing.

"Actually, I appreciate your concern. But even though you are a trained athlete and you're probably physically able to carry Mikey out of there all by yourself, the two of us will have a better chance of success than either of us alone. I've come this far, Greg, and I'm going to finish what I've started.''

"I thought that that's what you'd say," he responded with a smile, "and I can't say that I'm too disappointed.''

"Who shall we contact then?''

"Uncle Dan's out, and you don't know anyone else in town, do you?''

She shook her head.

"How about Frankie? He's the kid working at the bus station.''

"Are you sure that we can trust anyone who lives in town?''

"I'm sure about Frankie," he replied. "Before you arrived, I was feeling pretty sorry for myself, because back home I was a real hotshot, a boxer and a rich one to boot. But here in Euphrata I was just an intruder. Nobody was telling me how great I was. Everybody was friendly and polite, but I never was able to get inside the bubble that surrounds this place. If you had been here long enough, you'd know what I mean.''

"I've gotten a force-fed course since yesterday.''

"What I'm getting around to is that Frankie and his family are the only black residents of Euphrata that I've come across.''

"It's a racial club, too?"

"Must be. No one's ever actually said so, but it seems fairly certain. And the proof is in the fact that he can't walk."

Cathy looked suprised. "I didn't know that. He was behind the counter at the bus station when I met him."

"An accident when he was four. Like Louise said, you don't see very many people in this town who are less than physically tiptop "

"What on earth could they be doing up there?" Cathy wondered in quiet awe.

"I don't know, but maybe we can find out this afternoon."

They were surprised by how little Frankie was surprised. He practically recited the story along with them, using the observations he had made during his years of residence. He wasn't totally blasé about the tale, of course, and had little knowledge of the disappearances Louise had chronicled, but it took very little persuasion to win his belief in their theory.

"Shoot, man, I've known for years that this place is just too healthy for chance to account for it all," he told them. "And I was pretty sure that the York house had something to do with it. Are you certain that the librarian's disappearing act is connected with this?"

"What other answer is there?" Greg asked, shrugging. "She took us into her confidence, so she'd never skip without telling us where she was going."

"I only hope that she isn't dead," Cathy added.

"Now we're taking you into our confidence," Greg pointed out. "This might well put you in danger, so you can tell us right off to take a long hike over a short pier, if you want to. We'll never breathe a word of this meeting to anyone else."

Frankie broke the relative quiet of the otherwise empty bus station and startled both of them with an abrupt, piercing burst of laughter. "Dempsey you and your entire family don't have enough money to buy me off of this one! I'm going up there with you!"

Greg tried to cover his surprise. "We can use all of the help we can get, Frankie, but do you think that's such a hot idea? I mean, we need you to be our *outside* man in case anything happens to us."

"You'll have to call Greg's uncle and the state police," Cathy said.

"I won't even get to be a sidekick in this? Greg, I've been trying to get into the York house for years. Don't you see, man? Whatever they're doing in there might be a cure for me. I might be able to walk again!"

Greg was shocked by his own thickness. "Phew, Frankie, I didn't think about it that way. But the real problem is . . . well, the mansion has a lot of rooms, and we'll probably have to check out most of them in a limited period of time."

"Yeah, so?"

"That's three floors, a lot of stairs . . . and no elevators."

The truth hit Frankie quickly, and the enthusiasm in his eyes faded. "I'm hell on wheels on the straight and level, but something of a hindrance on staircases, is that it?"

"I'm sorry, man, but this is for real," Greg

answered.

"Okay, your logic's impeccable, as always, but I'm still going. I've got a collapsible chair back here, so if you can get it and me in the miniature back seat of that hotrod of yours, I guarantee that I'll be able to get it out by myself. If you're not out of the house in an hour—or whatever time limit we decide on—I'll wheel back here and spread the alarm."

"Nobody will think anything's out of the ordinary when they see you on the street?" Greg asked.

"Why should they? I'm crusing around this metropolis all of the time. I'm an institution."

"What about your job?" Cathy added.

Frankie raised his voice. "Anybody here care if I take the afternoon off?" The question echoed throughout the empty terminal. "The tea's at three-thirty, right? I've got a bus at twelve, another at six, and six hours of dead time in between."

Greg chuckled. "I wish you'd put it another way. All right! I can't think of another argument against you, not that you'd listen to one anyway."

"You know me pretty well." Then he added soberly, "My friends, I hope this doesn't sound too pretentious, but I believe that this will turn out to be the most important day of our entire lives. And, Cathy, if this guy is your brother, I know that you couldn't have a better fellow helping you to get him out than this old punch-drunk codger here. I promise I'll do everything I can."

* * *

Pamela Durben felt sure that her husband was dead.

Kevin hadn't returned during the night after having been taken away by Carl and Jeroboam, and an hour or so after that, more than half of those starved, emotionally abused people who had been sharing the room with her had been led away by other men with guns and billy clubs. Albert had fought with astonishing fury, but a few powerful clouts upon the head had reduced him to a stumbling and manageable state.

Pamela had expected to be taken along, but the nurse had taken the time to explain that she was not ready for the celebration; her turn would come soon enough. Then the hallucinogenic gas was used once more, leaving her in the throes of those terrible waking nightmares.

When she came to, another person had been added to the collection, a small bespectacled woman who identified herself as Louise Simpson and seemed to be practically as ignorant of what lay ahead of them as Pamela herself. Since she was securely strapped into one of the large chairs, it was a safe bet that she could provide no help in any situation.

As slowly as the grinding drift of the continents, the night passed, and though there were no clocks or watches in the room, Pamela's own refined internal chronometer informed her of the passing hours. Morning finally came without any appearance by Kevin or the vicious animals who had taken him away. He's dead, she thought with an icy certainty. They made him tell someone else—that old man—about what he did to that poor girl fifteen years ago, and he was tried, sentenced, and executed in a small-town kangaroo court.

Pamela and the other remaining captives finally were allowed to use the bathroom and take their first nourishment of the day in the form of a couple of glasses of plain water. In spite of the terror and mental chaos that threatened to completely overwhelm her, she had to marvel at the medical properties of the gas. Less than a day before, she had been within a few breaths of dying, yet now she seemed to be half a year along the road to recovery. Though she had to be helped into the bathroom by Louise and another woman, the change over a period of hours was almost beyond belief. When she was strapped to the bed again, another treatment was administered.

When she recovered from the visions this time, Kevin was standing over the bed.

"My God, are you all right?" she cried, forgetting her situation and trying to reach up and clasp him to her.

He smiled reassuringly. "I'm fine, babe," he said. "In fact, I'm damned near perfect." It *was* Kevin, and this was no dream, but . . . there was something different, something frightening.

"I thought that they had put you on trial last night and then murdered you," she went on breathlessly. "I was so scared that I'd never see you again."

"Pammie, you wouldn't have believed it if you'd been there! I figured that I was in for hell last night—torture, maybe even death—but it was a party, a damn get-down-and-drunk party! It was like something from—"

"A party?" She couldn't believe her ears or his attitude.

"That's right. It was kind of a monthly celebration of the discovery of the gas with invited guests. And tonight's going to be—"

"Kev, that's enough now," Carl said from behind him.

Pamela gasped, suddenly realizing that the guard was there with the same gun as the night before, if not the same intensity of purpose.

"Sure, Carl. I didn't mean to overstep my limits," Kevin responded almost pleasantly. He looked back to Pamela. "I was a hit down there, honey. You should have heard how they cheered and applauded. And all that I did was tell them about what the others and I did to Angie with, you know, a few details that I didn't have time to go into before. Anyway, they hung on every word, and I even started to remember things that I had intentionally buried about it, little tortures that we played—"

"Kevin!" she screamed. "Listen to yourself! What's happened? Last night, you were crying when you thought about it, and you even swore to me that it was a lie."

The odd new gleam in his eyes failed to dim. "Oh, it was true, all right. Surely you realized that. Haven't you asked me often enough about this Angie I mumbled about during the nightmares? Well, I don't think that I'll be plagued by those anymore."

"But . . ."

"Relax, babe. You see, I think we've got a real chance of getting through this. We might be able to offer a certain entertainment value to the establishment that will give them a reason to keep us topside instead of putting us down here with the others.''

"The others? What happened to them?''

"Oh, you all will see that tonight.'' He glanced at the five people who were still captive in the chairs.

Then Pamela knew the truth. He's gone, she thought. He's completely insane. The gas has taken the worst in him and it's magnified these qualities. He's one of them now—no better. I've lost him forever.

"Don't worry, Pammie. When I convince them to take me into the community, I'll put in a word for you, too,'' Kevin told her with an expression that she had never seen in the face of another human being until that moment.

Pamela began to scream then, and she didn't stop until Carl had taken her husband from the room and locked her away again with the other hopeless victims of this madhouse.

Chapter Ten

Midafternoon, Tuesday, July 11.

"It's going to get mighty hot under that," Greg observed as Frankie pulled a brown, Indian-patterned blanket over himself. He and the folded wheelchair were jammed into the Porsche's small rear seat.

"Just leave the windows down," Frankie grunted in response. "And remember, you've got fifty-five minutes. At fifty-five minutes and five seconds, I'm going to be zipping down the hill and doing my Paul Revere impression."

"I'll bet that the bus stop business is looking more attractive by the moment, huh?" Greg asked with a laugh.

"You two just be careful."

"Don't worry about us, man."

Cathy and Greg had expected the house to be virtually deserted at 3:40, since the daily tea seemed to start punctually. They walked across the spacious front porch and through the unlocked screen door without giving a thought to furtiveness. The honey smell hit Greg like a club.

"Can I help you?" asked a youthful voice from the comparative gloom inside the house.

They stopped and allowed their eyes to adjust. The speaker turned out to be a boy of about 14, and Greg recognized him as another town kid. Though he was standing now, it was clear that he had been relaxing in a chair close to the door with a comic book.

Strike one, Greg thought. "Hi. On door duty today?"

"That's right," the boy replied somewhat glumly, then brightened perceptibly. "But tomorrow I get to serve the tea."

"Hey, great. I'm Greg Hoode, and this is Miss Pettis. Miss Pettis is staying in the mansion."

To corroborate this, Cathy produced her room key. "I was going upstairs to change."

"Oh, sorry," the boy said. "I was just being careful, you know."

"Right, just doing your job," Greg forced himself to say in a friendly tone though he really felt like cursing. "We'll just be on our way."

With Cathy in tow, he rushed up the spiral staircase.

"Damn, I didn't think that they'd post anyone inside," he whispered after they were well away from the boy.

"Maybe he won't suspect anything," Cathy suggested. "There must be people coming and going all the time in this house."

Greg waved a hand at the empty corridors. "Not during tea time."

They continued through the cavernous dwelling and encountered no one until they had almost reached Cathy's room. As they turned the corner leading to the McKinley Room, they glimpsed Gretchen's small figure moving slowly down the hall away from them with a mountain of clean sheets in her arms; it seemed that changing bedding in the York mansion was a constant duty.

"Hello, Gretchen," Cathy called as she slipped her key into the door.

The answer was barely audible. "H'lo, Miss Cathy."

Gretchen's appearance triggered an idea within Greg. "How about the servants' passageway? If everyone except Gretchen is outside, we could go from room to room without being seen."

Cathy swung open her door. "The one in my room was locked last night . . ." Then, out of the corner of her eye, she saw how Gretchen was moving so slowly and painfully away from them. "My God, Greg, look at her!"

He turned, and even in the darkness of the unlighted hallway, he could see the deep, ugly marks on her bare arms and legs and the hobbling way in which she was walking. Unconsciously, his hands balled into fists. "Those animals," he whispered. And for an instant, Cathy was afraid of him.

"Gretchen!" she called. "Wait! What happened to you?"

Instead of answering, the girl appeared to be hurrying on, away from the two of them. An injury to her right leg caused her to limp badly however, and a seething Greg caught up to her in a matter of seconds as she opened the door to another hallway. He clutched her shoulder and turned her around to face him.

"Those bastards!" he shouted. The open door at Gretchen's side became the focal point for the rage that was flaring like a blast furnace within him, and he kicked it shut with such force that the thick walls of the corridor trembled.

Gretchen screamed and tried to pull free of his grip.

"Greg, for God's sake, you're terrifying her!" Cathy cried as she ran to the girl's side.

"No, no! I'm sorry, really. I won't hurt you." The young man's fury had changed to desperation in one flash of realization. The sight of the maid's swollen and discolored face had incited a fierce need for vengeance. In spite of his association with violence in its most basic form, Greg felt no attraction to it outside of the ring; still, he was able to see the kinship between what had happened to Gretchen and what he did in the name of sport, and he didn't like the view.

"Can't you control yourself?" Cathy demanded. "I thought that boxing taught you to channel your impulses." She pulled Gretchen's head onto her shoulder. "Shhh, it's okay. He won't hurt you."

"I-I . . . take it easy! I'm sorry," he said ineffectually. Then he stepped back and allowed Cathy to slowly calm the girl.

"Come on," she urged in a low but gentle voice. "Come into my room, and you can tell us what happened."

Gretchen shook her head weakly. "Go to work, please, let go," she whispered. "Trouble, um, please, or I get in trouble."

"I promise you won't. Come along." Cathy

slipped her hand beneath the girl's right arm and helped her to hobble into the bedroom. Greg followed, feeling both angry and shamed.

Cathy eased Gretchen onto the bed and carefully examined the bruises that weren't hidden by her short, plain dress. It was obvious that she had been beaten with a stick of some sort, leaving vivid stripes of yellow, blue and purple on the flesh of her arms and legs. The damage to her face seemed to have been done with hard fists however, and it was as bad as anything Greg had ever seen after a fight (and certainly worse than anything he had received in one). There were red, raw circles around each of her wrists and ankles.

But if any part of the evidence of the beating was the worst, if anything really sickened the two horrified young people in its savagery and really perverted connotations, it was the dozens of inflamed bite marks that had been forced upon all parts of the girl's body, including what they could see of her breasts. Those bite marks were human in origin.

"Gretchen, honey, who did this to you?" Cathy's voice was raspy with emotion. She had screamed at Greg for his reaction, but the same searing rage had been foaming within her, and it only seemed to be getting stronger.

Gretchen stuttered for a moment and then tried to stand, but Cathy gently and firmly held her down.

"You've got to tell us, Gretchen. What happened to you?"

"No, no," she sighed. "Go to work, please." But Cathy patiently repeated the question until the girl's resistance began to fade. "I-I don't remember . . . I fall on stairs, all the way down. Boy, I sure am stupid.''

"Is that the truth, Gretchen? You should always tell your friends the truth, and Greg and I are your friends.''

"He scared me," she said petulantly.

"I said I was sorry," Greg repeated. "I wouldn't hurt you. I've never hit a girl in my life. Don't you want to tell us who hurt you?''

"You know I trip . . . on the stairs . . .'' Her voice faded into silence, and she appeared to lapse into some kind of trance. Slowly, her green eyes began to glisten with unshed tears. "Hermie," she whispered faintly.

"Hermie?" Cathy asked in surprise. Even though Hermie had been the one to make the melodramatic entrance into Cathy's room during the previous night, she also had been the only resident of the mansion whom Cathy and Greg had seen show any affection for the girl, patiently helping her during the memory lapses and refraining from using the awful names that the other guests and family members regularly employed. "Did Hermie hurt you this way?''

Gretchen nodded slowly. "And somebody others," she whispered.

"Why?"

Getchen sighed heavily. "Being bad. I'm all the time bad and stupid.''

"You're not stupid," Cathy said firmly, "and I don't believe that you're bad, either. What did you do?''

"Came in here, in your room. Last night.''

"Of course. *You* pulled me over to the window! Why did you do that, Gretchen?''

Her voice was distant and somber. "So the ghosties don't get you. But Cook says no ghosties . . . so I come so you don't be like me. Work here, be stupid. Or put down there."

Greg was almost afraid to break the delicate rapport that had been established between the two girls, but he had to ask, "Put down where?"

Gretchen glanced at the floor. "I big mouth," she said. "Go to work now."

"Gretchen, would you like to leave here and go where Hermie and the old man couldn't hurt you?" he asked carefully.

Her swollen eyes flew to his face, and there was a clear plea in them. For a few seconds, she couldn't speak, but then her voice returned and her tone was flat and resigned again. "Got no place to go. Oh, Mommie, I . . . um, I think maybe I stay here 'til I die."

"We can get you out."

She laughed mirthlessly. "Hermie tells me where. Out of here to a nuthouse, whoosh."

Cathy stroked her hair. "Maybe we could find your family. You must have some family somewhere. Help us, Gretchen, so that we can help you."

She looked at the two of them, questioningly.

"Take us through the servants' passageway," Greg told her. "Show us where Earl is and where the people are put down."

She shook her head quickly, frightenedly. "Ghosties . . . the other people . . ."

"I won't let anyone hurt you," he promised. "I'm a very good fighter, and I'll take care of you."

The room fell silent. Knowing that words

would do no more convincing, Cathy took the girl's right arm and held it before her unblinking eyes. Six deep purple streaks ran through the smooth whiteness of her flesh like serpents in snow. Taking into account the way people seemed to heal at an accelerated pace in the mansion, this had to have been a terrible beating.

"Help us," Greg urged.

With a slight shudder, perhaps at her own temerity, Gretchen stood, limped across the room to the servants' door, and opened it.

The service corridor was a rather narrow and gloomy affair. Unlike the richly carpeted main halls, this second series of passageways consisted of bare wooden floors with a naked overhead bulb every 20 feet or so for illumination. There were no windows to break up the montony of the walls, though every so often they passed a marked doorway. Cathy's door had read, "McKinley Room."

"We're looking for Earl, Gretchen," Cathy said carefully. "Do you understand?"

Gretchen continued to pad softly down the hallway as she worked this over in her mind. Finally, she nodded.

"Is he inside the house now?" Greg asked.

"Asleep," she replied. "Sleeps all a' time."

"That could be as a result of the operation," Cathy pointed out hopefully.

"Sure, but remember that most babies sleep a lot," Greg cautioned her. To Gretchen, he said, "Can you take us to him without letting anyone else know that we're in the house?"

That seemed to catch her off-guard. "Who?"

Greg smiled wearily. "Earl."

"Oh, um, yep. I can do that. I think I can."

"Let's get to it, then, before Frankie has the National Guard storming the house."

At the first set of stairs that they encountered, Gretchen put her right arm around Greg's shoulders and began a relatively brisk descent. They reached the second floor landing and passed it. The ground floor approached, and both Cathy and Greg were surprised when Gretchen led them past it and deeper into the bowels of the house. The house, it appeared, was firmly set within the large hill that formed its foundation.

"I think I'm beginning to understand what she meant by being 'taken down there,' " Greg whispered to Cathy as he half-carried the little maid further down the stairs.

At the next landing, the stairs ended. Gretchen moved into the corridor that serviced a floor that Cathy and Greg hadn't known to exist. It appeared to be identical to the three above, at least from this side of the walls, and they began what developed into a long, silent trek. After several minutes, Gretchen suddenly began to appear very confused.

She stopped hobbling and turned to face them. "Who . . . ?" she asked helplessly.

"Earl," he said aloud. "You know, the 'baby.' "

"Oohh," the girl sighed. "One time I could think of things . . . I could remember . . ." She blinked and pointed to a door marked *Catoptric Room*. "Is this it?"

Cathy looked questioningly to him, too.

"Shoot, I couldn't even guess," he said. "I've

never met Mr. Catoptric. We can try it, I suppose."

"Just a minute," Cathy told him. She reached into her purse and withdrew the gun. "We may need this."

Gretchen caught her breath quickly. "I don't like that," she whispered.

"Man, you *are* committed to this," Greg stated with a touch of awe.

"I hope you haven't doubted it," she answered.

"Have you ever shot it before?"

She shook her head negatively.

"Ever fired any gun?"

"No."

"I was a member of the Greater Atlanta Gun Club for four years," he said. "Mind if I see it?"

She handed the small weapon to him. "I'd feel more secure if someone experienced were handling it."

"Twenty-two," he stated as he checked the gun. "Not much power or range, but dangerous enough if aimed at the right target."

"Would you keep it?" she asked.

"If you want me to."

"And, Greg . . . if the time comes to use it, promise me that you will."

"I'll do what has to be done," he answered, unknowingly repeating a vow that Cathy had made to herself.

Gretchen asked tentatively, "I don't get . . . you don't go . . . bang-bang to Miss Cathy? To me?" Obviously, she had seen guns fired before, and she was not eager to repeat the experience.

"No, no. Don't worry."

Inwardly, Greg was recoiling at the thought of again encountering that 25 or 30 year old "baby," and if the "baby" were indeed the recipient of a brain transplant operation . . . He turned the knob.

It was pitch black in the room beyond. Feeling blindly to the right side, he failed to find the light switch. Only then did he recall that this was the service door he was using, not the main entrance to the room.

"Gretchen," he said from within the room, "can you help me find the light switch?"

She limped by him in the darkness and, being much more familiar with the surroundings, quickly located the switch and flipped it.

"Jesus," Greg shouted in abrupt pain and surprise, the cries of the two girls matching his.

The switch had ignited an entire battery of high-voltage lights on the room's ceiling, and the intense power of them had been caught, tossed about, and strengthened by the peculiar design of the room. Its interior was covered with mirrors, while still others—spherical, cylindrical, convex, and concave—were positioned about the room without any apparent regard to planning. The illusion was one of dazzling vastness, as if they had stepped into the middle of a hollow star. The light raced throughout its reflective cage like a meteor from the heavens.

The three saw thousands of pieces of themselves scattered about the reaches of the room.

"Please, please, we go out of here!" Gretchen cried frantically as she tugged at Greg's arm. "We break something in here—I breaked some once, and Hermie will—please!"

This sounded like a good idea to Greg, and he
pushed Cathy ahead of him. Gretchen waited
until they were in the hall to switch off the light
and hurry out to join them, then Greg swiftly
closed the door behind her.

"A hall of mirrors," he said. "No home should
be without one."

"Professor Kasha, he . . . works with lights,"
Gretchen explained. "Catches lights."

"He must be the one who thinks he can create
perpetual motion," Greg said.

"Earl wasn't in there, Gretchen," Cathy told
her. "Don't you know where he's sleeping?"

The maid began to rub her forehead with one
hand, perhaps trying to draw the memory up and
into her grasp. "I forget. I just can't . . . you see,
I don't come down here to work too much, 'cept
Hermie says. I don't think I know anymore . . ."

"We'll just have to check every room then,"
Cathy decided very calmly.

Greg whistled. "We'd better get to it. We're
losing time fast."

They came across bedrooms, work rooms, and
rooms that had no apparent function. Gretchen's
memory seemed to have seeped entirely from her
mind, and the names on the doors generally were
of little use. When they found one room marked
Remedial, Cathy ventured a guess that this was
set aside for some type of education, and Greg
laid off of the obvious wisecrack in deference to
Gretchen. He pushed the door open, and a fog of
honey-scented air billowed out to envelope them.

The smell was strong enough to gag the young
man. "What in the world is in there?" he gasped

Cathy, who was not so much bothered by the

aroma, peered around him and saw a large room, softly lighted, filled with low, deep-cushioned couches, and containing a thin, reddish vapor that hung languidly in the air. Three people, two women and a man, were lying asleep on the couches.

"It looks like a community bedroom," she said.

"The Clinic!" Gretchen said excitedly. "S-sick people, hurt people, they get better here, quick!" She hobbled into the room and began to take deep, long breaths. A smile bubbled into her bruised face. "Ooh, I feel good!"

"Greg, this is strange," Cathy whispered slowly. "This is like last night, when I had the dream . . ."

Greg felt himself being transported into a dream, too, one of his from the night before involving a woman wrapped like a mummy. He shook his head to clear it. Scanning the rose-tinged atmosphere of the room swiftly, he spotted a metal dragon's head like the one in Cathy's room on the opposite wall. Red smoke was curling from its nose and mouth.

"Gas!" he shouted. "Get out and close the door!"

Cathy moved a little unsteadily back into the service hall, but Gretchen seemed to be much more affected by the vapor. Giggling, she hopped further into the room and began a sort of joyous dance in spite of her injured leg. She appeared to have forgotten all about the search or the possibility of escape.

"Gretchen!" Cathy called loudly. "What are you doing? Come out here!"

"I don't hurt," she said, laughing in response. "This will help me, make me better."

"We can't leave her in there, Greg. Somebody will find her before we can locate Mikey."

"Yeah, that'd be just my luck. Hold this." He handed the pistol to her. Taking a breath of clean air, both to guard against the drugging effects of the gas and to insulate himself from the repulsive smell, he sprinted into the room to where Gretchen was continuing her jubilant dance.

"I think I can fly," she was singing. And the way she leaped high into the air on legs that had been trembling with pain only seconds before almost gave that impression.

Greg caught her around the slender waist in midair and carried her toward the door.

"No, no, no!" she cried as she cuffed his head and shoulders. "I think I know it now. I can almost say it."

"Not right now, babe," he grunted.

As soon as they had cleared the doorway, Cathy slammed the door. She had breathed only a whiff of the vapor, but it had so quickly taken hold of her in that brief exposure that she wasn't at all surprised by Gretchen's reaction to it. Greg lowered the girl to her feet away from the door and then had to grab her wrist before she could escape back into the room.

"I need it," she said, pleading with him. "I can hurt too much now. Please, please!"

"Not now," he nearly shouted. "We've got too much to do and only a little time. If you give us away, we could all be in serious danger. Do you want that? Do you want Hermie mad at you again?"

Terror flooded her eyes. "Oh, no! Don't let her hurt me again . . . you punch her hard, okay? You help me!"

He urged her along the corridor. "If we keep moving, she'll never know that we were down here."

"Okay, okay," she whispered. "I . . . sorry. I can't keep it inside anymore . . . I can't remember."

"The hallucinations are leaving her," Cathy told Greg. "God, they're so realistic, but her mind is clearing now."

"In a manner of speaking," Greg said under his breath.

Nothing of interest turned up in the next four doorways they checked, but they stumbled upon an awesome sight when they opened a door marked *Arena,* descended a flight of stairs, and switched on the lights in one of the largest rooms any of them had ever entered.

"Holy cow," a stunned Greg whispered. "It looks like an indoor football stadium." Indeed, had they been standing in a domed sports arena, the impact would have been much less, and though it wasn't as large as that, the description was still an apt one.

The room ran the entire length and width of the mansion, and it was a good 25 feet from the smooth concrete floor to the heavy wooden ceiling. Though there were a number of huge tables stored to one side and literally thousands of metal folding chairs stacked next to them, it seemed relatively unfurnished otherwise. At one end of the long chamber sat a block structure that resembled a miniature temple, and at the other was a large wooden stage or platform of some kind.

"What is this place, Gretchen?" Cathy asked.

"Oohh," she sighed, "this is . . . the gathering place, the party . . . last night . . ."

"They probably host indoor teas down here," Greg conjectured. "Music, dancing, drinking, debauchery, the whole list. And Euphrata is such a quiet little place."

"They put people down here," the maid whispered.

"Here? Is this where it happens?"

"Uh huh."

"Cath, maybe we'd better check this out. If the Yorks are killing people here, townspeople or travelers like Mikey and Nona, there may be some evidence of it, and that's what we'll need to get the state police in here."

Cathy stared into the vast room and saw nothing that interested her. "We've got to find Mikey first," she said.

Greg glanced at his watch and saw that she was right, of course. "Gretchen, they didn't bring Earl in here and put him down, did they?"

She tried to say, "No," but her voice deserted her, so she merely mouthed the word and shook her head.

"It's an impressive place, but I don't see a soul down here," Cathy pointed out.

"You're right," he said. "Let's go."

Gretchen climbed the stairs somewhat reluctantly. "They have fun down here," she said in a melancholy tone. "One time I watched. I hided and watched. But last night, they hurt me here. Too many people . . ."

Anger boiled within him again, like an old friend. Instead of saying anything, however, he gently took her hand and led her into the corridor above.

They knew the very next room was the most important one they had located so far. Unlike the other doors they had passed, this one was unmarked—and also locked.

"They wouldn't have locked Earl away for the entire time that they were gone," Greg said thoughtfully. "He has to be fed and . . . changed and stuff."

"This is just the service door," Cathy responded. "It could be that Welsh didn't want the servants disturbing him at his work. Whatever is inside must be important. Can you open this door, Gretchen?"

The girl's brief exposure to the gas in the Clinic already had produced remarkable results, clearing the wounds on her face and lessening her limp. Scowling purposefully, she put both hands against the solid wooden panel and began pushing mightily.

Cathy had to hide a smile as she took Gretchen's shoulders and pulled her away from the door. "No, honey, not that way. I mean, do you have a key to open it, a passkey?"

She quickly felt the empty pockets of her dress. "Nooo," she admitted in disappointment.

"I guess we have to skip this one," Cathy said, her voice heavy with frustration. "But if he isn't in any of the others—"

"Give me a little room," Greg interrupted. He stepped up to the door and carefully targeted the space just above the useless knob, then he drew up his right knee to his chest and kicked the door as hard as he could.

Greg often had laughed at the exaggerated heroics of the movies wherein the pretty boy protagonists burst through the heaviest of doors by simply laying their shoulders into them. He realized that wood was harder than flesh and bone, but he had thought that a foot in a shoe would be a different story. If he had been wearing army boots, his theory might have been better served.

A bolt of pain shot up his leg as his tennis shoe crashed into the door, but he gritted his teeth and kept quiet. There had been no real damage done, and he had heard the door crack a little. He kicked again. The door, not having been reinforced in any way, ripped free of the lock and swung inward into the dark room.

"Gretchen, get the lights, please," Greg said. While she and Cathy were busy with this, he quickly flexed and straightened his right leg several times and then tentatively shifted his weight onto it. Nothing broken.

The light flickered on.

"Damn," Cathy sighed.

It was a large storeroom. Against one wall were a number of clothes racks containing coats, suits, dresses, shirts, skirts, and slacks of all styles and colors. Shoes filled an entire corner of the room, and another was taken up by a very big table over which was draped a cloth the size of a theater curtain. Everything looked clean, but none of it seemed to be new.

"This is just a storage room for old clothes," Cathy said. "Let's go on before our time is up."

"Just a second," Greg said. He managed to

cross the room without limping and then threw the heavy cloth back on one side of the table. This revealed hundreds of purses and wallets, all neatly laid out in rows.

"What on earth . . . ?" Cathy began.

Gretchen's eyes grew wide, and she backed quietly into a corner.

"Don't you see what this is?" Greg asked. "These things belonged to the people—the people who disappeared around here. This is the evidence we need to show the cops." He began quickly rifling through the material, and Cathy eagerly joined him.

Most of the contents of the wallets and purses were missing, apparently appropriated by the Yorks and their accomplices. There was no money to be found in any of them.

"We've got to get this to the police," Greg repeated.

"How will we ever get it outside without being seen?"

He opened a man's brown leather wallet. " 'William James Tomy,' " he read from the driver's license. "This is it! The driver's licenses and credit cards. We'll take forty or fifty of these, the cops can match the names against those of the missing people, and they'll have to believe us. Grab some!" He swiftly began combing the stolen bags and billfolds for the plastic cards.

Less than half a minute later, Cathy gave a short, wordless cry and dropped the blue purse she held to the floor.

"Hey, what's the matter?" Greg asked.

She thrust a driver's license into his face. Its picture was the face of the bride from the wedding photo. "That's Nona, Mikey's wife! See? 'Nona Marsha Byers'! She hadn't had the chance to have her last name changed, yet. They *were* here, and these monsters killed her!"

"Bring it along. We've got enough now, and that will prove that the Yorks are involved in kidnapping and murder. Come on."

"Oh, no!" Gretchen cried from the corner into which she had retreated. "We go to jail. We be punished."

A thought froze Cathy. "You didn't have anything to do with all of this, did you?" she demanded.

"N-no," the girl answered. "But I live here."

"Gretchen, don't you understand? You're not in trouble, and the police aren't your enemy. Lord, you're as much a victim as Mikey and Nona. You were probably kept as a baby by these lunatics for domestic help after they murdered your family. They work you like a slave, terrorize you, beat you, and . . . well, heaven knows what else."

"My family?" she repeated in a whisper.

"That's right. Let's get it in gear, ladies," Greg ordered brusquely as he flipped off the lights. "We've got some very important people to see."

Cathy stepped outside the property room. "Not yet, Greg. This license means that Mikey really was here, and I'm certain now that he's Earl."

"The police will take him into custody—"

"Before the Yorks really kill him? We've got fifteen minutes left, and I'm going to find him!"

"All right," he said in a resigned tone, "but let's please hurry. Okay?"

Two doors later, they discovered the listening room. It was packed with expensive and sensitive electronic eavesdropping equipment that included cameras and microphones capable of tuning into any room in the mansion. It was clear from the various signs of recent occupancy—empty coffee cups, a portion of a sandwich, a small sofa and other items—that this was a popular recreation spot. A little spying can be very relaxing.

"Talk about your dumb luck," Greg said. "If anybody had been tuned in on your room yesterday when you showed Gretchen that picture, we all could be six feet under now."

"This is the source of Noleta's psychic powers," Cathy said. "She knew our names because she had been listening in on us."

"More incriminating evidence." He looked at his watch. "Ten minutes to zero hour."

"You can go tell Frankie about all of this," she replied. "In fact, you can take all of this to the police. I've got to stay here and find Mikey."

There was a grimness to his brief laughter. "I won't run out on you now. After all, we've got those ten minutes."

And they needed only one minute more to enter the next room and find Welsh's elaborately equipped operating room and the sleeping adult-infant. Cathy ran immediately to the makeshift crib in which he lay.

"Would you look at all of this," Greg said in stunned fascination. The room was as large as three ordinary ones, and it was crowded with beds, machines, and medical paraphernalia. "There's enough stuff here to start a hospital."

"Doctor is a genius," Gretchen parroted in

obvious respect. "He can look into people, fix . . .
oh, so many wonderful . . . I wish I was smart
like doctor. Not so stupid, like me."

"Doctor will probably be spending the night
behind bars—and plenty of other nights, too. Be
thankful that you're not . . . uh, involved." He
walked to a huge wall cabinet.

Surprisingly, this was not locked, and when he
twisted the knob, the doors slipped open silently
and smoothly. Greg was not prepared for the
sight of anything shocking when he stared into the
shadowy recesses of the cabinet, but Dr. Stephen
Anthony Welsh was interested in brains; in fact,
he collected them.

Greg's eyes bulged in shock, and he almost
screamed. Before him on six wide shelves sat glass
jars, the size of five gallon cans, and in each jar
floated some portion of a human head.

Some were evidently whole, down to hair and
lashes, while others were simply naked brains or
portions of them. All were grotesque, even those
which seemed to be sleeping in the greenish
preserving fluid. They were male and female, old
and young. Three even had intact eyes that were
wide open and gaping accusingly at him.

"Oh God oh God oh God," he hissed to himself, trying hard to hold on to it. He wasn't sure if
he could keep from fainting.

Behind him, Gretchen, who was moving much
more freely and energetically now, bounced
toward him. "Whatcha looking at?" she asked
innocently.

Not her! She'd go to pieces, he thought as he
slammed the doors closed. Jesus, don't let Cathy
know, either! "Uh, nothing much; just some

more equipment," he said. "You wouldn't be interested in it. Run back to the door and make sure no one is coming."

"Can I stay with you?" she asked with the innocent faith of a six-year-old. "It's scary by myself."

"How could I turn down that face? Sure, you can stay with me." He ran the sickening tape through his memory again. None of them belonged to Mikey—at least not the ones with faces left.

Taking Gretchen's arm, he walked her away from the terrible cabinet. "Let's see how Miss Cathy is doing."

She had gently awakened the man and now was trying to get him to focus on the picture of Mikey and Nona. The man had had a bowel movement which stank overpoweringly, but she seemed not to notice.

Gretchen did. "He stinks," she whispered with a shy little smile.

"Shh."

"Mikey?" Cathy asked softly. "See the picture? See the man, Mikey?" She cradled his head in the crook of one arm. Her voice was so full of emotion, so brimming with hope, that Greg began to feel that it would be best for them all if that *were* Mikey lying in his own waste, even if it meant that he had been through the nightmare of that hideous operation. Welsh had claimed that he had already performed the procedure. If anyone could salvage a mind and a soul from the hell that the moving of a brain from one body to another must have created, Cathy certainly was that woman.

Of course, what was left of Mikey could just as well be floating in a jar behind those doors back there.

"What do you think?" he asked in a dry whisper. "Is it him?"

She ignored the question. "Mikey, listen to me. That's your name. Michael Nathaniel Lockwood. Do you remember? Look at the man's face."

The eyes of the man in the bed had been vacant until that moment, but they suddenly fixed on the framed picture. He reached out with uncoordinated slowness to take it from her. He drew it close to his face, still gazing at the images of the smiling man and woman, and moaned in a low monotone. Then he put the corner of the frame into his mouth.

Cathy began to cry. Cursing silently, Greg took the photograph from Earl. He knew what he had to do now, to make certain forever, and he began feeling through the man's longish hair near the back of his skull. He found nothing, as he had expected.

"Cath," he said, "this isn't Mikey. There aren't any scars on his scalp."

"If they put him in that special room . . ." she weakly began.

"No. Even when a wound heals that fast, like Gretchen is healing right now, it leaves scars, and there's nothing to indicate that he's had brain surgery of any kind. There's no evidence . . ."

"It could be!" she cried.

"It's impossible. Not even here, with the gas. No one could have done that operation alone."

"I know that, but . . . you're right." The tears streamed down her cheeks.

Gretchen padded to her side and began rubbing her shoulder. "What's wrong, Miss Cathy?" she asked. "Can I help for you?"

Greg ushered her to the door. "Her brother is dead, Gretchen," he whispered.

"I'm sorry. I don't have any brother."

"She'll be all right in a little while. She just has to accept the idea. Again. Let's wait in the hall."

It didn't take very long for Cathy to compose herself. In a way, it was something of a relief. She had given Mikey up to death once and had dealt with her grief, but the idea that he had survived, even in an altered form, had also ressurected those painful memories and emotions. What kind of life would it have been anyway? Especially if he had never progressed beyond the mental capacity that poor Earl displayed. At least, he was at peace.

She soothed the child-man to sleep again and quietly left the room in which she had lost her brother for a second time.

"We've got just about enough time to get to Frankie before he sounds the alarm," Greg said, "but we're going to have to leave right now."

Gretchen smiled hopefully. "We go away from here? Find my family?"

"Maybe you'd better stay here so as not to give anything away before we can get the police task force alerted," he told her.

Her face clouded. "I got to stay? With Hermie?"

"What if they find the door you kicked in?" Cathy asked. "Even if they don't suspect us now, they may figure that Gretchen had something to do with it, and since she obviously couldn't have done it herself, who's the most logical selection?''

"Yeah, what about that?'' the maid chimed in.

"Okay, so you can go with us,'' he relented. "Do you need to get anything to take along—like shoes, for instance?''

She looked at her feet. "No more shoes. In the cold days, I had some . . . I got a blanket. It's blue.''

"I think that will be safe enough on its own,'' Greg stated with a grin. "Let's go ''

They hurried up to the ground floor and managed to slip through the lobby without being noticed, the doorkeeper apparently on a break. Frankie was just working his chair out of the Porsche when they reached it. Storing the chair in the trunk and adding Gretchen to the passenger list, they drove quickly away from the mansion.

Cathy's eyes lingered on the house for a long time however. Everything was almost over now. She had discovered at least a part of the truth, but there was still a definite sense of loss.

"Good-bye, Mikey.

Chapter Eleven

Late afternoon, Tuesday, July 11.

"I suggest that we get out of town as soon as possible," Greg said. "We can drive to Tiverton and alert the state police there."

"Good idea," Cathy said quickly. "That's the way Louise was going to handle it."

"And you see where it got her," Frankie observed. "I say get our tails over to the sheriff's department right now. There may be some townsfolk involved in this, but, take my word for it, Sheriff Reed is as solid as they come, and he can have those murderers locked safely away before they can scatter to the four winds, which is exactly what's going to happen as soon as they find the door that our version of Bruce Lee kicked in."

Greg bit his lower lip. "Maybe no one will be down there for the rest of the day."

"Maybe—but maybe not." The young man

looked at the ten faces on the driver's licenses he held—ten people cut down by madmen. "And the animals who did this will slip away and never be found."

"We could phone," Cathy pointed out.

"And use the long distance operator and have it all over town in two minutes."

"You sound like you don't *want* us to leave town," Greg muttered. Suspicion had entered his overall view of life like a corrosive cloud, and he didn't like the way it felt.

Frankie caught the hint. "Right, Mr. Hoode," he said hotly. "Why don't you just take me about a hundred miles to the middle of nowhere and dump me, so you won't have to worry about the cripple taking any of the glow of triumph away from you when this hits the papers?"

Greg chuckled aloud. How could he have suspected Francis Albert Holloway? "No chance of that, man; then I'd have no one around who sings worse than I do." He turned into a restaurant parking lot and cut the engine. "What do we do, friends? Go to the local cops or drive straight through to Tiverton?"

"I don't want any of them to get away," Cathy admitted. "Maybe Frankie's right, maybe this Sheriff . . ."

"Reed."

" . . . Reed is capable of handling the situation."

"What's to handle?" Frankie questioned. "You take a dozen good men to the mansion and arrest everybody in sight, then sort 'em out afterwards. Money and a big name count for just so much, even in a small town like Euphrata, you know.''

"Cathy?'' Greg prompted.

"It's all right with me,'' she responded, "just as long as we do *something.*''

"Gretchen?''

The girl had been staring at Frankie in obvious fascination for much of the ride, and she didn't snap out of it even at the sound of her name.

"Well,'' Greg continued, "I'd say that the resolution has passed with only one abstention. First, I'd like to use the phone over there to make sure that Uncle Dan is home. Any objections?'' No one raised one, so he slid out of the car.

For a short time, everything was quiet within the vehicle. The three young people sitting in it were on the precipice of the biggest event of their young lives, and they knew it. Cathy's blue eyes seemed filled with the realization that something had ended for her even as something else was about to begin. Frankie looked intense, prepared, and, perhaps, a little eager. Gretchen's short sojourn in the Clinic had permeated her body with enough of the miraculous gas to have taken away the pain of her injuries, along with most of the visible evidence of them other than the most vicious of bite marks on her neck and chest.

The childlike girl didn't seem preoccupied with any of the momentousness of the upcoming hours. Instead, she appeared to be utterly captivated by Frankie. Very casually, she leaned across the back seat of the car and scratched the right side of his face with her nails.

"Yeow!'' he shouted, more surprised than hurt. "What's the matter with you, little woman? You some kind of vampire or something?''

Gretchen's eyes widened in fear, and she stared from his uninjured cheek to her fingers. "S-sorry, please, sorry!" she gasped. She pressed herself against the side of the car and lifted her knees defensively before her. "I . . . sorry," she repeated.

"Well, you don't have to run up the flags of panic," Frankie muttered as he rubbed his cheek.

Though she had said nothing, Cathy was clearly amused by the occurrence, so Frankie leaned forward and whispered, "What's going on with this chick? Is she a space cadet or something?"

"I don't think that Gretchen has ever seen a black person before," Cathy answered. "She was checking to see if you were wearing makeup."

"Raised in a lily-white environment or what?"

Cathy sobered. "Yes, she was, and it's been a very harsh life for her."

Greg returned to the car with a mildly puzzled expression. "I got him," he said as he climbed behind the steering wheel. "I filled him in on the situation briefly, and he asked me to get over to the house as soon as possible. I think he's afraid that the Yorks will try to stop us from contacting the police."

"Who's not? Why don't you let us out at the police station and scoot over to his place?" Frankie suggested. "I can get the troops moving while you pacify Uncle Dan's fears."

"That's right, Greg. We need to get the law into this as fast as we can," Cathy said. "Frankie and I can take care of explaining everything to them, because I'm sure we'll have to do a lot of talking to convince anyone of this wild story."

Greg drew in a deep, uncertain breath. "Hokay, but I don't mind telling you, I don't care very much for the idea of splitting up right now."

"Relax, man," Frankie advised him. "We've got 'em by the short hairs now. Nobody's going to shut their eyes to these licenses and credit cards."

The police station was four blocks away. It was a small, unobtrusive building that could just as well have been a post office. Even the parking lot seemed to be a miniature version of the real thing. Greg pulled into it and stopped before the front door.

"The police probably are going to try to get you to go with them to the mansion, to point out the hidden rooms and all," he said as he helped Frankie into his chair. "Turn them down flat until I get back."

"My, my, he does get protective, doesn't he?" Frankie remarked.

"I'm serious, you guys! We've stumbled across the worst bunch of maniacs since H.H. Holmes and the Chicago Murder Castle, and if the wallets and purses are any yardstick, the Yorks surely have outdone him. When they realize that they've been discovered, they're going to be as bad as rabid dogs, and I don't want you going back up there." Though ostensibly he was talking to all three of them, he was looking only at Cathy.

"But *you* plan to make the charge up Murder Mountain, right?" she asked perceptively.

He smiled. "I wouldn't miss it for the world."

Frankie began rolling toward the entrance to the station. "We'll be here when you get back from your uncle's, but there are no promises after that.''

Greg suddenly realized that this was the moment. He stepped up to Cathy and took her face in his hands. ''You be careful,'' he said softly. Then he kissed her, and he could feel her kissing back.

''Don't keep Uncle Dan waiting,'' she whispered. Then she kissed his cheek and began to follow Frankie. ''Come on, Gretchen.''

The girl was standing next to the car, but she swiftly ran to Greg and clutched his arm. ''No jail! Please, no jail!'' she begged urgently. ''Go with you, please! Please!''

''You'll be fine here,'' he assured her. ''Go inside with Miss Cathy and Frankie.''

''No, don't leave me. You said you would help me!'' Her voice seemed on the edge of hysteria again, apparently a frequent condition with Gretchen. She clung to him like a frightened child, which was exactly what she was. ''You promised!''

Greg looked at Cathy and shrugged.

She laughed. ''You certainly are irresistible. Just don't start a complete harem before you get back.''

Shaking his head, he led Gretchen back to the car and drove away.

Cathy and Frankie entered the police station together. The front desk was occupied by a youngish man who seemed absorbed in a daytime serial on television. He didn't look up from the screen until they reached the desk.

''Help you?'' he asked. ''Oh, hi, Frankie.''

''Afternoon, Wally,'' Frankie replied. ''Is

Sheriff Reed in his office?"

"Yep, but I don't think he wants to be disturbed."

"Well, you'd better wake him up, because we have some heavy-duty business to discuss with him."

"Nothing I can handle, is it?"

"Murder," Cathy answered. "Lots of murders."

The officer stood. "In that case, we'll just do some disturbing, won't we? Come on."

He led them down a short corridor and sharply knocked on the door at the end of it. Without awaiting a response, he opened the door and entered.

A large, grizzled-looking man in a uniform was sitting at the room's one desk with a newspaper spread out before him. He glanced up and said, "What's the problem, Wally?"

"Sheriff, these two kids need to talk to you about a murder," Wally answered.

"Is that right?" The sheriff stood and revealed himself to be a massive bear of a man. "Tell me all about it. I'm Sheriff Baxter Reed."

A thought occurred to Greg when he and Gretchen were almost at Daniel Hoode's home. "Gretchen, do you know Sheriff Reed?"

Apparently she hadn't been out of the York house very often during her short lifetime, because she seemed to be captivated by all of the new sights and sounds of little Euphrata. Her eyes sparkled with the wonder of it, and Greg had to repeat his question.

"Sheriff?" she responded.

"Yes, Sheriff Reed. Have you seen him in the mansion, during any of the teas or parties?"

For a moment, she seemed to be concentrating, but then something, a bird or a sign, caught her attention, and she said, "Pretty."

He grasped her hand with unintentional force. "Gretchen, listen to me. Have you ever seen the sheriff at the house?"

"Ouch," she said, trying to pull her hand free, but he wouldn't let go. "Bang-bang?"

"Yes, yes, the policeman, the man at the jail!"

She nodded slowly. "Whooosh, yes, he doesn't like me . . . he hit me, play games with the gun that hurt me . . . big man, and scary, too."

Greg hit the brake so hard that he and the girl almost bounced into the windshield. "I'll be damned! And I left her there!" As he looked up, he was literally shocked to find himself sitting in front of his uncle's home. "Stay here in the car. Understand?" he shouted. "Wait for me right here, Gretchen!"

She nodded with big, frightened eyes.

Throwing open the door, he sprinted across the front lawn.

The sheriff called in four other men to listen to Cathy's story. She told it quickly and clearly, omitting only the now-irrelevent details of the possible brain transplant, and when she was finished, Reed was thoughtfully drumming his fingers on the desk top.

"Miss, that's one hell of a story, if you'll pardon my French," he said in his deep voice. "It's almost unbelievable."

"But it's true!" Cathy cried. She held up a

handful of plastic-coated licenses and credit cards. "I swear to God it is, and those people have been trapping innocent travelers and doing heaven only knows what to them for years."

"Miss, I *know* it's true," he said. "I just can't understand how you kids could find out so much without alerting Cecil and every other York on that hill. Wally, you and Loomis take these two back to the mansion. Roy, Conrad and me will get over to the Hoode place and intercept the other boy and that little bitch of a maid."

Cathy felt as if someone had punched her in the stomach.

Frankie screamed, "Oh yeah, you bastards, I should have known," and took a big swing at the man nearest him. He missed, tipping over in his wheelchair, which the cop kicked away from him.

"Come along, girl," another policeman said as he took Cathy's arm.

She reacted out of instinct; there was no planning in the move, and she had never considered cheerleading training as any type of self-defense education. But when her right leg flashed up higher than her own head, the heel of her shoe crashed into the chin of the startled policeman with enough power to separate the man from his senses. He dropped lifelessly in front of her.

"Damn," Reed said in disgust. "Loomis, will you take this little lady back to the mansion, please, while we revive Mr. Wolcott?"

A second policeman moved toward her, this one sharp-eyed and ready. Cathy abruptly remembered the gun in her purse—Greg had returned it to her before they left the mansion—and desperately tried to reach it. The policeman ripped the purse from her shoulder and tossed it across the room before she could open it however. When he was close to her, Cathy waited until just the right instant and then launched the high kick a second time. It missed.

The cop ducked aside and brought up his left arm in a fast, sweeping motion that caught her just below the knee and sent her falling over a chair and to the floor.

"We don't need to make this so hard, baby," the man said with an evil smile. He extended one hand to help her to her feet.

Cathy took the offered hand with the intention of using the leverage in some constructive way, but as she rose, she realized that the weight advantage was just too much in his favor. Instead, she feigned unsteadiness and clutched the back of the wooden chair with both hands.

"Take it easy," Loomis told her. "I'll be glad to give you a hand."

So she hit him with the chair. Using an hysterical sort of strength that was suddenly pumped into her arms, she spun about with the chair at shoulder level and crashed it into the back of his head. Unlike countless movie props, this very real piece of furniture did not fly to pieces when it struck the man's skull, but Loomis almost did. He sprawled across the top of the sheriff's desk like a rag doll.

"What a bunch of monkeys," Reed grunted as he walked toward Cathy.

She swung the chair again, but he caught it with one hand and wrapped the other paw around her upper left arm. "I think we've played this game long enough. You others tie up the nigger boy—

gag him, too, so we don't have to listen to his shit
—and then see if you can drag these two Sleepin'
Beauties out to a patrol car. Looks like they'll be
spending tonight in recovery instead of at the big
party.''

Cathy tried to scream, but he was ready for
that, too.

Greg charged into the house like a wild bull.
''Uncle Dan!'' he shouted at top volume. ''We've
got to go. We've got to get Cathy and Frankie
away from Reed before he can do anything to
them. Then we've got to get to Tiverton and alert
the state police.''

Daniel Hoode appeared at the doorway with his
tanned face flushed with excitement. ''Greg,
thank God you're all right. I couldn't believe—''

Greg took his arm and began pulling him
toward the front door. ''We don't have time for
that. We've got to get out of here. God, the entire
town is in on this.''

Daniel pulled up at the door. ''All right, Greg,
but we'll need two cars for everyone. The keys to
the T-Bird are on my bedroom dresser.'' He
turned back toward this room.

''I'll get them.'' Greg actually ran over the sofa
in his haste to reach the bedroom. He was filled to
bursting with the fear he felt for Cathy's safety.

He snatched up the keys and raced back into
the den . . .

. . . where Paul Lattwig stood waiting for him.

''Afternoon, Hoodlum,'' Lattwig said
pleasantly. He was dressed much the same as
Greg, in jeans and pullover shirt, but he was bare-
footed. ''I hear you've been a busy, busy little

hillbilly today.''

"You just get the hell out of my way, Lattwig," Greg ordered. "I don't have the time to trade insults with you."

Lattwig began moving lightly on the balls of his feet, doing understated but meaningful stretching exercises. "Better make time, Hillbilly, because you've been upsetting some very important people, people who I need to make points with. You and I are about to settle this in a fair fight."

Greg's eyes narrowed and his lips curled into a thin smile. "You're in on it, huh, Paul?"

"Man, I'm up for a full membership tonight."

"And to beat me in a fair fight would put you over the top, right?"

"The way I figure things, this will just about do it."

"Let's get on with it then." With a flick of his right hand, Greg threw the key ring directly into Paul's face. The latter tried to duck, but the keys hit him right in the middle of his forehead and sent him stumbling back, howling with pain. Greg followed his advantage by shoving Paul over a heavy armchair. "Outside of the ring, there is no such thing as a fair fight, buddy," he stated.

He turned to the front door and saw a scene that sucked the life out of his body and mind. His uncle, Daniel Hoode, was standing next to his car and wrestling with a struggling and already gagged Gretchen, trying to tie her hands behind her back. He was involved in this . . . all of this . . .

"Oh, God," Greg whispered in a voice that cracked with emotion.

Then something hit him in the small of his back

and sent him reeling into the wall. He tumbled to the floor and looked up to see Paul Lattwig standing over him. Blood from a cut on his forehead was leaking into Paul's eyebrows.

"Get up, Hoode!" he commanded. "We're not finished yet!"

The numbness in Greg was burned away by fury. "Okay, sucker, you've got it," he hissed.

The den was spacious, giving them plenty of room, and they went about the deadly serious meeting without preamble. Paul took the offensive. He was sure that his refined art of karate, with its varied attack and combination of hand and foot techniques, would quickly overcome the comparatively crude discipline of boxing. He therefore was somewhat surprised when Greg rather easily avoided his assaults using a nimble backward motion.

"What's the matter, Hillbilly, lost your nerve for this sort of work?" he asked tauntingly.

Greg made no reply.

Paul screamed piercingly and launched a round kick at the other's head. Greg ducked the move and threw two powerful punches to Paul's kidneys as Lattwig's momentum carried him completely around. Paul grunted with the impact and whipped a hard backhand punch into Greg's face, connecting solidly. When he leaped about to face Greg, he saw with satisfaction the blood that was beginning to flow from his opponent's lips.

"Now we're even," he stated.

"You going to fight or talk?" Greg asked.

Paul charged again with a flurry of punches and kicks, Greg blunting the effect of most of them and responding with shots from both hands that landed with stinging force on Paul's body and head. Paul began to lose the drive that had characterized his initial attacks, and a new, confused expression crossed his rapidly bloodying features. He had never expected this.

Deciding to forsake technique for pure muscle, Paul took two vicious punches to his face and leaped in to envelope the smaller man with his corded arms. For a short moment, the two of them struggled in this manner, wrestling more than fighting, until Greg jerked upward with the top of his head directed straight into Paul's nose and mouth. The blow was a stunning one that drove the bigger man staggering away blindly. He lashed out immediately with a sidekick, but Greg avoided it with ridiculous ease.

"I'm going to kill you!" Lattwig gasped in blazing pain and rage.

It was time to end this, Greg realized. Cathy was in danger of losing her life—if she weren't dead already—and his uncle had just betrayed him. Nothing was going to stop him from bringing the full measure of his vengeance on this whole damned town.

When Lattwig attacked him once more, Greg deftly avoided the blows, doubled a hook to Paul's side, straightened the man with a hard right uppercut, and then kneed him in the groin. Paul instantly dropped to his knees, bellowing hoarsely.

"You cheater!" Lattwig cried, somewhat ludicrously in that deadly serious situation. "You're a boxer. You're not supposed to kick."

"Tough," Greg responded as he swung his right foot in an arc that whipped it around to clip

Lattwig's left temple and leave him unconscious on his back.

Now for the hard part, Greg thought as he turned to the door.

It was filled by a tremendously tall, broad figure. "Come with me, *Jugend,*" Gerhard Klopstock said in that bottomless voice.

Greg recalled the shy giant of the day before, apologetic for his appearance and ashamed by the fear that he inspired in people. That guy had never hurt anyone.

"Get out of my way, Gerhard," he said gruffly as he squeezed by the colossus and onto the front porch. What would he do next? How far would he go against his own relative to save a girl whom he hardly even knew?

Greg had no warning at all of the danger to come when one of Gerhard's mammoth hands caught him by the back of the neck and threw him against the outer wall of the house. His last sight was his Uncle Dan fighting to get the now thoroughly hogtied Gretchen into the open trunk of a police car.

And then he was as completely unconscious as Paul Lattwig.

Chapter Twelve

Greg had never been knocked out before, not in the ring, not in the gym, not even in street fights or everyday accidents. He had been shaken from time to time by solid punches and even knocked down once, but as a fundamentally sound defensive boxer, he had endured remarkably little punishment.

It wasn't at all like going to sleep. The loss of consciousness was, of course, totally abrupt, and the state that he entered was a cold, dreamless void.

When he began to drift back to consciousness, he was tightly bound and lying inside a cramped and black prison filled with sharp metal implements, the overpowering stench of gasoline, and a small, wriggling creature that made mewling sounds as it was thrown against and on top of him by the motion of the traveling prison. It took another minute or so before he was able to understand that he and Gretchen were in somebody's car trunk and on their way to the mansion. He struggled, but was unable to loosen the ropes around his ankles or the metal handcuffs that pinned his wrists behind him.

The remainder of the ride was brief, however. Moments after the car stopped, the trunk popped open and he saw Gerhard and Uncle Dan staring down at him. He naturally couldn't speak because of the gag, but he could tell by the expression on Daniel's face that the accusations fired by his eyes were reaching their target.

"Greg, don't you understand? I had to do it," he said in a plaintive voice. "I had no choice."

"Let us take them," Gerhard rumbled. "We have to get ready for the *zeremonie* tonight."

The induction of new members, Greg reminded himself. *I wonder if they have to kill somebody before they're admitted to the group?*

Gerhard leaned over and plucked Greg out of the trunk as if he were weightless. He tossed the young man over his right shoulder. Daniel followed suit with Gretchen, who was squealing lustily in spite of her gag.

They were inside a wide, high-ceiled building that Greg took to be the York garage. Gerhard had to bend both at the shoulders and knees in order to fit through a doorway leading into the mansion. When he reached a descending staircase, he began trotting down with an energy that threatened to bounce the breath right out of Greg's lungs; fortunately, the trip was not a long one, and they reached their destination within seconds. It was a room on the basement floor which he and the two girls had not searched in their afternoon exploration. Its door was marked *Furniture*.

"Good evening, my friends," the giant said jovially as he placed Greg in an armchair. "We have brought more guests to keep you company."

"Greg! I thought you had gotten away," Cathy cried in alarm.

Greg focused on his surroundings and discovered that the room was packed with both old and new furniture of all design and that in nine of the larger chairs sat Cathy, Frankie, and Louise Simpson, as well as six people he didn't recognize. The wrists of the captives had been strapped to the arms of the chairs and a restraining strap had been looped below their arms and across their upper chests. Otherwise, everyone seemed healthy, even if some of those unknown to him looked terribly thin and haggard.

"Damn, man!" Frankie spat. "You were our only hope, Gregorio."

Daniel appeared at the door carrying Gretchen, obviously somewhat winded. The girl had stopped fighting and adopted a forlorn, completely limp posture. He dropped her into another empty chair.

Gerhard reached into one pocket and produced a gun that was almost lost in the immenseness of his hand. "Now, your *Onkel* will untie you and secure you to this chair like your friends. If you resist or try to escape, I shall shoot you. You will not be killed, but I assure you, the wound will be most painful."

While Daniel nervously unlocked his hands and strapped them by leather wrist restraints to the chair's arms, Greg stared unwaveringly at Cathy. When the gag was removed, he asked in a dry voice, "Did they hurt you?"

"No, I'm all right," she assured him.

"You should have seen her, Greg," Frankie said. "She was great! She took out two of those turkeys before they got her."

"It did a lot of good, didn't it?" she added glumly.

Greg continued in a flat tone. "Mrs. Simpson, I'm glad to see that you're still with us."

"For now," the bespectacled woman responded.

"I only wish that Cathy and I had found this room this afternoon. We might have been able to free you and these other people before it . . . before things went this far."

One of the three women Greg didn't know choked back a sob.

Daniel Hoode was sweating heavily, and his face made it clear that he was experiencing a personal battle within himself. "Greg, son, I'm sorry that I had to do this to you, but you must understand—"

"I understand that a man I trusted, a man I loved almost like a second father, sold me out," he said coldly.

"But I had to," Daniel stated in desperation. "Don't you see? I had cancer, I was dying! When I found out about this place and the way that that natural gas can heal any kind of disease or injury, I knew that this was my only hope. And, good God, it worked! I'm completely cured!"

"And all you paid for it was your soul, right, Uncle Dan?" he asked bitterly. "And our lives."

"No, don't say that. Sure, I paid money, but I didn't mind that, and I think . . . I think I can save you." He looked at Gerhard, who was standing aside like a golem. "I'll talk to Cecil. He's in charge, and I'll convince him that, since you're family, he can trust you not to tell anybody about the gas. We'll pay extra, and you can move here to Euphrata with me and become a full member of the fellowship."

"And what about them?" Greg asked, inclining his head toward Cathy, Frankie, Louise, Gretchen and the rest.

"Well . . . they'll have to be silenced, put down, but believe me, once you've participated in the ceremony, you'll forget all about them."

"Get the hell out of my sight," Greg exploded. "I hope you choke on that damned gas."

"Son, be reasonable."

He tried to kick his uncle, but the man jumped back, out of range. "Don't ever call me your son. Get away from me," Greg screamed.

Gerhard placed a hand on Daniel's shoulder and said, "*Mein Antsbruder,* take care of the maid, and we will join the others in preparation for tonight."

"Uh, yes, of course," Daniel mumbled, as if still stunned that Greg had refused his offer.

When Gretchen had been secured to a chair, the two men left the room, but Gerhard paused as he bent to ease himself through the comparatively small opening and smiled. "Relax now, little friends," he told them. "We will be back in a very short time to introduce you to the greatest moment that your dull young lives have ever known."

As soon as the door closed, Greg began working on the wrist straps immediately, but the heavy leather was too strong to snap, just as the thick arms of the old chair were too solid to work free in the short time that he felt certain they had. Still, he continued to try. What else did he have to occupy his time?

"What's this ceremony, Gretchen?" he asked as he worked.

She had been silent since her gag was removed, but the fear that was consuming her was manifested in the continual trembling of her entire body.

"Talk to me, Gretchen," he snapped, his voice filled with frustration. "What's the ceremony?"

"P-party," she replied. "Big party, and they put the people down . . . I hided once and saw it . . ."

"Perhaps I can help," Louise said wearily. "I've had the opportunity to speak with our fellow captives today, as well as some of the people who are holding us here. From what I've gathered, the ceremony is held once a month and is called a lodge meeting as a sort of code name. Apparently, it's intention is to commemmorate the original discovery of that incredible healing gas, though actually it's a mass orgy in which a large portion of the town participates. It takes place in a vast room on a level below this one."

"We saw the room," Cathy said.

"Yes, well, the details are not very pleasant," Louise continued hesitantly. "There seems to be eating and drinking—a lot of drinking, since surprisingly the alcohol acts to counteract the narcotic effects of the gas, even though normally alcohol is a depressant—as well as just about any other form of entertainment that you can name.''

''You don't have to tell us any more if it's too painful for you,'' Cathy whispered sympathetically.

''That's all right, dear. We all need to know what we're facing. Perhaps it will help us come up with some kind of plan. Well, another part of the festivities involves confessions. Each month, out-of-town people are collected by the police and other community groups and imprisoned in this room. On the night of the ceremony, these people —we—will be taken down to the gathering and forced to confess to the worst things that we've ever done in our lives.''

''Confess?'' Frankie shouted angrily. ''What have *we* got to confess next to what these bastards are doing? Are they all crazy?''

''It's the gas. It causes everyone to heal so fast here,'' Cathy responded.

Louise nodded. ''That must be it. We know that it can cause absolutely unbelievable regeneration in negligible period of time. I've been here only twenty-four hours, and already I can perceive a change in my myopia, a condition which normally doesn't respond to anything other than surgery. I actually would be able to see much better without my glasses now, if I could somehow remove them. And we have the example of Mrs. Durben.'' She indicated a young woman strapped in a chair close to her. ''Mrs. Durben was seriously injured in a traffic accident only yesterday morning, yet she's almost completely recovered.''

Greg paused in his struggle with the leather straps to glance at the woman. She certainly didn't seem relieved or happy at her remarkable recovery, and in her eyes he detected a cold rage that was at least unsettling and at most extremely dangerous.

"During the height of the ceremony a pump is turned on, and the gas, which apparently has been tapped beneath the house, is released into the auditorium," said Louise. "It causes the most vivid and incredible hallucinations."

Of the assembly, only Frankie had not ever experienced a brief bout with these terribly sharp and powerful dreams.

The woman continued to explain what she could to those about her; it seemed that talking was a minor release, a way to temporarily assuage the mounting tensions of the approaching night. "It also seems to inhibit aging. I presume you've seen Cecil York? Then you know that he's almost a hundred years old, yet he has the energy and physical attributes of a man half his age. Did you know that Baxter Reed, the sheriff, is eighty-nine?"

"The sheriff?" Frankie asked incredulously. "Shit, we're sitting on top of the biggest discovery in the history of medicine. This could change the whole world."

"Yeah, except that the wonderful Euphratans are committed to keeping it their little secret," Greg said as he gave the strap on his right wrist a powerful but ineffective jerk.

"Save your strength, Greg," Louise said. "Unfortunately, that chair is old, sturdy and made to last."

"We'll see," he answered in a low tone.

"So this gas heals injuries and disease, keeps you young, and burns your brain to a crisp, right?'' Frankie asked.

"So it seems," Louise replied. "Apparently, long-term exposure to it works on the central nervous system to produce all manner of psychological disorders. Notice the pervasive honey smell around this house and the grounds? That's it.''

Cathy sighed. "That's what makes Noleta believe that she's a diplomat's dead daughter and causes Gretchen's retardation—'' She cut herself off abruptly. "Oh, I'm sorry, Gretchen.''

The little maid blinked back tears and whispered, "I want to go away from here. T-to my room, please.''

"It heals the body and destroys the mind," Louise observed. "Yet the local townspeople fight one another for the opportunity to act as unpaid servants here, while all provisions, furnishings, and labor are eagerly provided free of charge. The greatest wish of any Euphratan is to be invited to the monthly festivities, like the one that was held last night when nine of the people being held here were taken down there to participate—where we will be taken tonight.''

Frankie snorted loudly, as if to rid himself of the smell that permeated the entire hill. "Why tonight? If it's once a month, why don't they just hold on to us until August?''

"I take it that this is a special annual service for inducting members and giving the younger residents full adult status.''

"I know of one local who will have to wait until next year for full membership.''

Frankie's eyes brightened. "Lattwig? You took Lattwig?''

"He wasn't saying much when the fight was over.''

"Hot damn, I wish I'd seen it."

"I wish I could get to a telephone," Louise remarked. "All I would have to say is 'Operational Triangle is go,' and this place would be swamped with state police in minutes."

"Don't bet on it," Cathy said. "Before Reed put Frankie and me into the trunk of the patrol car, I heard him tell one of his flunkies to call the long distance operator and instruct her not to take any calls from Greg without checking with him first. It's likely that the rest of us are on that list, too."

"So the state force will eventually investigate this, but it'll be too late for us," Louise said with no longer any pretense toward optimism. "By then, we'll simply be evidence buried out there somewhere."

Cathy asked the question that they all needed answered. "You do believe that they're going to kill us then?"

Louise closed her eyes; for the first time, she seemed on the verge of breaking down. "I won't lie to you, dear. After all that I've come across in my own investigations, after what I've heard from these people here, and after what I've seen of these monsters just today, I have to think that they're going to use us to satiate their perverted tastes for torture and molestation, and then they will kill us and bury our bodies somewhere on this hill."

"Nooooo," Gretchen sighed almost inaudibly. "Not buried. Put down there."

"She's been saying that since yesterday," Greg told them. "They took her down there last night during the ceremony and raped and beat her, but we haven't been able to get much of the story

from her. What do you mean, 'put down there,'
Gretchen?''

In reply, she began crying softly.

It was 8:00 when the seven men came for them.
Four held guns on the group while the other three
released them from the straps.

"What are you going to do with us?'' Cathy
demanded as she slowly rubbed her wrists. She
recognized one of the armed men as Loomis, the
policeman she had knocked unconscious with the
chair.

One of the men nudged another in the ribs. "I
can think of a few things that we'll be doing with
you, you can bet on that," he replied with an ugly
leer.

"You touch her and I'll tear out your wind-
pipe," Greg said darkly as he stood up from his
chair. A gun was immediately thrust into his
back.

"I ain't going nowhere without my chair,"
Frankie stated firmly.

"You wanna stay chained to that thing?"
another man asked.

"My wheelchair, you dork!" Frankie replied
scathingly. "I can't walk."

"Oh, I forgot. Never mind. Your buddies can
help you."

With the handguns pointing the way, Greg and
Cathy lifted Frankie from the chair and slipped
his arms about their shoulders. Another man
placed a cautionary hand around Gretchen's arm,
and the remaining seven captives were ushered
into a group so that they all left the room
together.

It was rough when they came to the staircase that led them deeper into the earth, and since none of their amused guards volunteered a hand, Greg was forced to lift Frankie in his arms and carry him down the steps as if he were a child. It seemed that the young man's fear and anger over the coming ordeal was matched by his embarrassment.

Their destination was, as they had expected, the huge room in the depth of the house. What they hadn't been prepared for was the sight of at least 5000 people, men, women and older adolescents, all dressed in bright green robes with hoods that covered their heads.

"Holy mackeral," Frankie whistled. "This looks like a monks' convention or something. Half the damned town must be here."

"Shut up and keep moving," one of the guards ordered as he jabbed Greg's back with the barrel of his gun.

As they moved into the vast room, the crowd seemed to notice their arrival almost as a single organism and, as if on cue, began clapping their hands in a slow rhythm, something like a death-knell.

"I'm sorry, sorry, sorry," Gretchen whispered, as if attempting to chant herself away from the situation.

"Greg, we've got to do something," Cathy said under her breath.

"I second that motion," Frankie added.

Something, but what? Greg demanded of himself.

The thunderous clapping of the assemblage became even more like a death theme to the nine people as they were prodded across the floor toward the wooden stage at the eastern end of the long room. Several other robed figures, including Hermie and Cecil York, were waiting on the platform. When the crowd began to utter a sustained, wordless, gutteral cry, the combination of that and the clapping stretched the captive's nerves to almost unbearable limits.

"Stop it, stop it!" Louise Simpson screamed. A guard shoved her roughly onto the steps that led to the platform.

Cathy, Greg and Frankie, and Gretchen followed, but when the remaining six captives reached the steps, they were directed away from the stage by a pair of the armed men. Once the first five were standing atop the platform, they had no time to question the reason for this separation, because they were again confined by straps to chairs awaiting them there. These were simple-framed wooden affairs reminiscent of electric chairs.

Hermie stared happily at them for a moment. There remained in her nothing of the good-natured, congenial hostess who had welcomed Cathy and Greg to the house only the day before. She stepped to the front of the platform before the five captives and shouted, "Attention, everyone!" Even with the noises of the huge crowd and the lack of public address system, her voice carried to every corner of the acoustically designed room. "It is time now for the Prelude. Take your places!"

With a rehearsed precision, the 5000 people sat corss-legged on the hard floor.

Hermie surveyed the gathering with a beaming

smile, and finally Cathy was able to see the glitter of insanity that had been missing from her eyes before that instant. She was just as mad as Noleta or Welsh.

"I know the words!" she yelled ecstatically.

"I know the words!" the adult portion of the assembly roared back deafeningly.

"And now you, the novitiates who seek the Fellowship, will understand how we of this blessed land have been entrusted with the very secrets of God!" She stepped away from the front of the stage. "Welcome, then, our father, the sourse of our glory and power! Welcome Grandfather Cecil!"

The mass audience began slapping their hands on the smooth floor and chanting, "Grandfather Cecil, Grandfather Cecil!" in remarkable unison. Cecil York, looking even more like a lost little monkey in his voluminous robe, took Hermie's place at the front of the platform.

He raised his arms high above his head, and the room grew silent. "I know the words," he almost whispered.

The response was immediate and ear-shattering. Cathy bit down hard on her lips while the crowd's shouted reply rolled over her like a river of glowing lava. Then everything fell silent once more.

"We have tonight the opportunity to admit thirty-seven new souls into full membership in the Order," Cecil continued, "but first we must hear the best of the collected tales that have come to us in the year that has just passed. Tonight we shall have two truthful memories that will stir the blood of every real member of the fellowship!

"Listen well, you who wish to become one with us, for you are being tested. Your eyes will reveal what your heart feels, and only the brave and the involved will be selected to enter into the fold of the blessed, to share throughout eternity the wonders of this heaven we have been given by divine dispensation. Bring them forth!"

Greg saw a stirring in the cluster of people immediately before the platform where the remaining six captives also had been bound to chairs, and three men stepped from among them on their way to the steps. Two were evidently captives, while the third was directing them from behind with a handgun. Greg didn't recognize any one of the trio, but the young woman Louise had identified as Mrs. Durben called "Kevin!" to the largest as they passed among the chairs. The tall, bearded, brown-haired man glanced back and smiled bravely at her.

Once on the platform the first captive, a slender, pale man with a stubbly gray beard and long, silver and black hair parted in the center, stepped to the forefront where Hermie and Cecil had addressed the audience. It was apparent that he was going to deliver his so-called truthful memory first. The guard, who was the only person on the platform with a drawn weapon, stood next to him, though he hardly looked either vigilant or concerned that his charges might try to escape. Kevin Durben casually moved aside so that he was just next to Greg's chair.

"Hey," Greg hissed while the crowd applauded the slender man before his speech began. "Hey, mister, don't look at me. That guy with the gun isn't paying any attention to you. Get his gun and threaten the old man with it. That'll be our ticket out.''

Durben heard the desperate whisper and looked down at the tightly strapped boy at his side. ''Do what?'' he asked.

''We've got to try, man. They're going to kill us.''

In response, Durben placed his forefinger to his lips and said, ''Shh, it's about to start.''

Greg stared back at the man with his mouth hanging open in shock.

Cathy expected a short sordid story to be told by the first man. She had heard enough from those who had been captured before her to understand that, for some reason, the gas that these people habitually inhaled heightened their capacity and need for cruel, physically torturous activity as well as stories about such activity, so she knew that whatever this man had to tell would be the sickest, worst thing he had ever done. But how bad could it be? Really, what kind of horror would the average man inflict on his neighbor during his average life? She expected a bloody war story. She got worse.

The man was a hobo who had been picked up by the ''Euphrata Welcome Wagon'' when he had the misfortune to jump from a freight that was taking on water in Euphrata, but he also was a drug user who had early turned to crime to support his habit. If what he recounted were true, the worst thing that he had ever done had taken place in Denver, Colorado, when he and four other reckless addicts had taken over an all-night restaurant in their search for money. They killed the staff and diners immediately and hid their bodies in the back of the isolated truckstop café, and then they had simply waited out the night, robbing and murdering everyone who was unfortunate enough to stop in for a cup of coffee.

It was clear that the man enjoyed the telling. His eyes took on an almost religious gleam as he recited the tortures, rapes (both heterosexual and homosexual), and inevitable murders inflicted on 18 people. It was the worst thing that Cathy could have imagined; at that instant it seemed worse even than her own impending death.

She looked at her companions in this forced audience. Louise seemed ready to vomit, and Frankie was muttering curses to himself and directing them at the Yorks and anyone connected with them. Greg looked pale, not frightened so much as revolted and incredulous, while poor little Gretchen was weeping quietly and apparently not hearing any of it. Cathy knew that she looked as bad as any of them.

Then she looked at the Euphratans. They were enthralled. Their faces glowed with pleasure, and occasionally, at a particularly vicious juncture or vivid description of some mutilation, they would applaud. A few of the younger disciples appeared to be repelled by the tale, although against their fervent desires, and some even looked as if they soon would be violently ill, but these formed an almost infinitesimal minority. I'll bet they don't make the grade tonight, Cathy thought.

Greg again tried to get through to the man standing near him. "Listen, mister," he whispered almost loudly enough to be heard by the others on the platform. "You've got to stop this. You know we're dead if we don't do something. If you won't go for the gun, at least loosen this strap—just this one on my right arm—and *I'll* tackle him!'' He honestly felt that in all of the attention being paid to the energetic story-teller, he might have the chance to free himself and overpower the man with the gun before he could be gunned down. ''I swear we'll take you out of here with us.''

Once more, Kevin Durben looked down at him. His heavy beard split open with a frown and he said, ''If you don't shut up, I'll have to tell the sheriff that you're trying to ferment unrest . . .''

''Are you crazy?'' Greg demanded too loudly. ''They're going to kill you—and your wife, too!'' One of the men who had ushered him in overheard and cuffed Greg painfully on the ear. ''You bastard!'' Greg spat. This brought only a harder rebuke.

Finally, the speaker ended his account and was greeted with a roar of cheering and applause that seemed capable of lifting the roof and the heavy mansion atop it right into the night sky. Cecil walked to the man's side and placed one un-wrinkled, unspotted hand on his shoulder.

''What do you say for this story, my children?'' he shouted. ''Has he earned a place among us?''

The responding yell of approval left no doubt as to their decision, and the man began crying with joy. When Cecil told him to go and mingle with his new brothers and sisters, he didn't bother with the stairs but leaped from the three-foot plat-form to the hard floor to be instantly swallowed up by laughing and shoulder-clapping Euphratans.

''The next candidate!'' Cecil ordered. Kevin

Durben strode into position with an eager smile on his lips. In the milling crowd below, his wife emitted a heartbroken sob.

Now Cathy was certain that she couldn't be surprised or shocked. The first man had recounted 18 murders in which he had taken part without detection, so there was nothing that this speaker could say that would top that for depravity, unless it was the firebombing of a nursery school. And once more she was wrong.

Durben's story did involve murder, but only one. His victim was raped and tortured over a period of months, but these activities weren't actually much more imaginative in execution than what the drug addicts had done to the café staff and diners. What made it so much worse to Cathy's ears? Perhaps it was the fact that the torture had been such a drawn out affair or that the victim had been an innocent young girl not much older than herself. Or maybe it was the admission that these had been children acting in wanton cruelty against another child. Whatever the cause, Cathy found herself crying along with Gretchen before Durben was half-finished.

Greg listened with emotional numbness. It was sort of like absorbing an extremely hard punch to the temple, one that sends you into a kind of gauzy nothingness. Why was it so much like a physical blow? Because he recognized, hidden somewhere deep within, a flickering kinship with Kevin Durben.

Would he ever have done the same if given the opportunity and the way out of it? Never! But still, he could almost understand how Durben had come to do what he had done to that poor young woman.

He had read and been fascinated by most of the novels that Durben named, but that was fiction! He never would have done anything like what this grinning devil was recalling to a bunch of slavering idiots.

At that moment, Greg suddenly realized that he was right about himself. He wouldn't have taken part in an abduction and murder, not even if a hundred friends had tried to bully him into it. He boxed because he liked the sport, not with intent to hurt or maim, and if he ever did kill, it would be in self-defense, the defense of someone he loved, or out of need for retribution. Never for pleasure! Even in the middle of all of this insanity, he experienced a tiny flash of satisfaction—he was not Kevin Durben and he never could have been.

Greg closed his eyes, as if this action would also shut out the gut-wrenching sounds of the story and the crowd's reaction to it. It did neither, but that image blinked before his inner sight again— the mummy, the girl inside the tape. My God, that's Angela! he screamed silently. How did I know? This is the first time I've heard it!

Greg, the mummy said to him.

His eyes flew open, delivering him from one impossibility to another. Durben was describing how he had beaten the girl to death with a rock, the crowd was almost orgasmic, and Cathy was crying at his side, only two feet away but too far for him to reach out and touch her pale and trembling hand.

I'm going crazy, he told himself.

Greg, she said again, *only you know, only you understand. Only you can save me.*

"What? What do you want of me? What can I

do?'' he cried aloud. The man with the gun slugged him in the back of the neck.

Angela continued to speak, though she was fading now. *I'll come to you later, if you'll let me. Don't reject me, Greg. I have no one else. If you don't help me—us, this will be our fate for eternity. Remember me.*

Then she was gone.

Durben finished his tale with a mad laughter that totally replaced the heart-rending sorrow he had felt in his first telling of it, and oh, how they appreciated it down there, the whooping, waving, clapping mob. They enjoyed his memory of the death of one young woman more than the 18 that the first speaker had supplied to them. He was a member of the Fellowship even before Cecil stepped up to ask for their decision, and he flew down the steps to share the moment with his wife. She spat on him.

"Now, my children, our business of the evening begins," Cecil called to the 5000, and immediately the huge room fell silent. "The telling of the true and only story has come to its time, but there are those who are not yet ready to hear it. I saw them while the new members spoke, those who were shocked and sickened by the purity of our gift. *You* saw them! Let those of weak constitution and incomplete understanding be cast out of this holy gathering. I say it!"

At the signal, the crowd operated again in synchronization to drag to their feet 16 young men and women who had had the poor taste to display basic human traits such as compassion and revulsion. These were shoved, punched, and slapped unmercifully toward a rear exit by the jeering disciples. They had proven themselves unworthy of the blessing, so by the time they had managed to escape, they were bleeding and crying in pain and humiliation.

A great cheer marked their expulsion.

Cecil calmed the service again. "With sixteen weak eliminated, this means that tonight we have the opportunity to admit twenty-one advanced new souls into full membership in our glorious Fellowship," he continued. "But first the Story must be told!" He paused and closed his eyes, letting the memories come rushing back to him.

"This is it," Greg whispered to Cathy, "the reason for the whole nightmare." With his inner voice, he added, Go to him, Angie; haunt that son of a bitch and not me. He received no answer.

Cecil began. "It took place sixty-eight years and one day ago, when the world was quiet and men knew that God lived in the heavens and not in the earth. Tiverton was a hamlet and Euphrata, our Euphrata, only a dream. This dream would have been stillborn had not Providence shown to me the gift of perfect health and healing.

"We were digging in the good earth, my brothers and I, preparing the foundation for a huge dwelling to be inhabited by the atheistic A.H. Hotchkiss and his people. We knew of the great caves to the south, the Wyandotte cavern and others, but we knew nothing of such caves here in the body of this mountain, until the very ground gave way beneath our feet.

"We fell like angels hurled from heaven before the beginning of the world. Virgil York, the oldest and tallest of us, the father of six poor motherless children, vanished into the earth first, and in trying to save him, young and fair-haired Lionel was dragged into the black maw as well."

Cecil fell quiet for a moment, and the entire assemblage could hear Hermoine York sobbing at this story she had heard dozens of times in her 46 years.

Cecil then went on. "I stood over the dark opening to death, and even as I cried my brothers' names and called out for help from the other workmen, I began to smell the sweetness of the holy vapor that only God Himself could have placed there. It was minutes before I recalled that everyone else had left the building site early that day, leaving the three York brothers to carry on alone, and even then I couldn't bring myself to leave Virgil and Lionel in that pit to fetch other help. I screamed their names but was rewarded only with silence. I prayed to the Good Lord in the dying red sun as no man had prayed before or since, but no one seemed to hear my prayers. Then I crept to the edge of the opening in hopes of spying my brothers, and the earth took me as well."

Cries of anguish broke out in the audience, and several of the younger members began to whisper, "Grandfather Cecil."

He waved them to silence. "Though my brothers had lost their lives, in death they saved mine. I fell through eternity only to land like a flaring comet atop their mangled bodies on a narrow ledge above the endless depths. They cushioned me so that I was spared death, though my back was broken and all of the bones on my right side smashed to dust. I, too, surely would have died had not I been enveloped by the wonderful vapor.

"I lay in blackness and agony for one night and most of the next day before my fellow workers discovered the three apparently lifeless men one hundred feet below the surface of the earth. When they finally sent down a man on a rope, he himself almost died when I raised my torn face from the blood-soaked ground and asked for water. Eighteen hours after I should have died, I was nearly half-healed of my mortal injuries, and, my children, that very opening is there, at the far side of this room!" He stabbed a forefinger at the block enclosure near the west wall of the chamber. A spontaneous eruption of cheering rattled the ceiling again.

The demonstration was so powerful that it was well over a minute before even Cecil could quell it.

"But that was just the beginning," he roared like a miniaturized lion. "Hotchkiss, the unbelieving disciple of worldliness, refused to accept that the Lord had placed this miracle in Euphrata for a special purpose. He told the few neighbors that this was his land, and that he would reveal its secrets to the entire, profane world—to the infidels, the Negroes, the Orientals, and the fools who trust in worldly things. He would not listen to the voice of reason, and so when his rebellion threatened the revocation of this most blessed of gifts, we, the believers, took the issue in hand by acting as God had intended.

"There was a second opening into the caves below revealed to us by providence, and since it seemed not to contain the same amount of healing ether, we recognized that its destiny was to be a recepticle for those who would prevent the proper use of the blessing. With a ladder, we gave our sacrifice to the earth. We put Hotchkiss, his wife, his sons, and his daughters into the mouth of that cave that lies beneath this platform on which I stand!''

The eruption resumed, but Greg was still able to hear Cathy crying out, ''Oh, Jesus, they put them down there to starve!'' and he immediately knew what lay in store for them once the ceremony was over.

Cecil drew himself up to his full height of less than five and a half feet and literally screamed in triumph, ''These are the words! Heaven *is* Earth! We are the Chosen! We give ourselves to the Blessing, we pledge our lives to its secret and its defense, and we remove those who would betray its glory to the masses! As we have done in the past, so shall we do in the future!''

The celebration literally exploded then, with the robed people leaping to their feet and dancing in joy. From one of the numerous doors leading into the chamber, a dozen men appeared carrying kegs of some sort of beverage, and they were instantly engulfed by the members of the Fellowship, each begging to drink from the kegs. It wasn't difficult to realize that this must be the alcoholic drink that was used to ward off the sleep-induced effects of the gas. The main event was rapidly approaching, obviously.

''Defenders of the Blessing!'' Greg shouted at the top of his lungs while he surged upward against the confinement of the straps. The acoustics were so good that he actually was heard by a good part of the crowd. ''Murderers and rapists, that's what you are!'' The noise level of the room dropped abruptly, as the people turned to stare at him. ''You keep the greatest discovery of all time your own little secret, while you commit crimes that would make decent men and women vomit with revulsion. You don't *defend* the secrecy of the gas; you seek out innocent people to use in these barbaric ceremonies and to rob to increase your own wealth! What's divine about that? What's to prove you more worthy of the blessing than some reptile crawling on its belly through the slime?"

"Don't get 'em mad, man," Frankie hissed.

"What difference could it make now?" he replied. "These animals are going to kill us no matter what we say or do."

"We kill no one," Cecil proclaimed.

"Forcing people into a hole in the ground to starve or die of thirst and exposure isn't murder? Don't try to justify your murders to me, you sanctimonious little jackass!"

"Below us is the opening provided by God to receive those unworthy of the Blessing!"

"Below us is a cave!" Cathy screamed. "That gas comes from another cave or another part of the same one, and it belongs to the entire human race, not some twisted little fraction of it. Can't you see what it's done to you?"

"It's given us the miracle of perfect health."

"It's driven you insane."

"You will be silent," Cecil thundered indignantly.

Greg's voice was now lower in pitch, but it still carried throughout the hall. "And you and everybody like you can go straight to hell!"

Hermie reacted with furious speed by slapping his face with much more power than the armed guard had employed.

"Bring the nectar to the platform," Cecil commanded. "Let these traitors who will pay most severely for their crimes drink deeply so that they will not be offered the escape of sleep when the time for their penance arrives."

One of the men carrying the liquor quickly brought his keg to the stage and filled a tin ladle with it. He shoved this into Louise's face. "Drink it all," he ordered.

She tried to turn away, but the man grabbed her head with his free hand and then pressed the ladle between her lips while the keg dangled from a strap that crossed over his back and shoulder. Louise reluctantly swallowed and began coughing violently, but the man roughly forced her to drink all of the yellowish liquid.

Greg didn't want to lose consciousness anyway, so he readily accepted the next cup and swallowed it. It tasted like strong—and bad—beer.

Cathy could hardly stand the taste of the stuff, but she forced herself to drink some of it.

Frankie seemed pleased when the cup reached him. He gladly took a huge mouthful of the beverage and then, when the man was expecting no further trouble from him, spat every drop of it back into his face. He laughed in high-pitched, almost hysterical mirth even as the furious man and one other guard worked him over with their fists. Greg struggled like a man possessed, but he was unable to loosen the leather straps about his wrists and chest; finally, a bleeding and only half-conscious Frankie was forced to drink.

Last, a terrified Gretchen was half-strangled by the beer that was forced down her throat and splashed over much of her body.

"Now we will try the accused," Cecil shouted. "These five here have proven themselves to be wolves among us, hiding beneath the guises of friendship and concern, while in truth they seek to destroy our world." He paused in his speech to make a slow, dramatic walk before the five prisoners, and his eyes danced over them like twin barrels of a loaded gun. He stopped in front of Frankie and then stepped behind the chair which held him. "Here, we first have a resident of our own community, a man who could have overcome both his youth and his race to bring more glory to this very ceremony, a man who could have been one of us with the use of his legs restored to him had he not chosen to ally himself with the outside forces of chaos and evil. His name is Francis Holloway, and my words are that he has proven himself a devil through his undeniable perfidy!"

The crowd drew in a breath that seemed to suck the air from Frankie's own lungs and screamed as one, "Put him down!"

"Yeah, I would have as much chance of cracking this club as I would of walking on a highwire," Frankie shouted back at them. "You can all go to hell!"

Cecil clutched a fistful of Frankie's hair and used it to jerk the young man's head back sharply so that the two of them could stare eye to eye. "Hold that evil tongue or I'll order it cut out of your pagan mouth, boy!"

"Screw you!" Frankie answered.

Hermie placed her right hand on Louise's head. "And this is Louise Simpson, who lived among us as one of us, who was given charge over the local library and who was permitted to instruct our children what to read and think. All of this while she was spying on us, collecting filth against the day that she would bring her foolish theories to the outside authorities. Shall she be freed, knowing the type of damage that she could have done to our way of life?"

"No, no, put her down! Put her down!" the audience chanted wildly.

"You won't get away with this. You'll be caught and punished," Louise responded. She whipped her head violently from side to side and finally threw off her now unneeded eyeglasses so that she might see her executioners with perfect vision for the first time in her life.

"We will do what we wish when we wish," Hermie whispered with delight in the woman's ear. "You'll see that soon enough for yourself." Her hand slipped down the front of Louise's dress and between her breasts, drawing an anguished cry from the bound woman.

Sheriff Reed, the tallest man in the chamber due to the absence of Gerhard and looking like a muscular Jeroboam in his green robe, stepped behind Cathy and bellowed, "Catherine Lockwood! A girl who came to us in disguise to try to expose our wonders because her brother had brought about his own death in his effort to escape with our secret! A cunning and remorseless little harlot! How should we repay her traitorous crimes after she has been made to provide a sacrifice for the ceremony!"

Again the cry came, "Put her down!"

Reed smiled coldly. "Yes, but afterwards."

"You savages! You murdering scum!" Cathy shrieked. At that instant, she was more caught up in the fury that was inspired by her brother's death than in her own immediate danger.

Reed roughly caught Greg by the back of the

head. "And beside her is Gregory Hoode, the nephew of one of our own members, a boy who was within a day of being welcomed into our number, until he conspired with this treacherous slut to bring about our destruction. What is his fate to be?"

"Put him down!"

Certainly it was no surprise to Greg. His eyes searched for and found Daniel, even though the man looked so much like any other member of the mob in his ridiculous robe. He was standing next to Diana Meredith. "What are you going to tell them, Uncle Dan?" he called. "When they ask what happened to their son, how will you explain? That I ran away with the village whore?"

Daniel covered his face with the voluminous sleeves of the robe, and Diana put both arms about his shoulders. Greg didn't care that the man was crying.

Cecil took the last position in the line of captives. He looked down at the trembling girl with a harsh, deadly smile. "And what of this little one?" he asked in a surprisingly restrained voice. "This child, who was without family or guidance when we took her and gave her a home and love? This child who was allowed the rare privilege of living among us and serving the Blessing every day of her life!" Now his voice began to rise toward insanity again. "This creature who has received much only to repay our efforts with indefensible treachery?"

"Please, please, please," Gretchen begged desperately. "Please, I go to work now . . . no trouble, ever again, I work hard, please!"

"Put her down," the maddened audience demanded.

Gretchen, too, sought and found the face of a supposed friend amid the wild-eyed mob. "Please, Cook, I sorry! Help me here!"

Borden Davis, "Cook," had been lost in the emotions of the mob, but as he looked into those sweet, guileless green eyes and then at the pinioned hands which were working so helplessly and eloquently, his face went pale. For half a second, it seemed that he might speak for her, but then something more powerful overcame the need and he dropped his head, unable to meet her gaze.

Gretchen's heart broke. "Please don't let them put me down there! Cook?"

"Has she the mentality to be held responsible for her treason?" Cecil asked.

"No!" Greg suddenly exploded. He knew that this was her only hope. "Of course, she doesn't. What happened was my fault. I convinced her to help us, to come downstairs wth us. She's just a baby. You can't kill her for something I caused!"

Noleta Thrush broke from the howling pack, ran to the edge of the platform, and slapped her open hand down on the wood with a sound like a gunshot. "She must be punished! That is our ruling! Put her down!"

"I'm sorry, sorry!" Gretchen cried.

"I think not," Cecil stated in a cool tone that still carried more power than any voice that had spoken before him. "Have we not mercy among our many gifts? The effects of the holy vapor and the efforts of the most brilliant brain specialist that the human race has to offer have not been able to free her poor little mind from the convolutions of her stupidity. She paid her penance last night, and that shall extend even to the deeds she performed against us today. I rule that we shall free her to return to her household duties.''

"That is not the law. We ruled!'' Noleta shouted without thinking.

Cecil turned his eyes on her, which immediately set everything into perspective. "Perhaps you should like to take her place in the sentence then, my dear?'' he asked.

Terror electrified Noleta's features. She dropped her head submissively and backed into the anonymous safety of the huge group, frantically repeating, "Please forgive me, Grandfather Cecil, please forgive me.''

Cecil responded with a short nod toward the man who had brought the keg of liquor onto the stage. Gretchen watched in apparent incredulity as this man quickly unfastened the straps at her wrists and ankles. Greg was watching him closely, too, though his eyes were locked on the Lugar that the man wore in a small holster belted outside the robe. His guts boiled with the need to reach that gun and the impotence that prevented him from moving.

Cathy thought. She had thought that perhaps Cecil York had actually displayed some human compassion in allowing Gretchen to go free, in addition to a bit of affection for the retarded girl, but when she looked at the old man's face as he watched Wally loosening the leather bonds, Cathy realized that compassion and affection had had no influence on his decision. She also knew that this would not be Gretchen's last participation in a ceremony.

"Rise and leave us, little one,'' Cecil told the girl, "and always remember the grace shown to you here this night, as well as where your allegiance must lie throughout the unending future.''

''Thank you,'' Gretchen whispered as she took Wally's hand and stood. She still looked so frightened—then, with a sudden speed and craftiness that Cathy and Greg had never suspected her to possess, she clawed at the eyes of the startled disciple with one hand and snatched the gun from his belt with the other. Wally cried out and staggered back, clutching his face.

''You little savage,'' Cecil gasped in disbelief. ''You'll be beaten for that severely and tied up again—''

''You sh-shut up!'' Gretchen screamed. Holding the gun in both shaking hands, she shoved it directly into his face. ''No more! No more beating, n-no more of any . . . you l-let them go, right now, or I shoot you! You let us go away from here!''

The entire assembly gasped.

''Hot dog, girl,'' Frankie chortled. ''Get us out of here!''

''Unstrap me first and then give me the gun, Gretchen,'' Greg said urgently but not loudly enough to panic her.

''Y-yes, Mr. Greg,'' she said, nodding. ''Let him go!''

She was trembling like a leaf, and there was a good chance that she would have missed the old man had she fired, but Cecil's expression went from surprise through indignation and right into scared stiff. It left no doubt that he felt himself to be an instant away from a death that he had planned to postpone for perhaps centuries. Not even the gas could cure a bullet in the brain.

"N-now!" she commanded with terrified authority.

"Release them," Cecil croaked.

With the physical assurance of a powerful athlete, Baxter Reed took a single step toward Gretchen and swung his own gun like a blackjack.

"Gretchen!" Cathy screamed.

The barrel of the weapon struck the girl's skull with a dull and ghastly sound that brought cries and curses from the captives. Gretchen fell like a cardboard mannequin and lay as still as death on the platform. She was hardly even breathing. Reed picked up the fallen gun, thrust it into the hands of the bleeding man, and slapped him viciously across the face with an open hand.

"You be more careful next time, Wally," he ordered gruffly. "That's the second time today you've let a little girl get the best of you."

"Yes, sir, I will," Wally answered, red-faced with pain, humiliation, and anger.

"You son of a bitch!" Greg spat. He leaped forward in the chair and strained with every muscle to free himself. He wanted to hit Reed so badly that his body ached for it. "You and me, just the two of us! We'll put on a show for the rest of these idiots. Give me the chance, and I swear I'll kick your fat butt up between your ears!"

Reed's reply was offhanded and cool. "Shut up, kid, or I'll turn Gerhard loose on you again. Continue whenever you're ready, Father Cecil."

Cecil shook himself like a wet dog and seemed to resume breathing. "Yes!" he shouted. "See the fates that befall the treasonous and what will befall all who pervert the uses of the Blessing. Take these evil profligates to the preparatory rooms and attire them for the ceremony. Then will the vapor be released and the celebration begin, while they pay for their actions.''

The room was flooded again with wildly joyous cheering, and the captives were released from the chairs by wary armed men; none of them would be caught the way that Wally had been. The captives were forced from the stage and driven through the midst of the frenzied crowd, with Frankie being carried by one of the thugs and the unconscious Gretchen over the shoulder of another. The disciples, whipped nearly to madness and shouting all kinds of curses and epithets, began pressing forward and actually hitting and spitting on the five. Greg's heart was pounding with rage and fear, but even as he tensed the muscles across his back, the guard assigned to him placed a gun against the rear of his neck.

''Do it and you'll be dead before you hit the floor,'' the man promised.

Greg's eyes sought and found Cathy's. This was it, the roll of the dice that would decide if they lived or experienced an agonizing, lingering death below the ground, effectively buried alive.

And he didn't have the shadow of an idea about what his next move would be.

Chapter Thirteen

"But we can stay here now," Kevin shouted over the excited buzz of the crowd about him. "I did it, babe. I convinced them."

Pamela was strapped into a chair in front of the stage; to either side of her sat five other unfortunate prisoners, all virtually ignored by the happy members of the Fellowship. The annual celebration promised to be something far beyond the smaller monthly gatherings.

"If you just promise to abide by the rules, move with me here to Euphrata, and contribute the proper respect to the Yorks and the traditions, I'm sure they'll let you stay above ground." He continued to speak to her through an urgently happy smile. "You're my wife, and since I'm a member—"

"It really was true," Pamela said wonderingly. "I thought . . . I prayed until just this moment that you made it up to save our lives, but I can't fool myself anymore. But I can forgive you, Kevin, even of that, if you'll just get us out of this nightmare. We have to get away before that damned gas ruins your mind completely.''

''Damned gas?'' he respeated with a stunned look. ''Pam, that gas is what makes this the perfect place. No more disease, no more injury! Christ, we might live forever because of that gas. And everything else that Euphrata has to offer . . .''

''What? Dehumanization? These people are monsters, Kevin,'' she said, desperately trying to penetrate the deranged shield that had formed about his mind. ''They rape and torture and kill for pleasure. Come back to me, Kevin. You could never live with that on your conscience.''

Their eyes met, and for the only time in her entire life, Pamela felt total and utter hopelessness. ''I've lived with it for fifteen years,'' he said, and there was no trace of regret or sorrow in his voice.

''Well, I can't.''

He smiled. ''Then, I guess you'll go down to hell tonight, won't you?'' He turned and walked away from her.

Pamela dropped her head almost to the strap that was cinched so cruelly across her chest.

When the five captives reached the west wall and passed by the block structure that covered the shaft that Cecil had fallen into sixty-eight years ago, the man carrying Frankie turned to the right and the man holding the gun on Greg shoved him in that direction. The others went to the left.

"Hey, hold on a minute," Greg said, stopping abruptly.

"You want to die right here, boy?" the guard asked tightly.

"I want to find out what in the hell is going on. Where are they being taken?"

"None of your business, loudmouth! Move it!" The man cocked the gun.

Hermie York was accompanying the woman, and she stopped both groups with a wave of her hand. "Gregory, we are not barbarians, you know," she said. "You have to change into your robes, so we're providing separate dressing rooms."

"How utterly civilized," Frankie commented sarcastically. "I wonder how long these stinking robes will stay on us?"

"That's just something that you'll have to find out for yourself, isn't it?" she replied.

"Let's go," the man behind Greg ordered.

Greg tried to summon up a comforting smile for Cathy, but he didn't feel successful at it.

The room into which he and Frankie were taken was not actually a dressing room. Just as the holding cell earlier in the evening had proven to be a furniture storage area, so did this turn out to be a workshop of some sort, one cluttered with carpenter's tools and sawdust on the floor. Greg immediately took stock of the tools, but he realized that a hammer or a handsaw made a mighty poor answer to a pistol. Someone had left several extra emerald-colored robes on a ratty old sofa, and Frankie was dumped unceremoniously next to them.

"Get undressed," the man with the gun

ordered.

"Get bent," Frankie replied.

The man calmly aimed the gun in the boy's direction and squeezed the trigger. The explosion sounded like the end of the world in that small room, and a spot no more than five inches from Frankie's head was blown all the way through the sofa. Frankie threw himself to the floor, and Greg threw himself at the gun.

He pulled up short when the barrel was pointed at his forehead.

"I'm not going to say it again, boys," the man told them.

Frankie began cursing under his breath while he unbuttoned his shirt.

Cathy, Louise, and Gretchen were taken to Professor Kasha's esoteric chamber of mirrors. Louise was struck speechless by the awesome sight. Cathy was again gripped by the sensation of freefalling through a sky filled with clones of herself and the mild nausea that came with it.

"Okay, boys, that will do just fine. Run along now," Hermie told the men who had brought them to the room, after one had placed Gretchen on the smooth glass floor.

Sheriff Reed opened the door to the huge auditorium and waved the others out. "I'll be right outside, Miz York, in case you need me."

Hermie smiled coldly. "I'm sure there won't be any problems with the girls, but thank you, Sheriff."

Immediately, a shot rang out from one of the other rooms, causing Louise and Cathy to gasp aloud. Hermie simply chuckled.

"Sounds as if your boyfriend resisted a bit too much," she said. "Just the way your brother did."

Cathy was barely able to find her voice. "Why . . . ?"

Hermie shrugged. "It was just a couple of days until the monthly ceremony. We needed sacrifices, and your brother and sister-in-law were available. We planned to take them on the night of the ceremony, as we usually do with guests, but when your brother came down the morning after checking in and said that he and his wife would be leaving after breakfast, we realized that we would have to act quickly. They fit our needs so nicely.

"Your brother left to gas up the car, and while he was gone, we took the woman. She was no problem. When he returned, we intended to take him as well, but he fought—my, how he fought, even though we had drugged his breakfast with one of Tony's concoctions. The end result was that he was killed during the struggle. Tony hit him in the temple with a hammer."

Cathy felt the hot tears rising in her eyes like acid, but she held them back. She wouldn't cry, not in front of this monster.

"It was self-defense, I assure you. Well, the woman was in hand, but your brother was entirely useless to us for the ceremony. We have no dealings with the dead. Some said to drop him into the cave, but that would have been a sacrilege. We were planning to bury him in the stables until the sheriff arrived and suggested that we might get rid of the body and the car and forestall any official investigation into the disappearances by dumping them into the Ohio. He and

Wally drove to Tiverton and ran the little car into the river after smashing the windshield and leaving the passenger door open. Then Wally made the call to the Tiverton police."

"B-but . . . his head . . ."

"Oh, Tony kept that for study and dissection. He's very interested in heads and brains, you know. I believe he has part of it in a jar in his lab."

Finally, Cathy knew all of it, and her grief was multiplied rather than eased. "I hope that you die in agony," she whispered.

Hermie grinned. "That's quite possible, but you'll never see it. Now, take off your clothes and put on these robes." To add emphasis to her order, she withdrew a handgun from beneath her own robe.

"It will catch up to you," Cathy went on. "You can't go through life hurting and killing without paying for it some day. You and that crazy monkey of a grandfather will see the time when all of these ghosts are given the opportunity to avenge themselves. And Mikey and I will be among the first."

Hermie's smile vanished, and her lips grew thin and white. "I told you to get dressed."

It was Cathy's turn to smile, and it drove an icy spike into Hermie's heart.

Greg had once told a friend that, if faced with certain death, he would go down with all guns firing, rather than as some docile martyr with his hands tied behind him and a bullet in his brain. It had been easy to say and had sounded good, but it was proving to be very difficult to back up.

But that was how he was going to go.

Why? Because he didn't want to starve down there? Because he felt that he had to do something to give Frankie and Louise and Gretchen a chance? Or was it really because he realized in the depths of his soul that he had to do anything to get Cathy out of this alive?

It was clear that the cops weren't going to rush in at the last second in cinematic fashion and that Uncle Dan wasn't going to experience a change of heart, so the whole matter was up to him.

The second man who had brought him into the room was swearing while he helped Frankie struggle out of his pants. Ignoring the first man, the one with the gun, Greg moved in on the pair as if to offer his aid.

"Let me," he said, carefully positioning the second thug between himself and the pointing weapon. "It's not hard if you take your time."

"If this geek would help a little," the man complained.

"Inhale a walnut, fungusbrain," Frankie said.

"Here we go," Greg said, then he kneed the stooped man in the face.

Pain laced through his leg like a shock of electricity, but the damage to the man's nose and mouth was much worse than any little injury he might have sustained. The man's head shot up and back, allowing Greg to catch him by the hair and throw him with crazed strength at the gunman, who was only four feet away. The gun roared once and the pair went down with arms and legs flailing.

Greg had no time to think, but instinct told him that he had to keep moving and make things happen, or he really would be dead and so would Cathy. He leaped onto the struggling bodies with

his own fists and feet adding to the madness. He
heard neither the screams of the wounded man,
the bellows of the gunman on the bottom, or his
own wild cries, but strangely he did hear Frankie
shouting, "Get them, Gregorio, go, go, go!"

The gun was trapped somewhere between the
two men, but Greg quickly remembered they were
in a workshop. His right hand found a hammer
on its own initiative, and he brought it down on
the writhing mass just three times before both of
his opponents lay still. He didn't know if either or
both of the men were dead, and, actually, he
didn't give a damn.

"You did it, boy. You saved our asses!"
Frankie laughed. "It was beautiful, man, the
most beautiful thing I've ever seen."

"We're not out of it yet, Franklin," Greg
pointed out while rolling one man off the other
and retrieving the gun. "We're still in this place
with about five thousand unfriendlies surrounding us."

"Hell, yeah, but I like our chances a whole lot
better now." Frankie's elation then cooled when
faced with the reality of the situation. "We've
still got to get the women out of here, Greg. We
can't leave them with those crazies."

"Don't intend to, chum." Greg checked the
gun and found four shots left, laid it on the sofa,
then pulled his shirt over his head.

"What's our plan, man?" Frankie asked.

Greg slipped off his shoes and socks and
dragged a green robe over his head. It felt like a
tent. "I'm going out there incognito, if you'll
pardon the expression, to find them. Also I'm
going to ask one hell of a contribution from
you."

"Say it, Greg. I'd swim in burning oil to get back at those animals."

"How well can you get around without your chair? At all?"

Frankie rolled from his back to his stomach. "I have to go with my arms alone, and that plays hell with my elbows, but I can cruise pretty good this way."

"Good. I want you to find a phone and get the Tiverton police up here as fast as possible—make that the state police. You'll probably have to climb the stairs to the ground floor."

"It's as good as done, but what about the long distance operator? Everybody at the place knows my voice, and if Reed's warned them, they'll never put through a call for me."

Greg sat heavily on the sofa. "Damn! We've got to have them or we'll never get out of this town alive."

"Maybe if *you* called . . ."

"Nah. I've made enough calls to Atlanta in the last month to be instantly recognizable. I've even tried to date a few of the operators." He looked at the gun, trying to concentrate. If he left the house long enough to get to the telephone office and force someone to put through . . . no, not without Cathy. The inspiration hit him without warning. "What if we get another local to make the call for us? The operator won't refuse to put through a call for someone she doesn't suspect."

"Sounds good, but how do we pick this person? And how do we know that he or she isn't involved in all of this? I don't mind telling you, there are some pretty surprising faces getting ready to play Marquis de Sade out there."

"Shit, that's the truth. What about your

aunt?''

"You can bet my entire family is on that list alongside of us.''

"Wait, what was it that Louise said? That she was the only person in town who wore glasses? Do you know any other handicapped people around here?''

"In Euphrata?'' Frankie snorted. "Forget it.''

Greg literally pounded his head with the heel of one hand. It was there, if only he could dig it out.

"Stern! Ed Stern, the motel man! Call him!''

"Why Ed?''

"He's bald!''

"So?''

"So this gas must also cause the regrowth of hair or keep it from falling out. Look at Cecil—almost a hundred and even with that crew cut, you can tell he's hairy as an ape. And Uncle Dan was losing his hair before he moved here. Stern must not be involved or he'd still have all of his.''

"All right! But what do I tell him?''

"The code is . . . 'Operation Triangle is go.' Tell him you're working for Reed or something, and he'll trust you because you steer so much business his way. Get him to call the state police in Tiverton with that code, and then get the hell out of this house.''

Painfully, but with surprising quickness, Frankie elbowed himself to the hallway door, dragging his limp legs. He stretched up his long right arm to twist the knob. "I can make you a stone promise as to the first part, Greg—I *will* get that call out—but I ain't pledging anything about what happens after that.''

Greg started to press the issue, but he saw the

intensity in Frankie's eyes. "Okay, man, do what you have to. We'll get them."

"All of them," Frankie added. He pointed at Greg and received a confirming thumbs-up. Then he crawled through the door and into the black hallway beyond.

Greg took the gun in his right hand and drew it back and up into the long, billowing sleeve. After making certain that the two breathing bodies on the floor were still safely unconscious, he opened the door that led down to the auditorium and moved carefully into the milling crowd.

"Now, get her into this," Hermie ordered, tossing another robe to an already dressed Cathy. She was speaking of Gretchen.

Cathy stepped to the side of the still girl. "Lord, she's as cold as ice. I think that animal fractured her skull."

"So what? She never used that part of her anatomy very effectively anyway. Put the robe on her."

Louise helped Cathy to gently roll Gretchen to her side. The small girl groaned in pain, and her eyelids fluttered uncertainly. "My head hurts," she whispered weakly.

"Shh," Cathy responded. "They'll open the vents to the gas in a little while, and then you'll feel better."

Gretchen's eyes opened, and she stared upward in obvious surprise. "Cathy?" she asked, and her voice sounded different and strange. "Is that you?"

"That's right. Take it easy; we have to get this robe on you."

In spite of their restraining hands, the girl sat up and rested her face in her hands. "God, my head is throbbing. What happened?"

How ironic, Cathy thought. In the last hours of her life, a vicious blow to the head has allowed her to regain her faculties, one of those remissions Noleta mentioned. "The sheriff hit you, Gretchen."

"Who?" she asked. "The, uh . . ." Her voice faded away as she gazed at the mirrored surfaces that surrounded them.

"Hurry up," Hermie snapped.

Gretchen's eyes seemed to glaze over while she looked at the countless images of Cathy, Louise, Hermie and herself. "Where am I?" she sighed. "Yes, oh yes . . ."

"Can you stand?" Louise asked.

"I'm all right," she answered, and she stood almost unaided to prove it.

"Gretchen, I'm sure you know what will happen to you if you don't do as you're instructed—" Hermie was cut off by the sharp report of yet a second gunshot from the direction of the room where the boys had been taken. She looked that way automatically. "That Greg must really be putting up a fight.'

Like a little wildcat, Gretchen threw herself onto the older, larger woman. Hermione had absolutely no time to defend herself before she was knocked back into the nearest shimmering wall and then driven to the floor. Gretchen's voice became a shrill and inarticulate wail as she punched, slapped and scratched Hermie with both hands to reduce her features to a bloody pulp. It seemed that at any instant Gretchen even would resort to using her teeth on the woman.

Only once did Hermie manage to push away the crazed form and half-aim the gun at her chest, but even then Gretchen was swift enough to kick out and connect with the woman's chin. Then she clutched two fistfuls of Hermie's hair and began slamming her head repeatedly into the floor. Before Cathy and Louise could react, Hermie was unconscious, the mirror below her was shattered, and the gun lay free near her right hand.

"Good heavens!" gasped Louise. "Gretchen, that was amazing!"

"We've got to get out of here before they come for us," Gretchen said. She snapped up the gun and removed the clip as if she had been handling firearms most of her life. Her face quickly registered disappointment. "Damn it! Empty! She was threatening us with a gun she hadn't even reloaded!" In a fury, she threw the gun from her and smashed yet another mirror.

"Don't!" Cathy cried. "We can still use it to bluff our way out of here after we find Greg and Frankie."

Gretchen scrambled after the weapon, muttering. "That's right. We'll make them let us go."

But the door suddenly flew open to reveal Baxter Reed holding a pistol that they were very certain *was* loaded.

"You little demon," he grunted, seeing Gretchen astride Hermie's motionless form and reaching for the empty pistol. "I think we've had just about enough trouble from you for one night. Stand up."

Gretchen slowly complied, her eyes glued to his gun.

Reed raised it menacingly. "Now, come here."

* * *

Monty Loomis loved these ceremonies. He never missed one. When old man York made his way across the hall to the block building housing the vapor pump, Monty led the ringing cheers, and when he unlocked the heavy metal door, Monty was right there at his side to help swing the panel aside. In fact, it was a good bet that Monty got the first lungful of the scarlet gas after the pump was switched into operation.

He already had something of a buzz from the three cups of nectar that he had gulped down, so it took only seconds for the hallucinogenic properties of the gas to begin to work their magic on his mind. He was envisioning himself leaving the mortal world behind and soaring right through the mansion above into the moonlit sky.

He sobered in a fraction of a second when something painfully hard was jabbed into the center of his back and a voice filled with hate whispered, "Just flinch, man, and I'll blow your spine through the front of your chest. Then I'll put another slug into your brain."

"What?" Monty asked numbly.

"You're going to take me to where the women are, the women who are to be put into the hole, understand?"

"They're right there, in front of the platform!"

The weapon knifed against his backbone. "The others! Cathy!" the voice hissed.

"Sure, no trouble. Just take it easy!"

"Right, but I'm going to take you out if you make the first mistake," the other promised in a cold tone that sounded awfully menacing to Monty. "Remember that."

Monty was terrified. He was a sheriff's deputy who had never fired his gun, and he knew that not even Grandfather Cecil's vapor could save him from a bullet in the brain. "Just follow me, Brother, and stay real cool. I wouldn't do anything to give you away, I swear."

"If you do, it'll be the last thing you ever do," the voice told him.

They walked together at a slow, leisurely pace through the sea of mind-tripping disciples.

Greg had been right. Frankie had to climb to the ground floor before he could locate a telephone. He did examine a couple of rooms near the workshop before coming to this conclusion, but as much as he dreaded the ordeal, he realized that his only option was the damned staircase.

It was a real bitch. His elbows were torn and bleeding, and he didn't want to think of what the abuse was doing to his numb legs. Then, when he had almost reached the ground floor landing, his luck went on hold and he fell, like some movie stuntman, all the way to the bottom again.

He lay at the foot of the staircase for a long time, bleeding, bruised and probably broken. His lips were pouring blood, he had lost at least one tooth in the fall, he felt sure that more than one rib on his right side had been fractured, and his left ankle hurt like hell. Man, he was licked solid. He'd never make it up that mountain in this shape, and even if he did, he would be way too slow to do Greg and Cathy and the others any good. But he was determined.

Painfully, he dragged himself back to the stairs and resumed the long, torturous climb. He was halfway up this time when the mind-boggling truth of what he had felt after the fall slapped him in the face. *His left foot hurt!*

He looked down at the grotesquely twisted foot and almost fell again. He hadn't had so much as a twinge from either of his legs or feet in 12 years, and now his ankle was hurting!

Frankie threw back his head and roared with laughter. That damned gas was working! After only a few hours of exposure to it, there was nerve regeneration in his dead legs, and in a few days. . . God, he might even be able to walk again!

He never recalled completing the climb or opening the door to the ground floor. His jubilant spirit carried his body through the trial like an eagle soaring with a mouse. He found a telephone moments later in a deserted bedroom and, remembering the dozens of calls made from the bus stop, he dialed Stern's motel.

Ed was suspicious at first, as well he might be, and this led Frankie to doubt Greg's assertion that the man was not a part of the insanity at the York mansion, but when he followed the suggestion to invoke Sheriff Reed's name, the motel owner perked up instantly. Frankie told him that a huge drug bust involving out-of-town dealers was underway on the York property, and that since he himself was participating, he was in no position to wait for a long distance call to go through.

It was a half-assed tale from all angles, but not nearly as wild as the truth, which Ed never would have accepted. Finally, the moderately gullible Stern agreed that he would do his duty as a citizen of Euphrata, phone the state police department in Tiverton, and declare "Operation Triangle is go!"

After all, what kind of trouble could he get into by anonymously telephoning the police?

Frankie thanked him for his courage and hung up. One job taken care of. Now, he was determined to fulfill the second part. Greg had instructed him to get his butt safely away from the house, but he knew with a deep certainty that Greg and the women would never find their way through 5000 maniacs without some sort of diversionary tactic to help them. But what?

He crawled into the hallway that connected with the garage, searching desperately for an answer and now feeling faint sensations in both legs. The garage contained a half-dozen vehicles, none of which he could drive—yet. He couldn't call his Aunt Martha, because she would charge right up here and plunge into the thick of things, and he couldn't risk her safety that way. He had to do something on his own, some quick and radical stroke.

He saw the gas can sitting alone in the corner.

It was half-full. It was also as dangerous as hell. But this was a radical situation, to say the least. Okay, he had to do something, and this was all that was presenting itself.

Frankie was sweating bullets, both from effort and nerves, as he pushed the can ahead of him into the night and then spread the gasoline all around the outside of the garage. Trailing a small stream of the fluid away from the house and into the safety of the yard was next to impossible, but he did it without a second thought. He was some 60 feet from the mansion when the metal can went dry. He tossed it with all of his might back toward the house behind him.

There had to be dozens of ways out of the auditorium, if all of the doors he had seen down there were any indication, but he still couldn't shake the feeling that he was starting a bonfire that would grill probably the best friend that he had ever known.

Frankie didn't smoke, though he always carried a box of matches for those bus passengers who did partake. He dug these out after rolling a few extra feet away from the rivulet of gasoline. He lit the first match and threw it at the gas.

It fell short into the dewy grass and sputtered out. A second followed suit. The third seemed to do the trick, but actually it had landed in an isolated pool of gas and flared out briefly before dying. Ah, but the fourth . . . Just as he was beginning to worry about running out of matches, the fourth hit pay dirt and created a river of fire that raced toward the garage faster than Carl Lewis could have. The building blazed up like the Fourth of July.

"Make it out, Greg!" Frankie screamed piercingly. "Walk over every last one of those suckers and get through! I'm waiting, man. I'm waiting for you to make it!"

Monty Loomis led Greg to Professor Kasha's mirror room only to find the door open and the kaleidoscopic interior empty except for the bloody form of Hermie York.

"I swear, kid, Baxter brought them here!" Loomis said, on the verge of panic. He really didn't want to die. "I ain't lying to you."

But Greg was elated. "She did it, by God! Cathy took the bitch apart and escaped up the stairs. Come on, you and I are going to take the same road up."

Just as he jerked Loomis into the room,

however, a roar went through the assembly behind them, one of sufficiently differing quality from the normal din to attract Greg's attention. When he looked back across the vast room, he saw Cathy, Louise, Gretchen, and Reed standing atop the platform before some kind of open trap door.

"My brothers and sisters," Reed rumbled loudly. The red-tinted air seemed to tremble with his words. "One of these traitors has attacked our beloved Sister Hermoine, and she must now pay for her sins by descending into the eternal depths."

The crowd cheered. Anything, even a brutal assault on one of their own number, was welcome if it resulted in more pain and terror.

"You crazy animals!" Gretchen screamed. Her face was white with rage behind the stark red blood that flowed from her lips and nose. Reed had already exacted a measure of revenge, it appeared. "You're all going to pay for what you're doing, what you've already done to me and all of the others. You'll burn in the electric chair. This can't go on—"

Reed slapped her.

As if galvanized by the sight, Loomis made a dash for freedom. He ran by Greg crying out in alarm, but he wasn't fast enough. Greg clipped his head with the gun barrel and dropped him in his tracks. Once Greg Hoode might have hesitated to take that action, but a lot had changed in only the last 32 hours or so.

"Nice dreams," he muttered as he slipped the gun up his sleeve and pulled the cowl as far as possible over his face. "Don't worry, gals, the cavalry is on its way."

Then he moved back into the milling collection of psychotics and toward the stage.

Reed was holding Gretchen by the hair with one hand and gripping the pistol with the other. Behind him, the big wooden trap door that led to the second cavern was open and a long rope ladder had been dropped into the darkness.

"My recommendation would be to kill her on this spot with our own bare hands," he shouted to the audience, many of whom were already tripping on the gas. "But our Father Cecil, who has been given the divine insight and who knows the Words, has decreed that no life be taken by us if it can be avoided, so instead this worthless tramp will descend into the hell that awaits all traitors and perverters of the Blessing!"

"Put her down!" the assemblage yelled in one voice.

Oblivious to Gretchen's cries, Reed dragged her to the edge of the opening and then released her, only to place the gun against her temple. "Climb or die," he ordered.

Gretchen started to step toward the awful hole, when Cathy suddenly realized that everything now was up to her. She couldn't wait for Greg to come charging up—he might be dead already—and she couldn't let this poor child be driven to her death by the beast at her side. Her plan was nothing other than the physical expression of the rage that had been born within her by all that these monsters had done to her and her loved ones.

"Reed!" she screamed.

Startled, he turned to her. And she threw herself at him.

The man weighed 235 pounds, more than twice as much as Cathy, but he was knocked backward by her burst of fury. As he staggered a step away, trying desperately to grab her, his right foot came down on nothing. He wailed and threw himself forward, but he had already overbalanced with that final step. The last thing that he did before disappearing into the gaping maw of the trap door was to fire his gun.

Something like a baseball bat swung by a giant hit Cathy in her right side. She spun like a child's toy on her way to the floor, and when she hit, even the breath that she had drawn to scream was knocked from her lungs. Something hot and wet ran into her hands.

"Cathy, oh my God, no! Cathy!" Gretchen cried hysterically. She dropped to her knees and tried to pull Cathy's hands from the wound. Louise was at her right elbow, attempting to help in any way that she could. Out among the stunned onlookers, a young man's voice shouted her name over and over.

Actually, there was very little pain. She felt numb all over and weak, but she wasn't hurting very much yet.

Greg fought his way through the confused crowd with his heart in his throat. He had seen it all—Reed's attempt to drive Gretchen into the hole, Cathy's heroic intervention, and then the gunshot that had knocked her to the floor—and abruptly it all seemed meaningless, even the safety of his own life. The crowd surged forward, either to try to rescue Reed or to take vengeance on the young woman, but he produced the gun and fired a warning shot into the air. They receded in a circular wave.

"I'll kill you all!" he shouted while he literally climbed over the bodies of those separating him from the platform. He took the steps in a single leap and fell to the floor at Cathy's side. "Take it easy, Cath, I'm right here. It's all right. Everything's okay. I'll get you out of here," he whispered.

In all of the commotion no one, not even those on the platform, heard the strange sounds that drifted up from the black hole behind them following the noise of Reed's body striking the earth so very far below.

"It's not too bad, I think," Gretchen said, though her tone betrayed her concern. Under other circumstances, Greg might have been struck by the confident, almost intelligent manner in which she was speaking, but under the circumstances he failed to notice.

"Yeah, this isn't bad at all," he agreed frantically. "Damn, this is nothing but a scratch."

"If we can only stop the bleeding, the effects of the gas should take care of the rest in minutes," Gretchen continued. She moved aside on her knees to allow him a view of the wound in Cathy's side.

"Get me . . . up," Cathy gasped. "We have to run . . . before they recover enough to . . ." Her breath failed her. Since Gretchen was leaning directly over her face, her limp white hair was hanging loosely across her neck, so that Cathy could see the thin, pink scar that came down behind her left ear, made a turn before reaching her neck, and circled up on the opposite side of her head. "Ohhhh, oh no . . ." Cathy groaned. And then she fainted.

"Get back," Greg ordered the two concerned women. He handed the gun to Louise, trusting her more to be able to intelligently wield it if necessary. "Take this. We're getting out of here now!" He slipped his arms beneath Cathy's back and legs and lifted her.

"I don't know how . . ." Louise muttered as she looked uneasily at the gun.

"Just point it and shoot it," Greg ordered. He stood with Cathy's limp form, and she seemed completely lost in the billowing robe. "Come on!"

They didn't reach the steps. The crowd had composed itself in that span of time, and a number of men and women were rushing up the stairs shouting insanely. Greg kicked the leader in the chest and sent him hurtling back into those following. But three other men with guns scrambled to replace him.

"End of the line, kids!" one said laughing.

At the other end of the room in the pump building, Cecil York shrieked, "Destroy them all! For these crimes, I commanded that the sentence of death is just! Kill them!"

"Oh, yeah," disciple Roy Barnes hissed as he raised his gun.

Amid the eager throng behind him, Daniel Hoode stared wide-eyed at the ongoing drama, but he said nothing and made no move to intervene.

Greg spun on his heel so that his body was between Cathy and Barnes, and his stomach seemed to fall out of his body when he saw what was waiting for him at the open trap door.

A human arm, as dead white as fresh milk, was rising out of the pit, and it wasn't Reed's tanned

and hairy arm. Another followed it, and then a
man's head appeared above the edge of the platform. The scalp was covered with heavy and
wildly unkempt black hair, and the wide, wide
eyes were blinking frenziedly in the light. The
man was uttering a sustained, gutteral moan.

"Jesus, look at that!" little Joseph Trout cried
from the stairs.

"Kill it!" Barnes screamed, and he began firing
his gun with mad inaccuracy at the spectral
figure.

A howl of terror and disbelief raced like
lightning through the assembly. Greg leaped from
the stage with Cathy, and Gretchen and Louise
followed in panic. They knocked down eight
hysterical disciples but managed to keep their
bare feet beneath them.

The men on the platform continued to shoot at
the apparition from the pit, but in their complete
hysteria, they missed every time. The deathly pale
man struggled onto the stage to be followed by
another after him, and then came a virtual geyser
of chalky humans of all sizes and ages. They
swarmed up from the blackness like gigantic
insects and began a cry of their own that rose in
pitch to rival the screams of the panicked
members of the Fellowship. This new cry was
"Die, York, die, York!" It spread terror among
the disciples like a raging wind.

"What's happening?" screamed Pamela
Durben, one of the six still bound at the foot of
the stage. Because of the angle, she couldn't see
the crouching white horrors on top of it, but she
could hear the shots and the swelling cries of fear.

"Dear God, who are they?" Louise shouted as

she tried to remain close to the others amid the ensuing chaos.

"The victims," Greg replied. "The people who've been put into the hole since the beginning. Somehow they survived down there, because of the gas. They've survived and multiplied for sixty-eight years!"

From behind them, at the east wall, cries of "Fire!" added to the overall cacophony. It sounded as if the world were coming to an end.

"Which way?" Gretchen yelled.

"You can't leave us here like this!" an imprisoned man cried.

"Yeah, oh God, we've got to let them go," Greg said. Still holding Cathy in his arms, he began trying to unfasten the straps that held the woman nearest to him.

With hysterical strength, Gretchen shoved his shoulder and set him staggering several feet away with his unconscious burden. "Go on and get her out of here. I'll do that," she screamed. "Go on!"

He looked at her stunned. "Gretchen, we can't leave you in this."

"You can carry her out, but I can't," she answered. "I'll meet you outside when I've finished here. Please get going, Greg. Louise, you take the gun and make sure that no one stops them!"

Louise grabbed his arm and tried to pull him toward the west exits, away from the fire that now could be seen billowing smoke along the ceiling. "For God's sake, Greg, we have to get out of this," the woman cried. "Which way do we run?"

"I . . . all right, but I'll come back for you," Greg called. "If you're not outside when Cathy's safe, I'll come back in here and find you."

Gretchen paused only long enough to give him an agreeing wave with her right hand before she returned to the buckled straps of the man in the chair before her.

"Where?" Louise repeated.

"The mirror room," Greg answered over the tumult. "It's near the central staircase, the quickest way up, and away from the fire." A sudden rush of shrieking people engulfed the three of them, and Greg was spun around. When he regained his balance, Louise was gone. He stared wildly all about, but he could see no sign of her in the scores of identical green robes that surrounded him. "Louise!" he shouted. "The mirror room . . . go through the mirror room!"

The thousands of Euphratans didn't seem to know which way to run, however, and the addition of the crazed and dangerous men and women from the cavern, continuing to flow up the rope ladder and through the trap door and attack everyone possible, only magnified the insanity of the moment. Greg struggled through the clamoring throng in his effort to reach the mirror room. He was nearly driven to the floor and trampled on several occasions, and once a complete lunatic tried to tear Cathy right from his arms. He freed one arm long enough to drop the man with a short left hook and then jumped over the unconscious body, still searching for a way out of the nightmarish danger.

By chance, Pamela Durben was the last of the six people freed from the chairs by Gretchen. She struggled fiercely, jerking the heavy chair across the floor, but the tight straps seemed to grow even tighter. She screamed at the girl, though she understood that the child was working as swiftly as possible. None of the robed Euphratans stopped in their frantic flight to help her, of course, and when the naked albinos from the pit flooded from the stage into the area about it, violently attacking men and women as they encountered them, Pamela felt certain that she was about to die. The girl was working on the chair next to her own, but that would take too long.

Suddenly Kevin stood before her, grinning with a sort of glowing joy. "Hi, babe," he shouted.

"Kevin!"

He began unfastening the straps at her wrists. "You didn't think I'd leave you trussed up like this, did you? Hold still!"

To Pamela, it was as if the nightmare had ended. This was Kevin who was risking his own life to save hers, rather than that giggling mutation that had been so happy to recite the details of his schoolboy murder; somehow the real Kevin Durben had returned to repossess his body and return as the man she loved again. When the strap was released from about her chest, she threw herself into his arms.

"Oh, sweet Jesus, it's wonderful to have you back," she whispered urgently as she rained passionate kisses on his face. She was still weak and hurt from yesterday's accident, but she knew that she had recovered enough to get out of all this madness now that she had her husband back. When they were safe, no one would ever again speak of his confession or that Goddamned book that had caused it all. "Let's go now, before they can—"

He carefully took her arms from about him. "Don't panic, hon. These troglodytes have been underground for a long time, so they can't see anything too well. You shouldn't have too much trouble getting away from them.

"*We,*" she corrected, pulling him by the hand.

He didn't move. "I'm not going anywhere."

Unacceptable reality threatened to drown her again. "What? You have to! We've got to get away from this horror before something else happens!"

He laughed. "This is my home now, Pamela. I wish you'd stay with me, but I won't try to stop you."

"But those monsters . . . the Yorks!"

"We'll clean up these bastards easily enough, and the Yorks are my people now. You must see that." He looked around, and even in the center of that tornado of panic and terror, he seemed to be contented. "This is . . . heaven, just like Grandfather Cecil said, and I'll defend it with my life."

"That's crazy," Pamela wailed. "It's the gas. It's driven you as insane as the rest of these creatures. The gas and that book!"

"Babe, I know you can't understand, because you're not as involved as I am, but the gas has freed me. This is what every man wants, really, deep down inside his soul."

Pamela couldn't speak. There was no answer for a statement like that.

Kevin planted a brief kiss on her forehead. "This is my home, but you'd better be on your way. The trogs are half-blind, but they're not totally helpless."

"Do you need some help?" Gretchen asked, as she ran over to the two of them. The other captives were free and gone by then. "What's wrong?"

Kevin thrust Pamela against her. "Gretchen, I'm a member of the Fellowship now, and as such I order you to take my wife out of this house. Make sure that she gets away without being hurt and then come back here. We'll need you to clean up when this is over."

"What?" Gretchen asked incredulously.

"Kevin . . ." Pamela began.

"Go, both of you," Durben commanded. He pushed the young women so hard that they tumbled together to the cold floor. Then he turned away and began to run toward the steps that led up to the platform as if eager to engage the swarming troglodytes.

Pamela tried to stand and rush after him, but Gretchen held her back and said, "No, let him go. There's nothing that we can do if he doesn't want to come with us."

"Let me alone! I've got to convince him!" Pamela actually began to struggle with the smaller girl when the blood in her veins was frozen by what she saw on top of the stage. Kevin gleefully had plunged into the mass of crazed cave dwellers.

He was, she later supposed, simply trying to defend his new home. He grasped necks, arms, and heads in his large and powerful hands and dragged the white-fleshed men and women to the open trap door to throw them, screaming, back into the darkness that had released them. He attacked with a reckless abandon and apparently without any regard for his own safety until the confused cave dwellers turned on him *en masse*.

Pamela was standing now, so that she had a clear view of it, but that same view paralyzed her. She was unable to make even a futile gesture to assist him as he was ridden to the floor by those writhing bodies and then swiftly broken by the terrible anger that fueled their hands and feet. She could only scream out his name as those hands pulled on his body with such power that terrible rents in his skin threw steaming geysers of his blood into the air. She couldn't even avert her eyes when his arms and legs and genitals were ripped from his trunk or when talons scooped out his eyes and flat teeth tore his face from his skull. Finally his head was literally twisted from his neck, and it was over.

Kevin Durben, who really had died 15 years before on a hot, late summer's night and lived in death since then, died for the second and last time.

"Oh, Christ," Gretchen whispered in awe.

"Kevin!" Pamela screamed.

When the murderous cave dwellers turned their dark and gaping eyes toward the two women, Gretchen clutched Pamela's arm and practically dragged her along into the flow of terrified Euphratans.

Greg and Cathy had made their way to the block enclosure, but they could go no further due to the fact that some idiot with a gun was firing shots into the wooden ceiling in order to turn back the escaping horde like a cowboy herding cattle. Greg stretched his frame to its tallest in order to peer above the heads of those ahead of him, but what he saw was almost as awful as the rampaging cave people behind him. The furious

and armed obstacle turning back the panicked
crowd was Hermione York.

"Get back!" she shrieked wildly, waving the
gun. "No one is leaving here until Grandfather
says so!"

"Oh shit," Greg sighed.

When Kevin Durben died, a psychic blow
crashed into Greg's mind like an invisible truck.
He grunted deeply and stumbled several feet
toward the block temple, almost dropping his
precious burden as he did so.

He's dead, the mummy cried into his brain, and
even with his eyes open he saw her again. *Now
there is only you, Greg, only you, or we are lost
forever and ever.*

Jesus Christ, what do you want of me? he
begged. I don't even believe in ghosts!

First, you must save yourself, she answered.
*You are our only hope, and you can't allow your-
self to be destroyed now. Later, you will understand how . . . and why . . .* She faded away again.

"Greg, it hurts," Cathy said weakly as she
began to regain consciousness. "It hurts so
much."

He actually shook his head to rid it of what he
felt to be waking nightmares caused by the gas in
the air. "Hold on, honey, we're almost there," he
whispered to her. Maybe if they circled around
the block building . . .

In fact, they had made their way to the building
and halfway around it when fate again thrust its
way into their path. First, Gretchen appeared out
of the morass, along with one of the former
captives, Durben's wife; then the murderous side
of the coin landed, on this occasion in the form of
Cecil York. His hood had been torn from his

robe, and there was blood gushing from a mean gash in his cheek, but he had a rictal smile of pure insanity on his face and a gun in his right hand when he stepped out of the structure that covered the gas vent.

"Vile spawn of Satan's loins!" he bawled, and the four young people, who had halted at his appearance, knew with certainty that the old man at last had descended into irrevocable madness. "You brought this upon my house, and you shall pay for your treachery with your lives!" He aimed the gun toward them with a steady hand.

"Put that down, old man," Greg spat, twisting Cathy to one side, out of the line of fire. "It's all over now. This place is going up in flames, and if you don't get your ass out of here, you'll be charred along with it."

To his left, Gretchen also moved carefully to one side, obviously trying to draw his aim to herself and away from the others. "Cecil, killing us won't do any good anymore. It's too late for anything to help. Get out of here before the police arrive."

"Police?" he repeated hysterically. "What fear I from human authority? *I* know the words. They were told to me in this very spot sixty-eight years ago. I am beyond human laws . . ." He turned his face to the ceiling, and they could see the insanity spilling from his face even as the saliva ran from the corners of his mouth. "I know all of the words, and I am God!"

"Grandfather Cecil!" Hermie York called, appearing out of the chaos as if by magic. She rushed into the little building and joined him in front of the very shaft down which he had fallen on a summer day so long before. She grasped his free arm. "The house is on fire, and the demons are rising from the pit. We have to escape!"

He wrestled the arm free. "I'll never leave this blessed spot. God directed me to it so that I could become God. I shall defend it against all infidels. I am Cecil York, the Chosen One, and I know the Words!"

"But Cecil, they're coming! They're . . ." Hermie's eyes widened in sheer terror and her voice dissolved into an animalistic howl at the sight before her.

Greg snapped his head around in time to see a group of at least a dozen of the naked apparitions from below the earth lunging forward at full charge and chanting, "Cecil York! Die, Cecil York!" Then they hit him.

Greg immediately was driven to the floor inside the block building. Cathy screamed as she was ripped from him, and Gretchen cried out her name in horror. Greg tried to stand, but a bare foot smashed into his face and knocked him back to the floor. He grabbed the foot, twisted it, heard the snapping of bones, and then fought his way to his knees.

Cathy was buffeted by the assault as if she had been a piece of flotsam on the ocean waves. Agony was exploding in her side, and madness threatened to engulf her. She thrashed about with her arms, only to have them stamped upon. "Greg!" she cried.

"Cathy!" he responded. But he was still swamped by the wild pack of men and women struggling to reach Cecil, the focus of all of their hate.

"I've got you," a voice said in Cathy's ear. She felt a small pair of hands on her shoulders, pulling her out of the delirium. It was Gretchen. "Don't worry, I've got you," she repeated.

Then, in a split second packed with all of the terror and frenzy that was imaginable, the chortling Cecil York fastened himself to Gretchen's back and three huge cave dwellers engulfed the entire group. Reality tilted. The floor left Cathy's back, and directions became inverted. Gretchen was holding her and screaming, Cecil was clutching Gretchen and laughing, and the three troglodytes were gripping them all in maniacal fury. They rose as one body and fell as one.

The vent over the gas shaft was open. The shaft itself had been bricked about, but a four foot hole remained like some gaping mouth. The cluster of struggling people tumbled into this hole.

One of the cave dwellers vanished into the opening without a sound. The other two scrambled free before going over the side and then fled when Hermie fired a shot over their heads from Cecil's fallen gun. Cecil dropped into the shaft, taking Gretchen with him in a death's grip, and Cathy fell on the very edge atop the wide lip of the shaft, half in, half out, with Gretchen's fingers digging into her like iron claws. She began to slide toward the point where she too would plunge after them.

"Cathy!" Greg shouted as if that were the only word his mouth could form. He leaped ten feet and caught her legs just before she could slip over into eternity.

She was being torn apart. From her wounded waist down, she was still in the block house, but her upper body was dangling downward with the combined weight of Gretchen and Cecil threatening to rip her arms from her shoulders. Cecil was cackling now in total lunacy.

"I can't die," he was calling out. "I know the Words!"

"Hold him! For Christ's sake, don't let him go!" Hermie shrieked.

Cathy groaned with pain far worse than any she had ever thought possible. Greg tried to speak, but his entire being was concentrating on holding her out of the shaft.

Still, the thick robe began to rip in his hands and she began to inch into the mouth of death.

"No!" he managed to shout. If he stood to get a better grip, she would disappear forever down there.

Then another voice spoke to Cathy. "Cathy," Gretchen said with surprising calm. Her face was only a couple of feet from Cathy's, and the strain of holding Cecil's weight in addition to her own was glistening in her features. "Reach back and take Greg's hand. He'll pull you up. Don't fall. Goodbye, Kitty Cat." And then she opened her own hands.

"Mikey!" Cathy screamed.

They were gone, both of them, into the darkness.

"Mikey, oh God, Mikey!" Her grasp on reality blew in and out of her mind like flower petals in a storm. Greg quickly dragged her back onto the floor, but she fought with him to return to the shaft. Hermie was wailing piteously, but Cathy didn't hear her. She simply continued to cry Mikey's name repeatedly until Greg lifted her into his arms and ran with her from the pump building. Then she could only weep.

It couldn't be him, Greg told himself continually. He fled from the auditorium, through the surrealistic mirror room, and into the service hallway which was filling with black smoke. Cathy was in his arms and confused Pamela Durben by his side. And all the while he was silently repeating, She couldn't have been Mikey!

He found the staircase and charged up it. The smoke was hot and acidic, thick enough to cause him to cough heavily, but Cathy cried into his shoulder unaffected.

Damn, damn, damn, it couldn't have been him!

He kicked open the door on the ground floor and staggered into the lobby. Just one more door and he would be free into the night air.

"Good evening, mighty warrior!" a familiar, booming voice said. Hearty laughter flickered throughout the words.

"Gerhard," Greg whispered. The man hadn't been below at the ceremony, but Greg had been too busy to notice this absence.

The nearly eight foot giant stood at his full height in the center of the lobby. Other robed men and women darted around him and into the darkness beyond the door, but he seemed to notice only Greg, Cathy, and, by association, a transfixed Pamela.

"The game is up," Gerhard stated in his heavy accent. "Soon the entire world will know of this place and its miracles, and people such as I will be hunted down like wild things. But you will pay for what you have done this night with your blood . . . and theirs.''

"Run, Greg," Cathy pleaded. She didn't seem to care about herself anymore. "Put me down and get out of here!"

Greg surveyed the motionless giant and found him to be unarmed. Though it might be time to run, he realized, he would never make it around this monster carrying Cathy, and he sure as hell wasn't going to leave her here. Besides, something feral in his soul was calling out for this meeting.

Walking coolly to the sofa, he placed Cathy upon it as gently as he was able. "Don't worry," he whispered, "it's almost over." To Pamela, he added, "While I have him occupied, get her out of here." She nodded with wide-eyed, numb agreement.

Grinning, Gerhard positioned himself before the room's only outside exit, effectively sealing them inside with him.

Greg sighed. There was going to be just one way out for any of them. While there was plenty of distance between the two, he pulled the robe over his head to give himself more freedom of movement. Gerhard didn't charge him when he was in this most vulnerable position, so he dropped the robe to the floor rather than throwing it into the big man's face. He wiped his damp palms on his thighs and then raised his clenched fists.

"Any time you're ready," he said.

Gerhard nodded, and then he leaped.

By all rights, it should have been over as swiftly

as their first encounter. It should have been a cakewalk for the man with two feet in height and reach and 330 pounds in weight over his opponent. It should have gone many ways other than the one that it did.

Gerhard was a raging behemoth, maddened by the destruction of his perfect life by these inter-lopers, and he presented an obstacle more like a mindless force of nature than a human adversary. But Greg Hoode was a coldly ferocious devil.

Using his own natural advantages—speed of hand and foot and coordination—Greg avoided the giant's rushes and frustrated his efforts to turn the meeting into a deadly wrestling match, where Gerhard's overpowering strength would have made a quick end to the conflict. When he did find himself enclosed by those massive arms, Greg used headbutts, knees to the groin, all of the maneuvers that would have guaranteed him expulsion from a boxing ring to hurt Gerhard and then wriggle free.

Then he fired back. He used his knees and feet, but most of all he struck with his fists. His combinations rattled off of Gerhard's chest and raked his stomach, and when the huge head came down to within range following brutal body shots, he blasted that, too.

It took only two or three minutes, though this was long enough for the smoke to spread into the lobby, and then the match was decided. Gerhard roared and stormed, swung and cursed, and finally he staggered. The opportunity came like a dream out of Greg's imagination. Gerhard was standing before him, doubled to only half of his erect, exaggerated height and swaying ponder-ously, almost out on his feet. His incredibly long jawline hung before Greg's hungry fists, entirely unprotected.

This is it, Greg thought giddily. Then he launched the hardest right cross that he had thrown in his entire life.

His hand shattered like crystal, sending waves of agony surging throughout his body, but Greg laughed with the sensation. After what he had been through tonight, nothing could ever hurt him again. And besides, what his eyes beheld wiped away everything but exultation. Gerhard Klopstock was nose-diving into the thick, royal purple carpet with all of the grace of a falling redwood.

It was over.

Epilogue

Early morning, Wednesday, July 12.

Of course, it wasn't over; it was only just beginning.

The York mansion was besieged by various municipal vehicles, and the occupants of each of them were certain that *they* had the legal right and obligation to carry out their duties before anyone else interfered. Fire trucks cut off state police cars, who in turn waved off arriving radio and television news crews. Brilliant lights played over the exterior of the blazing mansion and picked out the flood of panicked refugees from inside. Most were dressed in exotic green robes and screamed in inarticulate terror, as if all of the spirits of Hell were pursuing them, while some were stark naked, as pale as clouds, and apparently completely crazy. A number of these had to be shot down without mercy before they could savage the stunned police and firemen. The scene reached nightmarish proportions.

Somehow the police gained control over the situation—they did have the guns, after all—and organized matters enough so that the fire department was able to douse the fire before it consumed the entire building. About half of the once-majestic York Manor was gone forever, though.

The state police knew why they were there to some extent, and they quickly began arresting everybody in sight, especially the naked albino maniacs, and calling in even more backups to help them. It looked as if all of Euphrata was running in screaming hysteria about the grounds, and though obviously they couldn't collect everyone, they were going to do their best to get the most important members of the huge group cuffed and on their way to Tiverton. It was clear to them that the local police force was involved in the situation up to their collective necks.

Through a fortuitous set of circumstances, Louise Simpson, who had been separated from the others in the maelstrom that had developed in the cellar, made her way safely out of the mansion and proved her identity to a high-ranking police officer. Since she was their main contact in "the Euphrata Affair," she was listened to with courtesy, if not outright acceptance. At her insistence, Frankie, Cathy, Greg, Pamela and she were soon gathered into a patrol wagon which had been converted into a makeshift ambulance and sent, with screaming sirens and flashing lights, on their way to a hospital in Tiverton.

As they left, the state national guard began to arrive to help in the containment efforts and impose a news blackout about the little, inconsequential town of Euphrata, Indiana.

* * *

It was dark in the van.

Cathy was lying on one of the two parallel couches, unconscious, and a medically trained policeman was attending to her. The bleeding from her wound had stopped, and though she seemed very pale, the cop assured a worried Greg that her heart rate and breathing were both strong and encouraging.

Pamela Durben lay on the opposite couch, awake but seemingly very close to lapsing into shock, and the policeman kept one eye trained on her. To either side of the woman sat Frankie and Louise, neither of whom appeared to be injured, though Frankie did show some badly scraped forearms and elbows. His ankle was broken, of course, but he was making very little of it and even appeared to be stimulated by the pain. It was the first such that he had been forced to endure below his waist in a long time.

Greg sat just by Cathy's head. His face was somewhat bruised and bloodied by his encounter with Gerhard, and his broken right hand had already become swollen and discolored. Like Frankie, he was making very little fuss about his own injuries. It could have been that the narcotic effects of the gas were lingering in their systems, but in Greg's case, his concern for Cathy overcame any self-pity. He sighed wearily, closed his eyes, and leaned back against the side of the speeding van.

"I guess it was pretty bad in there, huh?" Frankie asked tentatively, his voice low so as not to disturb the others.

A grim smile came to Greg's lips. "Yeah, it was bad. I don't know if we would have made it out if you hadn't set that fire."

"Hell, man, to get Cathy out of there, you would have walked over Satan himself."

"I think maybe we did."

Following a moment of silence, Louise asked softly, "Do you know what happened to Gretchen? I looked all over and described her to the police, but no one could find her."

Greg's voice was a dull croak. "Gretchen's dead."

"Shit!" Frankie responded. He slammed the edge of his right fist against the side of the van, causing the cops in the front to glance about nervously and Pamela to start as if waking from a dream. "Those damned, damned bastards . . ."

Louise dropped her head. "The poor little girl."

Greg said nothing. There was no reason for them to know.

The rigors of the night seemed to have taken most of the life from Pamela, and when she tried to sit up, it wasn't at all difficult for Louise to restrain her with merely a hand on her shoulder. "You should rest now," the older woman said. "We'll be at the hospital in a few minutes."

"I need . . . I need to ask something," Pamela answered weakly. She pointed to Greg, having forgotten his name. "I need to ask you."

He leaned across the aisle, resting his elbows on his knees and carefully positioning his right hand on his left thigh. "What is it?"

"You know about this stuff, this gas, don't you? You know what it does to people?" There was an obvious pleading tone in her voice.

He shrugged. "I saw what it did. I don't know how . . ."

"But it did drive people insane, didn't it? I

mean, it made that girl retarded and turned those people in the cave into killers."

"I suppose that's what caused it. It's the most incredible thing I've ever seen."

She drew a deep breath. "Then that's what happened to Kevin, isn't it? He might have made some mistakes when he was young, but he's never been that way since. He wouldn't enjoy hurting or killing anyone, so that gas just drove him insane, didn't it?"

In less than two days? Greg thought. But he answered, "We know how fast it works, so that must have been the reason he changed. But I don't believe that any of us have to worry about that kind of effect on us."

Just that admission seemed to relieve the woman, and she settled back onto the couch, eyes closed. "I knew that he wasn't Kevin anymore. That gas twisted his thinking and took what that book had done to him and magnified it. Kevin is dead, but he died in the wreck, not down there, not like that . . ." She drifted into sleep.

One effect of exposure to the gas upon certain individuals was the dramatic strengthening of psychic abilities, the strengthening that had come to a mentally leaden Jeroboam Chaliapin while eluding an envious Noleta Evangelista. Two of the people in the rushing van experienced such a heightening before they reached the hospital. To one, the episode was an ending, to the other it was the first step of a quest.

Greg

Greg didn't want to sleep in the police wagon. He wanted to stay awake and be there for Cathy, should she come to and find herself frightened, alone and in pain. But the police medic had insisted upon giving him an injection of pain killer when he saw how badly broken the young man's hand was. Greg slipped into unconsciousness before he even realized that it was creeping up on him.

She appeared gradually, as if undergoing a difficult shift from one plane of reality to the plane that Greg inhabited. She was still wrapped in the tape, of course, and though he couldn't see her face, he knew her.

Hello, Angie, he said.

Can I speak to you now?

Yes. Explain it to me, please.

I can say only that our hope lies in you now, Greg. There's no one else in the world who can right the wrong that was done to us and release us from this. If you refuse, we will be lost.

I don't believe in ghosts, Angie.

But we believe in you.

I didn't kill you. The man who did is dead now himself. Why can't you take your revenge on him?

He's not here with us.

Then why can't you rest in peace?

We don't search for revenge, Greg, but salvation.

Then why come to me?

I am real, even as I was real when my life was cut off before it could fully begin. I ask you now to give back to me that denied portion. I don't know the answer either, Greg, but I do know that you will have the ability and the opportunity to correct this terrible wrong and that you must willingly accept this duty. If you refuse to help us, we will go through eternity fettered and denied and condemned.

I don't know . . . I don't know what to say to
you . . .

I'm real, Greg. Barbara is real.

Barbara?

*The girl in the book who was killed by the
children. You read it, so you know. It was the
inspiration for my own death.*

But she was only a character, a part of one
man's imagination!

*She gained reality through my death and
through the years of suffering that Kevin and the
others endured. She is here with me.*

Greg saw her, a girl who had never existed.
Like in the novel, she was bound and gagged, but
her eyes were uncovered, and the look in them
seemed to draw the life right out of his heart.
God, to be forever like that . . . Why me? he
repeated.

*We can't say other than to point out that you
knew the passions that were the cause of all of
this, and you were strong enough to turn away
from them. You have strength of spirit. You have
our fates to decide.*

But I have no idea what you need!

*And you will have to search for it. You can
refuse now, simply close your heart to us, and we
will depart, never to reach across the gulf to
anyone again. We will be truly dead then. Or you
can help us. Please say that you'll help us, Greg.
Save us.*

What was there for him to say? The entire
world—and the world that waited beyond it—
seemed to be crashing in upon him, demanding
his life so that theirs might be spared. All of these
questions and no answers. Still, there was only

one response that he could ever have given. Greg gave his answer.

I'll help you. I'll do what I can, though I have no clue as to what is necessary. God help us all.

Emotions poured into the young man from the two girls, one an invention, the second a victim of that invention. He felt their gratitude, hope and joy flooding through his being, but most of all he knew their love.

Thank you, Greg. We must leave for now, but we know that your strength and love will be our redemption. Remember us.

I won't fail you, Angie, and you know that I could never forget you.

Then the two visions were gone, and Greg sank into a real sleep.

Pamela

While Greg met his ghosts within the framework of the present, Pamela leaped ahead in time. It was two years later, May 17th, a rainy Friday afternoon, and Pamela was about to end a mission that had haunted her since that terrible night in the York mansion.

The cab pulled to a stop before the quiet-looking, well-kept house, and the driver looked back at his lone passenger. "Here we are, ma'am. Should I wait for you?"

Pamela glanced at the meter for the charges and then doubled it to include the man's tip. Money was no worry to her now and never would be again. "That won't be necessary, thank you. I don't know how long I'll be staying, but I'll call your company when I'm ready to leave."

The driver took the money through the open slot in the glass partition, noted the size of the tip, and said, "Thank you, ma'am! Let me get the umbrella out for you."

"Please, don't bother." Pamela pulled her rain scarf over her hair and looked out at the light drizzle that was settling from the gray sky. Perhaps that was what she really needed, to walk in the rain more often; it might help to wash this obsession out of her soul, that is if today's visit didn't work. "Well, thanks a lot," she said, opening the door and stepping into the rain.

She took her time as she crossed the walk that led to the front porch. Even the rain needs a fair chance to work its magic.

Was she doing the right thing? The entire trip was woefully spur of the moment and ill-prepared. When she could no longer wrestle with the demons of that night and what had happened to her husband and why, she had called the publishing company on impulse to get an address for the author of that cursed book, and being Pamela Durben (which was a very big deal these days), she had received an almost immediate reply.

It was not a recent address, as the publishing company's last contact with the man had been 16 years before, but it was enough of a start. She could have checked further, called his home or hired private detectives to gain a perspective on the man she would be accusing, but she was afraid that her anger and need for vengeance would not survive the effort. This was something that had to be done face to face and as soon as possible.

Naturally, she had wondered why the man hadn't published anything other than that single novel, but she liked to think that what he had done in that single novel had somehow come back to haunt him in a way that even a printed sequel couldn't dispell. The last name on the mail box was correct, and Pamela was confident that the long suffering was about over for her.

She crossed the porch and rang the bell.

The woman who answered seemed to be about 60. She was small, no more than five-foot three, and a touch overweight, as if she, too, had about ten pounds that she continually promised to lose. Her hair was fine, black, and pulled rather severely back by ornate combs. Her eyes were brown and lively.

"Good afternoon," Pamela began. "My name is Pamela Durben, and—"

"Oh, I know," the woman said excitedly. "I saw you coming up the walk and I recognized your face from television, from all of the news programs and documentaries. Won't you please come in? Excuse my enthusiasm, but I must tell you, you saved my life."

Wrapped in a cloud of bustling excitement, Pamela was ushered inside the warm and neat home, seated on the comfortable living room sofa, and calling the woman Emily (by request) before she could get around to the purpose of her visit. She could feel her sense of commitment eroding before this warm welcome, but she steeled herself to say what she felt had to be said if the past were to be ever truly laid to rest.

Emily brought tea and bisquits from the kitchen while Pamela was wording the speech in her mind. "So you can see why I feel that you— and those other young people who discovered and publicized the Euphrata Vapor—actually saved my life," the older woman stated with the same ebullience that had carried her conversation from the first. She sat in an armchair facing Pamela.

"The doctors were quite open with me. If it hadn't been for the treatments with the vapor, I wouldn't be speaking with you today."

Pamela sipped her tea, which really was very good. "Well, when I have nightmares about that night, I can always console myself with the knowledge that millions of people are benefiting from what we uncovered," she admitted. "I'm glad that it was of use to you."

Emily nodded thoughtfully. "Of course, I didn't mean to minimize what you went through that night. It really must have been horrible. I know that you lost your husband, and I'm sorry. It just seems that sometimes the good things in life cost so much . . . All that aside, though, I fear I've been monopolizing the conversation. What can I do for you, Ms. Durben?"

"Pamela, please," she said. "Actually, Emily, I've come to see your husband."

The other woman looked slightly startled. "My husband?"

"Martin." Taking a short breath, she plunged ahead. "I want to talk to him about something he wrote that ruined my husband's life and almost destroyed mine."

Emily looked physically hurt, her eyes changing in an instant from bright to clouded with sorrow. She stood and walked to a beautiful fireplace that was flickering comfortingly in this damp and slightly cool spring afternoon.

Something seemed to give way in Pamela and she began to speak of things that she had sworn to herself never to mention. The whole story broke from her like floodwaters through a breached dam, the adolescent reading club, the way that they came across the novel, what they were incited to do, what they did, and the effects that the horrendous crime had worked on each of them. She cried a little, but when Emily made no response and stood with her back to Pamela, gazing evenly into the fire, she found that she couldn't hold back even the most irrelevant details of what she had discovered on that night.

When the story was told and she found herself regaining her self-control, Pamela said, "I know that Martin is not legally or even morally responsible for what happened. I also have to come to the conclusion that making an author responsible for his fictional creativity would deprive us of more in the way of freedom of thought than it would provide in safety. But these logical arguments can't ease my feelings. I have to see the man who thought that writing this," she produced a worn, well-thumbed copy of the novel that had been found in the ruins of the York home in her husbands effects, "in the name of entertainment justifies what it caused a decent and loving man to do."

Only then did Emily turn to face her, and the woman's expression was an odd mixture of sadness and relief, for she had just learned a truth that had worried her for many years. "Pamela, Martin didn't write that book to cause pain or suffering for anyone," she said quietly. "It was a novel, nothing more."

Pamela felt the dam filling again, threatening to burst and sweep her away again. "Let *him* tell me that," she said, more sharply than she had intended.

"He can't. He died sixteen years ago."

It was Pamela's turn to stare in disbelief at the other woman. She'd never even considered this

possibility. Why not? Was it because it meant that
he had escaped her wrath, her moment of
vengeance? Her voice was weak with surprise and
a considerable amount of pity when she said,
"I'm sorry. I didn't know." Much of the pity was
for herself. "I must seem terribly ridiculous to
you—and cold-hearted."

"Not at all," Emily replied. Her tone had
remained comforting throughout the confession,
even though much of the content of it had been
harshly directed toward a loved one whom she
had lost. She crossed the room and sat again close
to Pamela. "I won't lie to you. I really don't
believe that Martin incited the murder any more
than did any of those other books that your
husband's group read, because though writers can
help a person to . . . to recognize himself, they
never create what isn't already there. The man
who went on to other murders—Wesley, was it?
His personality would have driven him to that had
he never heard anything worse than the Bible. But
I'll tell you what I *do* believe. I think that you've
helped yourself greatly just coming here and
telling me this."

"It doesn't feel that way."

"Not now, perhaps, but it will. Give yourself
time. And you have eased a burden that I've lived
with for a long time, too."

Pamela sat up straight and blinked her damp
eyes until they were clear again. "What do you
mean?"

Rather than answering, Emily took a tiny key
from an apron pocket and unlocked a drawer that
was built into the coffee table that sat between the
two of them. Inside were a number of papers,
many old and yellowing, and she selected two

which she then handed to Pamela.

"These are photocopies," she said. "The police have the originals, though they never were able to make good use of them. We received them in a packet in December, after the girl's body had been identified in November. Martin had taken sick three months before, though he seemed to be improving, and he had great hopes that he would fight his way through it. After he saw these, something went out of him. He died the next February."

Pamela looked in horror at the slightly faded copies in her hands. The first was taken from a newspaper article that had been roughly cut. It described the discovery of the identity of 19-year-old Angela Leona Broughton, whose body had been found a month earlier in an Ohio forest, and it went into detail concerning the various, unthinkable tortures that she had been subjected to before being beaten to death by a heavy rock found at the site. Atop the article and about its margins were the words, "You made me do this!" written again and again in the much younger but still recognizable hand of Kevin Durben. The second sheet consisted of eleven snapshots taken of the girl while she was bound but before she had been wrapped in the tape. There was no doubt as to their authenticity.

"So, you see," Emily continued, "you had your revenge anyway. I'm certain that knowing that this had taken place contributed to Martin's death, and, just like Kevin, he had his nightmares before the end came. He even mentioned Angie once or twice."

"I didn't want revenge. I didn't come here for that," Pamela said pleadingly. "You've got to believe that.''

''I do,'' Emily assured her. She patted her shoulder and took the photocopies from her trembling hands. ''At last I can burn these and be done with it.''

''Don't . . . don't you think that you should keep them in case the police need them for some reason?''

''The police? Are you going to tell them about this?''

Pamela took the copy of the novel from the table and replaced it in her purse. Soon the fire would get this, too. ''I just assumed that *you* would.''

''Kevin is dead, and from what you've told me, his death was no easier than Angela's, if quicker. What about the others?''

''Wesley's dead, as I said, and so are Peter, who committed suicide, and Michele, who was murdered. Mona and Derick were tried and convicted of killing her after I provided some information anonymously last year, and though the truth didn't come to light completely—the prosecution worked on the love triangle theory— they both received life sentences.''

''The third girl?''

''Donna, Donna Jeptha. I haven't been able to locate her. I've used detectives and everything, but there's just no trace of her. I'm convinced that she's changed her name and moved away maybe even out of the country.''

Emily began sipping her tea again. ''I would imagine that she's suffering her own punishment.''

Pamela wanted to force this finally into the past, but there were still questions to consider.

"What about Angela's parents? Don't you think that they would want to know why their daughter died?"

Emily paused. "I can't answer that. All I can say is that you have both put my mind at ease and stirred up extremely painful memories by coming here today. You'll have to decide for yourself whether or not the truth would be worth what they would have to go through all over again. I wouldn't want to see Martin's name brought up in connection with something like this, but I won't fight you if you decide to reveal it all to them."

Tomorrow, Pamela thought, another thing to do on some far tomorrow. She started to stand. "Well, I thank you for your time, Emily, but I should be—"

"Must you leave so soon?" Emily asked, and Pamela could see in her eyes the desperate need for company at that moment. "If you stay, we could talk for a while, sort of help one another through it."

Pamela smiled. "Of course. I'd be glad to stay a while."

And so they talked and cried and even laughed a little over the ways that tragedy had linked their lives and taken someone of incalculable worth from each of them. Late in the afternoon, the sun came out.

When Pamela returned to her home following that meeting, she found a message from Greg Hoode, whom she hadn't seen in two years. In it was perhaps the most wonderful news that she ever could have received.

Thursday morning, July 13.

Everything was white.

She was surrounded, engulfed by fluffy whiteness, as if she were floating inside a cloud . . . or was a part of one. The sun streamed through the window across the room onto the crisp sheets that covered her and created the illusion of glowing whiteness.

Cathy Lockwood awoke.

"Hi," Greg said softly. He was standing next to her bed, dressed in a blue shirt and jeans.

"Greg," she responded through lips that were thick with sleep and medication. She stretched out her hand to him.

He took it in his left, and she noticed that his right was encased in plaster and supported by a sling around his neck. They were in a hospital.

"So you remember me, do you?" he asked with a lazy grin. "How do you feel?"

"Fuzzy," she said. "I feel like . . . like I've been tossed inside of a feather bed for a week."

"You've been asleep for almost two days. We're in a hospital in Tiverton."

Tiverton, Tiverton, she thought, is that near McKeesport?

"You look great," he continued. "Pink and healthy and . . . They took out the bullet and told me that there'd be no complications, but you did get a free appendectomy."

"Bullet?" she repeated. The ugliness began to return. "What's happened? Where . . . ?"

"Monica and her parents are having breakfast with my folks in the cafeteria. I wanted us to be alone together first so that we could talk about it."

"Talk about it?"

"About what happened. Everything." He

sighed. "The state police arrived just as we got out of the mansion, and they rounded up two or three thousand people who were there that night, including most of the people who came up from the cave, though I've heard that there are still some wandering in the woods trying to hide from the sun. Can you believe that they survived down there? God, they found a river and ate fungus and mushrooms and fish, but the gas really was what allowed them to live through all of the years. A.H. Hotchkiss himself may still be alive down there. The authorities estimate that there are as many people living below Euphrata as in it. Ten thousand people! Jesus!"

Cathy remained silent. The memories were coming now. She didn't want them to, but she couldn't stop them.

"Of course, the press would have gone crazy if they knew all of the details," he said with a laugh.

"If they knew?" she asked. "It's been kept a secret?"

He shrugged, trying to appear more nonchalant than he felt about the matter. "Well, for now the government's saying that some kind of wild virus engulfed the town, and they've quarantined it and instituted a news blackout. We, Frankie and Louise and Pamela and I, have been getting daily updates from the special panel that's been interrogating us. They're really eager to get to you, too, but the doctors would have none of it and—hey! Frankie is regaining the use of his legs! The gas repaired the nerve damage that he suffered in that car wreck!" Even though I swore to you that nerve and brain tissue don't heal, he added silently.

"That's wonderful," she said with as much

emotion as she could muster at that moment.

"He says that he's going to try out for the next Olympic track team while I go for the boxing gold. Man, at least some good has come out of this. Uncle Dan's going to jail . . . Let's see, what else? Thousands of people were trapped underground for decades, most of them born down there—there were a number of murders, naturally—but if the doctors can figure out the makeup of that gas and duplicate its effects, it may prove to have been worth it all. Damn, it's just so fantastic . . ."

"The, um, mansion . . . did it burn down?"

He pulled a chair to her bedside. "About halfway. Frankie did that; he said it was the only diversion he could come up with on the spur of the moment. Wow, we sure were lucky the gas wasn't combustible. Nobody died, though—not from the fire, anyway. And now the whole world's going to be changed."

"Gerhard?"

"He was still out cold when the police got there, but he's okay now. Hell, his name isn't really Gerhard Klopstock, and he's not even German. According to Matt Shelby, one of the interrogation team members, he's Charles Patterson, a circus performer from Oakland, California." Greg laughed again. "The Gerhard persona was just a manifestation of the mental effects the gas had on him." He was growing even more excited. "But do you know who wasn't crazy? At least, not completely?"

"Who?" she asked with a faint smile.

"Noleta! She really *is* Noleta Evangelista, the diplomat's daughter. Somehow or other, the kidnappers wound up in the York mansion and were put in the cave, while she was kept above ground until she recovered. Then they sort of adopted her."

'What about Hermie?" Cathy asked, staring at the rolling green hills framed by her window. This seemed so peaceful, so real; all that came before certainly didn't.

"Locked up. The police found her in the auditorium standing over the shaft and crying. It seems that she jogged so much to keep fresh air in her system and counteract the mental effects of the gas. Joseph the midget is in custody, too, and Barnes, and Loomis, and Kasha, and Noleta. Boy, is there going to be a diplomatic flap over her when this thing becomes public!"

Cathy couldn't hold it back any longer. It overtook her like a flood and burst through her soul in a gush of tears. She covered her face with her hands, almost dislodging an I.V. needle in her left arm. "Oh, Mikey, Mikey! I dropped him and killed him! Oh, my God!"

Greg awkwardly stroked her hair. "Shh, stop crying, please," he whispered soothingly. "That's why I wanted to talk to you alone. We've got to work this out. Frankie, Louise and I haven't told anyone the whole story, yet. I haven't even told *them* everything that happened."

"But I dropped him into that hole and killed him."

"She's not dead."

Cathy lost her breath. After a moment, she sat up and said, "What do you mean?"

He looked away from her, and his discomfort was obvious. "*She* let go of *you,* remember? And when she fell, she landed on the same ledge that Cecil and his brothers had hit seventy years ago.

Virgil and Lionel's bones were still down there.
Anyway, Cecil hit it again, but this time he died
and his body cushioned Gretchen's fall just
enough to save her life. She was terribly injured,
but she lived, and by the next day, yesterday, she
had been exposed to the gas long enough to have
almost completely recovered. The doctors say
that she won't suffer any permanent disabili-
ties.''

This time Cathy deliberately pulled the needle
from her arm and then tried to swing her legs
from the bed. She still was awfully weak, and
Greg was easily able to hold her in the bed with
his one hand.

''Wait!''

''I've got to see him! He's alive!'' she cried.

His voice remained sharp and commanding. ''I
said wait a minute. Gretchen does *not* have your
brother's mind! Believe me!''

''But I saw the scar from the operation.''

''You saw *a* scar. Welsh did do some of his
damned experimenting on her—her skull has been
opened—but there's no other evidence of a brain
transplant. The doctors have told me about the
x-rays—''

''How do you know that anything would show
up on x-rays?'' she demanded. ''Because of the
gas, Mikey's brain didn't deteriorate after they
killed him, or he wasn't actually dead, and the
operation was performed, and the gas kept him
alive and allowed his brain to heal inside her skull,
like Frankie's nerve damage is healing, but there
was some severe injury that made him forget who
he really was and made him act so naive, and
when Sheriff Reed hit him, it jarred his identity
back—''

"I know she had some temporary recovery due to the blow," he interrupted.

"Temporary? What do you mean?"

He was silent for a time, remembering last night. He couldn't bring himself to look at her. "I . . . we are kind of like celebrities here, even with the government men, because of the way we cracked this thing and made public the existence of the gas. So I've managed to secure some . . . special privileges, like these clothes instead of a gown. I've seen Gretchen since Tuesday; I talked with her last night. Cathy, she *is* Gretchen and can't even remember seeing a picture of Mikey. She is as . . . retarded as ever—maybe worse."

In his mind, he turned to those few minutes in the girl's hosptial room, only a few yards from this one. Little Gretchen, wide-eyed with both wonder at her surroundings and fear of what was going to happen to her, had clutched a big white stuffed bear that one of the nurses had been allowed to give her and asked to please see Miss Cathy and Hermie and Cook. That was only Gretchen and no one else.

"Her mental state now doesn't prove anything," Cathy whispered.

"Why not? If she had anything left of Mikey in her, wouldn't she have recognized herself in the wedding photo?"

"Not necessarily. If you met yourself walking down the street, you probably wouldn't take a second look. Besides, she did seem to respond to Nona."

"Because she thought that she was pretty." He took her hand again. "Nona's alive."

She gasped. Her emotions were being batted about like a tennis ball. "Thank God!"

"She was in the cave, and she's come through it well, considering everything she went through. She didn't see Mikey killed."

"What does Welsh say about it all?"

"Nothing. He's vanished. He was in Milwaukee when the story about the so-called virus broke, and apparently he realized that his little medical nightmare had been penetrated. He and Alfreda dropped out of sight. They may never be found."

Cathy leaned back wearily into the pillows, her resolve crumbling. Maybe it would be better for Mikey if he were peacefully at rest rather than a dimwitted medical freak. Was her own selfishness prolonging this torture?

"Did Gretchen ever say that she was Mikey, when she was normally intelligent?" Without awaiting an answer, he pressed the issue. "Did Welsh ever say that he had used Mikey in a transplant operation? Did Hermie? Did anyone?"

She shook her head slowly.

He knew that whatever was left of her brother was almost surely floating in one of those jars like a preserved vegetable. "Don't be forced to bury him again, Cathy. It'll only tear you apart."

Then the last piece of evidence flashed into her mind. "Gretchen called me 'Kitty Cat,' " she said triumphantly. "No one else but Mikey called me that."

"Noleta's telepathy," he countered in a tired voice, not wishing to reveal to her what he now knew of geunine psychic ability. "The microphones."

"But I didn't show you the postcard in the house. We were in the yard, a long way from the mansion, and they can't have bugged the entire lot. I'm sure I never mentioned the name in the house."

Almost sadly, he reached into his left pocket and pulled out a small metal object. "Another result of my special privileges. A federal investigator let me have this yesterday in exchange for two hundred bucks."

"What is it?"

"A bug, a microphone. He found it in my car. They must have planted it on Monday afternoon, the first time we stopped there. I'm sure you and I brought up the nickname sometime while we were in the car. Either Gretchen also was an eavesdropper, or she heard one of the others mention it. Or maybe you muttered it in that weird dream, when Gretchen was waiting outside your door."

"I don't remember ever saying it . . ." The foundations of her hope were being washed away swiftly now. "Couldn't it be true?"

He shook his head. "She's only Gretchen, little Gretchen Collier, according to the missing persons records, who disappeared thirteen years ago when she was two on a drive from North Carolina to Iowa. They haven't found her parents in the cave yet, but she isn't your brother reincarnated—and she never was."

"Then why would she have tried to give up her life to save mine?"

"Probably because you had been kind to her when no one else even treated her as a human being. The blow from the sheriff's gun must have caused her to have one of those periods of lucidity, but, according to Noleta, she's been having those for at least six years and always knows that a relapse will invariably follow. Maybe she just couldn't bring herself to face life as poor, feeble-minded Gretchen the maid anymore.''

Cathy's voice was weak. ''You're sure there's no possibility?''

Of course I'm not sure, he screamed emotionally. There will always be that sickening suspicion and the cold feeling in the pit of my stomach when I look at the kid, but I can't accept that is could be true! Aloud, he replied, ''Completely.''

''I suppose you're right.''

''And you won't bring it up with anyone else? Not even with the police or the federal investigators when they start questioning you? It could ruin the rest of your life, you know.''

''All right.'' She closed her eyes and put Mikey to rest.

''What will I do now, Greg, without him?''

He squeezed her hand. ''Well, you have a full —and soon to be famous—life ahead of you. There's already talk of a financial settlement for each of us—you, Frankie, Louise, Gretchen, and me—based on the commercial uses of the gas. And you know that it'll be the biggest consumer hit of all time.'' But Greg couldn't help wondering if the government would decide to release such a potent substance to the general public.

''But that's just money. I'll still be alone.''

''The Pettis family loves you like their daughter and sister.''

''And I love them,'' she added.

''And you may be closer than you know to someone else who loves you,'' he said with a little embarrassment in his voice.

Cathy looked at him and smiled. ''I was hoping

that you would say that.''

Greg returned the smile. ''Hey, what else do we need?''